D0846797

MAGNIFICENT OBSESSION

"I demand you release me this instant!"

"I'm afraid you're not in any position to make demands, Sabrina."

"I'll have you thrown behind bars! You'll rot in prison for the rest of your days!"

Ian ignored her, taking the steps two at a time, marching down the second-floor hall and straight into the bedroom that had been prepared for her.

"Let go of me!"

He complied, tossing her to the bed. Sabrina came up with a growl, pushing her hat from her eyes, glaring at Tremayne. "Blackguard!" she shouted, trying to fight her way off the bed.

"Tell me the truth, Sabrina," he said, his warm breath brushing her lips with each word he spoke. "Tell me why you came back to haunt me."

SHADOW OF THE STORM

DEBRA DIER

LEISURE BOOKS NEW YORK CITY

To Don, who always believed in me.

A LEISURE BOOK®

June 1998

Published by

Dorchester Publishing Co., Inc.
276 Fifth Avenue
New York, NY 10001

ISBN 0-8439-4397-1

Printed in the United States of America.

Prologue

May 1856, New York City

The oak bough groaned beneath the girl's weight, a mournful warning whispered on the cool evening breeze, mingling with the soft rustle of leaves. Yet, the warning had come too late for Sabrina O'Neill. The branch snapped beneath her, tossing her from her perch above the heart of the maze garden, hurling her toward the gravel below.

Her body convulsed with a realization that sparked every nerve, that slammed her heart against the wall of her chest and sucked air from her lungs—she was going to die. She threw out her arms. Flapping like a fledgling tumbling from its nest, she fought frantically for purchase in the thick foliage. Limbs slashed at her, each a dark, angry demon clawing her legs, her arms, her hands, eluding her grasp. Leaves ripped from their mooring tumbled from her hands, spilling a sharp tang into the air.

From below, Sabrina heard a woman shriek. She heard the deep rumble of Ian's voice, his words lost in her own piercing scream of panic.

Suddenly, there was nothing but air streaming over her in a soft rush, nothing to save her from her fall. She clawed at the air, trying to snatch the last branch as it retreated from her. Fractured thoughts flickered through the fear flaring like fire in her brain . . . Ian . . . he would discover what she had done . . . she would die humiliated . . . broken and bloody at his feet.

Something hard whipped around her. A solid bulk slammed against her back before she hit the ground, her moan entwining with a gravely groan. For a moment she lay with her eyes closed, the reassuring roar of her pulse pounding in her ears. Alive! She was still alive.

Bayberry and spices and something else, something intriguing, teased her senses. Gathering her shattered wits, Sabrina became aware of the hard cushion of a male body beneath her, the warm embrace of strong arms around her. Great stars above! She had landed on Ian.

Sabrina turned in his arms, her knee colliding with something solid, dragging a moan from his lips. "Are you all right?"

Ian released his breath between clenched teeth as he looked up at her, his green eyes filled with moonlight and shadows. "Fine."

The husky whisper was less than convincing. What must he think of her? Heaven help her, she wasn't sure she wanted to know. "I'm sorry. I didn't mean to . . ."

"Just what were you doing spying on us?" Felicity Barton demanded.

Sabrina scrambled to her feet, gravel biting into her naked soles. Although she was only thirteen, Sabrina stood several inches taller than the indignant blonde, the harlot who had lured Ian away from the wedding ball.

"Where did you come from?" Felicity stared at Sabrina down the length of her slim little nose. "The kitchen? A snooping little servant spying on your betters. Well, Mrs. Van Cortlandt shall hear of this, and you will soon find yourself on the street."

The harlot definitely needed to be whittled down to size. "Mrs. Van Cortlandt is my aunt."

"I see. You're one of *those* people from Mississippi." Felicity tilted her head, moonlight falling across her features, turning her face to cold white marble. "Apparently they don't teach little girls any manners in the South. I doubt your Aunt Caroline shall be happy to hear of this."

Aunt Caroline would be scandalized, Sabrina thought, her throat growing tight. "I suppose you intend to tell her?"

"That's right." Felicity tilted her head, a smug smile curving her lips. "With pleasure."

Sabrina forced her lips into a smile, hoping she looked more confident than she felt. "I suppose I'll have to tell Aunt Caroline what I was doing out here." She cast a meaningful glance to the granite bench nestled amid the three wide crescents of rose bushes fanning out from the center of the maze. "And what I saw."

"How dare you threaten me!"

"I think you'd better go back, Felicity," Ian said, rising to his feet, brushing bits of gravel from his black coat and trousers. "I'll take care of her."

"Instead of catching her, you should have let her fall," Felicity said, pivoting toward him, her skirt swaying, swishing against her petticoat. "It would have taught her a lesson."

Ian shook his head. "Draw in your claws, little cat."

"Get rid of her quickly, darling." Felicity ran her hand down the studs lining the front of his white shirt as she spoke. "I'll be waiting for you."

Sabrina clenched her hands into fists at her sides. She had half a notion to knock the harlot on her plump backside. The woman had no right to paw Ian. Felicity slanted her an arrogant glance before turning toward the entrance of the maze, her yellow satin gown sweeping Sabrina's linen breeches as she sauntered from the garden, leaving Sabrina alone with Ian.

Sabrina was staring at him. She knew it. Yet, she could do nothing to stop. It didn't seem possible. Just a few feet away stood the living image of her dream; only Ian was taller, more handsome than that shadowy figure conjured in the realm of her sleep.

Roses swayed in the breeze nearby, sliding their perfume around her, stirring memories of home within her. Sabrina imagined she was standing in the gardens at Rosebriar, imagined Ian on one knee asking for her hand, imagined him telling her he loved her more than . . .

"You're Brendan O'Neill's baby sister, aren't you," Ian said, rubbing the back of his head, as though he were easing a tender spot.

"Baby sister!" Dreams bumped painfully into reality. She already felt foolish, worse than foolish. She had just witnessed the man she loved, the man she intended to marry, kiss another woman. And the way he had kissed her, with his mouth and his hands, pressing her back against the bench . . . it made her blush just to think of it. On top of it all, she didn't need to be treated like a child. Not by this man. "I'll have you know, Mr. Ian Tremayne, I was thirteen last April seventh. Hardly a baby."

"Ancient. I'm surprised you could make it up that tree, what with the rheumatism and all."

"Oooo, I don't know why I came out here."

A whisper of a smile curved his lips. "Just what were you doing in that tree, Brat?"

"Don't call me Brat!"

"Don't act like a brat, and I won't call you one."

"I don't intend to stand here and listen to you insult me." Humiliated, she marched toward the entrance, giving him a sharp look when he joined her. "I don't want your company."

"Well, you've got it." He bowed, pressing his hand to his heart. "After you, milady."

Sabrina pivoted on her heel, determined to ignore him as he walked beside her. Impossible! Easier to ignore the sun on a hot August afternoon. Without touching her, he surrounded her, the heat of his body shielding her from the chill; and inside, deep within her, she felt a foreign warmth flicker and burn, a callow candle kissed by flame.

Although she had played in her Aunt Caroline's maze a dozen times, tonight her sense of direction eluded her. Ian remained quiet, allowing her to lead, smiling gently as she led him into one dead end after another.

"Do you always go around spying on people?" he asked as they emerged from the maze. "Or am I special?"

"I wasn't spying!"

Moonlight caressed his features, illuminating the crooked curve of his smile. "Are you sure?"

Sabrina glanced down to her bare toes, fragrant, freshly cut grass curling in cool tendrils around her feet. "All right. Maybe I was. But you're lucky I followed you; that woman was about to hang you up in her smokehouse."

He tossed back his head, his black hair brushing his shoulders, his laughter vibrating the cool night air, each robust note a blade slicing her pride.

"Braying jackass! The two of you were meant for each other!" He grabbed her waist-length braid when she started to run, tethering her like a young filly on a rein. "Let go of me!"

He gave her braid a soft tug. "Not yet."

"I don't care to be made fun of," Sabrina said, twisting her braid, feeling the bite of tears in the back of her eyes. "Just let go of me!"

"I'm sorry, I didn't mean to make fun of you."

The sincerity in his lush baritone brought her gaze up to his face. He was smiling in a way that soothed her wounded pride, in a way that seemed to say he understood her youth and appreciated her innocence. "Well, you've been doing a good job for someone not trying."

"I'll do better," he said, dropping her braid.

Trying to hide her smile, she turned and marched toward the house, with Ian in step beside her. A waltz drifted from the ballroom, the notes streaming around them in shimmering strands, like mist rising in the moonlight. If she were older, she could be in that ballroom, she could be holding a dance card with Ian Tremayne's name written beside every dance, she could waltz with him here under the stars.

She loved him. In church this morning, she had taken one look at Ian and known he was the man for her. A slab of longing a mile wide settled on her chest when she realized she might never get the chance to dance with him, to taste his kisses, to be his bride. Seven short years separated them in age, but it might as well have been a hundred.

"That woman is no good. If you're smart, you'll wait for the right woman before you get married."

"I'm not planning to marry anyone for a long time." Ian gave her that special smile, a smile that seemed to shine only for her. "I wonder what you're going to be like in a few years. I have the feeling you're going to grow up to be quite a heartbreaker."

"No, I'm not. I don't like those fancy games women play. I'll give my heart to one man, and I'll cherish his love all my days."

Ian brushed the curve of her cheek with his fingertips, looking at her as though he could see the promise of the woman she would become. "And he'll be a very lucky man."

She hesitated a moment, collecting her courage. "If you're real smart, Ian Tremayne, you'll wait for me." She sprang to her toes, grazed his chin with her lips, then dashed toward the house.

"Hey, Brat!" he said, running after her.

She started to scamper up a shapely elm planted beside the house. If he laughed at her, she would die, just die.

"Brat!"

Sabrina paused on the ledge of her cousin Lucy's open second-story bedroom window, her heart pounding at the base of her throat. After taking a deep breath she glanced down at him. "What?"

Ian took a minute before he replied, smiling up at her, moonlight burning his features into her heart. "You just might be worth the wait."

She smiled. "You just wait and see, Ian Tremayne."

"I just might do that." Ian turned, shoved his hands into his pockets, and walked away from the big elm, softly whistling a waltz.

"Sabrina, you're going to get into awful trouble," Lucy said as Sabrina climbed into the room. "Mama says girls are always throwing themselves at Ian Tremayne. She says they'll end up in trouble. And . . . and you kissed him!"

Lucy was ten, far too young to understand. "One day I'm going to marry that man," Sabrina said, leaning on the windowsill, watching Ian Tremayne until he faded into the shadows near the ballroom. "He'll wait for me. I know it. I feel it in my heart."

Chapter One

October 1865, somewhere on the Mississippi River

She could delay no longer. Sabrina O'Neill stepped into the crowded main cabin of the *Belle Angeline,* closing the door of her stateroom behind her. The soft click of the latch cracked like a gunshot to her heightened senses.

Guilt. It didn't show, she assured herself. It wasn't a brand across her face, even if she could feel the heat of it searing her cheeks. These people, dressed in their fine clothes, sitting in this elegant room, seemingly safe—they couldn't know what she was about to do. But she knew. Oh, yes, she knew. No matter how hard she tried to forget.

A waltz swooped down from the orchestra perched on a platform at one end of the long room, colliding with the deep bark of male voices, the shrill notes of feminine laughter, pulsing against Sabrina's ears. Clutching the brass door handle of her stateroom, she fixed her gaze on her father and snatched at her retreating courage. He was depending on her. She was all he had left.

At fifty, nothing in Duncan O'Neill's appearance betrayed his age; not his dark red hair, untouched by silver; not his finely chiseled features, barely brushed by lines. Several women turned their heads to watch the tall, slender man as he passed. Yet, Duncan didn't notice. Sabrina knew he was already too absorbed in the hunt, too preoccupied by the coming battle. He shared none of her doubts. He savored the pungent wine of vengeance.

"It's about time, Kitten," Duncan said, smiling, offering Sabrina a glass of lemonade. "I started thinking you were hiding in there."

Sabrina accepted the lemonade, her linen gloves absorbing cool droplets from the damp crystal. The glass trembled in her grasp, slices of lemon and slivers of ice vibrating with her tension, spilling drops of lemonade down the skirt of her mint-green silk gown. "Which one?" she asked, clasping the glass between both hands.

"He's sitting alone, five tables behind me on the right. Do you see him?"

Sabrina nodded. The Yankee sat facing the orchestra with his back to her. Delaying just a moment longer, she took a sip, fresh lemon flooding her senses, the tart liquid cutting a path down her parched throat. "Wish me luck."

"Kitten, with your face you don't need luck."

She knew better. One wrong move and they would find themselves behind bars.

Something about the man seemed familiar, Sabrina thought, as she walked toward the Yankee's table. Gaslight flickered behind crystal globes high overhead, shimmering on hair blacker than midnight; the thick mane longer than the fashion, tumbling over his collar in silky waves. Broad shoulders stretched his dark blue coat, shoulders too thick to owe their breadth to the skill of a tailor. She wondered how tall he was. Even sitting he looked tall and straight and barely restrained.

In a moment she would see what features went along with those broad shoulders. She glanced down into her glass, swirling the ice and slices of lemon, feeling her stomach quiver. A little trip, a little splash, and she would have her introduction. Feigning clumsiness was the easy part. The difficult role began after she met her father's chosen prey.

Thunder rattled the walls of the room, its deep bellow vibrating the chandeliers, drowning the orchestra. Sabrina hesitated, startled by the sudden explosion. She glanced up at the skylights carved into arches above the staterooms, the reflection of the room clouding the etched glass.

A storm at night.

The realization sent a single shiver quivering along her spine, stirring memories deep inside her. It was over! She had to purge the fear. Yet, in two years she had failed to banish the night terror. How long would she be haunted by ghosts and shadows? she wondered. She had a horrible feeling she would never be free of the terror, never be whole again.

Sabrina glanced back in time to see the Yankee move toward the door at the far end of the room. The man she sought moved with a lithe, powerful grace: a panther prowling amid sheep. Something about him taunted her, teasing a distant memory.

Compelled to see the face of this haunting stranger, she followed him.

The wind whipped at his face, tugged at the hem of his coat, as Ian Tremayne stepped onto the deck. Charcoal clouds swirled in an indigo sky, smothering the full moon, shrouding the earth in darkness.

Memories swirled inside him, memories ignited by the roar of thunder, the flash of lightning, memories living in the darkest shadows of his mind. The taste of black powder spread across his tongue, acrid, mixed with the sickeningly sweet taste of blood. He clenched his jaw, breathing in the damp night air, trying to cleanse his senses. When would it end? he wondered. When would he be free?

Never. Some memories couldn't be escaped. A part of him would always live lost in shadows.

Light spilling from the skylights of the staterooms guided him toward the stairs near the enclosed paddle wheel. As he approached the stairs, the tiny hairs on the back of his neck tingled. Instincts stirred inside him, instincts conceived on the battlefield, born of necessity, nourished by blood and fear.

Lightning sliced the black sky, illuminating the earth in a flash of silver, spinning shadow into substance. In his mind Ian saw the flash of shells in the midnight sky, beautiful, like shooting stars; stars that fell to earth and ripped a man to shreds.

"Look out!" a woman screamed, her voice slicing through the air a heartbeat before the sky's artillery fired.

Instincts honed by combat seized command. Ian pivoted, his gaze flashing on the barrel of a gun, his fist catching the gunman's chin, snapping his head back. As the gunman weaved, Ian grabbed the arm holding the gun. With a violent thrust, he brought the arm down over his raised knee, the sharp crack of bone ripping the air. Even as the man screeched with pain, before the pistol hit the deck, Ian turned, sensing a second man's advance.

Steel glittered in the light glowing from the staterooms. Ian raised his arm, blocking the forward thrust of the blade. Steel plunged into his arm, slicing, searing his flesh, releasing the beast within him, tossing him back in time, back to a blood-drenched field.

Ian surged forward, slamming his fist into the man's jaw, lifting his assailant upward with the force, knocking him back against the railing. Before the man could strike, Ian attacked, ramming him with his shoulder, knocking the knife to the deck.

Through a red haze Ian fought, slamming blow after blow into the enemy, barely feeling the fists thrown against his own body. Low groans coupled with the dull thud of flesh connecting with flesh to rise above the howl of the wind. One final uppercut sent his assailant tumbling over the railing, into the swelling river, the man's scream rising as he fell.

Ian clenched the railing, staring into the dark, swirling river. The man was gone. He dragged air into his lungs, welcomed the cool spray of the rain striking his face, fighting to clear his senses, to chain back the beast. Someone touched his arm. He pivoted, drawing back his fist.

"No!"

His downward fist froze in midair, a part of his brain recognizing friend from foe. A woman stood before him, her arms raised in front of her face, a pistol clutched in one hand, the barrel pointing toward the sky. "Easy," he said, taking the pistol from her raised hand. "I never strike women who carry revolvers."

He stepped away from the railing, searching the shadows for the gunman. "Did you see where he went?"

"No, I was too busy looking for the pistol. I thought you might need help."

"I did. Thanks for the warning." He slipped the revolver into his pocket, a sharp stab of pain knifing along his arm. He gripped his left forearm, blood, warm and sticky, oozing through his fingers.

"Are you all right?"

"I'm fine." He examined the ragged tear in his sleeve, his blood a black smear against his coat.

She moved closer, a breath of jasmine rising from her warm skin. The light from the staterooms gave him only a hint of her features, a glimpse of pale shoulders, enough to make him want to see more. She was tall, slender, the way he liked his women. And he liked her voice. It reminded him of satin, and it was colored with a drawl that conjured images of wide white verandas in the moonlight.

"You're bleeding," she said, touching his sleeve.

The gentle touch sent a fresh wave of pain rippling along his arm. "It's not bad."

"Your arm needs tending. My cabin is right there," she said, pointing toward the row of staterooms lining the side of the ship. "Please, let me help."

"It's no more than a scratch." Still, there were worse things than being treated by a nurse with a satiny voice, he decided, allowing her to lead him across the deck, their heels rapid gunfire against the oak planks.

"Aggie!" she shouted, pounding on the locked door of her stateroom. "Aggie, it's Sabrina."

"And just what are ye doin' on deck?" Aggie asked, sliding the bolt. She pulled open the door, frowning when she saw them. "What the devil have ye . . ."

"Aggie, this gentleman was attacked by two men," Sabrina said, leading Ian into the small cabin, stepping into the glow cast by the lamp on the wall beside the door. "Please tell the captain . . ." Her words dissolved in a gasp as Sabrina looked up at Ian, her eyes growing wide, as if she suddenly found herself confronting a ghost. "You!"

Ian felt his own stab of shock, and it had nothing to do with recognizing her. As far as he could tell, he had never seen her before in his life, but no man with blood in his veins could ever see this woman's face and forget her.

"Brina, are ye goin' to keep starin' at the man, or tell me what ye'd like me to be doin'?"

"Please tell Captain Anderson one of the men got away."

"And what about the other one?" Aggie asked, planting her hands on her narrow hips, cocking her head, staring at Sabrina, a plucky sparrow confronting a startled swan.

"The other one should be halfway to New Orleans by now," Ian said, smiling at the little maid.

Aggie looked Ian over from the top of his shaggy mane to the tips of his polished black shoes, a smile curving her thin lips, carving deep lines into the skin at the corners of her blue eyes. "Seems t'me they weren't too bright, pickin' on a big strappin' man like yeself."

"Aggie, please hurry," Sabrina said, helping Ian out of his coat.

"I'm Aggie Fitzpatrick," she said, making a stiff curtsy, lifting one corner of her dark blue muslin skirt. "At yer service, sir."

"Aggie!" Sabrina said, her voice overlapping Ian's as he started to introduce himself.

"I'm on m'way," Aggie said, waving her hands as she walked toward the door. "But I don't see any need in hurryin'. Unless the hooligan wants t'join his friend, he won't be goin' anywhere." She mumbled something about impatient youth as she opened the door leading to the main cabin, leaving Ian and Sabrina alone.

For a moment Sabrina stood staring at Ian, her fingers curling against his coat as though she held something very precious in her hands. Her eyes were huge, filled with innocence and at the same time an ageless wisdom, reminding Ian of a doe hidden in a secluded forest. There was a look in those dark eyes, something he had trouble defining, perhaps because he rarely saw it. Not in the faces of the others, the women who each wanted a piece of him: his body to warm their beds, his gold to line their pockets, his initial added to their monograms.

What was it about this woman? A glow? There was something compelling in her eyes, flickering flames that came to life when she looked at him. A light of genuine affection? For a man she didn't know? "Have we met?"

She glanced down at the coat she held in her hands. "Yes, we have."

"Are you sure?"

"If you let me tend your arm, I just might remind you of the first time we met," she said, hanging his coat on a peg by the door, the dark blue wool nestling against red and white roses in the wallpaper.

His arm. He had almost forgotten his arm. She had that effect on him. "It's a deal." He sank to a high-backed chair near the door, settling against the stiff horsehair, watching her.

Sabrina threw open the doors of the rosewood armoire across from the double berths, then tugged off her white gloves. "Are you hurt anywhere else?" she asked, lifting a walnut box from the floor of the armoire.

"Just my pride." Ian plucked at his bloody sleeve, folding his arm along his waist, trying to keep from staining the red and white roses in the silk brocade covering the arm of the chair.

"I'm not sure why your pride should suffer." She set the box on the floor beside his chair and handed him a linen washcloth as she spoke. "There were two of them, and they were both armed."

Ian pressed the cloth to his bloody arm. "That's not why my pride is injured," he said, smiling up at her.

"Then why is it?"

Her hair captured the gaslight, each strand spinning into burgundy fire. "What self-respecting man would forget meeting one of the most beautiful women he has ever seen?"

She lowered her eyes, not a coy gesture, but one surprisingly shy. He wasn't used to that. Of course, lately he had been keeping company with women who considered love a business transaction. He liked it that way: a nice, clean exchange of gold for favors. He found it more honest than the women who preferred to sell themselves into marriage for the gold in a man's purse.

"Well, perhaps there's a reason you can't remember," she said, toying with the green satin ribbon at her waist.

Only if he had been drunk. And somehow, even then, he had a feeling he would remember this woman.

Thunder cracked and her gaze snapped to the door. She stood for a moment with her slender hand poised at the base of her throat, staring as though she expected something horrible to come crashing through that door.

Ian felt a stirring inside him, the awakening of a foreign instinct. He wanted to hold her, to stroke her shining hair, to tell her nothing would harm her, at least not while he had breath in his body. Never had a woman affected him this way, on such an elemental level, other than simple lust. He felt an odd sense of belonging with her, a kinship. Who was she?

Her gown rustled softly against what he guessed were satin petticoats as she walked to the rosewood washstand. He followed each fluent movement, imagining the curve of her naked hip, the supple length of her legs beneath the yards of silk and satin. "What's your last name, Miss Sabrina?"

"O'Neill," she said, draping a thick white towel over her arm. She poured water from the pitcher into the porcelain basin as she continued. "Does that help prod your memory?"

"Sabrina O'Neill," he said, rolling the name over his tongue like wine. "I'm afraid it doesn't."

She glanced over her shoulder, smiling, touching him deep inside; in places filled with shadows and cobwebs, stuffed with dreams stored away so long ago he had almost forgotten they existed. She tempted him to pull those dreams out of storage, tempted him to dust them off and hold them up to the light. It made him suspicious.

Since the war, since his ascent to the Tremayne throne, he had become the target of every unmarried woman in New York; an object to be examined, to be coveted and acquired. Strange what the thought of gold could do to a person. He couldn't count the number of handkerchiefs that had been dropped in his path, the number of times a woman had purposely tripped him to gain an introduction, the number of women who had pretended to swoon from the heat to be taken into his arms. One woman had even shown up at his doorstep feigning amnesia. And this woman claimed to know him. What was her game?

Sabrina lifted the washbasin from its cradle of white marble, hesitating a moment before approaching him. It was then Ian realized he was staring at her, the way a lion might eye a fawn. Dismissing his dark suspicions, he smiled, encouraging her to draw near. There was no reason to believe this woman was anything other than the beguiling innocent she appeared to be. "I know, we met at a masquerade ball."

"No." Again came that bewitching smile. She knelt beside his chair, resting the basin on the floor, her gown billowing around her with the soft swish of silk against satin. "We met in a garden. In the moonlight. A long time ago," she said, draping a towel over the arm of the chair.

He lowered his injured arm to the towel as she lifted a pair of scissors from the walnut box. "We met in a garden, in the moonlight, and I don't remember?"

Sabrina looked up into eyes the color of the first tender leaves of spring. For nine years this man had haunted her dreams. Still, the reality of Ian was nearly overwhelming. His presence filled the small stateroom, his vitality vibrating the air around her, his essence intoxicating her senses, coaxing her to draw him deeply into her lungs. She felt as though she had run miles and come to a sudden halt: dizzy, breathless, exhilarated. He was here! Ian was really here. And he was smiling at her.

"You wound me," she said, snipping at the linen above the wound. "A lady likes to think she's unforgettable." Even at the age of thirteen, she thought.

"Believe me, Miss Sabrina O'Neill, you are unforgettable." He laughed, the velvety rumble colored by a trace of self-consciousness. "So why can't I remember you?"

"I might have changed a little since we met." Sabrina peeled the sleeve and washcloth from his arm, folded the stained pieces of linen, and laid them on the oak planks that edged the red and white carpet.

She touched his torn flesh with the damp washcloth, the white linen blooming red. There was a time when the sight of blood would have made her swoon, but not now. Not since Vicksburg. Not since the day she had volunteered to help at the hospital. Not since the first time she had wrung blood from the hem of her clothes. Many things had changed since they first met. Perhaps too many.

"Did we meet in New Orleans?"

"No."

"Saratoga Springs?"

She glanced up, startled by the look in his eyes; he seemed to reach out and surround her, hold her, make her feel as though he could spend a lifetime just looking at her. Her heart began a steady throb just at the base of her throat. "I suspect you meet far too many ladies."

"Not like you," he said, holding her with a steady gaze.

With those eyes he could tear down any facade, shred any secret she might try to keep. This was a man, flesh and blood. Not a dream. Not a boy. Not a young girl's fantasy lover. He could destroy her, destroy her father if she weren't careful. She dragged her gaze from his, shielding her thoughts. She had to stop acting like a foolish schoolgirl, like a flighty old maid at her first glimpse of a man in a hundred years.

"Who are you?" he asked, brushing his fingers across her smooth cheek.

The soft touch rippled across the pool of longing deep within her. Who was she? Sometimes Sabrina wondered. She didn't resemble the woman she once thought she would be—the woman she had asked him to wait for a lifetime ago.

A waltz drifted into the room from the main cabin. There had been a waltz that night. Would he remember? It was foolish to think he would remember a silly little girl. Still, she hoped he might. "Do you remember attending Eleanor Van Cortlandt's wedding?"

"That was years ago."

His black brows pulled together over the thin line of his nose as he studied her, the right brow bearing a crescent-shaped scar at the outer corner of his eye. Yet it didn't spoil that handsome face, only gave it a more devilish cast, reminiscent of a swashbuckling pirate—an effect heightened by the roguish tilt of his full lips.

"In the Van Cortlandt garden, nearly ten years ago." Slowly his look of confusion shifted, dissolving into realization. "You!" He laughed, filling the small cabin with deep masculine music. Under the influence of that music her own lips curved into a smile. "So, we meet again, Brat."

Still smiling, she lifted a roll of white linen from the box and began to wrap his arm as she spoke. "I thought I asked you not to call me Brat."

"But it seems you still deserve the name."

She glanced up at him. "Do I?"

He nodded. "For making me think I had lost my mind. Only a crazy man could forget a woman who looks like you."

"Beauty fades," she said, lowering her gaze to his arm as she tied the ends of the bandage. "What we are inside remains a lifetime." And at the moment, she wasn't sure she liked what she was inside. She had lived with hate for so long, she wasn't sure what else was left in her. "Finished. The bandage should be changed in the morning."

He touched her cheek, his fingers drifting across her skin like a summer breeze. She lifted her eyes; his face was close, drawing closer. Her breath hovered at the base of her throat as he brushed the curve of her jaw with his thumb, as he plumbed the depths of her soul with his eyes. Deep inside, in a place of mystery, sleeping embers stirred, a flame flickered and bloomed, spreading a delicious warmth through her veins.

Cupping the back of her head with his hand, he urged her forward. He was going to kiss her, as he had a thousand times in her dreams. Only this was real. Warm and real and wonderful. He lowered his gaze to her lips, black lashes casting feathery shadows against his cheeks. He parted his lips, his breath spilled across her cheek in a humid stream, and then she felt the first touch of his kiss.

Like a sable brush barely touching canvas, he moved his lips against hers, stroking gently, fanning the flickering flames deep inside her. She felt suspended in time. Her body responded without thought, without practice, leaning toward him, instinctively seeking the heat of his body. So this is what it felt like to be kissed, she thought, to be touched by a dream.

"Thank you," he whispered, his lips brushing hers.

She had the odd impulse to thank him. The waltz grew louder in her ears. Ian pulled away, smiling at her. In a daze, Sabrina realized the door leading to the main cabin was opening, admitting a cold rush of reality, snapping the spell. She fell back on her heels, turning her head, hiding her blush, busying herself with repacking the remedy box.

From the corner of her eye Sabrina saw Aggie enter the cabin, followed by Duncan; then the captain filled the doorway. Aggie stopped at the head of the narrow berths, standing aside, allowing Duncan and the captain clearance to move farther into the stateroom. Captain Anderson smiled at Sabrina as she glanced up at him, his lips a naked curve in his bushy blond beard.

A former captain in the Confederate Navy, Captain Avery Anderson knew Sabrina and her father made a living by stripping Yankees of their gold. Yet he looked the other way. Yankee-skinning wasn't a crime as far as the captain was concerned.

While Ian sketched the details of the attack for the captain, Duncan stood near the bureau, watching, the keen look of a predator in his dark eyes. Sabrina could see her father missed nothing, not even the way Ian smiled at her, a smile meant only for her, a smile as private and warm and lovely as the kiss they had shared. Her father saw another meaning in that smile, Sabrina knew it by the look in his eyes; he saw his prey stepping into the trap.

"It'd be our pleasure if you'd join us in the main cabin for some refreshment, Mr. Tremayne," Duncan said as the captain lumbered from the stateroom.

Smelling blood, her father would be quick to move in for the kill. "Father, I'm sure Mr. Tremayne needs rest."

"No, I'm fine," Ian said, slipping into his coat. He glanced down at his torn and bloody sleeve. "But I think it might be a good idea to change."

"Excellent," Duncan said, smiling. "We'll meet you in the main cabin."

Sabrina's throat tightened as she led Ian to the door, words twisting, throbbing, trying to escape. She should say something, warn him. Yet how could she? How could she betray her father?

Ian stepped out of the cabin, then turned to face her, taking her right hand in his warm grasp. "I'm looking forward to becoming better acquainted, Brat," he said, before pressing his lips against the cup of her palm, his warm breath streaming across her wrist.

If only things were different, Sabrina thought, watching Ian dissolve into the shadows, feeling the warm imprint of his kiss fade in the cool evening breeze. If only she were still that innocent little girl filled with dreams and hopes . . . but things had changed. She had changed.

Chapter Two

"From the way that Yankee looks at you, Kitten, it should be a child's game to lead the lamb to slaughter," Duncan said after Sabrina closed the door.

Sabrina tried to draw a deep breath, the air creeping into her lungs in a trembling trickle. She stared at the photograph standing in a walnut frame on the lace runner covering the bureau. It was all she had been able to save from the house. Taken three months before the war, it showed a family standing between the white pillars of a two-story brick house. Her family. Her home. Now only memories.

Sabrina understood her father's need for vengeance. She shared it. She and her mother had returned home from months of living in a cave during the siege of Vicksburg to find Federal soldiers camped at Rosebriar. The position of the house and the captain's walk perched on the roof provided them a strategic view of the river just north of Natchez.

Sabrina and her mother had been allowed to stay, to witness the soldiers cutting down ancient oak and magnolia trees for firewood, to watch them trample the roses that had been her mother's pride, to know Union officers slept in the beds where her brothers had once slept; her brothers who now slept under the sod of distant battlefields. Her mother had died of pneumonia, listening to booted heels marching across the oak planks of the ballroom over her head.

A week after her mother's death flames ravaged the house. The Yankees had called it an accident. Only Sabrina knew the real reason an oil lamp had been tossed against one corner of the ballroom. A Yankee lieutenant had tossed that lamp. A Yankee who had tried and failed to win Sabrina's affections. A Yankee who couldn't accept defeat at the hands of one southern woman. It was etched in hate upon her memory, the image of flames soaring from the windows of her home, the firelight reflecting that Yankee lieutenant's smug smile.

The Yankees had destroyed her home. The Yankees would pay to rebuild it. That was the logic she had used to justify their actions. Yet now, after seeing Ian, that logic seemed hollow.

Sabrina turned to face her father. "I'd rather you didn't play cards with Mr. Tremayne."

Duncan stroked one edge of his mustache, the neat fringe the same dark red as his thick hair. "And why not?"

How could she begin to explain how she felt about Ian? About a Yankee? "He's an acquaintance of Aunt Caroline."

"So is most of New York," Duncan said, studying her closely. "But that isn't the real reason, is it?"

"Maybe she's just tired o' the stealin'," Aggie said, from her perch on the edge of the lower berth. "The child shouldn't be on these boats. She should take Miss Caroline's invitation, she should be livin' a decent life."

"I suppose she'd be happy living in the midst of the enemy," Duncan said, glaring at the old woman.

Aggie lifted her chin, returning Duncan's angry stare. "Are ye sure it's the Yankees yer worried about?"

"I can take care of my daughter," Duncan said, rapping his knuckles on the bureau. "I don't need Carrie's help."

"I'm thinkin' it's time ye and Miss Caroline made amends, at least for Brina's sake. Ye can't call . . ."

"Aggie, please," Sabrina said, rubbing her throbbing temples. She had heard the same argument before, a hundred times. The temptation to live with her Aunt Caroline beckoned to her day and night; she would have a home again, she would be near Ian. Yet she couldn't. There was too much animosity between her father and her mother's sister; the animosity of a man jilted for another.

"Sabrina, I don't understand your concern about this blue belly," Duncan said, turning to face her.

She had to make him understand. Ian had been with her every day for the past nine years, his memory helping her cope with the harsh realities of a world turned to ashes. In her dreams Ian had held her, had kept her safe; and she had escaped into dreams both day and night. There had been times through the long, bloody years when she wondered if Ian ever had been real, or just a dream conjured up by an imaginative little girl.

"Ian reminds me of who I once was," Sabrina said, looking up at her father. "He reminds me of who I wanted to be. And he forces me to look at what I've become."

"Damn!" Duncan threw open the door leading to the deck, the oak slamming hard against the wall, recoiling, nearly hitting him as he stalked from the room.

"My, but he has a temper," Aggie said, smoothing back a strand of hair escaping her tight bun, the light brown tresses streaked with iron. "Even as a lad he was filled with fire and pride. Too much pride to see what's right fer ye."

"He does what he can, Aggie."

Sabrina followed her father from the cabin. The storm had subsided to a steady rain, the moon peeking out from behind an ebony curtain, but in the distance, down the length of winding river, lightning flashed in the dark gray clouds. The storm wasn't over.

Duncan stood near the railing at the side of the ship, his hand braced on one of the carved pillars supporting the upper deck. He didn't turn when she approached.

"Father, please try to understand," Sabrina said, resting her hand on his back. He stiffened, his muscles growing tense beneath the smooth black wool of his coat. "From the first moment I met Ian Tremayne, I felt something special for him."

He didn't look at her, keeping his eyes focused on the dark, rolling shadows of the shore. "You were a child when you met him. You have no idea what sort of man he is. He might be down here raping what's left of this land."

"And I might be coddling a silly schoolgirl infatuation. But I need to know. I need to know the man he's become. I need to know if there's a chance for us."

He turned and pinned her with his intense gaze. "Have you forgotten your mother? Your brothers? Or do they fade in memory compared to this Yankee?"

"No, I haven't forgotten." She would never forget; memories were all she had. Rain misted her warm cheeks as she held his gaze. "But maybe it's time to stop fighting the war," she said, the words clawing painfully past her tight throat. "Maybe we have to give up our hate to feel whole again. Maybe it's time to start healing."

"Dammit, Sabrina! This man could've been the one who killed Dennis, or Brendan." Duncan raised his face toward the sky, moonlight spilling across his features, revealing the grimace of a man in pain. "I'll not have my daughter involved with any Union bastard."

She stepped back, his hatred lashing her, as powerful as a whip cracking across her face. "Father, I won't help you."

His lips curved into a smile, his eyes glittering with fiery rage as he looked down at her. "I won't need your help to skin that blue-belly skunk."

She felt as though she had been pushed from a high cliff; there was nothing to hold on to, nothing to keep her from plummeting into the chasm. Nothing but her love for Ian. "Father, please, I don't want a war between us."

"Then don't side with the enemy."

"I won't let you hurt him," she said, her voice barely rising above the wind. "I can't let you hurt him."

Duncan swore sharply. "You're in for a fall, Brina. Even if I didn't play cards with him, even if I let him walk away with his money, it wouldn't work between you."

"I think you're wrong. I can't explain it, I don't really understand it, but I feel as though Ian and I are destined for each other. I felt it the first time I saw him."

"You're destined for heartache with that one. And I won't let it happen." He tapped his clenched fist against the railing as he continued. "I'm going to take that blue belly for everything I can."

Sabrina slumped against the pillar, watching her father march toward the main cabin. Warm tears slipped down her cheeks, mingling with the cool mist. Perhaps in time she could make him understand how she felt, but for now, if he wanted a war, he would have one.

There was something about the elaborately carved white arches of the main cabin that had always reminded Sabrina of the Methodist church in Natchez. Every Sunday she had sat in the family pew, listening to Reverend Marshal preach to his flock. Tonight she sat at a table near the back of the crowded room, deaf to the music and laughter streaming around her, watching a white-uniformed steward place a single deck of cards and a tray of colorful chips beside her father. It had taken Duncan less than ten minutes to maneuver Ian into a poker game.

"Is this your first trip down our winding Mississippi, Mr. Tremayne?" Duncan asked, accepting a glass of bourbon and water from the steward.

"No, this is my second in four months." Ian nodded to the steward as the black man placed a snifter of brandy beside him.

"Speculating in land?" Duncan glanced at Sabrina over the rim of his glass as he spoke, his eyes betraying a trace of his hatred. "It's cheap enough these days."

Sabrina's hand tightened on her glass of lemonade. Ian was a good man, an honorable man, not some horrible old carpetbagger.

"I've been working with a few men, trying to reestablish the railroads in the South," Ian said.

Sabrina breathed again.

"I'd like to one day see a network of railroads across the country." Ian lifted his glass to his lips, the crystal capturing the gaslight, spinning rainbows along the rim.

"So, you're a railroad man," Duncan said, pushing a deck of cards toward Ian. To prevent suspicion, he never played with his own deck, but the ship's deck was still Duncan's deck. For a small fee, the bartender kept several packs of marked cards for him, as he did for the other men who made their living on the river.

"It's a big country, and right now too much of it is isolated," Ian said, accepting the cards. "I think trains will eventually be our best means of transportation, for goods and for people."

Duncan shook his head. "I prefer the comfort of the riverboats."

"We aren't far from matching it." Ian shuffled as he spoke, the cards coming to life in his long fingers, flowing effortlessly in rapid cascades of red and white.

Ian was no novice. Feeling a twinge of panic, Sabrina wondered if he would recognize her father's game.

Ian met her eyes as he started to deal, a smile lifting one corner of his lips, those lips he had so recently pressed against hers. She felt her panic drain, felt a fluttering excitement fill her. Suddenly the image of how Ian had kissed that woman in the maze garden blossomed in her mind, as sharp as the night it had happened.

Without looking away from her, Ian continued. "We are working on a system for carrying passengers in luxury, with drawing rooms and dining rooms, as well as staterooms. Trains will be like hotels on wheels."

Sabrina stared at his lips, each sensual shaping of his words, remembering. Ian had held that woman in his arms, kissed her with his lips, with his tongue, his hands sliding up and down her back, molding her shape to the hard planes of his body, drawing soft whimpering sounds from her throat. Heat shimmered across

Sabrina's breasts. She wanted to be held that way, kissed that way, by this man, only this man.

A bolt of electricity shot through her as she met Ian's eyes. He knew! She could see the awareness in his eyes. He could perceive her thoughts, read the secrets etched across her heart. And she welcomed him, laying bare her soul. He lowered his eyes, his gaze sliding over her lips, a silent promise.

"The railroads sound fascinating," she said, shocked by the breathless sound of her voice. "Not many of us get the chance to help shape a part of the future."

Ian shifted a card in his hand, his black lashes lowering, before his gaze returned to embrace her. "We all shape part of the future: our own, the people around us."

Ian was her future. Sabrina knew it, she felt it, just as she had felt it the first time she had glimpsed this man. They would have three days before they reached St. Louis. Three days to protect Ian from her father's vengeance. Three days to convince Ian she was his destiny.

The first few hands went to Ian, but that was all part of Duncan's strategy. It was the first act from a play in which Sabrina had performed too many times. The sheep were allowed to win, to gain confidence, to become bold with their bets; then they were stripped of their fleecy coats without ever seeing the shears.

Sabrina dealt the next hand, serving Ian four kings and her father a pair of deuces. Duncan looked at his hand, then glanced at Sabrina. She met her father's dark gaze with a smile. She, too, had been practicing with a deck of cards.

Duncan returned her smile, then leaned back in his chair, adjusting the cuff of his coat. "I'll play these," he said, when she asked him if he wanted any cards.

Sabrina knew her father had palmed his cards, knew he was now sitting comfortably with four aces in his hand. He had shown her the trick last week. Just one more added to his growing repertoire.

"I'll take two." Sabrina discarded two of her cards. As she dealt herself the second card, she flipped it face up, revealing the ace of hearts framed against the emerald green table linen. "Oh, dear. How clumsy of me," she said, slipping the ace into her hand.

"Yes," Duncan said, rubbing one corner of his mustache.

As they played, Sabrina became aware of a man sitting a few tables behind Ian. Thin dark brown hair streaked with gray was

neatly swept back from a wide brow, as if care had been taken
with each wispy strand. He stared at her, the look in his dark blue
eyes prickling her skin. His face was round, his cheeks fleshy,
although he wasn't a fat man; just a man who looked well fed,
like a plump bulldog.

The man shifted his stare to Ian, a frown digging into his
brow, his thin lips pulling into a tight line. The captain had
informed them the yawl was missing, the man who had attacked
Ian nowhere to be found. Yet it seemed possible this man was in
league with the scoundrels who had attacked him. "Mr. Tremayne,
there's a man staring at us," Sabrina said, keeping her voice low.

Ian glanced up from his cards, his eyes suddenly alert. "Where
is he?"

"Behind you," Sabrina whispered.

Ian slid a chip across the table, allowing it to tumble to the
green and gold Brussels carpet. As he bent to retrieve it, he
glanced at the table where the man was sitting. He straightened, smiling as he gestured for the little man to join them.
When the man arrived Ian introduced Sabrina and Duncan to
James MacDoughal.

"I thought you were going to spend the evening in the gentleman's cabin, Mac," Ian said, glancing up at the man standing at
his side.

"I thought it best to keep an eye on you, Major." Mac shifted
a suspicious stare from Duncan O'Neill to Sabrina. "Never know
where there'll be trouble."

"Mac has been with the family since before I was born," Ian
said, smiling at Sabrina. She was staring at Mac, as though she
expected the little man to pounce at any moment. "He's been my
watch dog. Even followed me to war."

"Someone's got to look after you, Major."

"You see what I mean." Although Sabrina smiled, Ian could
sense her agitation. Mac was making her nervous. "Go enjoy
yourself, Mac."

"But, sir . . ."

"Go on," Ian said, glancing up at his old friend. "I can take care
of myself. I doubt the O'Neills intend to hit me over the head and
toss me overboard."

Mac gave Ian a stubborn look before he turned and left the
room, his bowed legs strutting indignantly. Ian knew better than
to believe Mac would keep his nose out of his business. No matter what Ian said to the old man, Mac would do what he thought

was necessary to protect him. Still, if the O'Neills were all they appeared to be, there would be no harm in Mac's snooping. . . . *If.*

Ian glanced at Duncan as the older man raised the ante. O'Neill had wasted little time in drawing him into a poker game. Was Sabrina as innocent as she appeared? Ian wondered.

Sabrina sat staring down at the poker hand she held, one slender finger tapping the back of a card, her delicate brows etching a crinkle in the smooth skin. The shape of her lips, the pure oval of her face, the dark sweep of sable lashes against ivory cheeks, curves and angles stroked with a rich palette of color created a compelling canvas. It was easy to savor her beauty, difficult to see beyond it.

As though she sensed him watching her, she glanced up, meeting his eyes; her eyes dark, endless, vulnerable, so very vulnerable. There was promise in those eyes, promise of passion and more, so much more. With one look she chastised the cynic lurking inside him.

He followed the rise of her blush as it brushed dusky rose across the smooth skin of her neck, her cheeks, the lobes of her ears. He imagined her hair loose, the silken skeins spread across his pillow, her arms bare and reaching for him. He found himself breathing deeply, trying to catch her scent, inhaling a wisp of warm jasmine. Beneath the concealing mask of his clothes, heat flashed across his skin, flaring along his thighs, his belly, tightening his muscles, flooding him with need.

One kiss had left him craving more. He wanted to touch her, feel the warmth of her blush; taste her, feel her body close around him until he was drowning in the light of her innocence.

There was something special about this woman, something special in the way she made him feel, something he didn't want to label or question or think about. Not now. Not yet. He just wanted to enjoy it for a while. He wanted to believe in the little girl who had once told him she would love only one man. He wanted to trust the bewitching woman she had become. He glanced at his cards, noticing for the first time the royal flush Sabrina had dealt him. The lady was bringing him luck.

Chapter Three

It moved toward them, a creature of light and fire, gliding across the dark, churning water, casting brilliant golden light against the glittering waves. The *Belle Angeline* called to her brother, lifting her voice in melodious song. Sabrina rested her hands on the smooth oak railing. She lifted her face to the chilly evening breeze, listening to the answering call of the approaching riverboat, feeling Ian's warmth radiate against her side.

Three days with Ian had gone by more quickly than three heartbeats. After the first day her father had not interfered. Perhaps it had been her own skill with the cards that had convinced him to abandon the fight; that first card game had cost Duncan a hundred dollars. But Sabrina preferred to think her father was silently allowing her to reach for her dreams, even though he didn't approve.

"When I was a little girl we'd sit on the back veranda and take turns telling tales, watching the boats glide along the river." Sabrina smiled up at the man beside her, moonlight etching each feature of his beloved face into her memory. "Did you know each boat has a unique whistle, a sound all its own?"

Ian turned, leaning his hip against the railing, smiling down at her. "I never realized that."

A waltz drifted out from the main cabin, the graceful notes weaving around them in bright, silvery threads. Sabrina resisted the urge to lean against Ian, to feel his warmth close around her. "My brothers prided themselves on being able to recognize a boat by the sound of its whistle."

"And you?" he asked, smoothing a wayward curl back from her cheek, his fingers lingering beneath her ear.

"Oh, I never was very good at it." She wanted to turn her face into his hand, to press her lips to his palm, to hold his slender fingers pressed to her skin. She felt delicate, vulnerable, as though she had been turned to glass and one wrong move would shatter her into a thousand pieces.

Ian stroked her cheek where the moonlight kissed her face, brushing warmth against her skin. "Dance with me, Sabrina."

One last waltz. One last time in his arms. She turned toward the main cabin.

"Here, in the moonlight," he said, taking her arm.

She closed her eyes as he took her into his arms. He held her close, closer than propriety would allow. Yet here in the moonlight there were no condemning eyes. His warmth chased away the evening chill, his arms held her with a gentle strength that made her believe he could protect her from any harm. Yet he was leaving. Tomorrow she would have nothing but memories to keep her warm.

His movements were bold, powerful, those of a man who had conquered this dance long ago. The emerald velvet of her gown billowed as he swept her across the deck, leading her through a series of dips and turns, waltzing into shadows, swirling back into the moonlight.

"Last night I was thinking about the first time we met," he said, slowing their movements until they were merely swaying to the music.

Each brush of his body against hers was a whisper spoken against the fluttering flames deep within her. "I'm surprised you remember at all."

"It marked a first. Never in my life had a girl dropped from heaven into my arms. As a matter of fact, you are the only girl to ever drop into my arms."

Her cousin Lucy still kept Sabrina informed of Ian Tremayne's exploits. The man had most of the women in New York at his feet. Beautiful women, young, privileged, women who didn't make their living by stealing from rich Yankees. "I suspect you don't often lack companionship."

"You said I should wait for the right woman. I have."

Did dreams come true? The look in his eyes gave her hope; with hope came fear. If he knew the truth about her, would he look at her this way, as though she were special? She stared at the hand she held against his shoulder, unable to hold his penetrating gaze.

"Is something wrong?" he asked, pausing in the middle of the deck, still holding her in his arms.

She should tell him now, before it went too far. Yet as she lifted her eyes to his, the words crumbled in her throat. Dear lord, she couldn't bear to see the warmth in those beautiful green eyes freeze into disgust.

"Is there someone else?" he asked, a line forming between the sable wings of his brows.

"There's no one else. There never has been."

He smiled again, a smile she would always remember. "That's encouraging."

The air had turned thick, far too thick to draw into her shallow lungs. "Is it?"

"Very," he said, sliding his hands down her arms.

The warmth of his hands seeped through the velvet covering her arms, a token of the warmth just out of her reach. She wanted to rest her head against his chest, feel his arms close around her, forget the past, the present, live only for the future with this man.

"Sabrina, I feel as though I've known you all my life. Longer. You make me feel . . . I'm alive with you, whole when I'm with you. Only with you." He paused, resting his hands on her shoulders, lifting his thumbs to brush heat against her neck just above the lace-edged collar of her gown. "I love you."

The words were spoken so softly, the words she had heard him speak a thousand times in her dreams. At first she wasn't sure he had really spoken them.

"Will you do me the honor of becoming my wife?"

Sabrina bit her lower lip, holding back the words rushing across her tongue. How could she agree to marry him without telling him? And how could she tell him?

After a long moment he touched the tip of her nose with his fingertip. "You keep me in terrible suspense, Brat."

Light spilled from the staterooms through the etched glass of the skylights, gilding his features. She closed her eyes, shutting out the compelling beauty of his face. He was so good, so honest, and she . . . she was a thief. Did she have a right to marry this man, the man she had loved all her life, the man she would always love?

He slid his arms around her, holding her against his chest, resting his cheek on her hair. The scent of starched linen mingled with his own to stimulate her senses. She could feel his heart beating against her cheek. If only . . . Ah, how many had made that desperate plea at some time in their life? It could change nothing.

"I had hoped you might return my regard," he said, his lips stirring her hair above her temple.

Her heart constricted at the tone in his voice, so filled with love, so vulnerable. "I do. Oh, I do."

"Then marry me, Sabrina. I'll make you happy." He stroked the blade of her shoulder with his warm palm. "Let me spoil you. Let me give you a home, children, a family."

Tears welled in her eyes, slipping from the corners, absorbed into the smooth white linen of his shirt. She couldn't let him walk out of her life. She couldn't allow a few months of vengeance to destroy their future. If he loved her enough, he would understand. Somehow she would make him understand. Somehow she would show him just how much she loved him. "Yes," she whispered. "Yes, I'll marry you."

His arms tightened around her, and then he was lifting her, spinning her round and round, until her laughter trailed in the air with his, her bright notes in harmony to his deep tones. Whispering her name, he lowered her into the moonlight. He brushed his lips against her cheeks, kissing away every trace of her tears, before pressing his lips to hers, allowing her to taste the salt of her own tears.

A soft sound, akin to a sob, issued from her throat as she threw her arms around his neck, pressing the softness of her body against his straining hardness. He slipped his arms around her, pulling her close, enfolding her in his love. She moved even closer, her crinoline tilting, allowing her to press more fully against him, providing her a provocative suggestion of powerful male thighs outlined by velvet. She couldn't get close enough to this man.

With her arms locked around his neck, Sabrina held him, fighting the terror inside her, the terror that he might leave; it was there, like a beast crouched in the shadows just ahead, waiting to destroy her. If she could only make him love her enough—enough to understand, enough to forgive.

He traced the fullness of her lower lip with the tip of his tongue, coaxing her to open to him. And she did, parting her lips, welcoming the shocking thrust of his tongue. She felt his body grow tense, the thick muscles of his chest turning to granite against her breasts. He delved into the moist mysteries of her mouth, plunging and retreating in a rhythm her body understood. Her blood quickened. The echo of her heart throbbed in the tips of her breasts, pulsed in that secret place deep within her, tugging her along paths she had only glimpsed in dreams.

Without warning, he stepped back, holding her at arm's length, his breath forming puffs of steam in the cold night air. "Have mercy, Brat. Any more and I'm going to lose this battle I'm fighting to be a gentleman."

"Would that be so bad?" she whispered.

He tightened his grip on her arms. "Sabrina, I'm not sure you understand."

"I've been dreaming about you for nine years, Ian Tremayne." She ran her palms over his arms, kneading the taut muscles through his coat and shirt with her fingers as she spoke. "Are you going to make me wait another day to make my dreams come true?"

He rested his brow against hers, closing his eyes, his breath a warm mist against her face. "Are you sure?"

"I'm sure I love you," she said, lacing her fingers through his. "Let me show you just how much."

Ian's cabin, one of the two suites aboard the ship, was located on the Texas deck in the stern. Ian turned up the gas on the wall lamp near the door, transforming the sitting area near the entrance into a golden oasis, casting flickering fingers of light into the shadows beyond. Sabrina's skirt brushed his legs as she moved past him, the brief touch tugging on his vitals. Everything inside him was taut and tingling.

He leaned against the door, the latch closing with a click. At the sound, Sabrina glanced back at him, before lowering her gaze to the floor. Lamplight stroked the smooth contour of her cheek, slipped into the thick coils of hair at the nape of her neck. The bed stood against the far wall, four posts of brass reflecting the light with a subdued radiance, beckoning.

Leaning harder against the door, Ian pressed his palms to the smooth oak to keep from touching her. He watched her, wanting her, his muscles rock hard, his blood pulsating with the need to possess her. This had to be slow and sweet and gentle. Yet a part of him wanted to toss her to the bed, to plunge inside her, to cleanse himself in her beauty, her innocence. Loath to frighten her, to overwhelm her with his need, he knew he had to keep that side of him in check.

"Your cabin is very nice," she said, her fingers fluttering over the high back of a blue velvet chair. "So much room."

She took a few steps, moving away from him, skimming her fingers over the bureau, touching his razor, his comb, her fingertips coming to rest on the rosewood handle of his brush. For a moment she stood with her head bowed, cast in profile, the glowing posts of the bed framing a portrait of feminine beauty and innocence.

Sensing her anxiety, Ian felt his chest tighten. Was she having second thoughts? Did she want to leave?

"Ian," she whispered, turning to face him. "I don't know . . . I've never . . . I'm not sure . . ." She bit her lower lip, cutting off her tangled words.

It would come now, her nervous plea to wait until they were married. He could override that plea. He knew how to touch a woman, how to drown any reluctance in sweet, sensual persuasion. Yet he wouldn't employ those old tricks with Sabrina. Never with Sabrina. He would abide by her wishes. For once in his stinking life he would be a gentleman. God, he wasn't sure he could let her walk out of this room.

"I'm not sure how things begin," Sabrina said, her lips curving into a shy smile. "But I'd like very much if you . . . if you'd kiss me again."

Her soft plea was a match to kindling. Two strides brought him to her side, and then she was in his arms, her arms tight around his neck, her breasts warm and firm against his chest. Ian tasted the tenderness in her kiss, felt the love flowing from her like wine. With the thirst of a man lost in an endless desert he drank from her lips, feeling her love course through him in a sparkling stream, swelling, saturating, until his soul was filled with her radiance, until the shadows disappeared.

"I've never felt like this with anyone," he said, stroking her cheek with the back of his fingers. "You're my own red-haired angel."

"Love me." Tears glistened in her eyes. "Please love me, Ian," she whispered, pressing her lips to his.

She trembled against him, pressing even closer, as though she couldn't get close enough, as though she thought he might suddenly disappear. With his lips against hers, he tried to reassure her. Nothing could ever tear him away from her. Nothing as long as he had life in his body.

He pulled the combs and pins from her hair, letting them fall to the floor as he freed her hair, strands of burgundy silk over three feet long cascading down her back. "Beautiful," he murmured, sinking both hands into the thick, cool waves, cradling her head, losing himself in the dark, shimmering depths of her eyes.

Beneath her hair, he unfastened the velvet-covered buttons running down her spine, and began dealing with the feminine barriers shielding her from his touch. With a stroke of his palms across her satiny shoulders, he sent the gown gliding to the floor where it settled, disturbing the air with a soft sigh. As he pressed kisses along the curve of her neck, his fingers worked the laces of her corset, the ribbon and eyelets holding her petticoat in place.

Ian knew the intricacies of women's clothes only too well. Countless women had shared his bed, all experienced, all well versed in pleasure. Yet this was the first time he would ever make love. He came to her used, jaded, cynical; that man would die tonight in her arms.

Four pearl buttons succumbed to his fingers; he slipped her camisole from her shoulders, baring her breasts. The round globes glowed in the lamplight, her skin so fair he could see the faint tracing of blue veins carrying her life's blood, the tips as dark as ripe strawberries, growing taut and tempting under his gaze. He brushed his cheek against their firm warmth, touched her skin with his tongue, tasting her, feeling her sharp intake of breath before her moan filled his ears.

He adored her breasts, flicking the tip of his tongue across each small, ripe berry, taking her into his mouth, sucking until she was clutching at his shoulders, until he felt her hips move rhythmically against his.

He slid her soft cotton drawers down the length of her legs, smiling at the little pink rosebuds adorning the white garters holding her white cotton stockings in place just above her knees. Innocent. Provocative. For a moment he thought about leaving the stockings, but not tonight. Tonight he wanted to touch every inch of her silken flesh.

He knelt on one knee before her, cushioned by a bed of velvet and satin. After removing her shoes, after sliding each stocking from her long legs, he stared up at this woman who had stolen his soul.

When she tried to cover herself with her arms he took her wrists in his hands, holding her arms wide, allowing the lamplight to flicker over the pale globes of her breasts, the sharp curve of her waist, the slight swell of her hips; warm ivory satin waiting for his touch.

"Never hide from me, angel," he said, pressing his lips to the smooth curve of her belly. "Always give me your beauty, your love."

The silky strands of her hair brushed his hands as he caressed the smooth curve of her back, the pouting cheeks of her rounded behind, kissed her belly, worked his way lower. She issued a whimpering sound deep in her throat. He nuzzled the crisp curls crowning her thighs, inhaling the heady musk of her scent, delving with his tongue, savoring the spicy taste of her. Her hands dug into his shoulders, clutching at his coat in a wordless protest.

He couldn't stop. He had to show her how precious she was to him. "Let me," he whispered, brushing his cheek against the curls guarding her feminine secrets.

Sabrina could deny him nothing. She wanted only to please him, to give herself wholly to this man.

Wicked. Wanton. Wonderful! She felt all of this and more as she opened to him, allowing him to touch her in ways she had never dreamed possible. With his lips and his tongue and his fingers he stripped away the mysteries, sliding inside her, discovering, teasing a hidden bud of sensitivity until it bloomed beneath his touch, stealing her breath, liberating that part of her ruled by primitive passions. She arched against him, shocked and exhilarated by her own desperate pleas for something she didn't understand, something her body craved, something only he could give her.

And then it was hers, this gift he surrendered with his touch. Shudder after shudder racked her body. If not for his hands on her hips she would have fallen, collapsed as one devoid of bone and muscle. In one graceful move, he stood, lifting her limp body in his arms, leaving behind a heap of velvet and satin and cotton on the floor, the wool and linen of his clothes scraping her sensitized skin.

Cotton sheets cooled her back as he laid her against the bed. "Don't leave me," she whispered, clutching at his shirt as he started to pull away from her.

He kissed her, a soft brushing of his lips against hers, a brief pulse of warm breath against her cheek. "I'm not going anywhere, sweetheart." In contrast to his words he gently pulled free of her grasp. "But I'm wearing far too many clothes."

Sabrina turned to her side, hugging her arms to her breasts, trying to ease the ache centered there. She followed his every move as Ian stripped away his clothes, the chair beside him gathering the discarded trappings of civilization: a gentleman's coat, waistcoat, cravat.

Sabrina slid her legs over the smooth white sheet, anxious for the first touch of his bare skin against hers. He removed his shoes and socks. Under his long fingers the pearl studs of his shirt slipped open, revealing a growing wedge of black curls. The lamp spread golden light over the thick curve of his shoulder as he peeled away his white linen shirt. He tossed the shirt to the chair, a gold ring swinging from a chain around his neck, shimmering in the lamplight before settling like a glowing ember against thick black curls.

Sabrina stared. Raw power pulsed in the thick muscles of his chest, his shoulders, his arms. A thin white scar slashed a diagonal path across his broad chest, starting just below the ring, slicing black fur before disappearing into the waistband of his trousers—the trousers he was unfastening.

Sabrina felt her mouth go dry. She had to drag each breath past the constriction in her throat.

He turned from her to strip away his trousers and drawers. With her eyes she traced the contours she so longed to touch, the lush curve of his shoulders, his arms, his back, thick muscles flexing with his movement.

Black wool and white linen slid away from the taut curves of his buttocks, the long sweep of his legs, black curls shading the thick muscles of his thighs. Just looking at him started an intoxicating warmth flowing through her veins, tingling every nerve, pulsing with a hot, moist desire in that nameless place only he had ever touched. He hesitated a moment before turning to face her.

The lamplight pulsed against his skin, carving a pagan god from the shadows. Sabrina sank her teeth into her lower lip. No one had told her what to expect. From the mating of horses she had only a vague idea of what would follow. Her body trembled at the images flickering in her mind. Still, she wasn't frightened, only anxious to learn the secrets from this man.

She swept the length of him with her gaze, trying to absorb the towering strength of his aroused male body. Another scar, this one thick and puckered, sank into the skin high on his right thigh. Yet the scars could not tarnish his masculine beauty. Just as there was beauty in a soaring hawk or in a stalking wolf, there was beauty in this man. She wanted to touch him, to feel his strength, to know him as she had never known another human being.

When she lifted her eyes to his she saw the wariness in those dark green depths, as though he expected her to be frightened, as though he feared she might deny him. Didn't he know, she could never deny him. She lifted her arms in a gesture of welcome.

He moved toward her, the shadow of the bedpost sliding across his body. The bed dipped as he lay beside her, rolling her against him. "Hold me," Sabrina whispered, sliding her arms around his shoulders. "Please hold me."

"Forever," he promised, slipping his arms around her, holding her close, kissing her.

She wiggled closer, brushing her breasts against the fur of his chest, rubbing her hips against his, slipping her knee between his thighs. The hot imprint of his body smoldered along the length of hers. The rasp of hair against smooth thighs, the solid thrust of pure masculinity against her belly, heavy, throbbing with tantalizing heat . . . every inch of him foreign, enticing.

"Ian," she whispered against his lips, loving the sound of his name.

With her hands she explored the intriguing terrain of his body, memorizing every curve and line, absorbing the texture and heat of his skin, wondering if she had ever felt anything so wonderful in her life. She slid her palms over his shoulders, warm satin over solid oak. The big, smooth muscles of his back shifted under her touch. He jerked suddenly as she ran her fingers down the column of his spine.

"A ticklish spot," she said, before nipping his chin.

He smiled. "You're learning my secrets."

She looked up into his eyes, eyes darkened a deep emerald by desire. He was so beautiful, a knight from a young girl's dream, scarred in battle, sent to rescue her from loneliness. "I want to know all of your secrets," she said, sliding her fingertip down the column of his neck. "Show me your secrets."

"Sabrina," he whispered, closing his eyes.

With his lips and tongue and hands he cherished her, kissing every inch of her skin, stroking, murmuring words of love and praise, making her feel beautiful and loved, so very loved. With feathery strokes he brushed her inner thigh before he trailed his fingers higher, into the mahogany curls. Sabrina arched against him.

"I don't want to hurt you," he whispered, his lips brushing her shoulder. "God, I don't want to hurt you."

Yet he would. By the tone of his voice, she knew he would, and she didn't care. "Please," she said, sliding her hands down his back. "Make love to me."

"Sabrina," he whispered, moving over her. Black curls teased her breasts. His weight pressed her down into the soft mattress, his skin searing her, his heat seeping into her pores.

When he settled between her parted thighs she opened to him, lifting instinctively, trying to capture him. He held back, poised against her entrance. He kissed her throat, her shoulder, his hands lightly stroking her hips, driving her mindless with need.

"Please," she whispered, clawing at his shoulders.

She heard him draw a deep breath, ragged, pulled between his clenched teeth. He gripped her hips and lifted her, pressing against her moist flesh with his velvet heat, slipping inside her. Just barely inside her.

He conjured magic. He was a wind blowing over a calm lake, raising ripples and waves of pleasure within her, pressing into her, parting restraining flesh, stretching, filling her inch by glorious inch.

The ring dangled from its chain, brushing her breasts with warm gold. Instinctively she wanted more of this man, needing all of this man. She tried to arch to take him in fully. Yet he held her hips, controlling her, sliding in and out of her; each time giving her more and more of his power; each time pushing until she felt a slow burn of pain; each time withdrawing, leaving her craving the splendid, searing touch of his flesh.

She looked up into his beautiful eyes. In those eyes she saw every word he had ever whispered, every kiss, every caress he had given her in countless dreams. She felt the toll of his control in the fine trembling of his arms and knew it was only his concern for her that kept him from giving her what she most desperately wanted.

"Now," she whispered, smiling up at him, brushing her fingers over his shoulder. "All of you, now."

He closed his eyes, as if on a silent prayer, then looked down into her face. "My love," he whispered, before giving himself to her.

She cried out with the pure joy of their joining. The pain was fleeting, a moment of searing heat that flared, then died, then rose from the ashes as pristine pleasure. Together once more as they had been through the ages, two pieces merging, forging a whole, claiming a love willed to them by destiny.

"Ian!" His name burst from her lips over and over again as she rose to meet his sleek thrusts, following the animal grace of his powerful body, finding her own power in the pleasure she could give by answering his primitive call. And she did give him pleasure. She could see it in the narrowing of his eyes, in the harsh gasps slipping from his parted lips, feel it in the tension of each rippling muscle beneath her palms.

Soon all thought dissolved into a vortex of pleasure, swirling, spiraling inside her, each stroke of his body spinning her faster and faster, drawing her upward. He covered her lips with his, snatching soft sobs from them, coaxing her to an even quicker rhythm.

Her hands curled against his shoulders, sliding against his glistening skin, grasping him, trying to pull him with her as he sent her higher. One sharp thrust sent her soaring, ripped at last from the bonds of earth, tossed toward heaven, feeling him rise with her, filling her with heat and power, clutching her, as their bodies stiffened and arched and fought to remain as one.

She held him with her arms, with her legs wrapped around him, reveling in each tremble of his body. His muscles seemed to collapse one by one as he eased against her, resting his cheek against her moist shoulder. His breathing mirrored her own, his heart beating to the same rhythm, filling her ears with the steady throb, growing quieter, quieter, until sedate and sated.

"Are you all right?" he asked, lifting his head, his nose brushing hers.

"No." She smiled as his face pulled into lines of concern. "I'm more than all right. I feel wonderful. Wonderful!"

She slipped her hand into the damp waves at his nape and pulled him down for her kiss. Love nurtured by nine years of longing, sweetened by loss, rose from deep inside her, surging upward, filling her, flowing through her every vein.

She humbled him with the purity of her love, and at the same time she filled him with a glorious pride. "Sabrina," he whispered against her lips, shifting to his back, taking her with him.

She giggled as he hugged her, rolling her from side to side, his arms locked around her slender frame. It had never been like this before, and Ian knew it would never be like this with another woman. But then, he didn't intend to ever know another woman, not again, not after tasting heaven. He felt new, all polished and shining with hope. In love for the first time. In love for the last time.

"Can we do that again?" she asked, rubbing her hand against his chest.

Ian couldn't help but laugh at her innocence. She was like a child who had just tasted chocolate for the first time.

She frowned and tugged at the hair on his chest. "Just why is that so funny?"

"Because I intend to do it again, and again," he said, slipping his hand into her hair, the silky strands curling around his fingers. "Just give me a few seconds to recover."

She smiled, seemingly satisfied with his response. He ran his fingers over the soft curve of her breast, the rosy tip growing taut at the slight touch. Responsive, so sweetly responsive. She made him feel as though he could fight dragons with his bare hands, conquer worlds in her name.

"Are you glad you waited for me?"

"Hmmm, very."

She lifted the ring from its nest of black curls, turning it in her fingers, capturing the lamplight in the braided gold. "And this?" she asked, smiling down at him. "A memento from a former lady love?"

"The ring my grandfather MacClaren gave to my grandmother on their wedding day." He kissed the tip of her nose. "The ring you will wear tomorrow, my love."

Sabrina closed the ring in her hand, staring at her knuckles for a long time. "Love me, Ian," she whispered, looking into his eyes. "Please, love me."

The desperate plea stabbed his heart. He could see fear in her eyes, fear of losing him, as she had lost her mother and her brothers. She had suffered in the war. She didn't have to tell him; he knew. He could tell by the way she relished simple pleasures, like a cup of creamy sweet coffee or a chocolate-covered pastry filled with whipped cream. There had been months of deprivation, maybe years. He was going to make up for those years. He was going to spoil her, adore her for the rest of his life.

"I do love you," Ian said, shifting beneath her. "More than anything in the world."

Moist curls teased his flesh before he found the entrance to paradise, before he felt her close around him, surrounding him with sleek, quivering heat. He loved her again and again and again, swearing his devotion, loving her as though this would be the last time he would ever hold her.

Each time with Sabrina was a revelation; each time the pleasure mounted with nearly unbearable intensity, proving more exquisite than the last. Finally, when they were both too exhausted to do more, they lay quietly in each other's arms. In this Ian also found a revelation: just being near her, just holding her was more fulfilling than anything in his past.

"I was going to California out of St. Louis. On business," Ian said, when their breathing had returned to a normal pace, and she lay curled soft against his side, one pale thigh resting over his, ivory against bronze, her cheek nestled against his shoulder. "Should we make it a honeymoon trip? Or is there some other place you would like to go?"

"To bed," she said, nuzzling her nose against his damp shoulder.

"I think I might have released a tigress."

"A ravenous one," she said, taking a little nip of his shoulder.

One dark brow lifted as he looked down at her. "Still hungry?"

"No." She smiled against his skin. "I feel plump and happy, contented."

He shared that feeling, a lush contentment he had never before known, a sense of loving and being loved. A part of him was afraid it might all disappear, as though what he held was only a dream, a dream that would vanish with the light of dawn. With his fingers he started brushing designs on the back of her neck, drawing a soft sigh from her lips. "Do you mind moving to New York?"

"I'd go anywhere with you."

He held her closer, pressing his lips to her hair, breathing in her fragrance. "We'll visit your father, and Rosebriar, as often as you like."

Reality seeped into the dream, like cold rain dripping through the eaves of a cozy cabin, chilling Sabrina. Curling her hand against his chest, she closed her eyes, willing away the intruder. Not yet. She didn't want to think of reality yet.

"What is it?" he asked, cupping her cheek in his warm palm, coaxing her to look at him.

She managed to smile. "Nothing. I was just thinking it's getting late. Aggie will be wondering what's happened to me."

"Tomorrow I'm going to grab the first preacher I can find and make you my bride." He hugged her in his powerful arms, kissing her hard. "I want to hold you through the night, see your face in the light of dawn, love you through the day."

Dread drifted around her, like mist gathering above the river, a premonition of impending disaster so strong it filled her every breath, pervaded her soul. With the truth, Ian could have her arrested; he could have her father arrested. She rested her head against his shoulder, staring at the ring nestled against the springy black curls.

Tomorrow morning, when they docked at St. Louis, Sabrina would tell her father about their plans. After she and Ian left the ship, when she was sure her father was out of firing range, she would tell Ian the truth.

Ian loved her, she assured herself. He would understand. He had to understand. There was no reason to be worried, she thought, trying to chase away the doubts, the fears. None at all.

Chapter Four

"The captain said we'd be docked by nine this morning," Mac said, laying several of Ian's shirts in a drawer of the trunk that stood open near the bed. He pulled his watch from his waistcoat pocket, frowning as he glanced down at the dial. "Gives us a little less than an hour left on this boat."

Ian slipped a blue and white cravat around his collar, staring at his reflection in the mirror above the washstand. His own face seemed foreign. Perhaps because he was looking at the features of a man satisfied with his life, satisfied because of one red-haired angel. The woman was magic.

"You're in mighty good spirits this morning," Mac said when the younger man started humming a waltz.

"That I am," Ian said, looking past his own reflection to the image of Mac trapped in the mirror. The old man stood staring at him, his face puckered into a frown, a dark counterpoint to Ian's smile. "Mac, you shouldn't eat lemons for breakfast. People will think you're unhappy with the world."

Mac shook his head. "I'll be glad to be getting my feet back on solid ground, I will," he said, marching to the armoire. "And out of rebel territory."

Ian tied his cravat, smiling as he thought of Mac's suspicions. For the past three days he had been bombarded by Mac's warnings. The old man didn't trust any rebel. Especially if that rebel were a planter who rode around in style when most planters didn't have enough money to plant cotton. Especially if that rebel enjoyed playing cards. No matter what Ian had said, the old watchdog wouldn't let go of the idea that the O'Neills were up to "dark mischief."

"I've got a steward waiting," Mac said, carrying an armful of suits toward the trunk. "We can be off this ship in two shakes of a mule's tail."

"I want you to arrange to have a steward pick up a trunk from Miss O'Neill's stateroom," Ian said, smoothing his cravat into his ice blue waistcoat, turning to face his old friend.

Mac frowned, staring at Ian a full ten seconds before finding his voice. "And why would I be doing that?"

"Because the most beautiful woman in the world has agreed to become my wife."

The suits fell from Mac's arms, splashing brown and blue and gray across the blue and white carpet. "You went and asked that woman to be your wife?"

"Mac, I realize you're only trying to protect me, but I don't need any protection from Sabrina."

"Damn, damn, double damn," Mac mumbled, bending to retrieve the pile of cashmere and superfine wool. He tossed the suits over the top of the trunk and stood staring down at them. "I wish you hadn't asked her. I wish I didn't have to tell you. But I'm going to have to tell you."

Ian didn't like the tone in Mac's voice, didn't like the doubts it triggered in his own mind. "Tell me what?"

"I told you I was suspicious of the man," Mac said, glancing over his shoulder at Ian. "I thought he was a little too eager, the way he got you into a poker game right away. So I watched him. I saw him playing in the gentleman's cabin. I saw how smooth he handled the cards."

Ian felt as though the ground beneath him wasn't what it seemed, wasn't quite solid. At any moment it might vanish and send him tumbling toward a void, with nothing to break his fall into oblivion. "Get to the point."

Mac ran a hand through his hair, leaving a few wisps standing on end. "I did some checking. I figure a ship is like a little town. You want to know anything, you just got to ask the barkeep. So, last night . . ." He hesitated before turning to face Ian. "There ain't no easy way to say this, so I'm just gonna spit it out."

"That's what I'm waiting patiently for, Mac."

Mac took a deep breath and started at a dead run. "O'Neill makes his living on the boats, stealing from rich Yankees he takes at the table. Cheating with cards. The daughter lures them in, then the father takes their money."

"What the hell!" Ian said, grabbing the little man's collar.

"It's the truth, Major," Mac said, straining against the strong hands that were pulling him off the floor.

"I don't believe it!" Ian shouted, shaking Mac like a rag doll.

"I'm . . . sorry," Mac said, clawing at Ian's hands, his face turning red. "You're . . . choking . . . me . . . sir."

"Dammit," he said, shoving Mac away, trying to rein in his anger, his hands trembling with the effort.

"I was hoping I was wrong," Mac said, rubbing his neck. "But you have to know; she's after your money."

"There has to be some mistake." Ian grabbed his dark blue coat from the foot of the bed. "Maybe the man wanted to get back at O'Neill for some reason."

"I don't think so." Mac pulled a package of cards from his pocket and handed it to Ian. "The barkeep said he keeps several packs just like this for O'Neill."

Ian pulled the cards from the package and shuffled through the deck, studying the backs of the cards. His jaw clenched as he noticed the small black mark in the corner of the red and white cards, placed differently for the different denominations.

"They're marked in the corner, sir."

"I can see that, Mac," Ian said, shoving the cards back into their package. "I didn't lose any money to him. In fact, he lost money to me."

Mac shrugged, staring at Ian from beneath his shaggy brows. "Maybe the girl saw a way to get more than what her father could make at the table."

Ian's hand clenched around the cards. "You're wrong."

Mac shook his head. "I wish I was."

"I'll prove it." Ian shoved the cards into his pocket and stormed out of the cabin. He wanted to hear the truth from Sabrina. He wanted to banish the doubts before they had a chance to fester inside him.

Ian raised his hand to Sabrina's door, hesitating a moment before rapping his knuckles against the solid oak. A moment later Aggie opened the door.

"I was thinkin' t'would be ye, Mr. Tremayne," Aggie said, stepping aside, inviting him in.

Over Aggie's head, Ian saw Sabrina. At the mention of his name, she spun toward the washstand, her gown of white- and violet-dotted silk swirling around her. Leaning toward the mirror, Sabrina pinched her cheeks, the gesture so earnest, so innocent, so disarming, he felt some of the darkness lift from his soul. She had to be innocent. He couldn't be wrong about her.

When he entered the small stateroom Sabrina turned to face him, twin blossoms of color staining her cheeks, her breasts rising and falling in uneven rhythm beneath a veil of lace and silk. He had meant to bring her roses this morning, pink roses to match the blossoms in her cheeks. Instead, he brought her doubts.

"Aggie, why don't you go on in to breakfast," Sabrina said, taking Aggie's arm. "We'll follow in just a few minutes."

"But they won't be servin' yet. What do ye expect . . ."

Ian stood near the door leading to the deck, watching Sabrina usher Aggie from the room, their voices reflecting on his ears without penetrating. Sunlight slanted through the skylight behind him, carving a bright path across the carpet, seeking Sabrina. The sun worshiped her, touching her face with gold, embracing the shimmering strands of her dark red hair.

In his mind he could see her lying on his bed, her skin pink-tinged ivory against the stark white cotton, her lips smiling, her hands touching him, as though he were the only man in the world, the only man for her. Memories stroked his loins, memories of a woman opening to her first taste of love, opening with a sweet passion that had stolen his soul.

After Aggie left Sabrina stood for a moment with her back pressed against the door, smiling at him, an angel suspended in a sunbeam. "I was hoping you'd come early."

She moved toward him, smiling, lifting her hands, reaching for him. Ian couldn't move. He felt the weight of the cards in his pocket, felt it pull against his heart like an anchor.

"What is it?" Sabrina asked, hesitating a few feet in front of him, her fingers curling into her palms. "Something's wrong. Isn't it?"

Delay was senseless. The sooner he cleared up this misunderstanding, the better. He slipped his hand into his pocket and withdrew the package of cards, laying them face up in his palm.

"Great stars above," she whispered, pressing her hand to the base of her throat. "How did you get those?"

Ian glanced down to the cards, the cards she had recognized with some measure of horror. "It seems you and your father make a living by relieving Yankees of their gold," he said, his voice sounding strange to his own ears, his mind still refusing to believe the truth.

"Ian, I should have told you, I started to a hundred times, but . . . I was afraid."

She wasn't even going to deny it. The stark truth slammed into his belly like a hot poker. He took a deep breath before he tried to use his voice. "Afraid the fly might have escaped your web?"

"Ian, please try to understand." She flicked the tip of her tongue over her lips, leaving them moist, reminding him of things that needed to be forgotten. "We lost everything in the war. The Yankees burned our house. We needed money to live, to rebuild; it seemed . . ."

"And that's what you wanted from me. Money." He slipped the cards back into his pocket. When her memory taunted him, when he woke in the middle of the night reaching for her, the cards would serve as a reminder of her treachery, of his own foolishness.

Sabrina shook her head, biting her lower lip as though she was fighting against tears, color rising to stain her smooth cheeks. "I was going to tell you before we were married, I swear," she said, resting her hand on his arm, flinching when he jerked away from her soft touch.

If he didn't know better, if he hadn't learned how well she could lie, he would believe every word. Lord help him, he wanted to believe her beguiling lies. "You are quite a little actress, aren't you."

"I just wanted to wait, to give us a little more time. I guess . . . I guess I just wanted you to love me a little more before I told you." She drew a shaky breath. "Ian, you have to believe me, I love you so very much."

"Bravo! Nice performance. But not as well played as last night." He laughed, glancing away from her, looking into the mirror above the washstand. In the silvered glass he saw his image reflected beside hers, caught in the spotlight of the sun, two actors in a twisted tragedy.

"Ian, please, don't do this. Don't rip us apart."

Raw pain coiled around Ian's heart, twisting, choking, until his chest throbbed. "Trading your virginity was your way of making sure I wouldn't back out of the marriage."

"No. It wasn't like that. I only wanted to show you how much I loved you."

She knew where to strike to do the most damage, knew where he was the most vulnerable. Suddenly he wanted to return just a measure of the humiliation he felt, just a sliver of his pain. He pulled his money clip from his pocket and withdrew a wad of bills. "Here, this should pay for your services last night."

Her lips parted, her features twisting with pain, as though he had just rammed his fist into her belly. "How dare you!"

"Oh, I love your outrage, Miss O'Neill. If I didn't know better, I would think you were about to cry real tears."

"Ian, please believe me," she said, plump tears glistening on her thick lashes. "I love you. I never intended to deceive you."

Lies! He had never heard better, told more convincingly. "And I never really intended to marry you."

She stared at him with lovely, confused eyes.

"I knew about your little game the first time your father dealt a hand of cards. I played along. I wanted to see just how far you would go to get my money."

"You knew all along?" she asked, tears spilling down her cheeks, catching the sunlight.

He nodded. "You can't really believe I would marry a rebel," he said, running his fingers across the full curve of her breast, smiling as she gasped. "I would rather bring a viper into my home."

"Everything was a lie?"

"I figured my little ploy of asking you to marry me would get what I wanted. And it did. You were one hell of a tumble."

She seemed dazed, as though she had fallen hard and had had the wind knocked from her. "Then, last night . . ."

"Was immensely enjoyable. Although not much of a challenge." Ian dropped the bills on the chair by the door, noticing the few drops of his blood staining the arm of the chair. It was nothing compared to the way he was bleeding inside. "If you ever decide to change professions, I know of an excellent brothel in New York. With that pretty body of yours, you can make a fortune."

She closed the distance between them, slapping his face before he could react. When she drew back for another attack he grabbed her wrist, wrenching her arm behind her back, slamming her against his chest. Instantly, the firm globes of her breasts seared his body through the layers of clothes separating him from her smooth skin.

"To blazes with you!" she shouted, tossing back her head. "I wish I'd never met you, Ian Tremayne."

Ian stared into eyes filled with fury, wishing he could forget the image of those eyes drenched with desire. He needed to forget. He needed to purge the memory of her skin sliding against his, her body drawing him deep inside, her scent, her taste. A knife twisted in his belly.

He shoved her away, dragging a deep breath, trying to calm the rush of blood in his veins. "If you play the game, Sabrina, be prepared to lose."

"Get out!" she shouted, clenching her hands into fists at her sides. "Get out!"

"There's nothing here to make me want to stay."

Once outside, Ian leaned back against her cabin door, closing his eyes, parting his lips in silent anguish. He wanted to lash out, to hurt something as much as he was hurting inside. He wanted to go back inside and shake her, crush her luscious, deceiving body to his, bruise her lips beneath his kiss, force her to love him as much as he loved her.

He ran his fingers over the fiery brand she had left across his cheek, feeling the searing heat of the other brand she had left across his soul. What a fool he had been! What a damned fool! No doubt Miss Sabrina O'Neill had had a tremendous laugh last night. At least he had the satisfaction of knowing she wasn't laughing now.

Sabrina couldn't breathe. Pain constricted her chest, squeezing her heart, strangling her lungs. For one moment she had known love as she had only dreamed possible, in the next it was gone. Nothing but smoke. Nothing but dreams. Dreams shattered by one callous man. A knock sounded on the door, but she couldn't move.

"It's me, Kitten," Duncan said, his voice a low rumble through the oak door. "Sabrina?"

The door opened. Through a veil of tears, she watched her father move toward her.

"Sabrina," Duncan said, taking his daughter into his arms. "I saw Ian Tremayne storming back to his cabin. One look and I knew something was wrong."

Sabrina heard a sob, the pitiful sound of a creature in agony. Was that her voice?

"Tell me about it, Kitten. Did he hurt you?"

She had to pull together the pieces. She couldn't let Ian Tremayne destroy her. "He . . . he knew about the cards," she whispered. She swallowed hard, pushing back the tears constricting her throat. "He thought I was just acting."

Oh, how she wished she had been acting. She would love to slip out of this skin of Sabrina O'Neill and into another, one Ian Tremayne would never forget, one he couldn't hurt.

"I'll go after the bastard. I'll call him out."

"No," she said, grabbing his arm as he started to leave. "No more bloodshed."

"But, Kitten . . ."

"No, please. Promise me you'll let me deal with Ian Tremayne my way."

Muttering an oath, Duncan lowered his head. "All right. We'll play this hand your way." He stared at her a long moment, rubbing his mustache before he finally spoke. "What are you planning to do, Kitten?"

"I don't know." She slipped her tongue out to taste the bitter tear poised at the corner of her mouth. "But you can be sure Mr. Ian Tremayne won't like it."

Chapter Five

"So, you failed."

Bennie shifted on the wooden stool, trying to see the face belonging to that raspy whisper, the face of his mysterious employer. A single lamp burned on the wall near the door, casting his companion in purple shadows.

The room smelled of whiskey and stale cigar smoke. It was hot, too damned hot, Bennie thought, glancing to the windows, wishing he could throw back the drapes and open the windows and let the November wind blow into the room. He felt as though he had swallowed a hot coal and it lay burning in his stomach.

From the bar below the sound of women's laughter and male voices drifted upward, seeping through the wooden planks of the floor. Flannery's was one of the rowdiest bars in Five Points. More than once Bennie had bloodied his fists on one of his fellow patrons. More than once he had jumped some sucker in the alley behind the bar. It was the way he added to his dock worker's salary. But tonight he was here for a different reason.

"Like I told you, Ed got killed trying to take out Tremayne. The guy tossed him overboard." Bennie held up his broken arm. "I got this. I was damn lucky to get away at all. You never said taking him out was like taking on the Fifth Calvary."

"I warned you he would be difficult."

From the shadows Bennie heard glass slide against the wooden top of the round table. Black-gloved fingers pushed a glass and a bottle from the shadows where his employer remained hidden. A dark outline was all Bennie could see, a hat pulled low over a face, obscuring the features.

"Have another drink, Bennie. You look like you could use it."

That raspy voice scraped along his spine. Bennie grabbed the bottle and tipped it against the water glass, clanging glass against glass. His unsteady left hand spilled whiskey across the table, forming dark puddles against the scarred oak as he poured. The liquor was a fiery heat across his tongue, down his throat. He drained the glass, refilled it, then drained it once more. Maybe the whiskey would settle his stomach.

"Feel better?"

Bennie dragged the back of his hand over his mouth. He would feel better when he got his money and got out of here. "Look, I done what you asked. I earned the money you promised me."

"Tremayne still lives."

"Look, I ain't gonna go after that guy again."

"I suspect I will have to deal with him myself." His employer shifted in the shadows. "When he returns he shall have an accident."

"I want the rest of my money."

"I paid you to kill a man."

Bennie stood, his legs feeling queer, like two pieces of seaweed. He pressed his hand on the table, trying to steady himself, sweat dripping from his brow to mingle with the whiskey spilled across the table.

"Something wrong, Bennie? Perhaps something you ate?" A raspy whisper asked from the shadows. "Or drank?"

Pain gripped his stomach, twisting it. Bennie doubled over, wrapping his arms around his middle, groaning, falling, bumping the table in his tumble. Glass crashed against oak, whiskey spilled, the bottle rolled across the floor, coming to rest against the wall with a dull thud.

"What . . . what . . . was in there?"

"Arsenic." Wood scraped against wood. His employer rose. "I'm told it will be quite painful. But don't worry, Bennie, it won't last long."

"Damn . . ." His body convulsed. His stomach heaved. He vomited across the dirty oak planks.

"It might be amusing to see Tremayne this way."

Through his tears Bennie saw the outline of his murderer. He tried to crawl, tried to grab one black pant leg.

"Still, an accident would be better," the employer said, backing out of the dying man's reach. "If not nearly as amusing."

Darkness snatched at Bennie through the pain. His body convulsed once, twice. He fell still, his breath escaping like a balloon collapsing.

Eyes sightless to the world caught the light of the lamp, reflecting a figure dressed in black.

Chapter Six

"Are you trying to give away all your money, Ian?"

Gaslight flickered overhead, casting Ian's reflection onto one of the glass-paneled bookcases lining the walls of his Uncle Henry's library. Ian ignored his cousin Randal's last question. It was at best rhetorical, he decided, looking through the glass at one of the books standing on the shelf: *Murders in the Rue Morgue.*

For as long as Ian could remember Rand had devoured mystery novels, beginning with Edgar Allan Poe. As boys, Ian and Rand had raided this library on a weekly basis, searching for books they weren't allowed to read.

"I just don't understand how a man can work so hard at making a fortune, then turn around and throw money away."

Ian frowned at his reflection in the glass as he listened to Rand. His cousin was beginning to sound like an old tutor they once had as boys. In a minute he expected to hear Rand pound a ruler against the wall just like old Holworth.

"Eccentric. That's what people are saying about you. Ian, you can't rebuild the south on your own."

Ian stared down into his glass of brandy, listening to Rand's muffled footsteps as his cousin paced the room. Was this the same man who had helped Ian smuggle three prostitutes into the library at Harvard one midnight? Even now the scent of dusty tomes conjured images of painted lips, of pale white thighs spread wide in flickering candlelight.

"Rand, what Ian does with his money is his business."

"Father, it's not just the low interest loans. It's the homes for widows and orphans, for invalids from the war."

Rand paced to the open French doors, slashing with his hand at the green velvet drapes that fluttered with the breeze. He was three months younger than Ian, but right now he seemed older, older than his uncle, old enough to be his grandfather, for that matter. For the first time Ian noticed the thin strands of gray in Rand's light brown hair, the lines flaring out from his gray eyes.

"How many have you established, Ian?" Rand asked. "Three in the east, half a dozen in the south, a few God knows where. What is it, ten altogether? Twelve? Fifteen? There's even talk you intend to turn the house on Madison Square into a home for widows and orphans."

Four years. Ian had spent them at war, Rand had spent them in marriage. Somewhere in that expanse of time, in that collection of varied experiences, Ian had ceased to know this man.

"They're just rumors, right?" Rand said. "You aren't going to turn that house into one of your orphanages."

Ian smiled. "I am."

"Your father's house." Rand looked as though he had just witnessed a particularly grisly murder. "Ian, you could get a fortune for the land alone."

"It's a nice big house, with plenty of bedrooms." And Ian didn't have the slightest intention of ever staying there again, not in his father's house.

Rand closed his eyes, his breath escaping in a sigh. "You know, they're going to say you're crazy."

When had his cousin become so preoccupied with money? Ian wondered. He suspected it had happened soon after Rand had slipped a wedding ring on Delia Maitland's lovely finger. Delia was a furnace, requiring steady shovels of cash to keep her warm.

"We should all be that crazy," Henry said, leaning back in a leather wing chair near the lifeless hearth. "I'm proud of what you're doing, Ian."

Ian shrugged. "If we don't help the people in the south rebuild, if we don't help them feel they are part of this country again, then the war accomplished nothing."

Into Ian's mind drifted the vision of a dark-eyed angel with hair the color of a scarlet sunset. Money to rebuild. Sabrina's need had cost him his future. There were times when he wished he had never discovered the truth about her, times when he would give anything just to see her again, just to touch her one more time. Pitiful fool.

"Is something wrong?" Henry asked, studying Ian over the rim of his glass. "Did everything go well in New Orleans and San Francisco? You've been back two weeks and you haven't said a word about your trip."

"It was . . . completely uneventful."

"I'm glad to hear it." Henry rolled his glass between his palms as he studied Ian. "Maybe now you'll stay in town a while instead of roaming from one end of the country to the other. We haven't seen much of you since . . . well, since you came back from the war. You shouldn't make yourself a stranger."

Sometimes Ian felt like a stranger. He felt more at ease with people he barely knew than he did with his own family. He stared into the darkness beyond the French doors. A warm breeze drifted into the room, carrying the raucous rhythm of a reel, the strident sounds of laughter from the ballroom. Soon he would be expected to join those people, Ian thought, feeling his stomach tighten. He had known most of the people in that ballroom all his life, and yet they didn't know him. Not any more.

"I'm hoping you will take more of an interest in the bank," Henry said, smiling at his nephew.

"What's wrong, Father?" Rand's lips pulled into a taut line beneath the fringe of his thick brown mustache as he glared at his father. "Don't you think I can handle the bank?"

Henry lowered his gaze to his brandy snifter. "Profits weren't exactly what they should have been last year."

"We still managed to make a profit. So we made a few bad investments." Rand turned a slate-gray stare on Ian. "It could have happened to anyone. Even you."

Ian felt the old rivalry crackle in the air between them, the same rivalry he had felt when his own father would hold his brother Jon up as the shining example of all a man could hope to ever become. He smiled at his uncle. "I'm sure Rand is doing a fine job."

Henry rolled his glass between his palms, frowning at Ian. "You are the majority partner, Ian. Two thirds of the bank, two thirds of all we've invested in, is yours. You should take more of an interest in what is happening."

Being caught in the middle of another argument between Henry and Rand was not a position Ian cherished. "Right now I'm tied up with other business."

"Trying to convince the legislators to vote for the merger of the Hudson and the Harlem." Henry smiled, lifting his brandy snifter to Ian in a silent salute. "You see, I do keep track of what my boy is doing."

Like his grandfather MacClaren, Henry had always tried to fill the void between Ian and his father. Charity for a young boy without a mother, for a young boy without a father. Two sons and a daughter had been born to Everett and Brenna Tremayne. Yet it had taken Ian years to fully realize that his father had room for only one child, his eldest son, his heir. Ian's hand clenched on the brandy snifter as he recalled the last day he had spoken to his father.

Ian had returned home from Chancellorsville bearing the news of Jon's death. Heartbroken, Everett had retreated into a bottle of bourbon, spurning every attempt Ian made to console him. On the night before Ian was to return to camp, he had made one last attempt to reach his father.

Everett hadn't turned as Ian approached, hadn't shown any sign he even knew his son was there. He just sat there behind the desk in his study, staring at the unfinished portrait of Jon hanging above the mantel. Only when Ian touched his father's arm did Everett acknowledge his presence. He had lifted his gaze to his one remaining son and delivered the final blow, shattering any small illusion Ian had held.

"Why couldn't you have been the one buried on that battlefield?" Everett had asked, his voice slurred with bourbon. "It's your fault my son is dead."

The words had stabbed Ian as fiercely as cold steel. At that moment he had felt worthless, and so damn foolish. If only he hadn't spent a lifetime trying to be worthy. But he had.

Two months later Ian had received a letter from his sister, Ellen. A trip on the top step of the long staircase at home had ended his father's life, and any chance they might have had to ever reconcile.

"Ian, your father would have wanted you to run the business," Henry said.

Ian wanted nothing of the Tremayne dynasty. Jon had been the chosen one, the man destined to assume the throne.

"I'm not sure we can make a banker out of Ian," Rand said, grinning at his cousin, his eyes betraying another emotion. "This is the man who once said he would never be cooped up in a bank all day."

Ian met the defensive anger in Rand's eyes with a smile. He understood that anger, all too well. "A few years ago I never would have wagered you would be married, or be working in the bank."

Rand shrugged, glancing down to the floor. "Amazing what the right woman can accomplish."

The door opened as Rand spoke. Ellen paused on the threshold and smiled at her cousin. "It's that very reason I've come looking for Ian."

Ian frowned as Ellen marched toward him, the look in her green eyes alerting his bachelor instincts, instincts freshly honed on the strop of Sabrina's treachery. Gaslight flickered on her black hair as she moved toward him, apricot- and cream-colored silk flowing around her slender form.

"There's someone I want you to meet," Ellen said, taking the glass from Ian's long fingers. She set the glass on the walnut table near Henry.

"Not again. The last woman you wanted me to meet chattered like a magpie."

"This woman is different," Ellen said, smiling up at him. "The first time I saw her I thought she was perfect for you."

"That's what you said about the magpie," Ian said, meeting Ellen's smile with a frown.

Ellen had been fifteen when their mother died. Although still a child herself, she had tried to become a mother to her seven- and five-year-old brothers. At seventeen she had left them to start her own family. Still, after more than twenty years, some habits lingered.

"I just can't stand seeing you go to waste," she said, tugging on his arm. "You've been back in town for two weeks and you haven't attended a single function. You're going to end up a lonely old bachelor."

Ian sighed and bowed his head. "Only if I'm lucky."

"I won't allow you to become a hermit," Ellen said, ushering him out of the library.

A hermit. He had never imagined himself becoming a hermit, but now the life appealed to him. If you didn't let people near you, you didn't have to expose yourself.

"You should have your hair trimmed," Ellen said. "All you need is a ring in your ear to resemble a pirate."

Ian ran a hand through his shaggy mane. He had intended to schedule time to have it cut, but it kept slipping his mind. "Afraid the lady won't like me?"

Gaslight from the wall lamps reflected in her eyes as she looked up at him. "Darling, I don't know a woman alive who wouldn't adore you."

At least they would adore the Tremayne money, Ian thought.

Their heels clicked against alternating squares of white and black marble as he walked beside his sister. Doors of polished walnut blended with walnut wainscoting as they traveled a long corridor leading to the ballroom, the music growing louder with every step they took.

He glanced into the card room as they passed, wishing he could escape into that male refuge. It had been months since Ian had attended a ball. He wouldn't be here tonight if Delia hadn't insisted he attend. Delia loved balls. It gave her a chance to shimmer in the spotlight, and she wanted everyone to see her glow.

Before the war mothers were often cautious about Ian. Not only was he a second son, but he had the reputation of being "handsome as the devil and just as dangerous to a young girl," as he had overheard one matron express it. Now, after inheriting both the Tremayne and MacClaren fortunes, every matchmaking mama in town was steering her daughter in his direction. Amazing what money could do for one's reputation.

"You look as though I'm leading you to the gallows," Ellen said.

"Aren't you?"

Ian was beginning to think there was a factory hidden beneath New York, a place where debutantes were manufactured. Inevitably these young ladies, with their smiling faces and flirting eyes and empty heads, would ask him the same questions about the war. Why did everyone think a man wanted to talk about his grand and glorious battles? There was no glory in war.

"She really is remarkable. And she's a real English countess, the daughter of an earl. Three weeks in the city and Lady Julia Wyndham has New York at her feet."

Ian frowned. This morning his nephew had spent an hour sitting in his office, talking about the beautiful Englishwoman. "This wouldn't be the same English countess who has Tim on his ear?"

Ellen kept her eyes focused straight ahead. "Timothy and every other eligible man in New York."

"Perhaps you have more than one reason for introducing me to the lady?"

"I wouldn't introduce you to her if I didn't think you would like her." She glanced up at him, a frown crinkling the smooth skin between her dark brows. "And yes, I think she is wrong for Tim. She's older than he is, and far too sophisticated, far too stunning. I think she could hurt him very deeply."

Ian knew the reality of those words. Sabrina had ripped his heart from his chest, had left him empty and bleeding.

Ellen paused in the hall a few feet from the entrance to the ballroom, touching his arm. "Is something wrong?" she asked when he met her eyes.

"Nothing." Ian forced a smile to his lips. "I was just thinking of work, that's all."

"Burying yourself in work, avoiding your family, your friends. It isn't healthy. Sometimes I think you take those business trips just to get away from us."

He felt safe in business, in control. At least in business no one tried to force him to be something he wasn't. No one expected him to be the same idealistic young man who had ridden down Fifth Avenue with all the other idealistic young men, marching to war, so full of righteous indignation at the south's attempts to destroy their country, so ready to fight, so ready to die. Only he hadn't died.

"I miss that charming young man who used to tease me, who found pleasure in everything he did. I miss your smile." She hesitated, studying his face a moment before she continued. "I worry about you."

"There's no need to worry about me. I'm a big boy now, and I'm doing just fine."

"I'm always here for you, Ian." She pressed her gloved palm against his cheek. "I only want the best for you. I want to see you happy, settled."

Ian rested his palm over the delicate hand pressed against his cheek. "Have you ever thought some of us are destined to remain bachelors?"

"Not you. You always had so much love inside you. It would be a horrible crime if you didn't have the chance to give it to someone. We just need to find the right woman."

The right woman. A few months ago he had been certain he had found her: that one woman he was destined to meet, to love for the rest of his life. It seemed youth didn't have a monopoly on foolishness, he thought. Still, there were times when he wondered if he would ever be able to purge that red-haired witch from his soul. Sabrina still haunted his dreams, invaded his waking moments when he least expected it.

"I'm sorry, El." He wasn't ready to go back into that ballroom. He wanted to leave, to retreat to the safety of his lair, where no one could push and prod and ask for things he couldn't give. "I'm really not in the mood to meet an English countess tonight. Perhaps another time."

"Ian, please," Ellen said, grabbing his arm as he turned to retrace his steps. "I really do fear Tim has lost his heart to this woman. At least get to know her. You can do it better than I. Women sometimes wear a different face with men than they do with other women. You'll be able to see if she's right for Tim, if she's safe. And you might even find she's right for you."

Ian shook his head. "El, I . . ."

"I keep thinking of Preston Van Horne."

Ian frowned, remembering the young man. Six years ago Preston had put a bullet in his brain over the lost affections of one of New York's feckless debutantes. "Tim isn't Preston Van Horne. He has more sense."

"Does he? Do you know him so well?"

Ian stared at the open doors leading to the ballroom. He didn't want to be here. He didn't want to paste a social smile on his face. He didn't want to scrape small talk from the roof of his mouth. "El, I'm sure Tim has more sense than to . . ."

"You knew the boy who adored his Uncle Ian. The boy who spent summers with you at Dunkeld. The boy you took fishing and riding. The boy you built a tree house for."

Ellen's words conjured images in Ian's mind: misplaced memories of sunshine glittering on the river, of soft summer breezes tinged with the scent of meadow grass and wildflowers, of laughter and innocence. He had been Tim's hero, the big brother the boy had always wanted.

"You don't know the sensitive young man he has become. Please, stay a little while. Talk to this woman, see what you think. I feel so unequipped to handle Tim. If Paul were here . . ." Her voice trailed off, her eyes lowering to where she clutched his arm, her white glove a ghost against his black coat.

Paul Reynolds had been more than his sister's husband. He had been a good friend, a friend who had died with so many others, while Ian had come marching home. "All right."

Ellen rose on her toes and kissed his cheek. "I don't know what I would do without you," she said, slipping her arm through his before ushering him toward the end of the corridor.

She paused at the top of the three wide stairs leading down to the ballroom, searching the crowded room for Lady Julia. From their vantage point, Ian surveyed the room, wondering about this English countess, admitting some curiosity. According to his nephew, the lady was an angel.

Tier upon tier of cut crystal glittered in flickering gas jets high overhead, four chandeliers raining golden light on more than five hundred of New York's elite. Gilt-trimmed mirrors on white-paneled walls reflected the radiance of gaslight. This was Delia's idea of a small party.

The robust strains of a waltz flowed from the second-floor minstrel's gallery into the room below, mingling with laughter and voices raised in conversation. In the center of the room, men in black evening clothes whirled ladies in colorful, flowing gowns around the polished walnut dance floor. Ian wondered if he would ever feel comfortable in this setting again. Tonight he was an alien among people he had known all his life.

Ellen led the way across the ballroom to where a group of people were gathered near the wide French doors leading to the gardens. A semicircle of men surrounded the settee, each paying court to Lady Julia Wyndham, shielding her from Ian's gaze. He could say one thing for her: The lady was generating tremendous interest.

Two gentleman stepped aside as Ellen tapped their shoulders, revealing the lady to Ian's curious eyes. One look sent the air rushing from his lungs, as though a cannon shell had slammed into his chest. For a moment he could do nothing but stare, stunned by features he thought never again to see.

She smiled, looking up at him with those huge dark brown eyes that had haunted him day and night for months, her expression growing curious under his steady glare. Ian reacted on instinct, forgetting everyone, everything but the woman smiling up at him. "What the hell are you doing here?"

"Pardon me. I don't believe I understand your meaning."

Somewhere in the corner of Ian's mind, in a niche not clouded with rage, he realized there was something wrong with her accent. "I don't know what your game is this time, but it isn't going to work, Sabrina." He took her arm and plucked her from the yellow brocade settee.

"Sir, I'm afraid you have me confused with someone else," she said, tripping as he dragged her toward the nearest door.

Ian caught her, pulling her against his chest; his body jolted into awareness at the feel of her breasts snuggled against his chest. "Damn you!" he mumbled, setting her back on her heels as though she were poison.

"Just what is the meaning of this!" Caroline Van Cortlandt demanded, blocking Ian's way when he started for the door with Lady Julia in tow. "How dare you treat Lady Julia in this outrageous manner!"

"If you had any idea of the true nature of this woman, you might understand," Ian said, his long fingers tightening on Julia's arm.

"Sir, I'm afraid there has been some terrible mistake. If you would just release me, I'm sure . . ."

"Why the British accent, Sabrina?"

Her dark eyes shimmered with amusement. "Perhaps because I was born and raised in England."

"Ian Tremayne, unhand Lady Julia this instant!" Caroline demanded. She stretched her five feet two inches until she seemed to match Ian's six feet three.

Ian hesitated, confusion warring with anger in his brain. The men paying Lady Julia court stayed clear of his anger, preferring to watch the battle from a safe distance of several feet. Without looking, Ian was aware of them, of the other spectators gathering around them, of their sharp indrawn breaths and their curious stares.

"Mr. Tremayne, my arm is growing numb," the beauty murmured, smiling up at him.

"Ian, please," Ellen whispered, touching his back.

Ian dropped his hand to his side, holding the beautiful redhead in the taut tether of his gaze. He drew a deep breath, trying to gain some control over his emotions.

"Ian Tremayne, I have never witnessed more shocking behavior in my life," Caroline said, cocking her dark head. "I demand you apologize to my goddaughter this instant."

"There has been no harm done," said the lady in question, rubbing her arm, the imprint of Ian's fingers staining her pale skin below the scallop of cream-colored lace draping her short puffed sleeve. "It's obvious the gentleman has mistaken me for someone else."

"Is it?" Ian turned from Julia to face Caroline Van Cortlandt. "This is your niece."

Caroline lifted her brows slightly. "I am her godmother."

"This is your niece, Sabrina O'Neill," Ian said, correcting her.

"This is Lady Julia Wyndham," Caroline said, as though she

were trying to teach English to a backward child. "The daughter of one of my dearest friends. Her father was the Earl of Lanchester."

"Julia Wyndham," Ian whispered, staring down at Sabrina. "What game is this?"

"Game? I'm not sure what you mean."

"Don't you?" Gaslight glowed on skin as smooth as silk, shimmered on dark red hair, setting fire to the thick coils drawn back from her beautiful face. This was Sabrina. He had no doubt about it. "The accent isn't much of a disguise."

"I didn't realize I needed one." Lady Julia tapped the lace-trimmed edge of her fan against her chin. "It would seem Sabrina left quite an impression on you."

"Not at all favorable," Ian said.

She laughed. "Apparently not. I know Sabrina, or I did, many years ago. I believe we have the same color hair. Perhaps that's what has you confused."

"The same hair." He clenched his hands into fists to keep from touching her. "The same features." He lowered his eyes, raking her body with his gaze, showing his contempt. "The same figure."

"Really!" Caroline said.

"Remarkable. I have heard we all have a double in this world, though one likes to think one is unique," the lady replied, smiling up at him. "Please excuse me, Mr. Tremayne. Perhaps we can discuss this later. You see, I've promised this dance to the gentleman behind you."

The beautiful redhead stepped around Ian when he refused to move, taking Timothy Reynold's arm. Tim hesitated for a moment, staring at his uncle, before leading Lady Julia toward the dance floor.

"That was most unhandsome of you," Caroline said, glaring at Ian. "If you only knew the scandal of it all. Come, Lucy."

Lucy Van Cortlandt stepped around Ian as though he were a rabid dog. Caroline turned on her heel and marched away, leaving Ian staring at her stiff back, her words swirling in his mind. Just what did she mean by a scandal?

Ian turned, watching his nephew take that infuriating redhead into the embrace of a waltz. So this was Tim's angel. Ian's gaze drifted from her burgundy hair down the curve of her pale shoulder. Sapphire-blue silk hugged the swell of her breasts, the sharp curve of her tiny waist, before billowing around her hips and shrouding her long legs. But he knew what was beneath all that silk and linen.

Images clawed at his heart: fragrant hair laying across his pillow in waves of red silk; soft lips parted in welcome; lamplight flickering against pale breasts, the rosy peaks lifting in silent invitation; satin thighs parting beneath him, wrapping around his back, as he plunged into the tight, quivering core of her. A sensation close to pain twisted in his chest, then gripped him low in his belly.

"Well, you certainly made an impression," Ellen said.

"El, are you sure that woman is who she says she is?" Ian asked, his eyes focused on Lady Julia.

"If there is one thing I learned while growing up in this city, it was to respect, and fear, Caroline Van Cortlandt. If she says that woman is Lady Julia Wyndham, that woman is Lady Julia Wyndham."

Ian shook his head. "She can't be."

Ellen tapped Ian on the arm with her fan. "Please, try not to start a riot. I'll try to smooth things with Mrs. Van Cortlandt."

Ian turned and watched Lady Julia as she glided through a waltz in his nephew's arms. She glanced in his direction, her smile setting a vise around his heart. Impossible! It just couldn't be. No two women could look that much alike.

"Is it safe to approach?" Delia asked, coming up behind Ian.

Ian turned to face her, blinking as shards of light slammed into his eyes. Upon first glance he had the impression a chandelier was moving toward him. Gaslight tumbled from the ceiling, ricocheting against the diamonds in the tiara perched in Delia's dark hair, glittering in the diamonds dripping from her ears, in the thick blue-white stones circling the curve of her graceful neck, sprinkling light across the hundreds of diamonds covering the white brocade of her gown. Ian wondered if he were looking at Rand's profit from last year.

"I don't think I've ever seen you make a stronger impression on a woman," Delia said, slipping her arm through his.

"Have you ever met a woman who was the very image of another?"

"No." One delicate brow arched slightly as Delia smiled up at him. "But I have heard a few gentlemen use that pretense to meet a lady on occasion."

"Identical," Ian whispered, looking back at the woman calling herself Lady Julia. Did she really think she could stroll back into his life and trick him into believing she was another woman?

"Do you mean Lady Julia reminds you of another woman?"

"No. She is another woman. A Miss Sabrina O'Neill."

"You mean this Sabrina came to New York and convinced Caroline Van Cortlandt to go along with her masquerade?" Delia arched one brow. "Mrs. Van Cortlandt, the dragon of society?"

"She really is Caroline's niece."

A dark curl brushed her pale shoulder as Delia tilted her head. "I thought Caroline was her godmother."

"No. Sabrina O'Neill is Caroline Van Cortlandt's niece."

Delia shook her head. "Why would she do it? Assuming she isn't Julia."

"Revenge."

"Oh, I see." Delia snapped open her fan, smiling up at him over the gilt trimming the edge. "Did this woman manage to slip under your guard?"

Ian frowned, keeping his gaze on the woman he knew was Sabrina. She had managed to slip under his guard and plunge her sword right into his heart.

"Did you want to marry her?"

He tipped his head, glancing down at Delia, telling her without words the answer was none of her business.

"So you did." She snapped her fan closed. "I wonder what she has that I didn't."

"You preferred Rand."

"You had to be a hero. Rand had far more sense." She brushed her fingers over his white cravat, rolling the emerald he wore in the snowy white folds beneath her fingertip. "Pity we'll never know just what we both missed. Or will we?"

Upon her debut the year before the war, Delia had been the most popular debutante in New York. Like most of the other bachelors in town, Ian had escorted the beautiful brunette to a few functions. But there had never been any mention of anything beyond an innocent flirtation, until his return from the army. "Delia, I . . ."

"I know. Forget I mentioned it." She turned and stared at Julia a few moments before she spoke. "Have you given any thought to the fact that she could be Lady Julia.? It seems to me this Sabrina would try to disguise herself in some way, maybe color her hair. That is, if she were going to try to convince you she is someone else. And I still can't imagine Mrs. Van Cortlandt going along with any tricky business."

Neither could Ian, but it was just too hard to believe. He had to hand it to Sabrina for her choice of roles. Who would doubt the word of Mrs. Caroline Van Cortlandt? "I guess I'll just have to find out whether or not the lady is telling the truth."

"If she is this Sabrina, do you suppose she would resort to violence? Maybe even try to kill you?"

Ian shook his head. "No. She would want a revenge of a far more personal nature."

"Still, I suppose you can never be certain she wouldn't try . . ." Delia hesitated, her gaze fixing on something to Ian's left. "Oh, dear, here comes trouble," she whispered.

Ian dragged his gaze from Sabrina, frowning as he saw Felicity Strickland advancing toward him. There had been a time when Ian would have greeted Felicity with open arms. But that time had passed. It had ended five years ago, on the day she had announced her engagement to Jon. Felicity had decided she could have Jon, the Tremayne fortune, and Ian to warm her bed. Ian had ended the affair.

After Jon's death Felicity had tried to reconcile with Ian, but he had had no use for the beautiful blonde. She had become engaged to Walter Strickland as a last resort, an attempt at jealousy, an attempt to bring Ian to his knees. Ian had wished her well.

Eight months of marriage hadn't changed her. Felicity was still trying to convince Ian to rekindle the fires of an affair that had died years before.

"You're staring at her like a hawk eyeing a mouse. Have you fallen under the lady's spell?" Felicity asked, running her hand down Ian's arm. "I understand she has every eligible male in New York at her heels."

"Who?" Ian asked, knowing full well Felicity had been watching his every move.

"The Lady Julia Wyndham, as if you didn't know," Felicity said, jealousy shaping each word into a dagger. "I'm really not sure what all the fuss is about."

"I guess you're having trouble with your eyesight," Delia said, smiling down at Felicity. "I've heard it comes with age."

The look in Felicity's hazel eyes told Delia to jump from the nearest bridge. Her expression softened as she looked up at Ian. "Dance with me," she said, resting her hand on Ian's arm.

"You never did believe in waiting until you were asked," Ian said.

Felicity leaned against him, pressing her breasts to his arm, a full swell of flesh rising above the snug yellow satin of her bodice. "There was a time you didn't mind."

"Times change."

"They don't have to," Felicity said, lowering her voice to a husky whisper.

"I think they do," Ian said, covering her hand with his. He intended to pry her hand from his arm, but before he could Felicity's husband emerged from a small crowd of people behind her. Great; a jealous husband was just what he needed to make the evening complete.

"Good evening, Walter," Ian said, breaking free of Felicity's grasp.

Walter nodded, his lips twitching, bobbing one corner of his wide mustache, his dark gaze fastened on Ian's face. He could feel Strickland's rage; it was a palpable thing, as tangible as Felicity's hand had been on his arm. They were nearly the same height, yet Strickland outweighed him by at least twenty pounds. Ian wondered how well Walter could use his weight in a fight; he wondered if Walter intended to show him.

"I thought you and Mr. Elsbury were deep in conversation, Walter," Felicity said, facing her husband.

Ian frowned, wondering what business Strickland had been discussing with the legislator. It could mean nothing. And it could mean Strickland was looking for a way to sink their efforts to merge the Harlem and Hudson railroads.

Strickland stared at Ian, his dark head cocked at an arrogant angle. "I noticed some other business that needed attending." He moved toward his wife the way he moved toward everyone and everything, looking as though he intended to plow aside anything in his path. "Excuse us, I want to dance with my wife."

Strickland took Felicity's arm and propelled her to the dance floor. He pulled her into the embrace of the dance and dragged her with him around the floor. Although Ian couldn't hear the words, the expression on Walter's face shouted every angry word.

"That woman won't be satisfied until she sees you and Walter facing each other with pistols drawn."

Delia had spoken Ian's thoughts exactly. "She's harmless compared to Sabrina."

"Looks as though she already has Tim on a leash."

Ian's hands clenched into fists at his sides. Something dangerously close to jealousy nipped at his heart when he thought of

Sabrina with another man, any other man.

One way or another he would strip away her mask. And when he did he would make that beautiful red-haired witch rue the day she was born.

Chapter Seven

Three weeks in New York, three weeks of attending parties and dinners and balls, and Sabrina had finally caught sight of her prey. Excitement and fear mingled in her veins as she thought of the dangerous game she was playing; vengeance didn't come without risk.

Sabrina felt Ian's gaze on her and glanced in his direction, meeting his angry stare with a smile. As if he had any reason to be angry. She was the one betrayed, the one stripped of her last shred of dignity.

"I want to apologize for my uncle. I've never seen him like that."

Sabrina glanced up at her enemy's nephew. Aside from the fine, straight nose and prominent cheekbones, Tim bore little resemblance to his beautiful mother, or to his uncle. He was close to six feet in height and slight of build. With a lock of pale blond hair tumbling over his brow, he looked younger than his one and twenty years. "I'm afraid your uncle mistook me for someone else."

"It's hard to believe he could . . ." Tim paused, glancing at the couple dancing nearby.

"Dammit, Felicity!" Walter's sharp tone caught the attention of everyone within twenty feet. "What the hell is it going to take to purge Ian Tremayne from your blood? Will you still be pining over the man when he's six feet under?"

"Quiet! People are watching," Felicity said, her voice a harsh whisper.

"I'm warning you, Felicity, end it with Tremayne."

"Or what? You'll challenge him to a duel?" Felicity laughed, a cold, bitter sound that grated on the nerves like nails against a chalkboard. "Do you honestly think you're a match for Ian? Why he'd . . ." Her voice faded as they swirled farther from Sabrina and Tim.

Sabrina stared after them, watching the anger build in Walter Strickland's face. Fear nibbled at the base of her spine as his angry words echoed in her mind. Strickland looked as though he could kill a man.

"I hope you don't get the wrong impression about my uncle." A rosy blush rose from Tim's starched white collar to darken his tanned cheeks. "He's really a very fine man."

Sabrina smiled up at this handsome young man. "You are fond of your uncle."

"Uncle Ian is one of the finest men I've ever known. He was a hero in the war, saved hundreds of men and very nearly died doing it. And near the end he even acted as a spy, right in Richmond."

A spy. Lying. Deceitful. Treacherous. The profession suited Ian Tremayne perfectly, Sabrina thought.

"No one can ride like him, or handle a pistol like him." Tim's dark eyes filled with pride as he turned his gaze to where Ian stood on the edge of the dance floor. "I always wanted to be just like him."

Sabrina wondered what Tim would think of his uncle if he knew the man had a penchant for seducing and deserting innocent women. It occurred to her, destroying this innocent young man's faith in the scoundrel might be one of the things she would take as part of her revenge.

At the end of the dance Tim relinquished Lady Julia into the arms of the next gentleman on her dance card. Like shears snipping the bud of a rose, the war had severed Sabrina's youth. The parties she might have attended, the men who might have courted her, had shriveled and died just as Sabrina was blossoming into womanhood. In the guise of Lady Julia, she tasted the wine of things that might have been, dancing with one young man after another, smiling, flirting, keeping Ian in her sights, willing him to engage in battle.

Ian kept his distance.

One lovely young woman after another accompanied Ian to the dance floor, their jewels glittering in the gaslight, their Worth gowns brushing his long legs. Youth, money, position were their heritage. And they all wanted Ian Tremayne. Could one English countess attract his attention?

Since arriving in New York Lady Julia had received thirteen proposals of marriage. Rich men seeking a titled bride, poor men seeking a wealthy purse, old men, young men, all flocked around the English heiress. Ian Tremayne wouldn't keep his distance for long, she assured herself. Curiosity alone would draw him into her web. Yet midnight flickered and died without seeing Ian Tremayne approach the Lady Julia.

She was sick to death of watching Ian Tremayne and his harem, Sabrina thought as she climbed the wide oak staircase of the Tremayne mansion. She tossed back a lock of hair tumbling across her shoulder, the tresses escaping the once neat roll at the nape of her neck. Her hair hadn't lasted through the last reel. Neither had her toes.

She glanced down at the blue silk slippers peeking from beneath her gown, a dark stain marring one toe. Timothy Reynolds wasn't the best dancer in the room, she decided, but, he was one of the nicest young men she had met in New York, despite the fact that he had a scoundrel for an uncle.

One bedroom on the second floor had been reserved for use by the ladies at the ball. Against one wall stood a large four-poster bed hung with white brocade. The other furniture, the sofa and chairs, the vanities and chests, all were white, trimmed with white. A thick white carpet stretched to all four walls, which were paneled in wood painted white. Sabrina felt as though she were walking into a cave of ice.

Two girls stood near one of the vanities, watching as a third young woman sat primping before the mirror. Sabrina had attended the coming-out ball for one of the girls, a Miss Fanny Warren, the week before.

"Rouge!" Gloria Phelps said, bending to get a better look at what her friend was doing. "Alisa, you don't really mean to use rouge."

"Just a dab," Alisa said, smoothing the color across her cheek. She tilted her fair head, regarding her image with a smile on her lips. "No one will know."

The girls turned as Sabrina drew near. She smiled and greeted them, receiving a warm smile and a greeting in return from Fanny and Gloria. Alisa Rensselaer was different. Behind her smile, Sabrina saw the cool look of a lioness eyeing an intruder to her turf.

Before Lady Julia had arrived Alisa had been the most popular debutante of the season. Since Julia's arrival more than a few of Alisa's beaux had deserted her for the English countess. Sabrina's smile grew a little wider as she held Alisa's dark blue gaze. Pampered, spoiled, willful, the beautiful Alisa deserved to scrape her nose bumping against the English countess.

Sabrina took a seat at the vanity near Alisa, one of the four vanities provided for the guests. After waving away the maid who came to her assistance Sabrina set out to tame her wayward mane. Beside her the girls giggled and talked and primped. Parties and balls, striving to be the belle of the town, worrying about your hair and clothes and the empty line on your dance card; that was the type of life Sabrina had been destined to lead. But fate had dealt her a different hand. Sometimes she couldn't help but wonder why.

Instead of living a life of pleasure, at their age Sabrina had watched her father and brothers ride off to war. While the debutantes of New York had been planning their next ball, Sabrina had been scraping the garden to find enough food for the next meal. And then Vicksburg. Her palms grew damp as memories flooded her consciousness.

Sabrina brushed her hair, half listening to the girls' lively voices. She envied them, envied their innocence, their joy, their bright, secure futures. Her own was far from secure. She had spent every penny she had saved to finance this trip of vengeance, including the thousand dollars Ian Tremayne had tossed at her for her "services." But it would all be worth it to see that man humbled.

"Mama says the only reason Mr. Tremayne is back out in society is because he's looking for a wife." Fanny released her breath in a heady sigh. "Oh, I think he's the most handsome man I've ever met."

Sabrina's hand tightened on the brush, her heart tripping at the mention of Ian's name.

"There's something dangerous about him," Alisa said, her voice filled with excitement. "He's a wild wolf surrounded by tame puppies. You can just look at him and know he's killed a man."

"My father said Mr. Tremayne was a hero in the war," Fanny said. "Yet he won't talk about it. When I tried to mention the war he changed the subject. Isn't that odd? You would think he would want to talk about what he did."

A hero. How many men had he killed? Sabrina wondered. Perhaps Brendan or Dennis had fallen by his hand.

"Did you see how smug Gretchen Chambers looked tonight?" Gloria asked. "Just because Mr. Tremayne took two dances, and both of them a waltz. She thinks the man is going to ask for her hand."

"Not if I have anything to say about it," Alisa said, her voice growing sharp with determination.

Sabrina dragged the brush through her hair. The women of this town acted as though Ian were the last man on earth, the only eligible male in the city. No wonder the man was an arrogant buffoon. No wonder he hadn't come near Julia Wyndham.

Perhaps he *was* looking for a wife; one of these pampered little debutantes, with their perfect little smiles and their perfect little lives, Sabrina thought. And he could have them.

Yet the thought of Ian married to another woman pierced her heart as keenly as a blade. Why was she so horribly weak? Why did she let it hurt her? Dear God, she was so tired of hurting.

"You'll have to excuse me, ladies." Alisa rose from her chair like a princess rising amid her court. "Ian has asked for the next waltz, and I wouldn't think of disappointing him."

The girls giggled and teased Alisa as they left the room. Sabrina lowered the brush to the smooth white top of the vanity. Tears pricked the corners of her eyes. Perhaps she had been a fool to come here. Ian was no more attracted to her in the guise of an English countess than he had been in that of a southern woman. She had been convenient and easy. Far too easy. Just one more conquest.

She grabbed her hair and began to coil the thick tresses at her nape. The war wasn't over yet. Somehow she would catch that man's attention. Somehow she would make him pay for what he had done to her. Somehow!

When her hair was finished she left the room, prepared to do battle. The lilting strains of a waltz drifted into the hall swirling around her as she descended the staircase. Sabrina paused at the base of the stairs, glancing at the wide entrance leading to the ballroom. She knew Ian was in there, dancing with the beautiful Alisa. And she knew she couldn't go back in there. Not yet.

She turned away from the ballroom, escaping down a long corridor, seeking refuge from the music, from the laughter, from Ian Tremayne and his women. As she walked along the hall, Sabrina glanced at the marble statues perched on pedestals along the walls, bits of white linen strategically draped from the waists of a few of the bolder Greek gods, apparently to spare the sensibilities of the female guests. Her innocence no longer needed shielding. Not since she had met one of those pagan gods in the flesh.

Near the end of the hall, she paused at an open door, intrigued by what lay within. Only one of the three gaselieres burned within the library, the gas turned low, a timid light glowing on bookcase-paneled walls of polished walnut. Books, hundreds of books, beckoned to her from behind glass doors. Most of the riverboats had small libraries, but nothing like this, nothing like the library she had lost with Rosebriar.

Sabrina crossed the thick green and gold carpet, drawn to the books, peering through the glass like a child at a candy store. She opened a door and ran her finger down the spine of *Wuthering Heights,* wishing she could lose herself between the leather covers. With a sigh, she closed the door. Books would have to wait.

"Did your Aunt Caroline tell you it was safe to come in here now?"

At the sound of Ian's resonant baritone, Sabrina spun on her heel, clasping a hand to the base of her throat. He rose from a wing-backed chair on the far side of the room, his expression cloaked in shadows. "Mr. Tremayne, I didn't know anyone was in here."

"Didn't you? Your aunt just left. I assume she told you she was done with her little drama."

Sabrina had never intended to involve her aunt, but after hearing what had happened between her niece and Ian Tremayne, Caroline had insisted on becoming a part of the scheme. And it was like prying pennies from a miser to get Caroline to change her mind once she had it set. Even after Sabrina had pointed out the risks, even knowing her reputation could be shattered, Caroline had remained adamant.

"I'm not sure what you mean," she said, in all honesty. No one knew exactly what Caroline would do next.

"No, of course you don't."

He left the shadows, moving toward her, gaslight glinting on the anger in his eyes. She fought the instinct inside her screaming for flight, reminding herself of the many months she had been waiting for this confrontation. This was only the first battle.

A smile curved his lips as his gaze dipped, boldly sweeping her figure. Her skin tingled, as though he stroked her with his fingers; and deep within her flesh, in that part of her only he had ever claimed, a pulse fluttered to life.

When he lifted his gaze to hers those pale green eyes told her he knew exactly what lay beneath the layers of silk and linen veiling her figure, exactly how her skin felt rubbing against his, how exquisitely their bodies fit together. He raised his glass, tilting it toward her in a salute before taking a sip.

To blazes with the man! He had left his mark on her, a brand across her soul, a hunger for more than revenge. She hated him for that. If the arrogant scoundrel thought he could muddle her senses with one glance, he was mistaken, she thought, desperately trying to pull together her scattered wits. She would show him. Lady Julia Wyndham was one woman who would never succumb to his maddening masculine magic.

"Mr. Tremayne, if you have something to say, please say it. I find your vague innuendos quite tiresome."

His lips lifted in a cold imitation of his smile. "You really are very good. Have you ever thought of a career on the boards? You would make a splendid actress."

He paused less than two feet in front of her, close enough for her to see the black pinpoints of beard beneath the surface of his smooth cheeks, close enough to catch the intriguing scent of his skin. Too close. "You really are quite rude. Have you ever thought of learning the social graces? You might eventually make a passable gentleman."

"On the surface, perhaps. But we can't change what we are inside, can we?" He swirled the brandy in his glass, glancing into the amber liquid, a circle of fire rimming the glass: gaslight striking crystal. "Do you always wear that perfume?"

His question caught her off guard. "No, but I often wear it. One of the ladies who once attended my mother mixes the fragrance of jasmine with spices. It's just one of the fragrances she prepares for me, but it's my favorite."

"It's strange both you and Sabrina would wear a similar fragrance."

Odd, he had remembered her perfume. Was there more he remembered? Did she haunt him a little, just a fragment of the way he haunted her? "Are you sure it is so similar?"

Was there a flicker of doubt in his eyes? A waltz drifted in through the open windows. Sabrina thought of Alisa wandering the ballroom, looking for Ian, and her smile grew wider. "You intrigue me, Mr. Tremayne. It would seem you cannot look at me without seeing this other woman. Do I really look so much like Sabrina?"

"The resemblance is nearly beyond belief."

Nearly. "She made quite an impression on you."

"When I was twelve I was stung by a hornet. I remember that sting to this day."

Sabrina fought to keep the smile glued to her lips. "Did you love her?" One last bud of hope demanded she ask, demanded she be sure before she went through with the rest of her plan.

His mutilated brow rose. "You're very direct."

"It's one of my many faults." She held him with her eyes, daring him to speak the lie. "Are you going to tell me?"

"Does it matter?"

More than anything else in the world. "It might. No woman likes to think she is being constantly compared to another."

Ian studied her a moment, as if weighing his words carefully. Behind them, velvet drapes lapped in the breeze, dancing to the waltz threading around them. "Whatever Sabrina and I had was a lie."

"I see." It had been real for her, far too real. Although she hadn't realized it, until this moment she had hoped there was a chance to put the past behind them, had hoped she might have been wrong about him.

Foolish woman!

Feeling her mask slip, she turned away from him. The evening breeze fluttered lace curtains at the windows nearby, brushing several rosewood frames perched on a Duncan Phyfe table sitting in front of the windows. One photograph caught Sabrina's attention. She lifted the rosewood frame and tilted it toward the light.

A young man dressed in leather breeches with a tartan sash slicing his white shirt stood poised with lance in hand, a mischievous look in his pale eyes—Ian. Even as a boy it was clear he had been destined to break hearts.

She felt his approach, the air coming alive as he drew near, pulsating against her skin. He paused beside her, so close his arm brushed hers, warm wool against her bare skin. Her fingers tightened on the frame. "Was this taken before you became a cynic, Mr. Tremayne?"

"We all have a time of innocence. That was taken at the height of mine."

How she had once loved the sound of that deep voice. How she had once craved the sight of his face, the touch of his hands. "You look as though you were ready to go out and slay a dragon."

"I was." He took the frame, his fingers brushing her hand. "When I was thirteen I had the idea of holding a tournament, complete with jousting, archery, and fencing contests. I guess I wanted to be one of King Arthur's knights."

She could imagine Ian at a joust, imagine him dressed in shining armor. Only this knight had a black heart. A feudal lord, bold, arrogant, sure of his power, taking everything he wanted. A pirate. That was Ian Tremayne. "You must have been a romantic."

He set the photograph on the lace runner covering the center of the tabletop. "I suppose I was."

As he looked down at her, his defenses seemed to slip. For a moment Sabrina imagined seeing her own pain mirrored in his eyes. Emotions rose inside her: anger, pain, hate, love, thick veins twisting around her heart until her chest ached. She wanted to slap him, to kick him, to throw her arms around him and hold him, just hold him. What had happened to that romantic boy? Why had he become a scoundrel? She wished she knew. She wished . . .

"Why did you come here?"

He was safely encased in armor once more, prepared to slay her as though she were a fire-breathing demon. "To visit with my godmother."

His eyes penetrated hers, stripping away her mask, dipping into the well of longing hidden deep inside her. "You're good, Sabrina," he said, his voice as soft and smooth as plush velvet, his eyes as sharp and brittle as cut emeralds. "But it won't work. I didn't buy the little fable your Aunt Caroline tried to sell me."

"Caroline is my godmother." Sabrina balled her hands into fists at her sides. "And I'm not sure what you mean."

"The fairy tale about Duncan O'Neill and the Earl of Lanchester's wife. The one that implies you and Sabrina share the same father."

"Caroline said . . . I don't believe it. She would never say such terrible things."

"Apparently she is as much a liar as you are."

The man was so arrogant, so sure of himself, so . . . "How dare you," she said, slapping his face. "You horrible man."

Ian stood for a moment, feeling the imprint of Sabrina's hand scrawled in fire against his cheek, watching her rush from the library, leaving him standing in a wake of jasmine. What if she really were Lady Julia Wyndham? Then he had just made a complete ass of himself, he realized. He released his breath between his teeth. He wasn't wrong. Not about that little witch.

After a few moments, when the brand of her hand had cooled on his cheek, he returned to the ballroom. Sabrina was gone. He knew it the moment he stepped into the room. It seemed empty now, despite the hundreds of people swarming the floor.

"Did you see her?" Mac asked, coming up behind Ian.

Ian turned, surprised to see Mac holding a tray of champagne glasses. "What are you doing serving drinks, Mac?"

"Filmore said I should get a look at some English lady. Says she's one of the most beautiful women he's ever seen. Dark red hair, he says. So I came to take a look." His brow folded into deep lines. "And I'm telling you it's her, the woman from the boat. Did you see her before she flew out of here?"

Ian nodded. "According to Mrs. Van Cortlandt, the woman is Lady Julia Wyndham, daughter of a childhood friend and the Earl of Lanchester."

Mac shook his head. "I don't care what Mrs. Van Cortlandt says. That woman is the same one from the boat."

Sabrina was the image of her father. If Ian were to believe Caroline Van Cortlandt, Duncan O'Neill's lack of honor extended beyond a deck of cards. He didn't believe her for a minute.

"I'm thinking I might just ask a few questions about the girl."

Ian nodded, half listening to Mac, his thoughts focused on Sabrina. She was out for revenge. And he had little doubt she would use any means to get it. He would just have to make sure she didn't walk away with his scalp dangling from her belt.

A storm swept across the city a few hours before dawn, ripping the dark sky with jagged streaks of light, filling the quiet night with deep blasts of artillery. Sabrina tossed her head on her pillow, fighting against the terror coiling around her soul, the terror she couldn't escape.

In her mind she clawed at the wall of dirt as she had countless nights, trying to climb out of the pit, but it was too deep, the sides crumbling under her hands. It hit her, shovel after shovel of black dirt, hitting her head, her shoulders, filling the pit, burying her alive.

She couldn't see.

She couldn't breathe.

Artillery shattered the air. Sabrina screamed, fighting against the black rain falling around her, accumulating at her feet, rising to her shoulders.

Somewhere in the distance a gentle voice beckoned, a soft hand touched her shoulder. "Sabrina, wake up."

She came awake with a start, sucking deep drafts of air into her lungs. Through her tears she saw Lucy's face suspended above her, the soft glow from the lamp beside the bed casting flickering shadows across her cousin's concerned features.

"It's only a dream," Lucy said, stroking Sabrina's hair.

Only a dream.

The night terror didn't resemble a dream. Dreams were filled with light and wonder, fantasies your mind lived in the middle of the night. Sabrina took a deep breath, trying to chase away the fear congealing in her chest, trying to quiet the trembling of her limbs.

Lucy sat on the edge of the bed and took Sabrina's cold hand in her warm grasp. "Was it the same nightmare?"

The night terror, the nightmares that wouldn't go away, the nightmares that left her feeling vulnerable, alone and frightened. She hated them, hated her own cowardice. "It's always the same," she said, slashing at her tear-streaked cheeks with her fingers.

"How long have you had them?"

Sabrina sat up, pulling her hand from Lucy's grasp. "Too long," she said, wrapping her arms around her raised knees.

"Sabrina, I've been thinking." Lucy was quiet a moment, staring down at her hands. "Why not just come to live with us? Send Julia back to England. Be Sabrina again."

Sabrina rested her damp cheek against the white linen sheet covering her knees. Yellow brocade formed a canopy over her head and fell in lush swags at the four corners of the carved walnut bed. Staring at the silk gliding down the post at the foot of the bed, she tried to conjure up the memory of her own bed at Rosebriar.

Dark mahogany. Icy blue velvet. Gauzy netting. Had she once been able to lay her head upon her pillow and not fear what awaited her in her dreams? Or was that another person? A young girl who had believed in hope and love and dreams. Where was that girl? "Sometimes I'm not sure who Sabrina is," she whispered.

Lucy rested her hand on Sabrina's arm. "I know who she is." She smiled as Sabrina turned to face her. "She's brave. Strong enough to go after what she wants. She's spirited, like a thoroughbred. And when she walks into a room, heads turn, men crumble at her feet. She's everything I always wanted to be."

Sabrina dabbed at her cheeks with the edge of the sheet. One day she would conquer this fear. One day she would be whole again. "You have so much to offer. Don't ever try to be someone else. Especially not me."

"I'm worried about you. Please, just forget about Mr. Tremayne."

"Ian Tremayne stole my pride," Sabrina said, her hands forming fists against her knees. "And it was the only thing I had left. Now I'm going to do the same for him."

"Sabrina, you're going to get hurt. I know it."

"It only hurts to realize how great a fool I was. Can you imagine, sheltering a schoolgirl infatuation for all these years, believing I was in love with a man after knowing him only a day."

"Yes, I can," Lucy said, her voice barely above a whisper. "Sometimes a woman knows, with one glance. It's like seeing someone and feeling at that moment as though you have known him all your life, and beyond. You felt that when you first saw Ian. Don't blame yourself for loving him."

"I fooled myself into thinking I loved him. Now I can see him for what he is. Why, he isn't even as handsome as I thought he was."

Lucy's blue eyes widened, her lips parted, closed, then parted again. "You don't think Ian Tremayne is handsome?"

Sabrina glanced down to the sheet covering her knees. "He isn't handsome, not really," she said, fingering a flounce of embroidered lace that adorned the hem of the sheet. "Not when you see the arrogance behind his smile, not when you know his cruelty."

"Think about what you're doing. Send Julia away, come live with us. Mother would be so happy and I . . ."

"Lucy, the man planned to destroy me. He lied from the beginning. He told me he loved me. He said he wanted to marry me. All he wanted was another conquest." Sabrina gathered the lace in her hands as she spoke. "And I wasn't even a challenge."

"I don't understand how Ian could be so cruel. He's always been kind. I can't recall a party or ball when he hasn't taken time to visit with me, to invite me to dance."

"Well, for pity's sake. That doesn't make the man kind. You're a very pretty young woman."

Lucy shook her head, her light brown braid swishing against

the white cotton of her robe. "Sabrina, I know I'm plain. Eleanor was the pretty one."

Eleanor, Lucy's beautiful sister, had died giving birth to her first child. The little girl had survived her mother by a day. Standing in Eleanor's shadow hadn't allowed Lucy enough sunlight in which to blossom. In the three weeks since Sabrina had come to live with her aunt, she had grown to understand why Lucy preferred to stay at home and hide in a book rather than attend a party. It was easier to dress and act like a small brown sparrow than to try to live up to her mother's expectations.

"Beeswax! What you need is a new hairstyle, something softer. And gowns that complement your hair, your pretty blue eyes."

"I don't think anything will help," Lucy said, lowering her eyes.

"You'll see. When I'm through half the men in New York will be begging for your hand." Perhaps even the one man Lucy adored, Sabrina thought.

"I'll never be beautiful."

"You can't see how lovely you are. Just wait until the new gowns we ordered arrive."

"I've never enjoyed shopping so much." Lucy sank her teeth into her lower lip. "I want you to stay," she said, gripping Sabrina's hand. "I wish everything would . . . I wish I could make everything right for you."

"Lucy, you mustn't worry about me."

"This is a dangerous game you're playing. Hate is a powerful emotion, powerful and frightening. All it can do is destroy."

"All I need is to see the lordly Ian Tremayne knocked from his high horse." She paused, imagining Ian's face, imagining his expression when Julia Wyndham destroyed his pride. "And I'm going to do it. No matter what it takes."

Chapter Eight

Smoke curled from fragrant cigars, lifting, drifting to hang in blue-gray clouds around the crystal globes of the gaseliers suspended above the main salon of the Union Club. Built as a mansion by a man who long ago had lost his fortune, the elegant Fifth Avenue pile of stone and wood served as a gathering place for men still holding their millions. Men who knew fortunes could be made and lost in a day. Men who knew a wrong move on the exchange could turn their costly mansions into clubs for the survivors.

Ian stared down at his full house, absently fingering the stack of chips piled in front of him. It seemed Lady Julia had pocketed the hearts of most of his friends, Ian thought, staring down into his cards. If rumors at the club could be believed, she had received no less than twenty offers of marriage since arriving in New York. Sabrina was after more than a rich husband this time.

"I tell you, Strickland is up to something," Rand said, tossing a blue chip onto the pile in the middle of the table. "I hear he was in Albany again last week."

The woman was Sabrina; Ian was more sure of it than he had ever been. She could change her accent, but she couldn't change the sound of her voice. The way the sun slipped fire into her hair, the way she tilted her head when she laughed, the way she made him want to hold her in his arms and never let her go—these betrayed her lies. No, there could only be one woman with that power over him.

"Ian," Rand said, waving his hand in front of Ian's face. "Hello, Ian, are you there?"

Ian glanced at his cousin. "Is it my ante?"

Rand frowned. "You haven't heard a word I've been saying."

"Sorry," Ian said, glancing down at his cards.

In the past few weeks Ian had made an effort to become reacquainted with both Rand and Tim. Yet tonight he couldn't concentrate on being social. He couldn't concentrate on work. He couldn't concentrate on anything. Not with Sabrina haunting him.

"What is it, Ian?" Rand smiled, studying his cousin from across the round walnut table. "A lady? A very lovely lady with an enchanting English accent?"

Or was it a very lovely lady with an enchanting southern drawl? Ian stared at his cards, looking at the queen of hearts and the queen of diamonds as though they might foretell his future. He had been to more parties and balls and boring dinners in the past two weeks than he had in the past year. Ellen had convinced him it was his duty to watch over Tim, to protect him from Sabrina. Still, Ian had to admit there was another reason for accepting all those invitations, for enduring all those people. He wanted to see Sabrina. And each time he did see her, she was flirting with a different man.

Watching Sabrina flirt with other men did something to Ian's insides; his blood heated to the boiling point, an odd emotion curled around his vitals. It wasn't jealousy. He would have to care something for the woman to feel jealousy. He just didn't like to think of her ruining one of his friends, he reasoned. And Tim was high on her list of lambs to be led to the slaughter.

"He's just upset because the lady prefers me," Tim said, grinning at Ian.

Ellen had come to see Ian at his office yesterday morning, desperate, afraid Tim would elope with Lady Julia the same way she and Paul had eloped. Sabrina wanted a rich husband . . . she wanted revenge . . . marriage to Tim would serve both purposes. "She's isn't what she appears to be," Ian said.

Tim shook his head. "Uncle Ian, please, don't start telling me about Sabrina again. I'm telling you, you're wrong about her. Lady Julia Wyndham is an angel."

It was like looking at a young version of Paul when Ian looked at Tim. On a warm April morning, a lifetime ago, they had ridden down Fifth Avenue together, Paul, Jon, and Ian, brass buttons catching the sunlight as they rushed toward destiny. Paul had met his at Antietam. And Tim was about to meet his with Sabrina. Ian had to make the boy see reason.

"Sabrina O'Neill is an actress. She can make you believe anything she wants you to believe." She had made Ian believe in love, a mistake he would never repeat.

Tim's hand tightened on his cards, bending them inward. "I know you're only trying to protect me. But you're wrong about her. She isn't that woman you met on some riverboat."

Tim was young, reckless, completely unprepared to handle a woman like Sabrina. Hell, he was nearly a decade older, and he had tumbled headlong into her web. He had believed every lie. God help him, when he looked at that beautiful red-haired witch, he found himself wanting to believe every word. "If you would just look past her beautiful face, you might . . ."

"Uncle Ian, I'm not a little boy. I'm a year older than my father was when he eloped with Mother."

"And you're thinking you might like to marry this woman."

"That's right."

Ian issued an oath beneath his breath. "Don't be a fool."

Tim's cheeks grew red beneath his tanned skin as he met his uncle's clear gaze. "I've always admired you, Uncle Ian. But I won't let you come between me and the woman I love."

Ian fought to control his anger, resisting the urge to grab the boy around the neck and shake some sense into his head. "The woman is a liar, a fortune hunter."

Tim lowered his cards to the table, exposing his pair of jacks. "I won't have you talking about her this way."

Ian folded his cards and rested them facedown on the table. "She only cares about one thing: a man's gold," he said, struggling to keep his anger under close rein. "She's going to destroy you if you aren't careful."

Tim stood, his chair falling to the red and yellow carpet with a dull thud. "I demand you take back those words."

"Tim, think about what you're saying," Rand said, coming to his feet. "Ian is your uncle, for heaven's sake."

"I won't have him talking that way about the woman I intend to marry," Tim said, staring at Ian with murder in his eyes.

Ian's chest tightened. "Has she agreed to marry you?"

"Not yet, but she's given me every indication she will accept." Tim slammed his fist into his palm. "I won't have you maligning her. I demand an apology, or . . . or satisfaction."

"Think, Tim," Rand said, grabbing Tim's arm. "Ian can shoot the heart out of a coin at thirty paces."

"I don't give a damn!" Tim shouted. "I demand he apologize."

All conversation had come to a halt in the room. All heads were turned, eyes focused in their direction.

Ian came to his feet, aware of the narrow ledge on which he walked. He had no intention of killing his nephew over that redhead. By the same token, he had no intention of letting Sabrina walk down the aisle into the arms of Tim, or any other man, for that matter.

"I'll give you an apology the day you prove she really is Lady Julia Wyndham," Ian said, keeping his voice low, denying all except those closest to him his response.

Tim opened his mouth, then closed it with a snap. The angry light in his eyes faded as he held Ian's cool green gaze. "Dammit, Uncle Ian, she is Julia. I know it."

Ian took a deep breath. "You know she's a beautiful woman, enchanting enough to charm the serpent out of Eden."

Tim glanced around, his cheeks growing redder as he noticed he was the center of attention. "You're wrong about her," he said, before marching away from the table.

Ian sank to his chair, watching Tim rush from the room. Just what the hell was he going to do?

"A little disagreement between relatives?" Walter Strickland asked, moving to Ian's side. "Something about a beautiful woman?"

The tiny hairs on Ian's neck rose at the sound of Strickland's voice. He glanced up, meeting the man's brittle stare. "Nothing that concerns you."

Strickland smiled, a tight twisting of his lips that left his eyes as cold and dark as coal on a winter's day. "You always did have a way with the ladies. One day they'll be the death of you."

"You've got an enemy in that one," Rand said, watching Strickland walk toward the bar. "Still, I suppose if my wife were following you around like a she cat in heat, I might want to see you dead myself."

"Thanks," Ian said, lifting his glass of brandy.

"What are you going to do about Tim?"

"Keep him from ruining his life." And keep a beautiful redhead from marrying his nephew. Ian had an idea of how to deal with the witch, an idea that could explode in his face.

Sabrina paused, her pen poised above the sheet of paper, seeking the next words. Somehow it didn't seem right to tell her father about the parties and balls and dinners she had attended in the few weeks since she had last written him. These were things he had once hoped for her, things he could no longer provide.

Should she tell him she hated each party and ball and formal dinner, that each was only another chance to see Ian, another set of hours that dragged by while he lavished his attention on one woman after another? There were times when it was all she could do to keep from marching right up to the man and punching him in the nose.

"Writing to your father, darling?" Caroline asked as she entered the morning room.

"Trying to," Sabrina said, dipping the tip of her pen into the inkpot. "But I'm finding it difficult to think of something to say." Something that wouldn't reveal how much she hurt inside.

Caroline crossed the room, rose-scented toffee satin rustling with every step. There was a grace in her aunt's movements, a confidence Sabrina admired. Although Caroline looked delicate enough to be swept away in a strong wind, she dwarfed people who towered above her in height, sent shivers down the spine with a single glance, exiled anyone who crossed her from what she deemed proper society. Still, beneath that regal exterior, Aunt Caroline was one of the most caring people Sabrina had ever known.

Caroline paused in front of one of the open windows, staring through the delicate rose pattern of the lace curtains into the garden for a few moments before she spoke. "Please do give my warmest regards to your father."

"I will."

Ever since Sabrina could remember her father had become irritated at the mention of Aunt Caroline. When Mother and the children had gone to visit Caroline in New York Duncan had usually found an excuse for staying home. On the few occasions when her aunt had visited Rosebriar, Sabrina had sensed the tension that existed between her father and her mother's sister. There had been anger and something more, something that had disturbed a ten-year-old Sabrina, had led her to ask her mother about the seething animosity.

Rachel had smiled, looking at her daughter with gentle blue eyes. With the honesty with which she had approached everything, her mother had told Sabrina that her father had once been in love with Caroline; that small confession had devastated Sabrina.

It couldn't be true. Love came to a person only once, and it lasted a lifetime. At the time Sabrina had been certain of those childish sentiments. Now she knew better. Love was something awful, a hideous monster that could suck all the joy from your life and leave you nothing but a dried-up shell.

Caroline's cat stirred beneath Sabrina's skirts; she felt his thick gray fur brush against her legs as he stretched. A moment later he emerged from his green silk canopy, sauntering toward Caroline, long tail switching, plump white belly swaying, nearly dragging on the carpet with each step.

"So there you are, Mr. Darcy," Caroline said, raising one finely arched brow at her cat. "Seems you have abandoned me for a younger woman."

Mr. Darcy stretched, humping his back, sinking his claws into the thick blue and gold Brussels carpet. He began to rub himself back and forth against her skirts, trying to win the lady's favor.

"Seems he's just as fickle as most men," Sabrina said, watching her aunt lift the big cat into her arms.

"In some ways men are very much like cats. At least the interesting ones," Caroline said, scratching Mr. Darcy's neck, a throaty purr issuing from deep in his chest. "They can be warm, affectionate, but you must always remember they have hidden claws. They may seem to adore you, but they will still wander off at the first chance to dally with some female in the nearest alley. And, I'm afraid, most women find it intriguing to try to tame something that will always remain just a little wild."

"Some men can't be tamed."

"Ian Tremayne is more difficult than most." Caroline shook her head. "You mustn't get discouraged, dear."

A warm breeze breathed softly against the lace curtains that shielded the room from the bright sunlight, the fragrance of freshly cut grass drifting into the room. "I didn't realize it showed."

"Darling, you've been marvelous at every outing. No one would be able to know how much you're hurting inside." The breeze fluttered the lace curtains, brushing Caroline's skirt, filtered sunlight etching rippling roses on her face, on her toffee-colored gown. "But I know. I know what you're feeling each time you see Ian Tremayne with another woman. Your love for him feels as though it might strangle you. And at times you wish it would, wish the pain would just go away."

Sabrina wondered how her aunt could know. How could she realize the pain that had become Sabrina's constant companion; at times it was sharp and steely, at others, dull, coiling, like a snake squeezing the life from her. She had long ago given up hope that the crippling weakness would ever completely go away. Now she prayed she could squeeze all that pain into a small corner of her heart. "I loathe the man."

"No, you don't." Caroline kept her eyes focused on the garden, her fingers caressing the cat lovingly. "He's a part of you in a way no other man can ever be a part of you. And you are a part of him, even if he doesn't realize it now."

"I mean nothing to Ian Tremayne. I never did." Sabrina tapped the tip of the pen against her half-written letter as she spoke, dabbing dots of shiny black ink on the fine white parchment. "Things haven't worked out the way I planned. I thought I could waltz in here and make that man fall in love with me. A rich English countess, for pity's sake, how could he resist?" She glanced at her aunt. "But he has. He never even gives me a thought."

"Oh, yes, he does. I've seen him watching you. And there's a certain look in his eyes."

Sabrina stared down at the dark pattern she was making against the paper. "Hatred."

"Hunger."

Heat scorched a path upward from Sabrina's waist, burning her breasts, her neck, her cheeks, until even the tips of her ears felt as though they were on fire. "I can't believe I was ever that foolish," she said, keeping her gaze fixed on the letter she was slowly mutilating. "How could I have believed him. How could I have let him . . . what a foolish little girl I was."

"Love can make fools of us all." Caroline was quiet a moment before she continued. "Tell me, has your father changed much? I haven't seen him since that summer before the war. Is his hair still that deep, vibrant red? Or has he grown gray?"

Sabrina glanced at her aunt. "I don't think he has any gray."

"Oh," Caroline whispered, smoothing the hair at her temple, as though she were absently searching for the few strands of silver that had threaded their way into her thick dark-brown mane.

Sabrina realized at that moment the reason her Aunt Caroline understood the pain of a shattered love affair—she had lived it; she was living it even now. All these years Sabrina had believed it was her Aunt Caroline who had been the one to leave, the one who had broken her father's heart. But she didn't need the words to know what was inside her aunt's heart; Caroline was still very much in love. "You're still beautiful."

Caroline laughed, the sound terribly self-conscious in a woman who never showed a whisper of her vulnerability. "Have I told you how much I enjoy having you here?" She glanced back at Sabrina.

"Just the short time you've spent with Lucy has brought about a change. She all but sparkled at dinner last night. Why, William Melborne couldn't take his eyes off her all evening. I think it's only a matter of time before you convince Timothy Reynolds to notice her."

Sabrina laughed. "I didn't realize you knew what I was plotting."

"Very little escapes me, my dear." Caroline tilted her head as she stared out the window, a queen surveying her kingdom. "Mr. Reynolds would be very suitable for her, I think."

"So do I. But the first thing I have to do is convince Mr. Reynolds how very spoiled, arrogant, and unsuitable a certain English countess is." Sabrina shook her head as she wadded her mutilated letter into a tight ball. "It amazes me how many men are impressed by that Englishwoman."

"You sound as though she were someone else."

"She is. She's a pampered, spoiled aristocrat who has never known hardship in her life. I'd like to see her make coffee from toasted sweet potatoes, or dig up her own dinner and make do with a few pieces of cornmeal and stringy old beans." Sabrina tossed the crumpled paper into the wastebasket by the desk. "No, little Lady Julia wouldn't last a day without her servants."

Caroline was quiet a long while, staring out at the sunswept lawn, stroking Mr. Darcy, the deep rumble of his purr filling the room. "When this is over, no matter how it ends, I want you to come live with us. As yourself, of course."

Sabrina's heart leapt for the chance. Yet at the same time she realized it was impossible. "I couldn't."

"Yes, you can. It would be amusing to see people stare at my niece, so like the beautiful countess. Think of the mystery we would be creating."

Sabrina bit her lower lip. "One man would know the truth. He could ruin my reputation. If he hasn't already."

Caroline waved away her words. "Nonsense. What happened was his fault. How could he tell anyone without looking like a complete scoundrel?"

Sabrina shook her head. "It wouldn't work."

"Yes, it would." Caroline turned and paced a few steps before turning to face Sabrina, her satin gown swaying with each movement. "I want you to stay. Together, we can work through the difficulties."

"Father needs me."

"You are not going back to those dreadful riverboats." Caroline dumped Mr. Darcy on the seat of an upholstered armchair near the windows. After issuing a deep, throaty protest, the big cat stretched, then curled into a ball on the blue velvet. "We can coax your father to come here. I need a good, reliable man to run the shipping company."

Another year stretched out in front of Sabrina. Another year of endless journeys on the river, always floating, never setting down roots. A weight settled on her chest, a slab of longing as thick and heavy as a marble tombstone. "Do you really think I could . . . no, I can't see how it could work."

"Young lady, I am quite capable of making minor miracles come true," Caroline said, resting her hand on Sabrina's arm. "You need a fresh beginning. Now don't you fret about anything. Just trust your Aunt Caroline."

Sabrina smiled. It would be easy to allow her aunt to talk her into staying. She might even coax her father into coming to New York. For a moment she indulged in the fantasy, seeing her father beside her Aunt Caroline, helping run the shipping company. Perhaps they would marry and end the loneliness she sensed twisting inside her aunt, the emptiness she knew haunted her father.

"You know, I almost believe . . ." Sabrina hesitated as a knock sounded on the door.

At Caroline's invitation the butler entered. He delivered a small white card to Sabrina, telling her the gentleman was waiting in the gold drawing room, then stood by to await instructions.

"Which one of your admirers is it, dear?" Caroline asked, absently running the back of her fingers over Mr. Darcy's back. "Sabrina? Are you all right?"

Sabrina read the few lines scrawled below Ian Tremayne's name, then read them again before lifting her eyes and meeting her Aunt Caroline's concerned look. "It's from Ian Tremayne."

"I didn't think he would stay away much longer," Caroline said, plucking the card from Sabrina's numb fingers. She read the few lines quickly and looked at her niece with a wide smile curving her lips. "So he begs the pleasure of a few minutes of your time. This is wonderful!"

Sabrina barely heard a word; the sound of her blood pounding in her ears was nearly deafening.

"Dicken, tell the gentleman Lady Julia will see him," Caroline said, dismissing the butler.

"Do I look all right?" Sabrina whispered as Dicken left the room. "Perhaps I should change. Wear something a little more . . ." She fluttered her hands near her neck. "Something that bares my shoulders."

Caroline smiled. "I think an evening gown might be a little obvious at ten in the morning, dear."

"Yes, of course. Perhaps the blue silk," Sabrina said, touching the green satin bow that rested against cream-colored lace at the base of her neck. "The one with . . ."

"Darling, you look beautiful." Caroline took both of Sabrina's clammy hands. "Do you want me to go with you?"

Sabrina shook her head.

"Are you sure?"

This was her war, and she intended to see it through to the end. "I can handle Ian Tremayne." Sabrina forced her back to stiffen. "I'm no longer a naive little girl. The man will soon discover he has met his match."

"Yes." A slow smile curved Caroline's lips as she watched her niece march from the room. "I do believe he has."

Sabrina hesitated a few feet from the drawing room, an actress preparing to step onto the stage, a woman preparing to confront the man who had betrayed her. There was no need to be nervous, she assured herself, smoothing the skirt of her gown.

She had rehearsed this scene a hundred times in front of the mirror. She knew her lines. She knew the role she would play: remote, sophisticated, untouchable.

Ian Tremayne would soon discover Lady Julia was immune to his charms. With her little finger the English countess would lift him high, then drop him so hard he would shatter into a thousand pieces.

Sabrina smoothed the skirt of her gown, straightened her shoulders, and prepared to meet Ian Tremayne's hostility with Julia's icy poise.

Chapter Nine

Sunlight glittered gold and scarlet against the lush green leaves of the huge oak guarding the entrance to the maze garden. Ian stood in front of the windows of Caroline Van Cortlandt's drawing room, his hands thrust into the pockets of his buckskin breeches, his dark green coat hitched back at his wrists. He listened to the soft whisper of oak leaves on the breeze, inhaled the heady fragrance of freshly cut grass, and gathered memories; the images distant, indistinct, like faded watercolors.

Once there had been a girl, an enchanting child with long red pigtails, and brown eyes that were far too big for her little face. Yet in that young face he had seen the promise of the beautiful woman she would one day become, the woman who would one day steal his heart. She had fulfilled that promise.

Ian's muscles tensed when he heard her footsteps on the marble-lined hall, her heels tapping the floor in a steady cadence. She was marching, a soldier headed for battle. Without seeing her he knew she had paused just outside the room, knew she was preparing to face him, and he knew what she expected.

Long ago he had learned to evaluate an enemy, to find his weaknesses, to turn those weaknesses into weapons. Without looking he knew when she entered the room, knew she stood watching him; her gaze burned the skin between his shoulder blades and he had the uneasy suspicion she was imagining a knife thrust in his back.

"Mr. Tremayne, this is a surprise," she said, her crisp British accent dripping with frost.

Time to go to war. As he turned to face her, he felt the first volley of cannon fire explode all around him. The air shimmered with a heat that sizzled against his skin and seared him deep inside, the impact slammed against his chest, sucking the air from his lungs. The force of his reaction to her stunned him. In some ways she was more dangerous than any enemy he had ever faced on the battlefield. Yet this was a war he couldn't afford to lose.

"Have you suddenly remembered a . . ."

"Good morning," he said, moving toward her.

She hesitated, her lips parted, as though he had just interrupted a well-prepared speech. "Good morning." She drew a deep breath and started once more. "Mr. Tremayne, have you suddenly remembered a member of my family you have failed to denigrate?" Although she looked as though she wanted to retreat as he continued to advance, she held her ground. "Is that why you . . ."

He pressed the tip of his forefinger against her lips, rendering her speechless, her breath escaping in a warm stream against his skin. "Lady Julia, please allow me to apologize for my behavior the first night we met."

With an elegant sweep of her hand she pushed aside his hand. "Oh, and to what do I owe this change of heart?"

She looked regal, cool, unruffled. Yet the flutter of lace over her heart gave away her agitation. "I realize I was mistaken. Please forgive me for my behavior," he said, smiling down at her. *Always take your enemy by surprise.* And from the expression on the lady's face she was very much surprised.

"You were a heartless blackguard," she said, lifting her chin, retreating behind a mask of cool sophistication.

He nodded. "A braying jackass."

"A complete buffoon."

He lifted his mutilated brow. "That bad?"

"Worse."

"Forgive me?"

"I suppose, under the circumstances," she said, moving to a wing-back chair near the windows. "If I do, indeed, truly resemble Sabrina, you must have been shocked. And . . ."

She hesitated, as though the words were far too painful to speak, tracing a gold rose etched into the brocade with the tip of her finger. Ian stood watching her, feeling no need to fill up the silence with words. He wanted the lady to play out her hand.

"After what Caroline told you . . ." She bit her lower lip. "You must realize I didn't know about my father. I never realized my mother had . . . well . . . it was quite a shock."

She was good, Ian thought. A soft sweep of her sable lashes against her ivory cheeks, a little quiver in her voice; if he didn't know better, he would believe every word. The lying little witch. "I'm sorry I had to be the reason you discovered the truth."

She glanced up at him, a tremulous smile flickering on her lips. "I understand."

He wondered how long she had practiced to perfect that charming mask of wounded pride. "I hoped you might."

A breeze drifted through the open windows, lifting the ribbons dangling from the bow beneath her chin, brushing the green satin across her cheek. As he recalled, her skin was smoother than satin, smooth and warm and tempting. And the texture of her skin was just one of the memories he wanted to forget.

She stood framed by the tall mullioned windows, white lace curtains fluttering in the breeze. Filtered sunlight shimmered around her, as though it emanated from her, this angel who had descended from heaven. This angel who had led him into hell.

"You really are one of the most beautiful women I have ever seen in my life," he said, echoing the words he had spoken a lifetime ago, wondering if she would remember.

She smiled, that smug Lady Julia smile, her eyes betraying a spark of confidence, a look that said she knew she had him dead in her gun sights. Only this time he had come to the field prepared to do battle. "I'm not sure how I ever confused you with Sabrina O'Neill."

She glanced up, her startled gaze locking with his. "What do you mean?"

He smiled. Anger was the crack in her defenses, the way he would rip the mask from her beautiful face, the way he would send this fallen angel packing. "I took a closer look. And in time I noticed differences between you and Sabrina."

"Differences?"

"You were right. You both have the same color hair, but, as I recall, Sabrina's eyes are hazel. Not at all as beautiful as yours."

"Hazel?" she asked, taking a step back as he moved toward her.

He nodded, pausing a foot away from her. "Or they could have been green."

"Green!"

Ian rubbed his chin. "Maybe they were blue."

She stared at him, the flare of her anger naked in her dark eyes. "You mean you aren't even sure of the color of her eyes?"

Ian shrugged. "The woman was no more than a brief encounter aboard a riverboat."

"I see." She turned toward the windows, her back growing stiff. "Do you make a habit of seducing women on riverboats?"

"What makes you think I seduced her?"

She glanced at him over her shoulder. "Didn't you?"

"Sabrina was nothing more than a mercenary tramp."

"It seems to me, Mr. Tremayne, you are quick to judge people," she said, her voice strained with the effort to remain calm.

"It didn't take long to figure her out. One card game did it."

She fell silent, facing the windows, her shoulders rising and falling with each quick breath she took. "I wonder, why would you imagine she would come here? For revenge?"

Ian looked past her shoulder to the maze garden. "I suppose."

"People don't usually seek revenge unless they have been wronged in some way."

Women had a funny way of turning things around, he thought, a way of always making the man the villain. Even if he was just protecting himself. "Sabrina was playing with fire. Sooner or later she was going to get burned."

"And you just made sure it happened sooner rather than later."

He had taken her innocence. She had taken his heart. They were almost even as far as he was concerned. Almost. "She got what she deserved."

She pivoted to face him, smacking her hip against the small pedestal table beside the chair with enough force to set it wobbling. A crystal candy dish spilled from the smooth mahogany surface. It tumbled in the sunlight, spewing small white mints in all directions.

Ian stepped forward, snatching at the glittering crystal at the same time as Sabrina. Their fingers collided. Their heads bumped. The dish tumbled to the floor between them. It bounced once, then settled, rim down, on the thick gold and white carpet, unbroken, in a pool of sunlight, the deep facets of cut crystal radiating rainbows of shimmering light.

"Oh, dear," Sabrina murmured, rubbing her brow, staring at him, a blush rising from her neck to stain the smooth ivory of her cheeks.

The haughty mask of Lady Julia Wyndham was gone, and in its place was the face Ian had loved upon first glance, vulnerable and sensitive and so very lovely. He lowered his eyes, watching the quick rise and fall of her breasts beneath sea green silk and cream-colored lace, knowing those firm globes would also be stained with the dusky rose of her blush. God, how he remembered the warmth of that blush beneath his hands, beneath his lips.

Other memories assaulted him, memories he fought in vain to banish. Memories that made him long to hold her in his arms, to inhale the fragrance of her skin, to bury himself deep within her. Yet his memories were no more than illusions of innocence and love.

Damn the witch!

Damn his own aching need. He was ten times a fool, but he wanted her . . . even now, even knowing every caress had been a lie, even knowing she had no heart, he still wanted her . . . the woman he could have for the price of his soul. But he wouldn't allow her to steal Tim's soul.

He had to stop thinking of what might have been. He had to remember why he had come here. He had to remember Tim, and the scheme this little witch had for ruining his young life.

"I'm interested in getting to know you," he said, retrieving the candy dish from the floor, the heavy crystal warm from captured sunlight. He set it on the table as he continued. "Sabrina is in the past. Let's leave her there." And somehow he would force her into his past, force her image from his dreams.

She glanced up at him, smiling, but her eyes shouted another emotion as she met his eyes. He got the distinct impression she was calculating how many different ways she could carve him up for Sunday dinner. "I thought you might like to go for a drive this morning. I would like the opportunity to show you some of the countryside."

"Mr. Reynolds has spoken highly of his heroic uncle. I would enjoy a chance to get to know the legend in person."

And to take him down a few pegs, Ian thought, returning her smile.

"Please, allow me just a few moments to change."

He wondered if a lifetime would be long enough for a witch to change into an angel. "Of course."

Once again he wondered about that pretty little girl he had met in a garden in another lifetime. How had she turned into this beautiful, deceiving woman? Even her smile was practiced. Why hadn't he noticed how false that smile had been? Why hadn't he realized she was a deceiving little witch the night he had met her on the *Belle?*

In a few hours the lady wouldn't be smiling quite so brightly, Ian thought, watching her leave the room. In a few hours he would make sure she couldn't hurt his family. In a few hours, one way or another, he would end her masquerade.

A humid breeze, heavy with the fragrance of clover and wild flowers, brushed Sabrina's warm cheeks. They were riding north of the city, along a road lined with towering oak and chestnut and elm. Through the branches she caught glimpses of the river, sparkling like rippling gold in the sunshine.

Bowing to the heat, she bent a few rules of propriety and tugged off her gloves. If only she could open the first few buttons of her gown. A little air on her neck would be heaven, but a lady never bared her neck or shoulders during the day, silly as that seemed. Perhaps she had grown far too accustomed to doing as she pleased. It had never occurred to her to keep the first few buttons of her calico gown closed when she was digging in the garden at Rosebriar for something to eat.

She opened her hands on the skirt of her gown. What would he think if he knew he had paid for the elegant walking dress of icy blue silk? Her hand clenched into a fist on her lap as the carriage swayed and Ian's thigh brushed her skirt. Through her lashes she glanced at that masculine thigh, soft buckskin flexing over taut muscles as he shifted his leg.

Memories rose inside her, conjuring up flames from the embers of desire smoldering deep in her flesh. Memories of long, muscular thighs rubbing against hers, his warm skin roughened by black curls. Memories that should never have been made. How could she ever have been such a fool!

"How does it feel to have a city at your feet?" Ian asked, smiling at her.

Not half as enjoyable as bringing you to your knees is going to feel, she thought. "Everyone has been most kind in making me feel welcome," she said, coaxing her lips into a smile.

"From what I hear, most of the bachelors in the city are anxious to coax you to the altar." His smile curved into a devilish grin. "And a few of the married men are thinking of ways they might dispose of their wives. Of course, it isn't difficult to understand why."

The man had a pirate's smile. Why hadn't she realized he had a pirate's soul that day she had met him on board the *Belle?* "I would hope I'm not the cause of ladies disappearing all over the city."

The man couldn't even remember the color of her eyes! While she could close her eyes and see every detail of his face, every detail of his body, every detail of the way he had touched her, and kissed her, and loved her. . . . *No.* It hadn't been love. He was able to separate love from what they had done together.

She supposed it was natural for a man like Tremayne to reduce lovemaking to something primitive, a man without conscience, without honor, without a shred of human decency. She supposed he would call it lust. She wondered what he would say when Lady Julia showed him at least one woman was immune to his brand of masculine magnetism.

Ian pulled up, stopping under an elm tree along the side of the road. "That's the Grange," he said, pointing to a two-story house set back from the road.

The warm breeze wrapped his scent around her, spices and leather and something else, an illusive essence that tugged at her and whispered to a part of her she barely knew. That part of her divorced from reason. That part ruled by emotions she was trying desperately to ignore. "The Grange?"

"It used to be the home of General Alexander Hamilton," Ian said, staring across the long sweep of grass that rolled gently upward from the road before surrounding the house.

Although modest, the house held a subtle elegance; a captain's walk crowned the white wooden structure and verandas graced both floors in the front and rear of the house, and green shutters, the color of the thick grass, flanked each window. If only they could go back in time, she thought. If only they could knock on his door and convince him not to meet Burr on that dueling field. And it would be only one of a thousand things she would change if she could journey back in time.

"He planted that cluster of thirteen trees near the house to represent the original States of the Union," Ian said, resting his forearms on his thighs. "You can see they're all straight but one. They say that crooked tree is the one he planted for South Carolina. It seems appropriate enough, wouldn't you say?"

"Oh, and why is that?" Sabrina asked, glancing at him.

"South Carolina was the first to secede from the union Hamilton and many others fought so long and hard to create."

"From what I've read, there were many who felt the states had a right to secede." What did Ian Tremayne understand of South Carolina, or anything or anyone south of the Mason–Dixon line, for that matter?

Ian studied her a moment, a smile lifting one corner of his lips. "Have you read much about the war?"

"It was tremendous news in England." Sabrina glanced back to the house, trying to steady herself before she fell, before she gave herself away completely. "People took sides."

"People took sides here as well." With a flick of the reins he started the team of bays at a brisk trot, their harnesses jangling, their long tails switching.

She studied Ian's profile a moment, seeing nothing in the calm mask of his face, needing to understand this man. He had been part of her for so long, a part of her youth, a part of her dreams. This was the man she had loved most of her life, the man who had given her hope when all around her dwelt in despair, the man who had taught her the joy of being a woman and the pain of loving too much. And yet she didn't know this man at all.

"Why did you fight in the war? I thought most wealthy young men paid substitutes to do their fighting. Were you following your older brother?"

A laugh issued from deep in his throat. Yet the sound was anything but joyful. It reeked with self-loathing.

"My brother was the type of man who would carry a spider out of the house rather than kill it," he said, glancing at her.

The raw pain she saw in his green eyes touched an answering chord deep within her. They had shared the pain of that war, and she sensed he also had not been able to find peace after the guns had grown quiet.

"Jon knew none of the vices, none of the darkness that cloud a man's soul. To meet him was to like him, without question."

"I guess I don't understand how a man like that could ride off to kill men who were just fighting to protect their homes."

"He had some misbegotten idea he could protect his little brother." Ian lifted his eyes to a point high on the horizon, the muscles in his face and neck growing tense. "You see, I'm the one who had the burning desire to ride off to war."

"Why? Why did you feel you had to join the slaughter?"

Ian kept his gaze fixed on a distant point down the length of the winding road. A long silence ensued, growing taut as it stretched longer and longer, the steady thud of hoofbeats on packed dirt marking the passing moments.

"Did you think fighting a war would be exciting?" Sabrina asked, breaking the silence. "Did you hope to come home drenched in glory?"

"Glory?" Ian glanced at her, as though he had only just remembered she was sitting beside him on the narrow leather seat. "Anyone who thinks there is glory in war has never seen a man's face torn apart by a piece of lead, or a boy barely sixteen cut into pieces."

"I doubt many wealthy young men have seen the horrors of war from their Fifth Avenue mansions."

"I wasn't after glory."

He held her gaze a few moments before directing his attention back to the road. Miles slipped away beneath the steady tread of the horses, and still Ian remained silent. Sabrina resisted the urge to probe his wounds. Perhaps it was better to stay at a distance from the pain she sensed inside him. Perhaps it was better to remain a stranger to the man she had once adored. Familiarity with the enemy might prove fatal.

The forest gave way to a small town, then took dominance again, unbroken except for a few houses set well back from the road, large houses of granite and brick. Sabrina supposed these were the country retreats of the New York aristocracy, the merchant princes, the landed gentry. Here the war had been nothing more than a distant rumble. How she envied their ignorance.

"When I was a boy I would ride up here with friends," he said, the unexpected sound of his deep baritone startling her. "In this part of the country, all through here, battles were fought during the Revolution, blood spilled, mainly patriot blood. We would choose sides, and reenact those battles."

"When you weren't pretending to be a knight in Camelot," she said, the image of that romantic thirteen-year-old boy drifting into her mind, the young man she wished had never died. If only they could recapture the innocence they had both lost along the way. If only . . . if only wishes came true. But they didn't.

Ian stared at the shifting patterns of sunlight and shadow cast across the hard-packed road by the branches overhead, as though they were words to a story, a story he was compelled to read to her. "I went to war because I believed in preserving the union they fought so long and hard to create. I think the only mistake they made was in creating a union predicated on the fact that all men are created equal while still allowing man to enslave his fellow man."

Sabrina shook her head. "The south would have abolished slavery in time without intervention from the north."

"Perhaps." Ian fixed her with a steady gaze. "After abolishing the union."

"There were southern men who fought for independence from Britain as well as northern men, Mr. Tremayne," Sabrina said, her back growing stiff. "Men who felt it their right to dissolve any alliance that would force them to yield to a government in which they did not feel fairly represented."

Sunlight filtered through the branches arching overhead, dappling Ian with sunlight, splashing gold on his hair, his face, his shoulders. He studied her a moment, his eyes intense, probing, searching hers until she had to glance away. She stared at a white butterfly as it flit amid a patch of buttercups along the road. In trying to discover the man behind his mask had she revealed too much of herself?

"You hold strong views about the war and state's rights."

She forced her lips into what she hoped was a convincing smile. "My mother was from Mississippi, Mr. Tremayne. I'm afraid some of her views have rubbed off on her daughter."

"I see."

The breeze tossed his long hair into waves around his face, and she was struck with the sudden memory of how silky those waves had felt sliding between her fingers. Why had everything gone so horribly wrong?

"If I didn't know better, I would think you were from the south."

"But you do know better." *Careful, she had to be more careful,* she thought. It was a dangerous game she was playing. Although he was content to believe in Lady Julia at the moment, one wrong move on her part could change his mind. If she tripped, if he discovered the truth, her Aunt Caroline and Lucy would suffer right along with her.

Still, he didn't look as though he had doubts about Lady Julia. In fact, he was smiling, as though he was more than pleased with the company. Oh, she was going to enjoy seeing this man humbled.

Sabrina pressed her back against the carriage seat and stared past the trees to where the river rolled, a small white steamboat disturbing the smooth, glittering surface. How often had she imagined a day like this, a day in the sunshine with Ian by her side? She couldn't help wondering why; what perverse twist of fate had led her to love this scoundrel? Somehow she would purge him from her blood. Perhaps her freedom could only be bought by his pride.

"Are you getting hungry?" Ian asked as he turned from the road and started down a gravel-lined drive, flanked on either side by oak and chestnut trees.

"A little." As she spoke they rounded a bend and a house came into view, a majestic dwelling crowning the summit of a rolling hill. Gray stone rose from the banks of the Hudson River, shaping the stately walls of an English manor house. Tall gables reached toward the afternoon sky, the sun casting hundreds of mullioned windows into gold.

"I've had lunch prepared at my grandfather's house."

"You were fairly certain I would accept your invitation, Mr. Tremayne."

"I was hopeful, Lady Julia."

And arrogant. She could see it in his eyes, that utter belief in his own male beauty, in his snakelike charm. He was secure in the knowledge that the Lady Julia would soon be another conquest. "Your grandfather's house is beautiful," she said, molding her lips into one of Julia's little smiles.

He halted the horses in front of the house. "My grandfather built this house to rival an English earl's country seat and then named it for the small Scottish village where he was born." He set the brake on the carriage and jumped to the gravel drive. He paused for a moment, staring at the house before he spoke. "Dunkeld was a gift to his English bride, my grandmother."

As was the gold band she knew hung around Ian's neck, the ring she had once thought she would wear. His heels crunched against the gravel as he passed behind the carriage. How many other women had hoped to wear that ring? How many other women had given their hearts to this man, their love, their innocence? In a way she was like a knight of old, avenging the honor of every woman this pirate had ever ruined.

She rested her hands on his broad shoulders as he gripped her waist and lifted her from the carriage. That intriguing male scent teased her senses, and she found herself holding her breath. Not this time. She wouldn't be a fool this time. He set her lightly on the gravel drive, his hands lingering at her waist as though he had every right to hold her. She stared at the base of his neck, trying to control her emotions. The sheer arrogance of the man!

He lifted one hand, his fingers drifting over her cheek, warm and firm, as he brushed back a strand of hair that had escaped her neat chignon, while his left hand lingered at her waist. She resisted the urge to pull out of his embrace. It felt too familiar. It was far too tempting. Yet she stayed. Lady Julia needed to lead him on, to make him believe she enjoyed his foul company.

"Mr. Tremayne, I . . ." Her words dissolved as she looked into his eyes; they were cold and hard as emeralds.

"Tell me why you came here," he said, his hand growing tense against her waist. "Tell me what you want, Sabrina."

Chapter Ten

"Sabrina?" She stiffened in his arms, her huge brown eyes betraying her surprise before she regained her composure. "I thought we had settled that matter."

"We are going to settle it. Now." Ian didn't try to hold her as she broke free of his embrace. She put three feet of warm summer air between them before she turned to face him, her expression sculpted into a haughty mask of indignation.

She tilted her head, the movement allowing sunlight to streak beneath the brim of her white straw hat, painting golden light across the lower half of her face. "Why, Mr. Tremayne, I do believe you are obsessed with the woman."

He traced the curve of her lips with his eyes, remembering their shape beneath his, their taste. Obsessed was a mild word for what he felt for the witch. "I want you to stay away from my nephew."

"You want me to . . . is that what your visit this morning was all about?" Anger seemed to stiffen every muscle in her body. "I suppose I'm not good enough for your family. Is that it, Mr. Tremayne?"

"The boy thinks he is in love with you."

"That boy is a young man. A very handsome, extremely charming young man. Not at all like his boorish uncle."

The muscles in his neck stretched and throbbed as he fought to keep his emotions in check. "I won't allow you to destroy him, Sabrina. You will stay away from him."

Her eyes narrowed as she held his gaze. "You have no right to tell me to stay away from anyone."

The proud set of her shoulders, the mutinous thrust of her full lower lip, the glitter of unshed tears in her eyes—if he didn't know her for the actress she was, he would believe she was the hurt little girl she appeared to be at this moment. But he did know better. Experience had taught him well. She was a deceiving little mercenary and he wouldn't be fooled by her again.

"You intend to marry Tim, don't you?" he said, voicing the fear that clawed at his belly.

She looked away from him. "Yes, of course I intend to marry him. And you will have nothing to say about it."

"How much? How much do you want to pack your bags and get the hell out of town?"

She met his gaze, her eyes flashing the dark fire of her rage. "You think everything, everyone can be bought by your money." She turned, the skirt of her icy blue gown rustling against her petticoat as she climbed into the carriage. "I wish to leave, Mr. Tremayne," she said, grabbing the reins. "I'll have your carriage returned to you."

The cage bracing his emotions cracked. He advanced on her, snatching her from the carriage like a hawk snatching a dove from flight.

She pushed against his shoulders. "You have no right!"

With his hands planted at her waist, he held her several inches off the ground, her face level with his, her lips so close he could feel each pulse of her heated breath against his cheek. Her breasts skimmed his chest, searing his skin through his clothes.

"Release me this instant you . . . you . . . colonial oaf!" She twisted in his arms, trying to break free, brushing her legs against his.

Primitive need gripped every nerve, every muscle of his body. Raw hunger consumed him. He wanted her. Right here, against the carriage. He wanted to bury himself deep inside her. He wanted to feel those silken thighs wrap around his waist. He wanted to hear her moans, feel her shudders as he forced her to taste the same bitter desire that was choking him.

Was this what she had planned from the beginning? To prove the power she held over him? To bring him to his knees with his own maddening need? And he was falling again, bending to her will, surrendering his pride, his heart . . . not this time. He lowered her to the ground, but before she could move he planted his shoulder in her belly, her breath escaping in a whoosh as he lifted her like a sack of flour.

"Let go of me!" she shouted, pounding her fists against his back.

"I gave you a chance to end this war, Sabrina," he said, carrying her up the three wide stone stairs leading to the tall front doors. "You leave me no choice."

One oak door was swung open by his butler as Ian approached. Ian had little doubt the little scene on the front drive had been witnessed by his butler and probably half the servants in the house. Still, Ormsby betrayed no emotion.

Ian wondered if anything could break the butler's calm facade. As a boy he had often tried, but even finding fifty frogs in the china cabinet hadn't rumpled Ormsby. Ian smiled, remembering the sight of the butler opening the cabinet to a deluge of croaking, jumping, "green nuisances," as Ormsby had referred to them.

"This must be your guest, sir," Ormsby said, stepping aside to allow Ian to carry his guest over the threshold.

"Help me!" Sabrina shouted. "This man is abducting me!"

"The blue bedchamber has been prepared, sir," Ormsby said, without a whisper of emotion. "Will you be wanting . . ."

"So, you've arrived."

Ian turned to see a whirlwind advancing toward him in the shape of one Hannah Waycott. For as long as Ian could remember, the little housekeeper had been a part of his grandfather's staff. Now she did her best to keep Ian and his household in order. He grimaced as Sabrina landed a blow to the middle of his back.

"Is this why you've dragged us all to the country?" Hannah demanded. "Up to mischief again, young man?"

"Can't you see what he's doing?" Sabrina shouted, punctuating her words with sharp blows to Ian's waist. "Help me!"

"Up to preventing the lady from making mischief, Hannah." Ian retaliated with his open palm across Sabrina's behind as he spoke, yards of linen and silk cushioning the blow. Still, he won a satisfying cry of indignation from the lady.

Hannah shook her head. "I've seen you do plenty of . . ."

"We'll talk later," Ian said, starting down the hall. He had taken just about all the abuse he intended to take from the little wildcat slung over his shoulder. Despite Sabrina's continued blows, her wiggles, her shouts of protest, Ian didn't slow his pace as he marched down the passageway leading to a wide oak staircase.

"I demand you release me this instant!"

"I'm afraid you're not in any position to make demands, Sabrina."

"I'll have you thrown behind bars! You'll rot in prison for the rest of your days!"

Ian ignored her, taking the steps two at a time, marching down the second-floor hall and straight into the bedroom that had been prepared for her.

"Let go of me!"

He complied, tossing her to the bed. Sabrina sank into the thick feather mattress, her cheek sliding against the velvet counterpane.

She came up with a growl, pushing her hat from her eyes, glaring at Tremayne. "Blackguard!" she shouted, trying to fight her way off the bed.

Ian gripped her shoulders, shoving her down against the soft mattress. Sunlight streamed through the open windows, striking one cheek and leaving the other in shadows. Yet Sabrina saw the rage burning deep in his eyes, the rage that sent a ripple of fear through her. This was a man who had killed, a man who could kill again. There was something primitive inside him, something that both frightened her and aroused her in a way that shamed her to the core.

"Tell me the truth, Sabrina," he said, his voice deep and smooth as the velvet beneath her hands, his warm breath brushing her lips with each word he spoke. "Tell me why you came back to haunt me."

Sabrina twisted the counterpane in her hands. The truth would only get her burned at the stake. Her only hope was to hide behind her mask. "I am Lady Julia Amanda Wyndham, you imbecile."

Ian's hands tightened a moment on her shoulders before he released her. He moved to the foot of the bed where he rested his shoulder against one of the thickly carved mahogany posts. He let his gaze roam over her, lingering on the length of her silk clad legs, the embroidered lace at the hems of her drawers, exposed by the skirt that had twisted around her hips.

Heat flared in the heart of her femininity. She rose to a sitting position, tugging at her gown, shielding her legs. "How dare you! How dare you kidnap me!"

He looked into her eyes and allowed her to see the shifting flames of his emotions, the desire smoldering deep within him. "Tell me, Lady Julia," he said, his gaze drifting down her neck. "Are you a virgin?"

"Of course," she said, tossing the light blue counterpane over her legs, still feeling far too exposed.

"Perhaps I should test your honesty." He lowered his gaze to where she clutched the counterpane against her breasts. "You see, Sabrina is no longer a maiden."

No. Not since she had given her heart and soul and body to a scoundrel. Lord, she hated this man. Hated him for her own crippling weakness. "So you mean to rape me, to ruin me, to satisfy your obsession."

"I doubt it would be rape in the end."

The truth in his words battered her pride. She was far too vulnerable where he was concerned. "And when you have discovered your mistake? Then what?"

Ian shrugged, as though he didn't care, but she caught a glimpse of doubt in his eyes. As long as there was that fragment of a doubt she had a chance. "My family will have you tossed in jail for kidnapping me, Tremayne."

"Perhaps even flogged?" he asked, moving toward her.

Sabrina scooted back on the bed. "Yes. Perhaps even hanged."

He sat beside her, the bed dipping beneath his weight, rolling her thigh against his hip. "If I'm to be hanged for kidnapping, what more could they do to me for kidnapping and rape?" he asked, running his hand along her arm, trailing fire across her skin beneath the smooth blue silk.

Sabrina sank back against the pillows, her head hitting the headboard in her attempt to avoid his touch. "Have you no conscience?"

He lifted a lock of her tumbled hair, rubbing the silky strands between his fingers. "None where Sabrina is concerned."

"I am not Sabrina!"

"Aren't you?" he whispered, lowering his gaze to her lips.

Slowly he traced the curve of her lips, as though comparing their shape to some distant memory. Under that lazy perusal her breath hovered in her throat, desire curled in warm tendrils across her belly. "To blazes with you," she whispered.

A muscle flashed in his cheek. "I was damned to hell the moment I met you."

"Then let me go, before we are both ruined."

Ian dropped her hair and came to his feet. "I'm afraid it's too late for that."

She followed him with her eyes as he crossed the room. "What are you going to do?"

He turned at the door. "Tomorrow I'm going to hire the Pinkertons. They should be able to discover the truth about you."

A truth that would be far too easy to discover. "By then I shall be ruined."

"If you are Lady Julia Wyndham, I'll set things right."

He stood staring at her for a moment, Sabrina's fate hanging unspoken in the air between them. Her hands clenched against the counterpane she held at her neck.

"Good day, my lady," he said, before leaving her alone with her fear.

Sabrina closed her eyes at the sound of the lock sliding into place. She tossed aside the counterpane, came to her feet, and ran to the door. What would he do once he discovered the truth? Send her to prison? Or something worse?

"Tremayne! Let me go!" she screamed, pounding against the door. His footsteps, muffled by the hall carpet, grew more distant.

She tugged on the handle, knowing it was locked, praying some miracle would open it. It was pointless, she thought, resting her forehead against the cool oak, her fists throbbing.

Hannah was waiting for Ian at the base of the stairs, hands planted on her plump hips, blue eyes silently scolding him. He had seen that look a hundred times, usually after he had pulled some piece of mischief, like the time he had slipped into the hen house and glued all the eggs to their nests.

Aside from a few more strands of gray in her light brown hair, Hannah hadn't changed since the days of his youth, when she saw to it that he had his favorite gingerbread whenever he came to visit Dunkeld. "Any chance you made some of your fabulous gingerbread, Hannah?" Ian asked, giving her a wide boyish smile.

"My gingerbread can wait, young man." She tilted her head to stare up into his face as he drew near. "First you'll be telling me why you're holding that young woman against her will."

Ian rubbed his fingertips across his right eyebrow, feeling the scar left behind by the blade of a knife. Strange how the worst scars didn't show. "The lady left me no choice."

Hannah sniffed loudly. "Seems to me you've spent most of your life trying to rid yourself of some girl. This one you lock up in a room."

"This one is dangerous."

"That lovely creature?" She gave him a look filled with doubt. "And in what way?"

"Every way." He wasn't in a mood to recount his history with the lady. Yet he could see Hannah wasn't going to cooperate without some sort of explanation. "Her name is Sabrina O'Neill, but she'll tell you she is Lady Julia Wyndham. She came to New York for revenge and she doesn't care who she hurts in getting it. I'm going to stop her."

"Revenge?" Hannah's brow crinkled into a frown as she studied him a moment. "And what did you do to her? Why is it she came to New York for revenge?"

"I spoiled her plans." He glanced away from her, trying to hide his thoughts, knowing she could read him as easily now as she could when he was ten. "Take her something to eat, Hannah. And see if that beautiful witch needs anything."

She touched his arm. When he looked down at her she smiled, her eyes sad and knowing. "This woman is different than the others. And she's more than an enemy."

"Your eyes are too sharp, woman," he said, chucking her under the chin. "Now, go see about that redhead."

Like a caged tigress Sabrina prowled her prison. A big tester bed stood against one wall, dark mahogany posts glowing in the afternoon sunlight, lush blue velvet flowing from the canopy in elegant swags at each post. On the opposite wall, near a second door, a Chippendale highboy reached toward the scrolls etched into the ceiling. A matching armoire stood guard on the opposite side of the door.

Sabrina's pulse raced as she moved toward that door. It might lead to a connecting room, a room with an unlocked door. She threw open the door and stared into a small dressing room. It provided no means of escape.

Cursing under her breath, she crossed the thick wool carpet and rested her hands on the sill of the open windows. Warm air, tinged with the scent of roses, rushed into the room, brushing her warm cheeks, billowing the blue velvet drapes.

The house stood poised on the brow of a hill, surrounded by forest, overlooking the river. A white side-wheeler rolled down the shimmering water, gray smoke rising from twin stacks, curling upward along great stone columns that soared four hundred feet above the river. Below, starting a few yards from the house, hundreds of rose bushes lined a serpentine path leading to a white gazebo. It would be an ideal place to sit with someone you loved on a warm summer day and watch the river flow.

Did Ian ever go there? She thought of Alisa, of Gretchen, of Fanny, and a hundred other women who sought to become his bride. Who would one day sit beside him in that cozy little summer house, her hand in his warm grasp, her head nestled against his broad shoulder?

She closed her eyes, imagining Ian and his bride, trying to conjure his image with Alisa. Only the image she saw with Ian was her own. In her mind he smiled down at her, his eyes warm with love. Longing curled around her heart, squeezing until her chest ached. She shook her head, trying to rid herself of that false image. She was far too old to believe in fairy tales.

"Go away," she shouted as someone knocked on the door. A key rattled in the lock and she turned, preparing herself to go another round with her opponent.

"I'm Hannah Waycott, Miss," the plump little woman said as she entered the room, carrying a tray ladened with dishes. "I'll be looking to your needs while you're a guest."

"You mean while I'm a prisoner."

Hannah smiled at her. The fragrance of freshly baked bread trailed in her wake as she crossed the room to the writing desk near a second set of windows, the aroma opulent perfume to Sabrina's long deprived senses. "The master said you might like something to eat."

"Oh, he did?" Sabrina's gaze followed that tray. Thick slices of bread, still warm enough to melt the butter that had been spread lavishly over them, rested on a plate piled high with thin slices of ham and beef. And the tall glass of milk beside the plate looked cold, cold enough to form beads of sweat on the smooth glass. "I suppose I'm expected to eat like a good prisoner."

Hannah smiled. "You'll need your strength if you're going to spar with the master."

Sabrina felt her stomach grumble. "You can tell Mr. Ian Tremayne he can jump in the . . ." She paused, the sound of barking drawing her attention to the window.

Ian was walking down the sloping lawn toward the bluffs above the river and he wasn't alone. Three dogs accompanied him, two ranging several yards in front of Ian, one staying close to his side, and none of them looked as though they had the pedigree to step foot upon that manicured lawn.

"Ah, the pack has discovered he's home," Hannah said, moving to Sabrina's side.

The dog staying close to Ian reminded Sabrina of a newborn fawn, slender, delicate, with smooth, sandy-colored hair. She frowned as she noticed that the dog was favoring her rear left leg, limping with every step. "Is Tremayne in the habit of kicking his animals?"

"No. My heavens, no," Hannah said, pressing her hand to her heart. "The master found her a few weeks after he returned from the war. He rescued poor little Guinevere from a group of young brigands who were tormenting her, beating her with sticks and kicking her, trying to kill the little creature for sport."

"Guinevere," Sabrina whispered, watching as Ian casually brushed his hand over the dog's smooth head. Perhaps there was still a young boy looking for Camelot deep inside the man. She quickly dismissed the thought. There was nothing romantic, nothing noble inside this man.

"The black furry one with the white stockings is Byron, and the squatty little devil who looks as though he is kin to an over-sized pug is Shakespeare. Master Ian found both of them in the streets." Hannah folded her hands at her waist, smiling at the man who crossed the lush lawn as though he were a saint. "He always did have a weakness for strays. I remember once he brought home a bear cub whose mother had been killed by some hunter."

Sunlight streamed in golden shafts through the branches of oak and hickory and chestnut that dotted the wide lawn like a few remaining pieces left on a chess board of dark green and gold. Ian paused, his back growing rigid, his head coming up like a jungle cat sensing danger. He turned in a ray of sunlight slanting through the branches over his head, staring straight up at Sabrina.

"You should have seen his grandfather's face when Ian brought home that cub. Well, he . . ."

Hannah's words dissolved into a soft buzz in Sabrina's ears. She was aware only of Ian, of the way the sunlight caressed his features, the way the breeze lifted his black hair, making him seem as though he had come from another time and place, a distant realm of fantasy and dreams.

For a moment Sabrina forgot her anger, forgot her pain, her humiliation at his hands. Feelings surged inside her, warm, famil-iar, overwhelming. She wanted to touch him. Each breath of the fragrant air filled her with a horrible need to touch his face, his hair, his lips. His expression shifted, his features growing tense before he turned away from her, as though he couldn't stand to look at her.

Sabrina took a step back from the window, feeling Ian's rejection as sharply as a slap across her face. Would she ever learn to guard her heart? "Unless you intend to help me get away from here, I would like you to leave," she said, interrupting whatever it was Hannah was saying.

Hannah paused, her lips parted. "I'm afraid you won't find anyone here who will go against the master. You see, there isn't a man, woman, or child working for Ian Tremayne who doesn't care deeply for him."

Sabrina hugged her arms to her waist as she watched Hannah leave the room. The lock clicked in the door. She pressed her hands against the windowsill and stared at the empty space on the lawn where Ian had stood only a few moments before. He was gone, vanished into the dense woods. And she was left behind in this prison.

There had to be a way, some way to escape.

She thought about tying together the drapes and sheets and anything else she could find to form a rope ladder. Yet more than thirty feet separated her from the ground. Even if she could coax all that material to stay together, she had her doubts about making it down in one piece.

The breeze rustled the leaves of an ancient oak that stood near the house, slender wooden arms brushing the stones near the window. She stared at the tree, her lips curving into a smile as she noted the long, crooked limbs bobbing just a few feet away from her prison cell. It just might work. Tonight, in the shelter of darkness, she would show Ian Tremayne he had underestimated his enemy.

Chapter Eleven

Sabrina stood poised on the ledge outside her room, palms flat against the stone wall, bare toes curled against the cold stone beneath her feet. She had left her shoes and stockings and petticoats behind her in her prison cell along with the nightgown Hannah had brought for her. A warm evening breeze rustled the leaves of the ancient oak, lifted the hem of her gown, and skimmed across her skin, leaving a trail of gooseflesh. Slowly she eased herself into a kneeling position.

Just keep your eyes on that limb, she told herself, leaning forward to grab the nearest branch. *Don't look down.*

The branch bobbed beneath her weight as she crawled toward the massive trunk of the oak. A low moan whispered from the tree limb and shimmied along her spine, sparking memories within her. There would be no one to catch her this time, no one to break her fall should the limb give way beneath her. Holding her breath, inching her way along the rough bark, she prayed the branch would hold her.

Moonlight penetrated the thick leaves in places, giving her glimpses, dark outlines of limbs and leaves. Once at the trunk, she began to lower herself, stretching, searching with her feet to find the next limb, grasping each new bough with her hands, dangling a moment until she could find her next perch. Finally, she stood just ten feet off the ground.

Sitting on the limb, back pressed against the trunk, she lowered her legs over the side. When she was dangling by her hands, she released her grip, falling the rest of the way, thick grass cushioning her fall.

She rolled to her side, gasping for air, silently giving thanks. Skin scraped and bleeding, heart pounding, she resisted the urge to stay there on the soft, cool grass. She wasn't out of danger yet.

Coming to her feet, she tried to catch her bearings. On the far side of the drive the forest began, tall trees marching together, forming a dark wall. A silhouette in moonlight, the stables stood at the end of a graveled drive, a few hundred yards from the house.

No light flickered in the quarters on the second story of the long building; the grooms were asleep. From where she stood to the trees sheltering the stables was open ground. If she could get there without being seen, if she could take a horse, then follow the river back to the city, she might have a chance.

Ian couldn't sleep. He opened the liquor cabinet in his grandfather's study, a smile curving his lips as he poured brandy from a decanter into a crystal snifter. Strange, the house had been his for three years, yet it was still his grandfather's house. It always would be. Every stone, every piece of lumber had the stamp of Ian MacClaren.

Ian raised his glass to the portrait hanging above the mantel, silently saluting his grandparents. Rebecca Stanhope MacClaren smiled down at her grandson, her honey-gold hair falling in a long coil over her shoulder, blue eyes following his every move, as though she were ready to rake some mischief. She was lovely and headstrong, willful enough to defy her aristocratic father and marry a penniless Scotsman.

Ian MacClaren regarded his namesake with pale green eyes, his hand resting on Rebecca's shoulder, smiling as though he knew the secret of the ages. Perhaps he did. Perhaps that secret was in finding the right woman. At least his grandfather never had to worry that the lady he loved had married him for the size of his purse.

"I wonder what you would say, Grandfather, if you knew I had a beautiful woman locked in a bedroom upstairs," he said as he walked out onto the stone terrace. No doubt his roguish grandfather would have approved.

Byron and Shakespeare, who were both lounging on the stone terrace, glanced in his direction. Byron thumped his fluffy tail against the stone in welcome; Shakespeare merely lifted his eyes. The plump little beggar only found energy when it was time to eat. Ian sipped his brandy, enjoying the mellow heat sliding down his throat, listening to the chirp of the crickets. He had always loved it here. It had always been peaceful. Yet these days he couldn't seem to find peace anywhere.

Guinevere limped from where she had been lying by the open French doors to sit beside Ian. "You're a rare find, Gwen," Ian said, stroking her head. The dog closed her eyes, arched her neck, and pressed her muzzle against his leg. "A faithful female. Unlike my beautiful redhead."

He hadn't been with another woman since that night he had made love to Sabrina aboard the *Belle*. Not that there hadn't been opportunities. He had come close three times, with three different women, one of them a lovely red-haired widow in San Francisco, but she had been the wrong redhead.

After returning to New York he had even spent one evening in the Louvre, where he had spent many evenings on satin sheets with nameless women, but he had left the elegant bordello without taking any of the beautiful young women upstairs.

He wasn't sure why he was playing the role of a monk. Maybe he just didn't want to confirm his own terrible suspicion: Imitations wouldn't ease the ache inside him. Never in his life had a woman affected him this way. This hold of hers reached beyond his flesh, beyond lust; it dipped into the very core of his soul.

Of all the women he had known, why had he been destined to fall under the spell of this heartless witch? Why did she haunt him night and day? Why did he feel half alive without her?

"Tell me why, Sabrina," he whispered, gazing down into his glass. Why had she betrayed him? Money. He supposed after what she had gone through in the war, money had come to mean everything to her. He could almost forgive her. Almost.

"Just what am I going to do with you, Sabrina?"

A sharp bark from Byron dragged Ian from his painful reflections. The dog was standing, staring between the stone balusters at something beyond the terrace. Shakespeare soon joined in, dragging his plump body to stand on his bowed legs, his blunt nose pressed between the balusters, his deep bark joining Byron's sharp warning.

It was probably a deer, Ian thought, glancing out across the dark sweep of lawn rolling away from the house. "What the devil!" he muttered, seeing a woman running in the moonlight.

Sabrina was halfway to the stables when she heard the first shouts billowing from the house. She froze on the grass beside the drive, staring back at the house. Her heart slammed against her ribs when she saw a man emerge from the shadows of the terrace.

There was no mistaking Ian Tremayne's tall, broad-shouldered form.

Moonlight poured across his face. Even at a distance she could see the rage etched into his handsome features. She didn't want to know what he would do if he should catch her.

She turned, lifting her gown, running toward the stables, shivering at the angry bellows from behind her. Ian's shouts brought two men running from the stables. They paused a few feet from the building, stuffing nightshirts into their trousers, staring at Sabrina as though she were a ghost.

"Stop her!" Ian shouted.

She didn't intend to give them a chance. Tall trees smothered the moonlight as Sabrina crashed into the copse on the other side of the drive. Dark shapes loomed around her. Stones and twigs cut into her feet. Weeds grabbed at her ankles. Behind her an army thundered in the darkness, barks, shouts, footsteps drumming on her heightened senses, ringing with the roar of blood in her ears.

Sabrina bit her lip against the pain, against the horrible fear slithering up her spine. Something grabbed her hair, snapping back her head, tearing a scream from her throat. She turned to fight off her captor, her hands connecting with a bony branch.

"Over there!"

Her scream would lead them right to her. She tugged at her tangled hair, trembling fingers tearing the fragile strands. The crash of footsteps grew louder. With one last jerk she freed her hair.

Ian was close, so close she could imagine his hot breath beating on her neck. She plunged through the forest, like a vixen caught in the hunt, wild dogs nipping at her heels. Air colored with the scent of moss, of elm and oak and hickory, ripped through her nostrils, flooding her lungs. Something scurried in the twigs to her left—she tried not to think of the creatures residing in the darkness.

"Sabrina!"

She pushed on blindly, fear of Ian outdistancing all other fear. The moonlight seemed as blinding as sunlight as she emerged from the forest. Wild flowers lined the forest edge, Queen Anne's lace delicate snowflakes in the moonlight, buttercups, violets, and clover filling the air with sweetness.

Slabs of rock, patches of dirt and pebbles plunged toward the river, delicate saplings and clumps of weeds dotting the slope. Her feet throbbed as she stared down the steep, rocky cliff.

"Sabrina!"

The icy blue silk of her gown shone like a beacon in the moonlight. She started down the slope. If she could just make it to the river's edge, to the sheltering trees, she could . . . Stones rippled from beneath her foot; pain snapped through her ankle. With a cry, she tumbled to the ground, sliding on her side, stones tearing the delicate cloth of her gown, scraping her skin.

Pebbles and dirt slipped through her hands as she tried to stop her fall. Snatching a clump of weeds, she finally halted the punishing slide. She rolled to her uninjured side, drawing her knee to her chest, her hands reaching for her injured ankle. Pain throbbed just below her anklebone, stealing her breath.

"Dammit, Sabrina! You're going to get hurt out here alone."

She nearly laughed. A sprained ankle was nothing compared to what he would do to her once he discovered the truth. She couldn't let him catch her.

To her right, just above her head, the mouth of a small cave yawned, opening on a ledge of rock and dirt. Clawing with her hands, digging with her toes, she crawled toward that dark sanctuary.

Cool, hard-packed dirt met the cuts on her palms, eased the pain in her knees. Just inside the entrance of the cave she collapsed against a smooth granite wall, pressing her cheek to the cold rock, dragging air into her burning lungs.

Rocks tumbled past the mouth of the cave. She pressed her hand to her lips, holding her breath, afraid any noise might lead Ian to her.

Something stirred behind her, the sound of claws on rock scraping her spine. A snort rumbled in the cave. Her heart rammed into her ribs. After taking a deep breath she turned her head. Twin sparks of light shone back at her, reflected moonlight in a bear's eyes. Too terrified to scream, Sabrina began backing out of the cave.

Don't frighten him, she thought.

A low growl rumbled against the stone walls. Sabrina screamed. On the ledge she came to her feet. Pain ripped through her ankle as she started to run. Her leg folded beneath her, spilling her to the ground.

A growl roared behind her.

Fighting her pain, she stumbled to her feet. A paw lashed across her shoulder, knocking her to the ground, forcing the air from her lungs. Through the deafening roar of blood in her ears she heard a second growl lash the air, savage, different from the bear behind her. What other monster had come to claim her?

She lifted her eyes to find Ian standing on the ledge in front of her. Unarmed, he stood with his arms spread, his hands curled, his teeth bared, looking more fierce than the black bear standing at her feet. White linen stretched tautly across Ian's wide chest, the breeze ruffling the sleeves of his shirt, his midnight hair. He was magnificent, all wild, unleashed power and grace.

"Don't move," Ian whispered, never looking away from the bear.

Sabrina lay flat against the ground. Ian shouted and waved his hands, bellowing in a savage tone, moving until he stood on the ledge by her side. The bear grumbled. Ian took a step closer, shouting loudly, clapping his hands sharply. From above them she heard the sound of barking. Even the dogs were smart enough not to try to descend that cliff.

Sabrina glanced over her shoulder in time to see the bear drop to his front paws. Amid shouts from Ian, the bear retreated to the safety of his cave, his big body swaying with each hurried step.

Before Sabrina could utter a sound, Ian plucked her from the ground and tossed her over his shoulder. She rode the hard thrust of his shoulder until they reached the crest of the hill, where he lowered her to the ground.

"Damn foolish woman," he shouted, pushing the hair back from her face. He cupped her face in his hands, staring into her eyes, concern naked in the pale green depths. "Just what the hell did you think you were doing?"

"Escaping!" She pushed aside Ian's arms, hitting Byron's nose with her hand. The dog took a step back, then sat beside Shakespeare, who had already flopped on a patch of wild flowers. Guinevere kept her distance, staying a few feet to Ian's left, looking at Sabrina as though she thought the woman was a snake that might strike at any moment.

Ian examined every feature of Sabrina's face with his eyes, his fingers brushing her chin, near but not touching a small cut. "How badly are you hurt?"

She lifted her chin, meeting his concerned look with cold defiance. "Does it matter? I'm surprised you didn't let your bear have me for dinner. I suppose you keep him to impress your guests."

"I confess. I spend my summers training all the bears in the neighborhood. Would you like to see him dance the minuet?"

"I would like to go home."

He ran his hands lightly down her legs, coaxing gooseflesh to rise across her skin. She slapped away his hands. "Just what do you think you are doing?" she asked, trying to pull together the tattered pieces of her gown. One side of the delicate fabric was no more than shreds from her hip down.

"Apparently not what you think I'm doing," he said, grinning at her, his teeth showing animal white in the moonlight. He bent his head, wrapping his warm hands around her injured ankle.

She sucked in her breath, trying not to cry out in pain.

"I don't think anything is broken," he said, lifting his gaze to hers. "But it needs tending."

"Your concern touches me."

Chapter Twelve

Ian carried Sabrina back to the house, cradling her against his chest. She rode with her arms crossed, her head turned away from him, seemingly detached, while he was aware of every soft curve pressed against his body. When he thought of how close he had come to losing her . . . his arms tightened around her. The little witch had shaved ten years from his life.

Hannah met them in the entrance hall, her eyes growing wide as she saw Ian and his lady. He gave Hannah instructions, a list of what he would need to tend his guest, then carried Sabrina to her room.

The torn pieces of her gown parted as he lowered her to the bed, revealing the long, shapely curve of her leg, her skin glowing in the gaslight. She tugged at her gown, covering her legs as best she could. Yet it was too late for Ian. Memories swirled inside him, escaping the walls of their prison like smoke rising from a fire. One night with her, one night cushioned between those satiny thighs, and he was lost forever.

"So, just how did you manage to escape?" Using the question as an excuse, he turned to explore the room, hiding the incriminating evidence throbbing in his trousers. The woman could set his blood on fire with one touch.

He glanced over his shoulder. She lay against the pillows, burgundy hair tumbling wildly around her shoulders, a streak of dirt on her lovely cheek, her arms crossed at her waist, looking every bit a lost waif.

Yet there was something more about her, the defiant tilt of that lovely chin, the proud set of her slender shoulders. Here was a woman to fight for, a woman to stand at a man's side and forge an empire, a woman who could get into your blood and burn like a fever. Never in his life had he wanted more to hold her in his arms.

She could ruin him.

Perhaps she already had.

He rested his hands on the windowsill and stared out at the rose garden. As a child he had often found his grandparents sitting together in the gazebo, hands clasped, heads close together, watching the river roll past. Their years together had only strengthened their love. That's how it should be. That's how he had imagined it would be with Sabrina. Another illusion.

Wood scraping against stone brought his gaze to the oak tree. A smile curved his lips as he realized how the lady had managed to escape a locked room. "You always did have a penchant for climbing trees, Sabrina," he said, glancing over his shoulder at her.

Her chin rose a degree. "Mr. Tremayne, how long have you had this obsession with Sabrina?"

"Obsession? Is that what led you to New York?" He turned to face her. "What is your obsession, Sabrina? What will satisfy you? Revenge? What did you hope to win by coming here?"

"If you treated Sabrina in the same manner you have treated me, I can well understand the woman wanting to see your head on a silver platter."

"So you would like to see me dead."

"If I had a sword, right now I could skewer you myself."

"I guess I'm lucky you don't have a sword."

She released her breath in a hiss between her teeth. "You're so smug, so sure of yourself. Well, let me tell you this, Mr. Ian Tremayne . . ." She hesitated as Hannah entered the room, followed by a small, dark-haired maid.

Hannah's gaze darted from Ian to the girl lying upon the bed, then back to Ian, a small smile lifting the corners of her mouth. "Will you be needing any help?" she asked, dropping an arm-load of towels and sheets on the foot of the bed. A dark brown bottle and a carving knife rested on top of the load of linen.

"No. I can handle it from here. But I want you to have the front bedroom at the end of the hall prepared." Ian smiled down at Sabrina. "Although I doubt you'll be climbing many trees in the next few days, we'll change rooms just to take away the temptation."

The maid set a bucket near the foot of the bed, then turned

to follow Hannah out of the room. Ian lifted the bucket and approached Sabrina.

"I don't need your help."

"Your ankle needs tending," he said, lowering the bucket to the floor beside her, chunks of ice rattling against the metal sides.

"I can do it," she said, tugging away as he grasped her leg just above her ankle.

"All right," Ian said, lifting his hands in surrender.

Sabrina dipped one toe into the bucket of ice and water. The icy sting shot straight up her leg. She glanced up at Tremayne, who stood watching her, a crooked smile on his lips. Nothing would cause her to show this man any weakness. After taking a deep breath she plunged her foot into the bucket, gasping at the sudden shock of ice meeting warm skin.

"It should take some of the swelling down," he said, his voice sounding deceptively gentle.

"How comforting."

He laughed and lifted that wicked-looking knife. Gaslight from the wall lamp beside the bed shimmered against the blade as Ian wielded the knife against a sheet, cutting notches into one side. When he was done he dropped the knife to the bed, then began tearing long strips from the mutilated sheet, linen yielding with a scream.

"How long do you plan to keep me prisoner?" she asked, looking down at her palms, her skin scraped and sore. It had taken months after the war to smooth her skin, to make her hands look once more like the hands of a lady. One night with Ian and she was once again digging in the dirt.

"That depends on how long it takes for the Pinkertons to uncover the truth about you."

She curled her fingers, staring at her broken nails, afraid he would see the fear she couldn't hide. "And how long do you suppose that will take?"

"It will take little more than a week to travel to England. A few days to do some checking on the Earl of Lanchester." He was quiet a moment, the sound of liquid swishing in a bottle filling the silence. "Depending on how easy it is to find the truth once he's there, I would guess no more than two weeks, maybe less."

"Caroline will know you kidnapped me," she said, glancing up at him. He held a brown bottle in one hand, a folded piece of cloth in the other. "She'll have the police after you."

"I can handle your Aunt Caroline."

"She's my godmother." Sabrina clenched her hands. If anyone could handle Caroline Van Cortlandt, it would be Ian Tremayne. Her only hope was to escape.

"Lift your chin," he said, sitting beside her on the bed.

"What are you doing?" she asked as he lifted a cloth to her face. An odd scent of carbolic acid, camphor, and alcohol drifted from the soaked linen.

"Taking care of a few cuts. Hannah's own home remedy."

She snatched the cloth from his hand. "I prefer to do it myself."

"Pity," he said, glancing at a cut on her thigh. "There were a few places I was looking forward to tending."

"I have no intention of feeding your lechery, Mr. Tremayne," she said, dabbing the damp cloth against her chin, biting her lip against a sharp sting.

"No?" He laughed deep in his throat. "Then try not to escape again, my lady."

Although his lips held a whisper of a smile, his eyes smoldered with serious intent. She lowered the cloth, her fingers growing tense on the soft linen. "Is that a threat?"

He shook his dark head. "A promise."

"You don't frighten me," she said, hoping he wouldn't see through her lie.

"You saw what kind of trouble you got into this time. Next time you might not be so fortunate."

She smiled. "I hardly call being held prisoner by a barbarian fortunate."

"Lady, you haven't seen my barbarous side. At least not yet."

She glared at him as he knelt on one knee beside the bed. He was wrong. What could be more barbarous than seducing a woman, stealing her innocence, her dreams, her love?

Her gaze followed his hand as he reached for a towel. The knife lay against the pale blue velvet little more than a foot away, the blade glistening in the gaslight.

Ian lifted her foot from its icy bath, his warm hands searing her cold skin.

Sabrina stared at that knife, her heart pounding wildly against her ribs.

He wrapped a towel around her foot and ankle, handling her as though she were made of delicate porcelain.

She wrapped her fingers around the wooden handle of the knife.

"It should be all right in a few . . ." Ian hesitated, his words dying as she thrust the tip of the knife to the soft skin beneath his chin.

"Don't think for a moment I won't cut your throat," she said, forcing his head back, exposing the vulnerable column of his neck. "I'm angry enough to slice you into fish bait."

He didn't respond, perhaps because he was afraid any movement would slice his throat.

"You are going to order your carriage hitched and take me back to Caroline's. Do you understand?" she asked, prodding him with the knife. "I'm not afraid to kill you."

One corner of his mouth twitched. He grabbed her hand, his fingers wrapping like a vise around hers, clamping her palm to the handle. She struggled against his hold, but her strength was no match for his. A frustrated groan escaped her lips as he dragged the knife away from his throat.

"I hate you," she shouted, slapping him with her free hand, her palm stinging from the blow. In the gaslight she saw the dark stain of her hand bloom against his cheek, and the darker stain of blood trickle from the corner of his mouth.

He met her eyes, staring at her for a long moment before he spoke. "So you want me dead."

"I only wish to heaven I were a man," she shouted, twisting her hand in his grasp, trying to free the knife handle, which still rode flush against her palm. "Strong enough to take this knife from your grasp and plunge it into your heart."

"All right." With his free hand, Ian grabbed the front of his shirt. White buttons flew in all directions, spraying her chest as he cleaved the linen to his waist.

Sabrina stared, her heart throbbing at the base of her throat as he thrust his shirt open, exposing golden skin and sable curls. "What are you doing?" she asked as he jerked her hand, forcing the tip of the blade toward his chest.

"Giving you what you want, Sabrina."

She struggled to release the deadly knife, powerless against his strength. Slowly he drew her hand forward, pressing the tip of the blade against his bare skin. His eyes . . . they were the eyes of a man she had never seen before. This man was wild, reckless. This man didn't care if he lived or died.

"One thrust, Sabrina." He tugged on her hand. "It's pressed against my heart. Can you feel it beating?"

Was it her imagination or her own pulse or the throb of his heart she felt vibrating against her palm? "Do you expect me to cower, Tremayne?"

He smiled. With a sharp thrust he forced the tip of the blade into his flesh. Yet it was Sabrina's cry of pain that ripped through the room. Ian revealed nothing in the harsh lines of his face, nothing but a cold glitter in those strange eyes.

She stared in morbid fascination. Crimson welled from the wound, staining the silver blade. Blood slid down his chest in a narrow rivulet, clinging to crisp black curls, streaming past the thin white scar on his chest, staining the waistband of his dark blue trousers.

"How does it feel, Sabrina, knowing you hold your enemy's life in your hands?"

"Don't," she whispered, closing her eyes.

"One thrust and you can end it." He tugged on her hand. "One thrust, straight into my heart."

"Please," she whispered.

Time hung suspended between them. Aware of each breath he took, she waited, silently willing him to stop this madness. After an eternity he released her hand, giving her control. She tossed the knife across the room, the sound of metal hitting stone chilling the air as it struck the hearth.

"You're insane," she whispered, fighting against the tears searing her eyes.

He lowered his eyes, staring for a moment at his own blood, as though he were surprised to see the scarlet stain. "Yes. I suppose I am."

Without wiping the blood from his chest, he began binding her injured foot, his fingers deft, infinitely gentle as he wrapped long strips around her ankle and instep. Sabrina watched him, staring at his long, dark hands, hating him for making her feel weak and foolish.

When he was finished he stood and lifted a towel from the foot of the bed, then scrubbed the blood from his chest. She glanced up, looking into his face as he slipped one arm around her shoulders, the other beneath her knees. "What are you doing?" she demanded, pushing against his chest as he lifted her into his arms.

"Carrying you to your new quarters."

"You mean my new prison cell," she said, trying desperately to ignore the hard thrust of his chest against her side, his skin searing hers through the thin layers of cloth separating them.

"Have you ever seen the inside of a prison cell?" he asked, carrying her across the room.

"Unlike you, I have never had the occasion to break the law. Do be sure to tell me all about it when you are behind bars."

He shifted her in his arms to open the door, forcing Sabrina to throw her arms around his neck to keep from falling, her lips a warm breath away from his neck. His intriguing male scent tingled her senses and, much lower, deep in her flesh, she felt a stirring, a primitive response of woman to man.

She stiffened as he straightened, crossing her arms once again in front of her. Great stars above, this man was her enemy. She couldn't forget that again. If she did, she would be lost.

He smiled down at her, his eyes telling her he knew exactly what was happening deep inside her. "Sabrina and her father make a living cheating Yankees of their gold. An offense that could easily win them both a long stay in a federal penitentiary."

"How unfortunate for them," she said, hoping her fear was well disguised. "Yet it has nothing to do with me."

"Doesn't it?"

She turned her head, staring at the green silk covering the walls of the wide hall, oil paintings in carved frames passing in and out of her vision as Ian carried her, his chest brushing her arm with each long stride. "I grow tired of trying to coax a madman out of his delusions. Believe what you will and take the consequences."

"I've always taken responsibility for all of my actions, my lady."

And he would one day pay for his actions toward her, she thought. Somehow the prisoner would become the warden. Somehow!

He carried her into a room at the end of the hall. A brass oil lamp burned on a mahogany chest near the bed, casting flickering light across the burgundy silk covering the walls. Her heart thumped a steady tattoo against her ribs as he carried her toward the big four-poster bed. If only she could banish the memories. If only she could stop this horrible longing deep inside her.

He lowered her to the white sheets, then hesitated, his arms growing taut beneath her. Her heart pounded at the base of her throat as he leaned over her, his breath falling soft and warm against her cheek, his eyes tracing the full curve of her lips. Was he thinking of the woman he had betrayed? Was he remembering the few short hours they had shared in each other's arms? Or was he just hungry for another tumble—and she the closest female.

If he tried anything, she would fight him. But a flutter low in her belly told her just how tenuous her position was. She would have herself to fight as well.

He slipped his arms from beneath her, leaving cold the flesh so recently warmed by his heat. Shamelessly, she watched him as he walked toward the windows, devouring the breadth of his shoulders, sliding her gaze down the length of his back, touching his lean waist.

What was becoming of her? Had he turned her into a harlot? A woman who craved a man's touch at any price? Why couldn't she look upon this man and see only the treacherous scoundrel he was? Why did she have to see traces of the man she once adored?

"I'm afraid the view isn't as pleasant," he said, keeping his eyes focused out the window. He jammed his hands into the pockets of his trousers. "But the nearest tree is on the opposite side of the drive."

He fell quiet but made no move to leave. Moonlight streamed across his face, illuminating the flicker of a muscle in his cheek as he clenched and unclenched his jaw. She sensed the tension growing taut inside him, felt that same tension draw on her muscles.

Issuing an oath under his breath, he turned to face her. His gaze flickered over her face, hungry, filled with the same desperate longing that had become her daily companion. Electricity crackled in the air between them. Her skin prickled. She held her breath, waiting for the charge, wondering if she could manage to fight him. After an eternity he spun on his heel, turning away from her.

"I'll send Hannah up to help you prepare for bed," he said, leaving the room without glancing in her direction.

The lock slid into place and muffled footsteps echoed in the hall, growing faint and finally disappearing. She fell back against the pillows, staring up into the dark canopy above her head, thumping her fists against the mattress. Conflicting emotions warred within her heart. She felt cheated, frustrated, relieved, and at the same time furious.

Perhaps people were like horses. A stallion could smell a mare in season. Ian had given her a taste of temptation. He had left her with a woman's craving. Lord help her, she wanted that man to hold her, she wanted to kiss him, she wanted . . . She had to escape before she gave him the one weapon that could destroy her.

Chapter Thirteen

Sunlight streamed through the open windows behind Ian's desk, scorching a path across one oak-paneled wall of his office on Broadway. He lifted an unfinished sketch from the top drawer of his desk, his fingers leaving damp smudges on the paper. Shifting in his chair, he tugged his shirt, peeling the white linen from his damp skin. Lord, he hated the city in the summertime. It was time to retreat to the country. Yet he couldn't.

Two stories below, carriages, horse-drawn trolley cars, drays, and riders on horseback all crowded the street outside his office. Wheels and horseshoes clattered against granite, horses whinnied and snorted, bridles jangled, bells clanged, the noises colliding, mingling with a low drone of voices until the air vibrated in a steady pulse against his ears, aggravating the ache throbbing in his temples.

He rolled a pencil between his fingers, staring down at the sketch of a new parlor car, trying to fix his thoughts on business. Early this morning he had left his grandfather's house. He had escaped to the city. Still, he couldn't escape Sabrina's spell.

He glanced up from the sketch as Mac showed Elias Bainbridge into the room. Short, stout, with hair the color of a copper kettle, Mr. Bainbridge did not meet the ideal of a Pinkerton detective, but apparently he was good at his job. Good enough to be promoted to head of the New York office four years ago, at the age of forty-two. But was he good enough to find out the truth about Sabrina?

Yesterday had only served to heighten memories of her. The memory of her lips, her voice, her hot, tight flesh, quivering, yielding to the demand of his hardened flesh, had haunted him for months. Last night had been a mistake. Touching her had only made him hungry for more. And she wasn't immune. He could see it in her eyes, he could see her anger and more, a simmering desire that drew him toward her in a way no woman had ever done before.

Staying under the same roof, knowing that beautiful witch slept just a few feet away, had done nothing for his rest the night before. The few hours he had slept, she had haunted his dreams, coming to his bed, her dark eyes filled with desire, glowing with love, her luscious body soft and naked against his.

Memory sparked the kindling deep in his belly, flames licked at his loins, and he felt an all too familiar tightening in his belly. Damn! If he was smart he would stay clear of that witch until he was sure who she was. After that he intended to purge her from his soul once and for all.

At Ian's invitation the detective took one of the two brown leather armchairs in front of the oak desk. Sunlight simmered through the open windows, striking the oval glasses Bainbridge wore perched on his nose. He cleared his throat before speaking. "I understand you want us to find someone, Mr. Tremayne."

"Not exactly. I want you to . . ."

"I will see him!" Caroline Van Cortlandt said, shoving open the door to Ian's office.

"I'm telling you he's busy," Mac said, tugging on Caroline's arm.

Caroline glared up at the little man, her delicate nostrils flaring, dark color staining the crests of her cheeks. "You will take your hand off me this instant."

Mac stepped back as though she had punched him in the jaw. He stiffened, his face pulling into taut lines, looking like a bulldog about to fight for his territory. "Now listen here, Mrs. . . ."

"It's all right, Mac," Ian said, smiling at his old friend.

Mac pursed his lips. For a moment he looked reluctant to give in to this spitting cat, but finally he turned, leaving Mrs. Van Cortlandt on the threshold of Ian's office.

Caroline marched to the desk, blue- and black-striped poplin rustling against her petticoats, her gaze lowering to Bainbridge. "You will leave."

Bainbridge blinked up at her, then turned a startled expression to Ian.

"Mr. Bainbridge, perhaps it would be better if you waited outside," Ian said, smiling at the detective. "This should take only a few minutes."

Bainbridge didn't hesitate. He escaped as though he were being chased by hornets, closing the door behind him.

"What have you done with my niece?"

"Your niece?" Ian leaned back in his chair. "Do you mean Sabrina is in town?"

Caroline drew a deep breath, her eyes narrowing to blue slits. "You know very well who I mean. My goddaughter, Lady Julia Wyndham."

"What about her?"

"She took a ride with you yesterday morning and never returned." Caroline clenched her hands at her waist, black cotton gloves growing taut across her knuckles. "If you harm her, I will see you hanged."

Ian glanced down at the pencil he held between his fingers. "It would seem you have reason to talk to the police, Mrs. Van Cortlandt." He lifted his gaze to her stormy visage. "What did they say?"

Caroline lifted her chin. "I haven't spoken to them."

"I see."

"But I shall."

Ian nodded, his lips curving into a smile. "The police are hardly discreet. I'm afraid they will want to investigate everyone involved." He paused, holding her with his look, seeing the anxiety growing, mixing with the anger in her eyes. "And it's hard to tell what skeletons they might unearth. What scandal they may cause."

"I'm warning you, young man," Caroline said, resting her hands on the desk, leaning toward Ian. "If you harm her, I will destroy you any way I can."

"Rest assured, Mrs. Van Cortlandt, I have no intention of harming her."

"What do you plan to do?"

"Find out the truth." Ian rolled the pencil between his fingers.

"I see. You still refuse to believe she is Lady Julia."

Ian held her gaze a moment. He could see her anger and nothing more. One thing for sure: he didn't want to play poker with the lady. "I have found with some things that the only way to discover the truth is to go looking for it. And while I go looking for it, I don't intend to allow my nephew to ruin his life by running off with that beautiful redhead. No matter who she is."

Caroline studied him for a moment, and Ian had the uneasy feeling that those blue eyes of hers saw more than he cared to let her see. Where Sabrina was concerned his emotions ran far too close to the surface.

"What you have done will ruin her reputation."

"I'm sure you can think of something to protect her reputation."

"Oh, yes. I will think of something, Mr. Tremayne." She smiled, staring down at him in a way that made the hair tingle at the nape of his neck. "You can be sure of that."

Caroline spun on her heel. With head held high she marched from the room, leaving behind a whisper of roses, a trace of doubt. Ian wasn't sure what the woman had in mind, but he was sure he wasn't going to like it.

Elias Bainbridge knocked on the open door. Ian gestured for the detective to enter. The sooner Bainbridge got to work, the sooner Ian would have his answers.

Caroline glanced up from her sampler as her daughter entered her gold drawing room. Lucy wore one of the new gowns Sabrina had helped her choose, and Caroline had to admit, the choice was superb. A bodice of rose-colored silk trimmed with ivory lace bared Lucy's pale shoulders and hugged her slender waist before billowing into a full skirt of rose silk trimmed with three wide flounces of the same embroidered lace. Instead of Lucy's usual bun, her hair was caught at her nape in coils of glossy curls adorned with silk rosebuds and ribbons.

"Turn around, dear."

Lucy obeyed, turning slowly, her head down, her arms held at awkward angles at her sides.

"Darling, you look as though you are about to be hanged. I thought you would be thrilled to attend the theater with Mr. Reynolds."

"I would if he had asked me, if he weren't taking me because you insisted Julia wanted me to go as her substitute." Lucy clenched her hands beneath her chin. "If I weren't so worried about Sabrina."

"Sabrina would want you to go, darling. Julia's sudden illness will give you a chance to get better acquainted with Mr. Reynolds." Caroline had decided to allow Julia to contract a cold, a mild illness that hopefully would be over in a few days.

"But how can I go with him? How can I enjoy the theater when Sabrina may be hurt?"

Caroline dismissed her daughter's words with a wave of her hand. "Ian Tremayne isn't going to hurt Sabrina. Oh, he'll be angry when he learns the truth about her. And I have little doubt he will learn the truth." She jabbed her needle into the sampler and set it on the table beside her chair. "When he does he'll return her, unharmed. You see, the man is in love with her."

Lucy pressed her fingertips to her lips. "Do you think so? Do you really think so?"

"I have no doubt about it." Caroline rose from her chair and slipped her arm around Lucy's slender shoulders. "Now, you will have a lovely time with Mr. Reynolds. And don't you fret about your cousin. All she needs is a little time to bring that man to his knees. And if she doesn't, I will."

It was after midnight when Ian returned to his house on Fifth Avenue. He had managed to do it, he thought, as he shed his clothes in his dressing room. He had managed to resist the compelling urge to ride back to his grandfather's house, to ride back to that beautiful witch. Now, if he could only manage to sleep without being haunted by her.

Moonlight streamed through the open French doors leading to the balcony, guiding him across his bedroom, his feet cushioned by a carpet of varying shades of blue and ivory. Why the devil had the drapes been pulled around his bed, he wondered, throwing open the icy blue silk hanging from the canopy.

After tossing his robe on the chair near the bed he slipped between crisp white linen sheets. His leg brushed something warm and smooth, something his instincts immediately identified as a woman's thigh. "What the devil!"

"What took you so long, darling?" Felicity asked, pouncing on him, pressing her naked breasts to his chest. "I've been waiting for hours."

"What the hell are you doing here?" Ian asked, grasping her shoulders.

Felicity rubbed her belly against his, the damp curls crowning her thighs brushing provocatively against his skin. "Come on, Ian, can't you guess?"

"Dammit!" he mumbled, tossing her to the side. She grabbed his arm as he tried to get out of bed.

"Ian, darling. You can't tell me you're not lonely in this big bed."

Ian broke free of her hold and came to his feet. "Get out," he said, his voice low and deadly calm.

Felicity shook her head, her fair hair brushing the pink crests of her heavy breasts. "I'm warm and wet and ready for you, darling," she said, brushing her hand over her belly. "Do you remember what it was like, Ian?"

Ian felt the blood stir in his loins, his muscles growing taut. Sabrina had him hungry, haunting him day and night, filling him with a desire that throbbed in his loins like an open wound. Damn that redhead!

Felicity's gaze roamed the long length of him, lingering on that part of him under primitive rule. "My God, you're gorgeous."

At that moment Ian wished he didn't have the habit of sleeping in the nude. He snatched his robe from the chair, the emerald silk gliding like a sigh over his skin.

"Come back to bed, Ian," Felicity said, reaching for him. "I'll take care of that saluting soldier of yours."

Ian stepped back as her fingers brushed his thigh. He would become a monk before he slaked his lust with this woman. "Go back to your husband, Felicity."

"He's in Albany. I don't expect him back until tomorrow, so you see, no one will know."

Ian frowned as he tied the belt of his robe. "Why is he in Albany?"

"I'll tell you all about it when you come back to bed." She slid her leg over the edge of the bed, brushing his leg with her toes. "It's something you really should know all about."

"It's not worth the price." He grabbed her arm and hauled her from the bed.

"I like it a little rough," she said, slipping her hand inside his robe, running her fingers through the crisp curls covering his chest.

"I know," he said, grabbing her hand as it snaked across his belly. "Where are your clothes?"

"Darling, did you know Walter intends to sink your little plans to merge the Harlem with the Hudson?"

Ian's frown deepened as he looked down at her.

"I heard him talking with Elsbury the other night. It seems they've formed a little band of conspirators." She slipped her knee between his, sliding her free hand down the curve of his hip. "They intend to tell everyone they will vote yes on the merger, then vote no."

Her fingers brushed his belly and he grabbed her hand.

"Tell me, Ian, what does it mean to sell short?"

"It means selling stock you don't own."

"Really. Now I wonder why Walter and his friends intend to do that?"

He knew all too well why they intended to do that. "Where are your clothes?"

"I'm not going to tell you," she said, smiling up at him.

"Fine." Ian pulled the silk counterpane from the foot of his bed and tossed it around her shoulders.

"Ian, you can't mean . . ." Her words ended in a shriek as he tossed her over his shoulder. "Stop joking, darling, and put me down."

Ian ignored her, marching from the room with Felicity wiggling on his shoulder.

"Ian, you can't mean to toss me out," she said, as they started down the wide staircase.

Ian kept walking.

"You wouldn't dare toss me out. You wouldn't dare!"

Ian only hoped she had a carriage waiting. If not, he would have to let her stay until he could get one hitched.

Marble chilled his bare feet as he crossed the entrance hall. He threw open the front door, allowing a warm breeze to rush through the portal. In the shadows across the street he saw her carriage.

The counterpane slipped from Felicity's shoulders as he deposited her on the stone landing, exposing full, pale breasts in the moonlight. "Good night, Felicity."

"Damn you!" she screamed, clutching at the counterpane. "I'll see you in hell for this."

"No doubt you're hoping for company." He closed the door on her curses and threw the bolt.

"A man with your kind of luck with women ought to seriously consider becoming a monk," Mac said from the first landing of the staircase.

"I'm beginning to feel like one, Mac," Ian said as he started up the stairs. But that was going to change, just as soon as he learned the truth about his beautiful redhead.

Sabrina sat in a chair near the windows, staring out at the front drive, moonlight turning the gravel to a ribbon of silver. This morning she had awakened to find Tremayne gone. Confined to her room, she had spent the day trying to lose herself in a book, trying not to think of Ian Tremayne. She had failed miserably.

A warm breeze swept in through the windows, lifting a strand of her hair across her face, brushing her nightgown against her breasts as softly as a lover's caress. She crossed her arms over her chest. Images rose in her mind, of eyes darkened emerald with desire, of arms holding her in a powerful embrace, of lips firm and hungry upon hers. Even miles away, he haunted her. Would he always haunt her?

How long did he intend to stay away? she wondered. For her own good, she hoped he stayed away until she could escape this silk-lined prison. Yet a part of her, a shameful, reckless part of her, wanted to see him, wanted to touch him, to hold him, to possess him. Glancing up at the midnight sky, she picked one star, the brightest diamond in the heavens.

Star light, star bright . . . No. She wouldn't make a wish. Wishes were for little girls who still believed in their dreams.

Chapter Fourteen

"I knew he was up to something," Rand said, wearing a path in the Aubusson carpet covering the floor of Ian's study, crushing roses of ivory and shades of scarlet under his heels. "He wants to ruin you."

"I know." Ian sipped his coffee, his third cup this morning, the dark liquid warming his throat. "The proposed merger will have the stock soaring. So Rutledge and his little band of conspirators sell short. After the vote the stock falls, we lose our shirts, and the legislators and their associates buy the stock for next to nothing. The shorts make a fortune, and it's the last time a stockholder receives a dividend from either railroad."

Rand sank to one of the two wing-backed chairs in front of Ian's desk, morocco leather sighing under his weight. "So, how do you stop them?"

"We have nearly two weeks before the vote."

"Another two weeks for those bastards to flood the market with stock."

"I hope they do." Ian leaned back in his chair and followed a shaft of sunlight as it pierced the windows and flowed upward along the curving mahogany staircase leading to the second-floor gallery. Books lined three walls of the gallery. More books lined the mahogany shelves in the adjoining library; they were one of the few things he had taken from his father's house, old friends he couldn't leave behind. "I hope they dump all their stock and try to sell hundreds more they don't own."

Rand shifted in the chair, resting his hands on his knees. "You have an idea."

"I'm going to buy every share of stock I can get my hands on. And every contract for stock the shorts are willing to provide."

"It sounds reckless," Rand said, shaking his head. "The stock will fall through the floor."

"Not if there isn't any stock on the market." Ian rolled his coffee cup between his palms. Behind him burgundy velvet drapes fluttered with the warm breeze, carrying the scent of freshly tilled dirt from the rose garden. "We buy all the Harlem stock we can, lock it in a safe, and wait for the price to go back up."

Rand sat back, a smile slowly curving his lips. "The men who sold short won't be able to cover their shares."

"We'll own their contracts." Ian sat back, studying his cousin, weighing their chances. For his plan to work each man involved would have to risk a fortune. "I'm meeting with the Commodore, Jerome, and a few others in two hours. Before I do I need to know if you want a piece of it."

Rand released his breath between his teeth in a low whistle. "If it does work, there will be more than a few men ruined."

"I think that was their idea. Except we're going to change the names of those men."

"It's a gamble. But you could make a fortune."

"It will take sizable capital to gain a corner. Big investment, big gain."

"And even bigger risk." Rand lowered his eyes, studying the tip of his brown riding boot. "Why let me in on it?"

"You always liked a good gamble. And with Delia's taste, I figured you could use a few extra greenbacks."

"Ian, I wish I could come in with you on this, but . . . I'm a little short of cash right now. I'm not sure I could raise more than twenty thousand."

It seemed Delia was even more expensive than Ian had imagined. "How much would you like to invest? A hundred thousand? I could lend you the money."

Rand glanced across the desk, meeting Ian's eyes. "If you put up a hundred thousand for me, I'll pay you back out of the profits." The corners of his mustache twitched. "If there are any. If not, I'll pay you back by the end of the year."

"All right." Ian rose and looked down at Rand. "I don't need to tell you we have to keep this quiet. If word leaks that we know about the conspiracy, we lose everything."

"Right." Rand lifted his shoulders, as though he were trying to work out some tension. "If we don't lose everything anyway."

Ian smiled. "If it weren't a gamble, it wouldn't be any fun."

Rand groaned in response. Neither man spoke as Ian walked with his cousin to the front door.

"I almost forgot," Rand said, turning on the top step, his eyes growing narrow against the bright morning sun as he looked back at Ian. "Delia asked me to invite you to dinner tonight."

Ian shook his head. "Give her my regrets. I'm going out of town for a few days."

"In the middle of all this?"

"There's nothing to do once all the players are in place. After the capital is raised I could drop off the face of the earth and the deal would still go through." He wanted to see Sabrina, hear her voice, touch her. Lord knew he was a fool, but he couldn't stay away from the witch. "I feel like spending a few days at Dunkeld."

The sound of horseshoes on gravel rattled through the open windows behind Sabrina. She lowered the book she was reading and stood, trying her best to keep her weight from her injured ankle. Late afternoon sunlight slanted through the windows, striking her face with gold and scarlet. Lifting her hand to her brow, shielding her eyes, she stared down the drive.

A man atop a golden stallion approached the house, his black hair tossed by the wind, his long legs encased in buckskin hugging the horse's sides. Horse and rider moved as one, fluid, powerful. Ian lifted his face as though he knew she waited, his eyes seeking, finding her, setting her pulse to a dizzying rhythm.

Images collected in her mind, wisps of memories that had never been made. Or had they? It was as she had imagined countless times: Ian riding up the gravel drive of Rosebriar to claim her as his bride. An odd sensation gripped her, emotions swirling around her like a whirlwind, ripping her from the present, casting her into that imagined future. Or was it the distant past?

He paused on the drive beneath her window, locked in her gaze, caught in the spell spinning around them both. The rustle of the leaves in the breeze, the evening call of birds, the distant sound of the river faded. All she heard was the sound of her heart. All she saw was his face. He had come to claim her, her lover, her mate, as he had in countless lifetimes before. Never had she felt this powerful pull toward any other man. He beckoned to her senses and beyond. He touched her soul with magic.

"You're back!" Hannah said, running from the house, three dogs bounding out in front of her plump figure.

Like moonlight dissolving in the rays of the sun, the spell vanished. Sabrina stepped back from the window, pulling her gaze from her enemy, dragging air into her lungs. She pressed shaking fingers to her lips. This wasn't Rosebriar, and Ian wasn't going to claim her as his ladylove. Daydreams and wishes were for children. Ian had taught her that lesson, a lesson she would do well to remember.

She sank to the chair and lifted her book, determined to ignore the man when he came to her door. Studiously she stared at the open book, the words no more than black marks on a white page.

The rosewood clock on the mantel clicked away the seconds. She glanced at the crystal face. Ten minutes had passed, and Ian still hadn't come to her. Not that she wanted to see him. But the very least the scoundrel could do was see how she was feeling.

Another ten minutes passed before she heard the key rattle in the door. Taking a deep breath, she stared down at her book. The door opened.

"Mr. Tremayne, I do not wish . . ." She glanced up, meeting Hannah's smiling face, feeling the bitter bite of disappointment. "Oh, I thought you were . . . that man."

Hannah laughed. "So you've seen him."

"Lord of the manor? Yes, I've seen him," Sabrina said, glancing at the cloud of cream-colored silk cascading from Hannah's arm. "What have you got there?"

"It's one of Lady Rebecca's gowns. Master Ian thought you might like to wear it to dinner tonight."

"Am I to suppose he expects me to join him tonight?"

A frown worked deep creases into Hannah's brow. "Now, lass, have dinner with him."

She had a choice of having dinner with a scoundrel or facing the same four walls. "Tell Tremayne I do not have dinner with pirates."

"Lass, he really is a wonderful man, once you get to know him."

"I know him well enough," Sabrina said. *Too well.*

Hannah lowered her head, cream-colored silk flowing behind her as she left the room. A few minutes later she returned with the gown still draped over her arm and a folded piece of white paper in her hand.

Sabrina took the note and read the single line written in a slightly reckless hand. *Afraid of pirates?*

Sabrina glanced up at Hannah, who stood watching her, a hopeful expression on her round face. "Tell the man I am not afraid of him," she said, shoving the note into her book. "I simply do not wish to suffer his company."

Hannah nodded as she left, returning a few minutes later, plump cheeks flushed, puffing, carrying the gown and another note. Sabrina snatched the note, growing irritated with her own dissolving resolve. She didn't want to eat alone in this room. She wanted some conversation. She wanted to wear that pretty silk gown. And she wanted to see that pirate again.

I assure you, I know how to use a knife and fork. I never talk with my mouth full. And I promise not to bite. Please join me.

"Tell the man . . ." Sabrina hesitated as Hannah raised her hand.

"I'm getting too old to be running up and down those stairs." Hannah gave Sabrina a warm smile. "Please, have dinner with him. It will make my life much more pleasant."

Sabrina glanced down at the note she held between her fingers, tracing the elegant scrawl of his reckless hand, feeling a tingle of excitement race through her blood. Even sparring with the man made her tingle. "I suppose, if I'm to choose between having dinner with a scoundrel or facing these four walls the entire night." She lifted the hem of the gown. "Let's see how it fits."

"I'm sure it will be fitting much better than that gown of Nora's."

Sabrina glanced down at the blue calico cotton Nora had let her wear. Unfortunately the two women were not the same size. The gown pinched at her breasts, sagged at her waist, and fell halfway between her knees and her ankles. She wondered if the silk would fit any better.

To Sabrina's surprise, the cream-colored silk required few alterations. Apparently, Lady Rebecca had been slender up to the day of her death. With a few tucks in the waist the gown looked as though it had been made for her. Even the creamy satin slippers fit. At least the right one did. The swelling in her left foot prevented any hope of wearing a shoe.

Pale silk bared her shoulders; the tight-fitting bodice hugged her breasts and her waist, the gown plunging in a deep vee several inches below her natural waist. Two bands of blue silk rosettes decorated the hemline, and the edges of the sleeves, which fell just above her elbows. A small cluster of three rosettes rested a few inches below the hollow of her neck, adorning the modest, round decolletage.

From a cedar-lined closet in the attic Hannah produced a pair of lawn drawers and a chemise, plus five lace-trimmed petticoats designed to be worn with the gown. Considering the heat of the evening Sabrina decided one petticoat would do.

"It's been too long since I've had the pleasure of fixing a lady's hair," Hannah said, coiling Sabrina's hair into a thick rope.

Sabrina rubbed her finger over the smooth mahogany vanity, weaving a serpentine trail on the polished surface. "Then I take it most of Tremayne's women bring their own maids."

"You're the only young lady he's ever brought here," Hannah said, taking a hairpin from a white porcelain tray on the vanity.

Sabrina wasn't sure she believed that. Of course, it didn't matter. He hadn't brought her here to whisper tender words of devotion in her ear.

"I would brush Miss Brenna's hair every night before she'd go to bed. One hundred strokes. Ah, she had hair like yours, fine and thick, like silk, only ebony in color, like the MacClarens."

"You used to tend Ian's mother?"

"Aye. Right up to the time she died. Beautiful she was, bright like a polished diamond." Hannah's hand tightened against Sabrina's hair. "Why she ever picked that mean-spirited young man when she could have had her pick . . . ah, it still makes my blood boil."

Her Aunt Caroline had whispered about Everett Tremayne's numerous infidelities. She had also spoken of Brenna Tremayne as though the woman had been a saint. Brenna had been a devoted mother, an ardent supporter of the missions in the slums of the city. While working with the poor at the mission she had contracted the fever that had claimed her life when Ian was only a boy of five. "Pity Tremayne grew up to be the image of his father."

"The devil you say!" Hannah moved to Sabrina's side, still holding a handful of hair. "Master Ian is nothing like that silver-tongued, black-hearted son of a jackal."

"No?" Sabrina asked, lifting her gaze to Hannah's indignant scowl. "Then what do you call kidnapping me? The work of a saint?"

Hannah's lips pursed, her gaze lowering to the hair dangling from her hand. "He has his reasons, lass."

Not any of them as good as the reasons she had for escaping the man, Sabrina thought. She sat in silence, staring blindly at her image in the mirror as Hannah fussed with her hair.

"You look lovely," Hannah said, slipping small blue silk roses into Sabrina's hair, the heavy tresses swept back in a thick coil at her nape. "Ah, but I wish Master Ian would marry; I do miss having a missus to look after. The house craves the hand of a mistress."

Sabrina glanced down at the silver-handled brush laying on the top of the vanity, afraid of what her eyes might reveal. "From what I've seen, he's busy looking."

"Is he, now? Well, maybe he's already decided."

Maybe he had. Perhaps he had spent yesterday with Alisa, or this morning with Gretchen, or any one of a hundred other women. "It is of no concern to me," she said, determined to make the words the truth.

Hannah smiled at her in the mirror. "Seeing you wouldn't marry him if he were the last man on the face of the earth?"

Sabrina lifted her chin. "That's right."

Hannah shook her head. "Ah, but I have a feeling about the two of you. A feeling you are destined for one another. I thought it the first moment . . ."

Sabrina stood, frustrated, strangely uneasy with the turn of the conversation. "Ian Tremayne and I are enemies, and enemies we shall remain."

Hannah sighed, her eyes telling Sabrina she didn't believe a word of it. She ushered Sabrina to the door, supporting the girl's arm. Sabrina silently cursed the pain centered in her ankle, the pain that made her dependent on anyone. Hannah opened the door, and Sabrina froze.

Ian Tremayne stood near the open windows across the hall, black trousers hugging his long, muscular legs. A breeze swept in from the river, ruffling the sleeves of his white linen shirt, the long black silk of his hair.

Ian turned as they entered the hall, and she noticed he wore no cravat; his shirt was open at the neck, revealing a triangle of dark curls and warm-looking skin. One glance started a queer sensation quivering low in her belly, warm and pulsing and dangerous.

No matter how often she pleaded with her senses, she never seemed capable of ignoring this man's raw masculine power. Vitality vibrated from the man. He breathed excitement into her life. At a distance he could set her pulse racing. And when he touched her . . . she shouldn't think of such things.

He sent his gaze roaming over her, touching her face, the curve of her shoulders, the soft swell of her breasts, which rose and fell with each quick breath, betraying her agitation. Sunlight gilded one side of his face; the other was cast in shadows. Yet she could see his smile: warm, welcoming, and completely disarming.

"Ah, I thought you might have come up," Hannah said, stepping back from Sabrina. "You won't be needing me now."

Sabrina stared at Hannah's back as the little woman marched down the hall, leaving her standing alone with Ian in the dying rays of the sun.

"You look beautiful," Ian said, moving toward her.

"I don't need your help." Sabrina slapped aside Ian's outstretched hand as he reached for her arm, the movement causing her to lose her precarious balance.

She snatched for something to stop her backward tumble and found Ian's strong arm. He grabbed her arm, steadying her. Before she could catch her breath he swept her up into his arms.

"You are a stubborn woman," he said, smiling down at her.

"And you are a black-hearted rogue," she said, pushing against his chest. "Put me down! I don't need or want your help."

"I'm glad you decided to join me," he said, ignoring her protest and carrying her toward the stairs.

"I can see you dressed for the occasion," she said as he started down the wide, curving staircase. Without thinking she pressed the tip of her finger to the triangle exposed by his partially open shirt, brushing springy black curls before bumping against his warm skin. Her reaction was immediate, a sharp tug of remembrance that stole her breath and left her aching inside.

She snatched back her hand and looked away, staring at the pattern of gold diamonds cast upon the mahogany wainscoting by the windows above the Great Hall. She couldn't look at him. She knew he could read her every thought.

"Pirates never dress for dinner, my lady. Especially when it's summer and they are in the country."

She could hear only amusement in his voice. Perhaps he hadn't noticed her agitation. Perhaps he didn't realize the awful power he could wield over her senses. Just how was she ever going to overcome this weakness?

Ian carried her down a hall to the first room on the right. His dogs were waiting in the room, which appeared to be a study. Byron trotted over to him, poking Sabrina with his cold nose until she stroked his fluffy head. It was then she realized the dog had one blue and one brown eye.

Shakespeare lifted his head from the parquet where he was lying near the open French doors, but he didn't seem inclined to expend his energy to investigate his master's guest. With a thud he dropped his head back to the floor. Guinevere approached them with her head down, her tail tucked between her legs. She seemed anxious to be near Ian, but still she held back, looking at Sabrina with wary brown eyes.

"It's all right, Gwen, the lady isn't going to hurt you," Ian said, his voice as soft and soothing as if he was talking to a child.

The dog lifted her ears, took a step forward, then hesitated. For a moment she seemed to weigh her need to be near Ian with her need to stay away from the stranger in his arms. In the end she slinked back to a pillow that lay on the green and gold needle-point carpet near the marble hearth. After circling the green velvet pillow once, she lowered herself to the soft cushion and fixed a mournful gaze on Ian.

"It takes her a while to trust anyone new," Ian said, lowering Sabrina to a Queen Anne chair covered in rich emerald silk velvet.

Sabrina understood the dog's reluctance. Once you'd been hurt by someone it was difficult to trust again. Ian dropped to one knee in front of her and lifted her bound foot, warm, bronzed hands closing around her calf just above the bandage.

"What are you doing?" she asked, trying to jerk her leg from his grasp, pain shooting through her ankle at her effort.

He looked up at her, a whisper of a smile on his lips. "I'm trying to see how your ankle is."

Gripping the arms of the chair, she stared down at his dark head, allowing him to examine the fresh bandage Hannah had applied that morning. He held her foot, his long fingers brushing the bandage with such gentleness she lost her breath.

She forced air into her taut lungs and snatched for the protective shield of her anger. "I didn't realize you had taken medical studies, Mr. Tremayne."

"I learned how to tend horses when I was a boy," he said without glancing up at her.

"Thank you for the comparison."

He smiled up at her. Disturbed by the emotions he could resurrect inside her, she looked away from him, her gaze catching the portrait above the mantel; Ian Tremayne stood beside a woman seated on a white wicker chair.

Sunlight flowed through the French doors behind Sabrina, glittering on the painting, streaming across the woman's golden hair. Roses spread out behind Ian and his lady, the graceful columns of a white gazebo rising in the background.

So, Hannah had lied. Ian Tremayne had once brought a woman to this house, a very beautiful, very special young woman. "What happened to her?" Sabrina asked, jealousy curling around the base of her throat, choking her voice.

Ian glanced up at her, his expression reflecting his surprise. "Who?"

"The woman you posed with in the rose garden."

He frowned. "I've never posed with any woman in any garden."

"You lie? When the proof is hanging on the wall behind your head?"

Ian came to his feet, turning to glance up at the portrait above the mantel. He studied the portrait a moment before glancing at Sabrina, his eyes echoing the warmth of his smile. "Take a closer look at the gentleman."

Sabrina turned her head, staring at the books lining walnut shelves along the far wall, unwilling to see Tremayne with his former ladylove. And there was no doubt in her mind that that beautiful, fair-haired woman was his love. The artist had captured that tender emotion in the curve of his fingers on her pale shoulder, in the smiles on their faces, the look in their eyes.

"I think you rate yourself too highly, Tremayne. I would hardly call you a gentleman."

"The man in the portrait is my grandfather."

She glanced back at the painting. Pale green eyes looked down at her from a finely chiseled face, handsome enough to steal a woman's dreams. Yet upon closer inspection she noticed slight differences in this face and the face of the man standing in front of her. MacClaren's brow was a little higher, the nose not as finely chiseled, the lips thinner, less sensual. Still, the resemblance was remarkable.

"I wonder what he would think of you now, Ian Tremayne." She stared up at the living image of that oil painting. "What would he say if he knew you were holding a woman here against her will?"

"If I told you people used to call him the Green-eyed Devil, would you have your answer?"

"So you come by being a scoundrel honestly, is that it? Piracy passed on through the bloodlines."

"Oh, my lady," Ian said, resting his hands on the arms of her chair. "What am I going to do with you?"

"Release me."

"Never."

She pressed her head back against the soft velvet as he leaned forward, trying to avoid the kiss she knew would come, the kiss she knew she couldn't resist. His warm breath fell soft and sweet against her lips, tinged with brandy and his own intriguing scent.

"What would a true pirate do with a helpless woman, a woman completely in his power?"

He brushed his lips against the curve of her cheek, beside her lips. She caught her breath and fought to keep from turning her face, from capturing those warm, sensual lips against her own. "You'll see how helpless I am." She felt him smile against her cheek.

"Tell me. Would he take her in his arms? Would he strip away the silk of her gown, the linen veiling her luscious flesh?" He pressed his lips to the soft skin beneath her ear, touching her with the tip of his tongue.

She swallowed the sigh drifting up her throat, sinking her teeth into her lower lip to keep it under control.

"Would he stroke her skin with his hands?" He lowered his voice, brushing his lips against her ear, raising goose bumps along her shoulder. "Would he taste her with his lips, his tongue?"

Warm tendrils of desire curled at the base of her spine. "You wouldn't dare."

"Think again, my beautiful witch."

He was capable of anything. A fragile thread of doubt kept the beast at bay, a thread that could break at any moment. She pushed against his chest. "You make light of me, Tremayne."

"Do I?" Ian lifted away from her. "Do I indeed?"

Standing before her as he was, she couldn't fail to see the taut outline of his aroused flesh, pressing in a long, thick ridge against the black linen of his trousers. Heat flaring in her cheeks, she pulled her gaze from that tempting, masculine display, staring up into eyes that had darkened, like twin emeralds in firelight.

"Would you care for a drink before dinner?" he asked, moving toward a cabinet built into the wall near the door through which they had entered. "Some sherry, perhaps."

Just like that, he could change his mood. With a turn of his shoulder he could dismiss her, while she sat there with the blood humming in her veins. She had to learn to better control her emotions. Somehow.

"No thank you." She needed to keep a clear head. Byron rested his chin on the chair, nudging her arm with his cold nose. "You like attention," she whispered, stroking the dog's head, hoping to distract her thoughts from his infuriating master.

Ian poured a generous portion of brandy into a crystal goblet and drained it in one gulp, the amber liquid cutting a fiery path down his throat, failing to cool the flames raging in his loins. He had to control himself. He should have stayed in the city. He should have kept miles between himself and that beautiful red-head. Yet he couldn't, he thought, refilling his glass.

"Your grandmother was very beautiful."

He glanced over his shoulder. The position of her chair cast Sabrina in profile. Her head was tilted, her long neck arched like a graceful swan. Sunlight slanted through the windows, streaming in gold and scarlet across her, springing into flames in her glossy mane. Lord, she was beautiful. Yet more than her beauty attracted him.

"She was more than beautiful," he said, drawn back to Sabrina's side.

He looked down at her, seeing past her beautiful face. Her strength, her wit, her courage, her damnable pride had captured him. How many women would climb down a tree to escape her captor? How many women would devise a plan as bold and reckless as this masquerade to extract her pound of flesh? How many women could dominate his every thought, control his every desire?

Sabrina was his enemy. Yet he couldn't forget those few hours he had shared with her, wrapped in her arms, lost in her sweet flesh. Lord help him, he wanted her more than he had ever wanted anything in his life. And she wanted his money.

"She was born Lady Rebecca Stanhope, the daughter of an English marquess." He glanced up at his grandmother as he spoke. "Yet she gave up everything—wealth, family, title—to marry a penniless Scotsman."

"She must have loved him very much."

He glanced down at her, meeting her dark eyes with silent challenge. "He never had to worry whether she had married him for his money."

Her chin lifted, her lower lip growing plump. "Is that what worries you, Tremayne? Afraid a woman will marry you only for your money?"

Ian glanced down at his glass, seeing his reflection in the amber liquid. "It's been known to happen."

"I see. I suppose you have nothing else to offer a woman, not loyalty, compassion, love."

He tightened his fingers against his glass. "All and more to the right woman."

"And who is she? This right woman? Is she one of your pampered and spoiled debutantes?"

"Do you suppose she could be a lying, deceitful witch?"

"I'm not sure you would know her if she threw herself into your arms."

"Can we always trust our instincts?"

Sabrina looked up at the portrait. "She did."

"The gift they shared was rare." Ian stared at his grandparents, feeling loneliness echo inside him, in a deep cavern of longing, so dark, so very empty. "He came to this country with fifty dollars in his pocket. Together they built a shipbuilding empire that started with a single ferry he built with his own hands."

"You look envious."

He glanced down at her, meeting her dark eyes, startled by her perceptiveness. Did she realize how much he wanted to hold her? Did she realize he ached with need, burned with the agonizing flame of desire for her? "I suppose I am. When you inherit money you never know if you could have made it on your own."

She was quiet a moment, studying him, a crinkle appearing between her delicate brows. "You would have succeeded. You have his instincts, his drive, his ruthlessness, like a hungry lion." Her lips curved. "Or a pirate. You could also be called a green-eyed devil."

He raised his glass to her, his lips curving into a grin. "I'll take that as a compliment."

She glanced away, color rising to stain her cheeks. "Yes, I'm sure you would."

Ormsby entered at that moment to announce that dinner was ready. Despite her protests, Ian lifted Sabrina in his arms and carried her down the long corridor to the formal dining room. Yet there were no places set at the polished cherry wood table, which could easily seat fifty diners. He carried her across the dining room and through a pair of open French doors to the terrace.

A round table with a top of black marble and legs of wrought iron stood just outside the door. Two wrought-iron chairs padded with floral cushions sat at angles to the table, waiting for them. Atop white lace, crystal glasses shimmered in the setting rays of the sun, the silver candelabra in the center of the table glowing scarlet, its curving arms holding long white candles that had yet to be lit.

If he had asked her, he could not have provided a more inviting setting. How many women had lost their hearts to him in the moonlight? she wondered.

"Do you often entertain your guests alfresco?" she asked, as Ian lowered her to a chair.

He paused a moment, his hand resting on the curve of her back, and she wondered if he could feel the way her heart raced beneath his touch.

"I seldom entertain guests," he said, taking his place at her side.

"I suppose I should feel privileged."

He chuckled, the sound deep in his throat. "Still, I suppose you don't."

For a man unaccustomed to entertaining, Tremayne was a master at it. Despite her anger, she found herself enjoying his company, listening to tales of mischief performed as a boy, parrying questions designed to reveal more of her own past, creating a fairy-tale world for Lady Julia Wyndham, playing this game of hide and seek. He would learn the truth soon enough. She only hoped that by that time she would be gone.

As the sun faded in a last burst of gold and scarlet across the sky, Ormsby returned to light the candles. The music of crickets and the river surrounded them.

Dessert turned out to be whipped cream served in a flaky pastry covered with a thick chocolate sauce. She glanced at Tremayne as Ormsby set the plate in front of her. Had Ian remembered it was her favorite? Or was this simply coincidence?

Candlelight flickered across his features, revealing the challenge in his green eyes. Nothing was mere chance with this man. He was hoping she might slip, reveal herself in some way, end this game.

She glanced down to the pastry. What else did he remember about those three days they had spent together? "Where was the tournament held?" she asked, carefully diverting the conversation back to him.

A breeze blew in from the river, lifting perfume from the rose gardens. "We held it in a meadow a few miles away from the house," he said, smiling at the memory. "It took a week to set up the tents and stands, the playing fields. When we were done Lancelot would have felt at home. My grandfather was even more excited about it than I was. I think he secretly enjoyed the chance to be a king."

"Sounds like something my brothers would have enjoyed."

He paused, his water goblet suspended halfway to his lips. "I didn't realize you had brothers, Lady Julia."

Sabrina's hand twisted the napkin resting on her lap. Careful. She had to be careful with this man. "My brothers are dead, Mr. Tremayne."

One corner of his lips lifted slightly. "Oh, I see."

"They went down in a shipwreck with my parents. They were on a trip to Calais."

"And you survived."

Heat crept into her cheeks. "I didn't go. I . . . I had a cold."

"So they left you, and drowned on the way to Calais."

No. It hadn't been a shipwreck. Yet they were gone just the same. She glanced down at her water goblet, the damp crystal shimmering in candlelight.

Chills crawled along her back as memories clouded her vision. In the crystal Sabrina could see her mother's pale face, her blue eyes wide and searching, dazed, like a lost child. "Where are they, Brina?" she had whispered. "Why hasn't your father come to see me? Where's Dennis? Brendan? Don't they know I want to see them?"

Sabrina had bathed her mother's brow in cool water, knowing the fever was doing its deadly work. Mother had forgotten what was too horrible to remember. How could Sabrina tell her that Dennis was gone, killed in a peach orchard. And Brendan . . .

"Lady Julia?" Ian's voice drew Sabrina back from her dark memories.

She glanced at him, for a moment forgetting what he had said. "I beg your pardon."

He frowned. "You were saying your family was killed in a shipwreck."

Sabrina's throat tightened. "That's right."

"How terrible for you."

His sarcasm pricked her. He knew she had lost her mother, her brothers. He was cold and heartless and he just didn't care. "I didn't realize you would find the loss of my family so amusing, Mr. Tremayne," she said, tossing her tortured napkin on the table beside her plate.

Her chair scraped against stone as she shoved it back from the table. Her ankle crumpled beneath her as she stood. She lurched, grabbing the table to keep from falling. Ian was out of his chair and at her side before her low groan had vanished on the breeze.

"I don't want your help!" she said, pushing against the strong arm reaching for her. "Just stay away from me."

"Sabrina, I'm . . ."

"Get the blazes away from me!" she shouted, turning away from him. Forcing her back straight, she limped toward the door, clenching her teeth against the pain, which careened upward like a jagged knife with every other step.

"Let me . . ." he said, taking her arm.

She spun on her heel, lashing out with her open palm, slapping him across the cheek, the blow hard enough to snap his head to one side, hard enough to burn her palm. Frustration, rage, and pain soared inside her. She lashed out at her enemy, pummeling his chest, his shoulders with her clenched fists. He weathered the storm, standing like a stone statue, taking each blow, until her fists ached, until her tired hands rested impotently against his chest.

"You're horrible," she whispered.

"I know." The tenderness in his voice sparked something dangerous deep inside her, something she wanted to believe in but couldn't. "I know what it feels like to lose someone you love."

"Words, Tremayne. You know nothing."

He cupped her elbows with his hands, his touch achingly gentle. "My brother died in my arms."

So had hers. Dear Brendan, who had taught her to dance. Brendan, who could illuminate a room with his smile. Brendan had died in her arms at Vicksburg, while Yankees had slung shells over their heads. Pain twisted in her heart. She fought against the shameful tears stinging her eyes. This Yankee would not see her pain. "Let go of me."

He tightened his grip on her arms. "I can't," he said, his voice sounding oddly tortured. Without another word he lifted her in his arms.

Turning her head away from him, she crossed her arms at her waist, wanting nothing of his embrace, nothing of his warmth radiating against her. He carried her along the long corridor, up the staircase and to her room, as though a fire chased him. The bed had been turned down, the lamp on the bedside chest lit, spilling golden light across the white sheets.

He lowered her to that pool of gold, his arms taut around her, holding her close, his lips a breath away from hers. He whispered to her with his eyes, silent words of need, of desire, words echoing in her own heart. She fought the urge to slip her arms around his neck, to draw him to her, to ease the horrible ache that throbbed deep within her. Yet what he offered was a lie. What she needed he refused to give.

"I'll fight you," she said, her voice a harsh whisper, knowing she would also fight her own need.

His lips parted, and he looked for a moment as though she had plunged a knife into his ribs, then anger distorted his features, blurring all other emotions. He cupped her cheeks in his big hands and slammed his mouth over hers, his lips firm, punishing, demanding.

She grabbed his arms, trying to break free. She would not surrender to this man. She would not surrender to her own weakness. Yet . . . she wanted him, more than anything in her life she wanted this man.

Before she could lose the battle he pulled away from her, dragging the back of his hand across his lips, as though he wanted to erase the imprint of her kiss. He stood for a long moment, staring down at her, breathing hard, his eyes ablaze with rage and a desire he couldn't disguise. "The next time I have you, Sabrina, it will not be rape."

"You're insane if you think I will ever submit to you."

"Do you really think you can fight me and your own desire?" He smiled, a slow, sensual curve of his lips. "You want me. You want me between those beautiful thighs. I can taste it, Sabrina. I can feel it when I touch you."

Sabrina's hands clenched into fists at her sides, despising him for the truth he wouldn't allow her to hide. "I hate you!"

"When this farce is ended I will have you. And make no mistake, it will not be by force."

"I will give you nothing."

"Time will prove one of us wrong."

And time was her enemy.

Chapter Fifteen

Caroline Van Cortlandt glanced at the tall satinwood clock in the hall as she passed. Ten minutes to midnight. It was just like the man to barge into her house at this hour. It was just like him to cause trouble.

Pausing in front of the gold drawing room, she drew a deep breath. It had been nearly seven years since she had last seen the scoundrel. She only hoped he wasn't as handsome as she remembered.

He turned from the windows as she entered the room, broad shoulders thrusting back proudly. Tall and slender, just as she remembered. He didn't even have the decency to look old. He swept her figure with his dark brown gaze, drifting over her satin dressing robe as though he had every right. The man was just as impertinent as ever. And just as handsome, even with a full beard obscuring his cheeks.

"You shouldn't be here," Caroline said, fingering the lace at the top of her robe, feeling the throb of her pulse against the high collar.

"Where is she, Carrie?" Duncan O'Neill asked, moving toward her. "Is she ill?"

Caroline drew her lower lip between her teeth. "How long have you been in town?"

"Since the day after Sabrina arrived."

"Where have you been staying? Weren't you afraid someone would see you? You could ruin everything."

"I've got a room at a boardinghouse off Broadway. And with this bush nobody is going to recognize me," he said, running his hand over his bearded cheek, scratching his chin. "The damn itchy thing."

Caroline moved away from him, taking hold of the brocade

drapes. "Why are you here?" she asked, tugging the drapes closed, brass rings singing against the brass rod.

"To make sure my little girl doesn't get in over her head. Tremayne is a devil. Now where is she?"

"I don't know," she said, her voice barely above a whisper. He gripped her arm and spun her around to face him. "How dare . . ."

"Save your icy stares for someone who doesn't know you so well, Carrie," he said, his fingers growing taut against her arm. "Now tell me what happened."

"You will release me before I say another word."

He held her a moment before dropping his hand. "Well?"

Caroline took a seat on one of the sofas flanking the hearth. Duncan remained standing, staring at her with those dark, accusing eyes. With every effort to remain calm, she related the events surrounding Sabrina's disappearance, including her visit to Ian Tremayne.

"I don't believe he will hurt her."

Duncan slammed his fist into his open palm. "The man has already hurt her. I should have killed him long ago."

"Duncan, please," Caroline said, coming to her feet. "Please, don't do anything rash. I believe Sabrina is still in love with the man."

He turned and marched to the door.

"Where are you going?"

"To find my daughter!" he shouted over his shoulder.

"Duncan, please wait." She chased after him, following him down the long marble-lined hall, white satin billowing in her wake. "Duncan, please stay out of this. The way you're feeling you might . . ."

He turned at the door. She tried to stop and couldn't, skidding on the marble floor, plowing into him. His arms came around her and for a moment he held her, his embrace warm and familiar and more welcome than she wanted to admit. She stared up at him, watching the play of emotions in his eyes, seeing the fleeting ghost of the desire that had burned so brightly between them, before his expression grew closed and angry.

Frowning, he stepped away from her, dropping his hands to his sides. "The way I'm feeling, I just might send that Yankee back to hell, where he belongs."

Caroline pressed her fingers to her lips, watching him storm from her house. He always could leave her breathless. She closed the door, resting her brow against the cool oak. "Ian Tremayne, I hope you stay far away from town," she whispered. She didn't want to see either man hurt.

Ian slammed his fist into his pillow, a single feather escaping the smooth linen cover. Women! They were all alike, designed to twist a man into knots, destined to send him to an early grave. He turned to his side. Moonlight flowed through the open windows and billowing velvet drapes, cutting a wedge of silver across the swirls of aqua and ivory stitched into the woolen carpet beyond the foot of the bed, and through a second set of windows a shimmering wedge of light slashed across his chest.

Sabrina was flesh and blood; beautiful, yet mortal, like any other woman. No witch. Still, she had cast a spell, a spell he wondered if he could ever break. Why was it he had this odd feeling when he looked at her, a strange notion he had loved her before, in a hundred lifetimes?

With a sigh he flopped onto his back and tossed the sheet aside, allowing the breeze to ripple across his bare flesh. His skin tingled. His blood simmered. His loins ached. He felt like a stallion with the scent of a mare in his nostrils, a stallion trapped behind bars. And the cause of his misery lay sleeping just a few yards away. He turned to his side, putting his back to the cool moonlight.

He could have her. And in the end it wouldn't be rape. He knew women, knew how to touch them, knew how to coax moans of pleasure from their lovely lips. At one time he had considered it a fine art, something like riding or shooting or playing with the exchange.

But with Sabrina it had been different. For the first time it had been real. At least he had believed it was—a fool's illusion of love, a beggar's dream come true. Yet he hadn't been Sabrina's dream, just a means to an end. A bag of gold. That's all he had been to the beautiful witch. His hands clenched into fists.

For as long as he could remember he had had this horrible drive inside him, this need to be the best at whatever he did. Perhaps because he had always felt as though he could never quite measure up, he could never be as good as Jon. And he never had been.

Even when he graduated at the top of his class at Harvard, it still hadn't been good enough. Perhaps that's why he had resented his brother. Love and resentment and guilt at those feelings when Jon had died. Years later, he could finally see with some sense of distance the rivalry his father had established for his sons. Perhaps one day he would find peace in that realization.

His body dragged his mind back to Sabrina. Why didn't he take her? Why didn't he use her to quench the fire flaming in his blood? Because he might be wrong, he thought, slamming his fist against the mattress. Because she might just be an innocent woman whose only crime was looking like a deceiving little witch. In which case, he would be nothing less than a monster.

Sabrina had been the first virgin he had ever made love with, and he had taken her thinking they would be married. His conscience was clear in that regard. She had used her innocence to entrap him; he had just evaded the trap.

Yet Lady Julia Wyndham was another story. He wasn't anxious to add her complete ruin to his conscience. But if she pushed him too far . . .

He closed his eyes and willed sleep, praying his dreams would not be haunted by that beautiful dark-eyed redhead.

Sabrina rested her hands on the windowsill. Fireflies flickered in the trees across the drive, like lost fairies searching for home. Riding high in the sky, the moon cast silvery light across her face, shimmering on the single tear glistening on her cheek. She swiped at the droplet. Somehow she had to get away. Each day with Tremayne she stood the chance of revealing herself, and when she did . . . she shivered in the warm breeze.

But how could she escape?

Her breath caught in her throat, her gaze resting on the ledge just outside her window. If she could follow that ledge to another room, she might be able to slip out of the house before anyone knew she was gone. She stuck her head out the window and glanced in both directions.

The windows to her left were closed, but to her right, in the room at the corner of the house, they were open, the breeze billowing against dark drapes. No more than twenty-five feet separated her from a chance at freedom. She glanced down to the gravel thirty feet below. One slip and . . . she wouldn't think about that.

Without another thought she sat on the windowsill and swung her legs out the window. Slowly, carefully, she stood on the narrow stone ledge, balancing her weight on her healthy foot.

Rough stone bit into her naked soles as she edged along the ledge, limping, keeping her hands pressed to the stone wall, her gaze fixed on the next window. A gust of wind flung her unbound hair across her face, twisted her gown around her legs, threatening to pluck her from her perch. She froze, pressing her back against the wall, curling her fingers against the rough blocks, swallowing a shameful whimper.

There was no turning back.

With a deep breath she began again.

When at last her fingers felt the smooth wooden window casement she nearly screamed in relief. Just a few more steps. Gripping the side of the window, she slipped her foot inside the room. Balancing on the windowsill, she lowered herself, extending her injured ankle, sitting back against the sill. With a sigh she swung her legs around and stood, her feet sinking into a thick woolen carpet.

Her shadow cut a path in the wedge of silver flowing through the window behind her. Light shone from beneath a door on the far side of the room, guiding her to freedom. She started for that door, blind to everything else around her.

"What the devil!"

Sabrina froze at Ian's deep bellow. Glancing over her shoulder, she saw him rise from the shadows, moonlight from the second set of windows limning him, flowing across the curve of his shoulder, slipping light into his thick mane; a lion disturbed in his lair.

She turned, rushing toward the door, pain shooting up her ankle. Her hand touched oak. She turned the brass door handle and dragged open the door. In the next instant it slammed shut, a rush of air hitting her face.

"Devil!" she shouted, turning to face her captor, slamming her fist into his bare shoulder.

He grabbed her arms in strong hands. "Just how the hell did you get in here?"

"Let go of me!" she shouted, twisting in his grasp.

"Dammit, Sabrina! You crawled across the ledge, didn't you?"

"You have no right! Let me go!"

He turned, swinging her up over his shoulder. "Of all the reckless, foolish . . ." His words ended in a frustrated growl. "You could have been killed!"

"Let go of me!" Before the last word left her lips she was plummeting toward his bed. Warm linen tinged with his scent plowed into her face. She came up, pushing her hair out of her face, swearing under her breath.

"Just what the devil am I going to do with you!"

Not willing to give up, she scrambled off the other side of the bed. He had her before she was halfway across the room, wrapping one powerful arm around her waist, lifting her from the floor, dragging her back toward the bed.

"Let . . . me . . . go," she shouted, biting out the words, clawing at the arm around her waist, kicking, hitting only air.

He tossed her to the bed and pounced before she could move, pinning her to the mattress with his big body. "Blackguard!" she screamed, pounding her fists against his broad shoulders.

Mumbling an oath under his breath, he captured her slender wrists in his big hands, thrusting them high above her head. "Enough!"

Pinned beneath him, she became aware of each brush of their bodies, her struggles only bringing her in closer contact with his hardened muscles. She fell still, trying not to breathe, for each breath brushed her thinly clad breasts against his naked chest.

Moonlight splashed across his shoulders and one side of his face, transforming his skin to smooth, white marble. Yet he burned her like a shimmering white flame. She didn't need to see him to know he was naked. Twisted around her hips, her nightgown gave her little protection from the heat of his skin, from the rasp of dark curls against her thighs.

"What do I have to do, lock you in the cellar to keep you from harm?"

"I'll find a way to escape you, Tremayne!" She felt a change in his muscles, a shifting of warm flesh against her breasts, the brush of the gold ring he wore around his neck, as he transferred both of her wrists to one of his hands. "Let go of me, you big brute."

He pressed his lips to her neck, his warm breath stirring a strand of her hair, his lips curving into a smile against her skin. "Do you remember what I said I would do the next time you tried to escape?"

Sabrina swallowed hard, forcing down the fear crawling up her throat. "You don't frighten me, Tremayne," she said, trying to break free of his hold. It was like trying to break free of iron bands.

"I warned you," he whispered, before nipping at her jaw. "How far should I go this time, my lady? How much of the pirate do you chance to meet?"

"You can go straight to blazes!"

He chuckled low in his throat, a deep, sultry laugh that rippled along her spine. "Is this what you had in mind, witch?" he asked, moving his hips, pressing against her, allowing her to feel the beast rise inside him, growing long and thick and hot against her thigh.

"I had only one thing in mind," she said, feeling her flesh awaken to his touch. "Escaping you."

He pressed his lips to her neck, breathing in her scent, exhaling, his breath hot and moist against her skin. He slid his hand along her side, his palm cresting the mound of her breast, rubbing the sensitive tip before sliding lower. Sensation chased sensation deep within her flesh. Her body throbbed beneath his touch, her breath growing quick and ragged.

"Yet you came right to me. Is it fate?" he asked, his fingers curving around the top of her thigh.

"Rotten bad luck!"

He laughed, brushing his cheek against her shoulder. "Not from where I am."

He lowered his head, nuzzling her breasts through the thin cotton, taking one taut bud between his lips. Sparks collided in all directions as he rolled her nipple between his teeth, shimmering across her skin, gathering low in her belly, forming a pool of liquid fire.

"Let go of me!" she screamed, bucking beneath him.

He raised his head, thick muscles twisting against her breasts, as he surged higher, sliding his body against hers, branding her with fire, until his lips hovered just above hers. "Have you ever thought of the time we made love?" he asked, his voice low and husky.

That one night had haunted her dreams, had slipped into her waking thoughts when she least expected. "I have never made love with you, Tremayne. You or any other man!"

His hand tightened on her wrists. "Still playing the virgin countess?"

"If you weren't so blinded by your obsession, you would see it for the truth."

"Shall we find out who is wrong, my lady?" he asked, shoving his knee between her thighs.

"No!" she whispered as he settled between her thighs, his skin searing her flesh. He pressed against her, an iron spike wrapped in hot velvet. Warm honey flowed between her thighs, welcoming him, damning her. "Don't!"

She closed her eyes to the dark male beauty of his face, hiding her own desire, her other senses coming into sharp focus. His heady male scent, musk and spices, plunged past her nostrils, filling her lungs, seeping into her blood. She felt his muscles tighten where he touched her breasts, her belly, the inside of her thighs, warm skin burning her flesh, crisp curls sweetly abrading smooth skin.

Poised at her entrance he paused, pulsing with promised pleasure. Clenching her teeth, she fought the tremendous urge to arch against him, to capture all his power and strength.

"Your body betrays you," he said, sliding his heated length against her moist folds.

She bit her lower lip, trying to corral the moan sliding across her tongue.

"You're hungry, Sabrina. Has it been so long since a man has ridden these lovely thighs?"

"How dare you! How dare you treat me like some common whore."

"There's nothing common about you." He lifted away from her, coming to his feet beside the bed. "Do you still think I will have to rape you? If I wanted you, Sabrina, you would be mine."

His taunt was a saber slicing her pride. Moonlight flowed over him, carving every strong line and curve of his powerful body, shaping an erotic statue worthy of a master. "If you don't want me, Tremayne, why are you as hard as a railroad spike?" She covered her lips, shocked at her own outburst.

He laughed, the sound deep and husky. "Touché, my lady. It would seem my body hasn't any sense where one beautiful redhaired witch is concerned." He took her arm and dragged her from the bed.

Her breath escaped in a rush as he pulled her against the solid wall of his chest, his arousal pressing intimately against her belly. Had she gone a step too far? Had she managed to snatch defeat from unexpected victory?

"Next time I won't try to control the beast, Sabrina." He lowered his lips to hers, taking her mouth in a torrid kiss, stealing her will. "Next time I will take you. And I don't give a damn what you call yourself when I do."

Moonlight streamed through the open windows of Ian's bedroom, a silvery spotlight catching a man and a woman entwined in an embrace. From the shadows of the copse across the drive a figure dressed in black watched. So, Ian Tremayne had kidnapped the Lady Julia Wyndham. Interesting information. Useful information. Still, there was no profit in blackmailing a dead man. And soon Ian Tremayne would be dead.

Chapter Sixteen

Sabrina shoved a damp lock of hair back from her face before reaching for the porcelain pitcher on the washstand. Water tumbled from the pitcher, sloshing in the cream-colored basin, drowning the red tulips painted along the sides. At least it was passably cool. Unlike anything else in this oven.

Cupping her hands in the water, she splashed her face, letting water run down her neck, the cool rivulets streaming between her breasts, across her belly and down her thighs. If she wasn't afraid that the green-eyed rogue would barge in at any given moment she would tear off her nightgown.

She turned at a soft knock on the door. At Hannah's cheerful good morning Sabrina invited the woman into her prison cell.

"Oh, my, but it's warm in here," Hannah said as she entered Sabrina's bedroom, clothes piled across her arm, a pair of brown boots dangling from her hand. She glanced at the closed windows, then turned to look at her as though Sabrina had lost her mind. "It's a lovely morning. Why don't we just open the windows."

"Be my guest," Sabrina said, lifting her arm toward the windows.

Hannah gave her a curious glance as she laid fresh underclothes and a riding habit of buff- and tan-colored poplin on the bed. "Master Ian said you would be riding this morning," she said, setting the boots on the floor.

"Oh, he did," Sabrina said, crossing her arms at her waist, watching Hannah walk to the windows. Mr. Tremayne was far too sure of himself.

Sunlight penetrated the polished panes, slicing a wide golden path across the red and white roses blooming in the carpet. Hannah stepped into the sunshine and pushed against the windowframe. The window remained closed, as Sabrina knew it would. "They're nailed shut," she said when Hannah strained once more to force the window open.

Hannah pivoted, facing Sabrina with wide eyes. "Now why the devil are they nailed shut?"

"You can ask your master when you tell him I have no intention of riding with him today or any day."

Hannah frowned. "I suppose that means you'll be spending the day in here with a book."

Sabrina's chin lifted, her stomach growing tight at the thought of all day in this airless sweatbox. "I prefer my own company to his."

"Are you sure you . . ."

"Tell him he can take a running leap off the nearest cliff."

Hannah nodded, her lips twitching as though she was having a difficult time keeping the smile from her lips. "I'll tell him."

After Hannah left Sabrina lifted the bodice of the riding habit. Like the gown the night before, the scent of cedar lingered on the smooth cloth. Creamy braid circled each pearl button on the buff-colored bodice and fanned out from the center to form long diamonds.

Why had women's clothes changed so little in twenty years? she wondered, laying the bodice beside the tan-colored skirt. Her own riding habits gave her no more freedom than this antique. Unlike the days when she would ride in Brendan's breeches.

A smile curved her lips as she remembered days riding the lush green hills near her home. No one could catch her when she was atop Aidan's strong back. Where was he now? Often she wondered if her beloved horse had survived the war. She prayed he had found a comfortable home, a place where he would be loved and appreciated, even if it was with a Yankee.

"So, you've decided to hide in your room."

Sabrina's breath caught at the sound of Ian's voice. The scoundrel could move like a cat, without making a sound, sneaking up on her as though she were a mouse he was about to have for dinner. She spun on her heel, facing him, his tall, broad-shouldered form nearly filling the doorway.

He didn't believe in neck cloths, she thought, her gaze riveted on the dark vee exposed by his open white shirt. Or coats. And those riding breeches were just a shade above being indecent, she decided, her gaze flowing down his legs to the shiny dark brown boots clinging to his muscular calves.

He shifted, cocking one knee and resting his hip against the doorframe, the muscles in his thighs rippling beneath buttery-soft buff-colored leather. She became aware of the pulse throbbing in her neck, her blood growing thick and hot in her veins.

"Well, Countess?"

His sarcasm dragged her gaze to his face. He was smiling in a way that told her he knew exactly what effect he had on her. Well, he could go straight to blazes! "Do you ever knock, Tremayne?" she asked, retreating behind a stone wall of anger.

"Only when I'm sure I'll get an invitation."

He slid his gaze over her, from the tumble of hair cascading over one shoulder to her toes, repaying the look she had just given him. She stood under that long, lazy perusal with her chin lifted, her hands clenched at her sides, feeling like a slave on the block, determined not to cower.

She didn't have to look to know the damp cotton of her night-gown was nearly transparent, clinging to her breasts, her hips, her thighs. He expected her to scream and cover herself like a fright-ened maiden. She refused to give him the satisfaction, refused to let him know he could set her blood on fire with that heat-ed look.

"Have you had your fill, Mr. Tremayne? Or would you prefer I strip?"

He met her gaze, his eyes filled with shadow and light, like the forest at sunrise. "Now I really would take that as an invi-tation."

Sabrina fought the nagging trembling in her legs. "From what I've seen you don't need invitations."

One corner of his lips lifted. "If I didn't know better, I would think you were trying to tempt me into bedding you."

Was she? She turned away from him, hiding the doubt in her eyes. What was he doing to her? "I thought you were going rid-ing, Tremayne."

"I thought you might enjoy a ride, my lady."

Sabrina stared out the window. Across the drive elm and oak and hickory rose, lush green leaves swaying in a welcoming breeze. Beyond, the river glittered in the sunlight. "I would love a ride, but unfortunately it includes your company."

Ian's deep chuckle rumbled in the room. "Are you that fright-ened of me?"

"I am not frightened of you," she shouted, glancing over her shoulder at the smiling devil.

"I see. Then it must be someone else you fear. Perhaps yourself."

"Don't be ridiculous," Sabrina said, turning back to the window. Yet it was all too true. This man made her forget everything but the beating of her own heart, the rush of fire in her veins whenever he was near.

"Perhaps you should try being less stubborn. I have a long-legged mare saddled and waiting. Food packed. And . . ." He paused a moment before he continued. "And I would like very much to enjoy the pleasure of your company."

She turned to face him, wondering if his eyes would deny the sincerity in his voice; they didn't. "All you have to do is toss me over your shoulder and drag me to the horse."

He smiled, a wide, gentle smile, filled with honest warmth. The effect was nothing less than devastating; it hit her like a powerful right to her jaw. Why did the scoundrel have to have that smile as a weapon? It seemed to reach out and gather her in a net, to tangle her up in emotion until she had trouble thinking.

"I prefer to have you accept my invitation." He glanced around the room. "Still, if you prefer to stay here, I understand."

He turned, his hand on the brass door handle. He was going without her, leaving her in this hellish hot room where she could suffocate, while he enjoyed a ride in the fresh air. "I have no intention of spending the entire day in this steamy prison cell, Tremayne. Even your company is preferable to this."

He glanced over his shoulder, giving her his smile. "I'm glad to hear it, my lady."

Ian left, sending Hannah to help her dress. When Sabrina was ready Tremayne carried her from her room to the front drive, where a bay mare stood waiting for her at the hitching post. Stormy Lady was beautiful: tall, full-chested, holding her shapely head with an arrogance Sabrina would expect in one of Tremayne's horses. The golden stallion standing beside the mare tossed his head as they approached, his bridle jangling, his golden mane lifting on the breeze, the silk of his tail brushing the gravel paving the drive.

"He's beautiful," Sabrina said, wishing she could stroke his golden mane. As if Ian read her thoughts, he carried her to the stallion's side.

"Say hello to the lady, Cisco," Ian said.

The stallion bent one knee and lowered his head in a graceful bow, then tossed his head with playful arrogance.

"It is a pleasure to meet you, Cisco," Sabrina said, stroking the stallion's neck, smiling as he nickered in response.

Before the war she had spent nearly every morning riding her chestnut stallion, Aidan. She had been with him when he was born, had raised him from a colt. Every morning he would come running at her whistle, nuzzling her hand for the sugar she always carried in her pocket. "He reminds me of a chestnut I once had."

"What happened to him?"

Aidan had been taken by Union soldiers, along with all the other horses on Rosebriar. A dull pain throbbed in her heart when she remembered watching the confused stallion being led away from his home by a man in a blue uniform, a man just as cold and heartless as Ian Tremayne.

Aidan had struggled against the Yankee's hand, turning his head toward Sabrina, dark eyes silently questioning. And she had stood there, helpless. She still missed him, like a friend lost forever, a friend who had depended on her, a friend she prayed was safe and sound.

Sabrina kept her eyes focused on Cisco's silky mane. "He was stolen four years ago."

"I'm sorry."

She glanced up at Ian, surprised by his gentle tone. Looking straight into his eyes, she saw nothing, his emotions veiled, like a card shark holding four aces. "So was I. He was a good friend."

"Did you ever try to locate him?" Ian asked, lifting Sabrina to the mare's back. He turned and mounted Cisco in one smooth movement, the leather creaking under his weight. "The army kept records of property taken from civilians."

Sabrina gripped the reins. "Still living with your obsession?"

He grinned. Without a word he led the way across the drive and into the forest where she had plunged so recklessly on her first night at Dunkeld. Morning sunlight pierced the leaves overhead, transforming the demons of the night into gnarled tree trunks. Yet her demon rode beside her.

Emerging from the forest, Ian paused on the bluffs, raising a hand to shield his eyes from the sun, staring across the river to the stone columns of the Palisades. Primitive, forbidding, the dark gray stone permitted little to touch it, a few brave trees finding homes among the scattered rocks near the base. There was comfort in those savage stones, comfort in something solid, unshakable. A golden eagle soared from the gray stone columns, gliding on the wind, spiraling toward the water, searching for prey.

"The Palisades is just one more reminder of how insignificant we all are compared to the power of nature," he said, glancing at the woman beside him. A lock of hair had escaped the thick roll at her nape. The dark red tendril drifted with the breeze, capturing the sunlight, brushing her neck, her shoulder, the curve of her breast. He curled his fingers against his palm.

"Still, you wage a war against nature."

He dragged his gaze from that shimmering tendril of hair. "I'm not sure what you mean."

She glanced down to the shiny ribbons of steel hugging the shore. "You managed to lay tracks even here."

"Not me. I would have laid them inland, left the river unspoiled." This place was a part of him, a part of his youth, his innocence, a part of him he had left behind long ago. And this woman . . . she was also a part of him, in a way he wasn't sure he wanted to understand. "At least the cliffs keep the noise from the house."

"Why, Mr. Tremayne, I thought you were the one who wanted to lay track from New York to California."

He glanced at her, startled by her careless admission. "When did I say that, Countess?"

She glanced away, her back growing stiff, her hand growing taut against her reins. Was she remembering the night they had talked about his dreams? he wondered. He remembered. But then, he remembered everything about those three days he had spent with her on board the *Belle*. Too well.

"Really, Mr. Tremayne, you ask me to remember when you have uttered every word? How very arrogant of you."

He stared at her profile, admiring the proud tilt of her head, the defiant pout of her lower lip. A part of him wanted to believe in Lady Julia Wyndham. A part of him wanted a second chance with this woman. "I suppose it is." It was arrogant, not to mention profoundly stupid, to entertain thoughts of a future with this woman. But he couldn't seem to help himself.

They rode side by side along the bluffs, sending pebbles cascading over the edge, scaring a white-tailed rabbit away from his meal of clover near the edge of the path. Ian smiled as he watched the rabbit scamper through swaying Queen Anne's lace. It had been a long time since he had ridden these paths. Too long.

He needed this. He needed to fill his lungs with air fragrant with meadow grass and wild flowers. He needed to see that some things were exactly as they had been a lifetime ago. He needed to see Sabrina riding beside him. And he needed more.

He stared across the meadow that stretched between the river and the forest. The long meadow grass swayed in the breeze, the dark green blades entwining with delicate wild flowers of yellow and white. Ian knew there was a glade nestled just beyond the forest, a secluded paradise with a swimming pond his grandfather had made by damming the stream. He remembered many days spent lying in the long sweet grass, while the breeze licked the water from his skin.

He glanced at the woman beside him, imagining her lying naked on a bed of meadow grass and wild flowers, sunlight glistening against her damp skin. He imagined her dark red hair splashed across the emerald green grass, her arms spread wide, reaching for him, her legs wrapped around his waist, drawing him to the luscious heat of her body.

He felt his muscles tighten. Heat flared in his blood, flowed and concentrated low in his belly, where it pulsed and throbbed with each surge of his heart. He drew the fragrant air deep into his lungs. He had to fight this all-consuming hunger for her; it would lead only to destruction.

Sabrina stared at the copse of trees rising just beyond the meadow. The trees grew thick there, thick enough to hide someone. It would be hard to find someone in those trees.

"This is where we held the tournament," Ian said, smiling at her.

She tightened her grip on the reins, half listening as he reminisced about his three days in King Arthur's court. Was the mare fleet enough to outrun Ian's stallion? she wondered. This might be the only chance she would have to run. She was a good rider. And the stallion would have to carry Ian's weight. She glanced at the copse across the meadow. Once in there she might lose him. And if he caught her . . . it was worth a chance.

She pressed her heel into the mare's side, urging the horse into a full gallop. The horse surged beneath her, stretching her long legs. Sabrina leaned low, the mare's mane whipping against her face, excitement streaming through her veins.

She would show the man he couldn't . . . a sharp whistle ripped through the air. The mare came to an abrupt halt. Sabrina rocked in the saddle, grabbing the pommel to keep from spilling over the mare's neck, the sound of hoofbeats pounding with the blood in her ears. Before she could regain her balance completely a strong arm whipped around her waist.

Ian plucked her from the saddle as though she weighed no more than a child. The air left her lungs in a whoosh as she landed across the hard rails of his thighs, her cheek grazing the buckskin clinging to his calf.

"Trying to steal my horse?" he asked, resting the palm of his hand flush against her backside.

"Steal your . . . why, you . . . you . . . jackass!" she shouted, kicking her feet, pushing on his thighs, struggling to right herself. Cisco sidestepped under her reckless motions, snorting, tossing his head, his golden mane flying across Sabrina's shoulder.

"Easy," Ian said, grabbing her skirt in his hand, shifting his thighs beneath her, hard muscles sliding against her breasts, as he gave silent signals to the horse. The stallion halted under his master's command. "You'll have Cisco tossing us both."

"Let go of me!" she shouted, kicking her legs.

A warm breeze drifted across her calves, her thighs, her hips as he inched her skirt upward, bunching the yards of material at her waist, ignoring her twists and turns to free herself. "What are you doing?" she shouted, struggling to turn on his lap.

"What type of punishment should I deal out to a horse thief?" he asked, leaning his forearm across her back, pinning her against his lap.

Sunlight pulsed against her thinly clad buttock. Yet it was no more than a whisper of warmth compared to the scalding heat of his body pulsing against her breasts, her side, her belly. She sensed his hand poised above her, ready to strike. She tensed, clutching the top of his boot, kicking her feet, dreading the blow of his palm across her buttock. Yet she was completely unprepared for what he did.

He slid his open palm over the curve of her upturned bottom, stroking her through the thin cotton of her drawers, his heat searing her skin. That provocative touch rippled through her, tingling her skin, pulsing in her breasts where they pressed against his hard thighs. "You have no right!" she shouted, wiggling beneath his touch.

"I've had about all the nonsense I'm going to take, Sabrina," he said, his hand growing tense against one pouting cheek.

"You've had all the nonsense you're going to take!" she shouted. "Of all the . . ." Her words ended in a shriek as he slipped one arm beneath her, grabbed her hips, and turned her in his arms, draping both of her legs over one hard thigh.

Sabrina pushed her brown felt hat back from where it had slid across her eyes and glared up at him. "So you've had enough, have you!" she shouted, slamming both fists against his shoulders. "I'm the one being treated like a common street woman," she said, hitting him once more. "And the name is Julia, you arrogant, no-good . . ."

"Enough."

Although the word was spoken in a smooth voice that barely rose above a whisper, his eyes shouted at her. The angry glare in his emerald eyes made her forget what she had been about to say. The horse sidestepped, the movement rocking her hip against the saddle of Ian's loins; his arms tightened around her.

"Swear to me you'll make no more attempts to escape me," he said, leaning over her, his shadow falling across her face. "Or we'll end this farce here and now, my way." He smiled, a devilish curve of his lips. "I've always been partial to a tumble in the grass."

Sabrina swallowed back the curse rising in her throat; the look in his eyes told her one wrong word would send him plummeting past the edge. "All right. I give you my word. I will not try to escape you again." One corner of his lips curved upward, the arrogant smile forcing her to continue. "Today," she added, brazenly tempting fate.

His eyes narrowed; one corner of his lips twitched. She held her breath, waiting for his explosion of anger. What came instead was even more powerful. He tossed back his head and laughed, filling the meadow with deep, vibrant music, his chest vibrating against her breast.

"Oh, my lady," he said, resting his brow against hers. "What am I going to do with you?"

Sabrina stared at the dark hollow at the base of his neck. "I suppose setting me free is out of the question."

He smiled down at her. "I suppose," he said, brushing back a lock of hair from her cheek, his bare fingers a sensuous slide of warm skin.

With his eyes he traced the curve of her lips, his own lips parting, his breath warm and moist and sweet as the fragrant meadow against her cheek. Her mouth went dry.

The man was wild, untamed, a pirate misplaced in time. A pirate who took what he wanted. A pirate who would destroy her unless she found a way to escape her own horrible need. Closing her eyes, she turned her face away from him.

She felt the subtle shift of his thighs beneath her. Cisco moved beneath them, easing into position beside the mare. After lifting her to the mare's back Ian handed her the reins. "There, she's all yours again," he said, patting the mare's neck.

The mare nickered softly and bobbed her head, brushing his arm. Another female trapped by this man's masculine magic, Sabrina thought. "Until you decide to pull her under your spell again."

He glanced at her, sunlight streaming across his features, humor crinkling the corners of his eyes. "If only other females were so easily trained."

Sabrina's chin soared. "Is that what you want, Tremayne? A woman who will respond to your every whim? Broken of will? Spiritless? A docile little puppet at your command? Is that your ideal woman?"

He was quiet a moment, holding her angry glare, his own emotions and thoughts veiled. "Does it matter what I want?"

More than she wanted to admit. There was still an ache inside her, a raw, throbbing wound that only he could heal. But he would never heal her. "No, Tremayne," she said, turning her gaze to the trees a few yards away, hiding her emotions from him. "It doesn't matter to me what you want."

From the corner of her eye she saw him sitting beside her, watching her for what seemed a lifetime. Leather creaked as he shifted in the saddle. "We have a truce for the day at least. It's far too pretty a morning to waste on anger. Do you suppose we might try to enjoy the day?"

Sabrina drew a deep breath. Enjoying Ian Tremayne's company had never been a problem. No, far the opposite had always been true.

"Well?"

She lifted her eyes, meeting his warm gaze with cold defiance. "I gave you my word I wouldn't try to escape, Tremayne. I never said I was going to enjoy being with you."

"Pity. For I find I enjoy being with you. Perhaps more than I should."

What had he meant by that? He turned away, urging his mount toward the trees. The mare followed like an obedient puppy. No doubt the man was playing with her, as a cat plays with a mouse before devouring it, she decided, dismissing the warmth she had seen glowing in those beautiful green eyes.

The meadow dissolved into a thick copse of oak, chestnut, and maple. Sunlight pierced the canopy of leaves overhead, sprinkling light on the moss and ferns covering the rocky ground. A short distance into the copse Ian stopped, raising his hand. Sabrina pulled up beside him.

"Look," he whispered, pointing toward a narrow stream several yards away.

Water tumbled over rocks, the soft rushing sound rising on the air, mingling with the rustle of leaves in the breeze. At the edge of the stream stood a doe and her two fawns, long necks arched as they lapped the clear water. Sabrina held her breath, watching them.

A sound, a scent, a sense of danger, something alerted the doe. Her head snapped up, her ears springing straight up, her gaze turning to a point somewhere in the shadowy woods to the left of Ian. In a heartbeat they disappeared into the trees, mother leaping, leading her children to safety.

"We frightened them," Sabrina said, wishing they had stayed a few moments longer.

Ian glanced at her. "Something frightened her, but I don't think it was us. The breeze is in our faces. She wouldn't have caught our scent."

Sabrina glanced around the stand of trees, feeling a chilly breeze cross the base of her spine. They weren't alone; she felt certain of it. From the look on Ian's face she knew he sensed it, too, a presence hidden in the shadows.

"Are you getting hungry?"

"You're not going to eat here!" She had the sudden desire to be out of these woods, a desire to feel the sun on her face.

Ian shook his head. "There's a glade just up ahead. I haven't been there in years. But as I recall . . ."

Gunfire shattered the morning air.

Ian jerked in the saddle. He fell forward, grabbing his side, gasping for breath. Startled, Cisco reared, tossing his head, pawing at the air.

Sabrina stared in shock, the world tilting, slowing until each heartbeat seemed an eternity. Ian gripped the reins, fighting to quiet the horse, his soft groan of pain exploding in her ears like thunder. Cisco whinnied and turned, prancing in and out of a sunbeam. It was then that she saw the blood, bright scarlet spreading across Ian's side, staining white linen and pale buckskin.

My God! It was happening again. Gunfire. Bloodshed. Death. No, not again! Not Ian!

"Ian!" Sabrina shouted, riding to his side.

"Take care," Ian said, his voice a husky whisper. "Turn around. Ride out of here."

"But you're bleeding."

"Ride!" he shouted, his tone carrying the stern bark of command.

"Not until . . ."

The mare bolted as Ian slapped her rump. Sabrina grabbed the reins, ducking close to the horse's neck to keep from being knocked from the saddle by a low-hanging branch. Ian's horse plunged through the woods behind her. She kept glancing back, confirming that Ian was still in the saddle, assuring herself that he was alive, her heart pounding at the base of her throat. How badly was he hurt? Just how badly was he hurt?

When they cleared the woods she pulled up on the reins, turning to Ian. He swayed in the saddle, clutching his side, blood soaking his shirt, his breeches. She jumped from her saddle, her ankle collapsing beneath her, spilling her to the grass. Mumbling an oath, she dragged herself to her feet. Fighting her pain, she limped the few feet to his side.

Ian dismounted, clutching the pommel to steady himself. He turned as she touched his arm.

"Put your arm around my shoulders," Sabrina said, slipping her arm around his waist, her hand sliding against the warm sticky patch at his side.

"How's your ankle?" he asked, his voice a husky whisper.

"My . . . I'm fine," she said, staring up at him. "Just lean on me."

She could feel him trying to keep his weight from her shoulders, but with each step his strength ebbed. By the time they reached the shelter of a nearby oak he was leaning heavily upon her. He sank to the ground, bringing her with him.

Sabrina knelt beside him, her fingers trembling, stumbling as she worked the buttons running down his chest. Blood soaked the white linen, sticking his shirt to his skin. Breath froze in her throat when she peeled the shirt from his flesh, her eyes focused on the ragged hole in his side just above his waist. Blood flowed freely from the wound, sliding across his waist to soak into the ground beneath him. She searched for an exit wound and found none.

Ian glanced down at his side, frowning at the sight. "We need to stop the bleeding," he said, gathering the hem of his shirt in his hand. He pressed the linen against the wound and looked at her. "There's a tablecloth in . . . the saddlebag."

Sabrina rushed to the stallion as quickly as her injured ankle would permit. Her hand hesitated on the smooth leather saddle. If she mounted the horse, she could get away. And Ian would bleed to death. There was no decision to be made.

The horse tossed his head as she dragged the heavy saddlebags from his back. Ian lay with his back against the tree, one knee bent, one arm outstretched at his side, his hand resting palm up near a clump of buttercups. He was watching her with a wary look in his eyes, expecting her to mount, waiting for her to abandon him.

Anger and pain twisted like hot steel inside her. How dare he think she would leave him to die! "Who would have done this?" she asked, kneeling beside him.

He didn't seem to notice the anger coloring her voice. "I don't know. Poachers, probably."

"How did they mistake you for a deer?" She tossed back the flaps on the soft tan saddlebags. "Deer don't usually ride horses."

Ian shook his head. "Stray shot."

One saddlebag was packed with food, eating utensils, and a carving knife. In the other she found two pewter plates, a tightly rolled white linen tablecloth, and a bottle of cider. Using the knife, she sliced nicks into the tablecloth every few inches. Linen screamed as she tore the cloth into long strips.

"I suppose you realized Cisco would have stopped with a command from me, just like Stormy."

"You think that's the reason I didn't try to ride out of here? You think I would have left you here to die?" she asked, folding one strip into a thick pad.

He met her eyes. "I thought you wanted to see me dead."

She had seen far too many die, boys who deserved more than a shallow grave scratched out of some battlefield. "I wouldn't want to explain your death to St. Peter when I meet him," she said as she lifted his blood-soaked hand away from the wound.

Ian chuckled, his breath ending in a ragged gasp, his handsome features contorting with pain. "Remind me not to laugh."

Men died if they lost too much blood; she knew that truth too well. She pressed the pad to his wound, applying pressure, anger and fear making her less than gentle. Ian sucked in his breath. "I'm sorry," she said, keeping the pad taut against the wound. "But I have to get the bleeding under control."

"Who taught you how to do that?" he asked, his head lolling back against the dark gray tree trunk.

Sabrina stared at the pad pressed to his wound, blood rapidly staining the linen red. Careful, she told herself. Lady Julia hadn't been through a war. She sought a reason to cover her knowledge, snatching on the one he had given her while tending her ankle. "Our head groom taught me how to tend horses."

"It isn't the first time I've been treated by a horse doctor, but you are the prettiest one I've ever seen."

His blood was flowing like the Mississippi in spring. She folded another strip of cloth and pressed it to the blood-soaked linen, praying she could stem the flow.

"Lean on me," she instructed, taking hold of his shoulders.

Ian leaned forward, his head bobbing, his cheek coming to rest against her temple, his hand grazing her hip. She wrapped strip after strip around his lean waist, slipping her hands beneath the warm linen of his shirt, binding him tightly, her heart squeezing as her ministering dragged a ragged moan from his lips.

When she was finished he leaned back, resting his head against the tree. "Well done, my lady. You handled that as though you had done it before."

Sabrina turned away, hiding her thoughts. "I'll ride for help."

Ian took her arm as she tried to rise. "I don't think so."

"How far do you think you'll get with that wound? It must be three or four miles back to Dunkeld."

"I've been hurt worse than this and ridden farther."

"Mr. Tremayne, I give you my word, I will bring back help."

He shook his head. "Cisco will carry me just fine."

Sabrina sat back on her heels. "You don't trust me."

"No, I don't suppose I do."

Using the tree for support, he dragged himself to his feet, a moan crawling up his throat, escaping his rigid control. Sabrina sank her teeth into her lower lip. He dropped his forehead against the tree trunk, his Adam's apple bobbing, as though he were swallowing back the gorge Sabrina felt rising in her own throat.

His shirttails flapped in the breeze, a ragged flag of red and white. With his eyes closed, his face pulled into taut lines, he stood there with his brow pressed against the rough bark, taking control of his breathing until the ragged gasps were slow and rhythmic. Only then did he glance down at her.

Perspiration plastered black waves to his brow, the long ebony tresses curling around his neck. In his eyes she saw the determination of a wounded knight who refuses to leave the battlefield, or a pirate about to go down with his ship.

"Unlike you, I know the meaning of honor, Tremayne. Let me ride for help before you kill yourself."

"You don't know me very well, Countess," he said, offering her his hand.

She knew him for the scoundrel who had seduced her, who had stolen her heart, she thought, ignoring his outstretched hand, rising to her feet. That man had no honor.

He pushed away from the tree, drawing his shoulders straight. A single drop of perspiration slid down his neck and curved along his collarbone before disappearing into the tangle of black curls below. The white linen of the makeshift bandage was already blooming a dark scarlet. He would be lucky to make it thirty yards without collapsing, she thought. She curled her fingers into her palms to keep from touching him.

He staggered toward his horse. It would serve him right if the stubborn mule bled to death. It would serve him right if he fell flat on his face. He stumbled. She rushed to his side, catching his arm, steadying him before he fell.

"Thank you," he whispered, smiling down at her.

Would she ever learn? she wondered.

Chapter Seventeen

He would be all right, she assured herself, staring out the window at the white gazebo planted in the center of the rose garden. Ian Tremayne was too stubborn, too ornery, too vibrant to die. She shifted in the wing-backed chair, resting her cheek against the aqua velvet, settling her throbbing ankle more comfortably on the velvet-covered footstool.

The doctor had arrived more than an hour ago, chasing everyone from the room. Sabrina had gathered with Hannah, Mac, and Luther, Ian's head groom and her guard, in the sitting room adjoining Ian's bedroom. A warm breeze drifted across the garden, swirling perfume in the air, bathing her face with the heady scent of roses warmed by the sun. Another vigil, she thought, fighting the memories threatening to rip away her calm facade.

A groan of pain rumbled through Ian's bedroom door. Sabrina clenched her hands in her lap. What was happening in there? She would feel much better if she knew the doctor, better yet if she could be with Ian. If she were Ian's wife, nothing would keep her from his side. Nothing!

Byron nudged her arm with his cold nose, looking at her with sad eyes, as though he wanted to give her some comfort. Even the dogs seemed to know what was happening. Shakespeare was lying on the wooden planks in front of Ian's bedroom, his nose pressed to the crack beneath the door. And Guinevere paced back and forth in front of the door, limping, her ears pressed back against her sleek head.

"If I ever get my hands on the bastard who shot the major . . ." Luther's lips pulled into a thin line, nearly vanishing in his dark bushy beard. He raised his hands, his thick fingers curling into claws, reminding Sabrina of the bear she had met the other night.

"I'll kill the man with my bare hands."

Tremayne certainly had a way of inspiring loyalty in his servants, Sabrina thought. Or had that loyalty been inspired elsewhere? "Did you serve with him in the army?"

Luther nodded. "Me and Mac both. If it weren't for the major, we wouldn't be alive."

"Us and a lot of other men," Mac said, resting his forearms on his thighs, glaring at Sabrina. "You'll find no better than Ian Tremayne."

Sabrina stroked Byron's head and lifted her gaze to where Luther sat on the edge of an upholstered armchair, looking as though he wasn't sure if he wanted to sit or stand. "What happened?" she asked, her voice barely above a whisper. She wanted to know, and at the same time she was afraid of learning more about the man who lay bleeding in the next room. Afraid of feeling more for him than she did at this moment.

"We were trying to take Richmond, and old McClellan called for retreat," Luther said. "Well, our regiment never got word of it. That's the way of it sometimes. We went to sleep in the woods and woke up to rebel bugles."

Mac nodded. "Surrounded, we were."

"Well, the major, he doesn't scare easy. He told us to hitch up and get out before those rebels knew we were there. It took two days, two days of crossing enemy territory, before we made it back to camp." Luther curled his huge hands into fists. "And everything was a jumble there. Men separated from their commands, brigades, divisions all mixed up. That McClellan couldn't find his ass . . ." He caught himself, glancing over at Sabrina, his cheeks growing pink above his dark brown beard. "The general sometimes didn't command real well."

Sabrina couldn't help but smile at the big man, which made him blush all the more.

"It was a tangle," Mac said, shifting on the sofa. "And while the generals tried to sort through it all, the rebels set up artillery on a low ridge and began flinging shells at us. Just like ducks on a pond we were."

"Well, the major was furious. He mounted and started charging up that hill, all alone. Well, when we saw him, riding right into hell, the rest of us followed." A big grin split Luther's beard. "We sent those rebs running for Dixie."

"But not before a shell caught the major in the leg." Mac bowed his head, staring down at his clasped hands. "He nearly died."

Silence settled over the room like a black cloth, covering their heads, making each breath a fight for air. Sabrina pictured the ragged scar on Ian's thigh, imagined the pain he must have suffered. Was it any worse than the wound he had now? He would be all right, she assured herself. Dear God, he had to be all right.

"I'm not liking it one bit. There was those two men on the riverboat, that accident with the coach a few weeks ago, and now this." Mac shook his head. "Makes a man wonder if there's more than fate at work here."

"What accident with a coach?" Sabrina asked, glancing to where Mac sat on the sofa in front of the hearth.

"Someone nearly run him down. A coach with no lamp lit come out of the dark. The horses grazed the major's side, knocked him to the street, and the driver kept on going." Mac's brows met over his crooked nose as he looked at her. "Now, you wouldn't be knowing anything about that would you, miss?"

Sabrina shivered, remembering the chilling sensation she had felt just before the shooting. Someone had been in those woods, watching, waiting.

"Would you, miss?" Mac repeated, glaring at her.

The man hated her, and he didn't try to hide it, Sabrina thought. "I wish to see Mr. Tremayne behind bars, Mr. MacDoughal. Not in his grave."

"Leave the child alone, James MacDoughal," Hannah said, rising from the wing-backed chair across from Sabrina. "If not for her, Master Ian would be gone."

Mac nodded, mumbling under his breath. "Did you see anyone, miss?"

"No one." Sabrina glanced down at the dark stains marring her skirt. It had to be an accident. The alternative was far too frightening. "He said it was a poacher."

"Poacher?" Mac shook his head. "I'm thinking it's not likely."

Sabrina hugged her arms to her waist, shivering deep inside. She glanced up as Hannah placed a hand on her shoulder.

"Now, don't go letting MacDoughal get you all upset. If the master says it was a poacher, then it was a poacher." Hannah smiled, her blue eyes filled with gentle understanding. "I can't be believing anyone would want to kill a fine man like Master Ian."

Only Sabrina knew better. If her father had his way, Ian Tremayne wouldn't live past the sunset. And she had her doubts that Walter Strickland would mourn Ian's passing. How many other men wanted to see Ian dead? Who knew he was at Dunkeld?

"Come, child. I'll have a nice hot bath prepared and fresh clothes laid out."

"Not yet," Sabrina said, resisting Hannah's gentle tug on her arm. "I would like to hear what the doctor has to say."

Hannah's smile grew. "I see."

Perhaps too much, Sabrina thought. The door opened, hitting poor Shakespeare's nose. The dog scrambled to his feet and backed up, plump legs planted, blunt face lifted as he watched the doorway along with everyone else.

Dr. Brimley entered the room, his narrow shoulders hunched beneath his black coat, his face pinched and grim. He stared at Sabrina, thick white brows shading his dark eyes. She held her breath, waiting for the words she had heard too many times before. No one spoke. It was as if everyone dreaded what the answer to their unspoken question might be.

"Would you come in here a moment, young lady?" Brimley asked. "And you, Mrs. Waycott."

Sabrina rose and limped across the room, followed by the others. Brimley raised his hand, refusing passage to all but Sabrina and Hannah.

Sabrina paused on the threshold, the scent of blood heavy in the air, scraping memories from shallow graves in her mind. Clenching her fists at her sides, she forced her legs to move.

Sunlight flowed into the room through the open windows, tossing golden light across the man who lay on the big tester bed. His clothes lay in a bloodstained heap beside his tall boots on the floor near the chest beside the bed. A white sheet draped his naked hips.

Sabrina rested her hand against a thick post at the foot of the bed, drawing her gaze across Ian, feeling tight bands of fear twist around her heart. The towels that had been placed beneath him to protect the mattress were stained scarlet with his blood, as was his skin above the wide white bandage binding his waist.

He tossed his head restlessly against the white pillow, back and forth, his hand twisting into the sheet at his side, his lashes fluttering against his cheeks. Beneath the sheet his legs thrashed. What demon was he fighting in the darkness of his mind? Sabrina wondered.

A low moan slipped from his lips, lashing around Sabrina, drawing her to his side. Sitting on the bed beside him, resting one hand over his tightly clenched fist, she stroked his dark hair back from his brow. "You're going to be all right," she whispered, praying the words were true. Too many times in the past they had been a lie.

Ian drifted in and out of consciousness, swimming up through thick, throbbing pain, tumbling back into dark, rambling memories. He was on the field again. But where? Did it matter? In time they were all the same.

Which town? Which battle? Which piece of bloody ground would become his grave?

Faces swirled around him, friends and enemies. Blood hung sweetly in the air, mingling with the bitter taste of black powder on his tongue. Shouts, death screams of men, of horses, the rattle of gunfire, the roar of cannon, all rushing together into rolls of thunder crashing against his ears. Men going down all around him, spinning like tops, gasping for air, gulping their own blood.

So many dead. So many dying. They coiled around his feet, threatening to drag him down into their bloody ranks.

He lifted his face to heaven, the sunlight blackened by powder. When would it end? Dear God, when would it ever end?

Silence.

He stood alone in the light of dawn, his uniform bloody, some his own, some from the men he had killed. Mist rose across the once green meadow, curling around twisted heaps of dead men. All around him they lay, faces black with powder, red with blood, eyes open and staring at the rising sun.

Enemy and friend, each with the same blank stare, each sacrificed to a distant cause. How noble it had all seemed in another lifetime. How hard it was to remember those ideals when staring into those lifeless eyes.

He knelt, lifting one limp body into his arms. Jon stared up at him with cold blue eyes. As he cradled his brother in his arms, a figure emerged from the mist.

His father advanced toward him, scowling. "Why? Why didn't you take the ball, instead of my son?"

Ian stared down at Jon. It was his fault. All his fault. Pain knotted in his throat. A gentle voice whispered his name. A hand brushed his brow, soft and cool, tugging him from his nightmares.

Ian dragged open his eyes. Above him hovered the face of an angel, sunlight flowing across her dark red hair. She had come to claim him, to rip him from this earthly hell.

He tried to lift his hand, to touch her face, and felt darkness reach for him. "No!" He wouldn't be torn from her, not again.

Yet the dark void beckoned, pain swirling around him, dragging him under, pulling him away from his own red-haired angel.

"Ian, can you hear me?" Sabrina whispered, brushing her hand across his damp brow.

"He'll drift in and out through the day. Maybe the next," Dr. Brimley said, glancing over Sabrina's shoulder. "You know how to tend a wound, young lady. If you hadn't stopped the bleeding, the gentleman would be dead by now."

Sabrina stood, turning to face the doctor, clenching her hands at her sides. They were close to the same height, though with his stooped shoulders, Brimley seemed shorter. "Is he going to live?"

Brimley glanced down at his patient, his face carved into solemn lines. "It was a clean wound; nothing vital was damaged. Yet . . ." He drew a deep breath. "If his lungs stay clear, I think he has a reasonable chance."

A reasonable chance. The words plucked at her heart. She had heard them before. He couldn't die! Not Ian.

Ian's lashes lay in thick black crescents upon his cheeks, his skin tinged with a gray pallor, the full curve of his sensual lips parted. Sabrina watched the rise and fall of his chest, silently assuring herself that he did, indeed, live. The doctor gave Sabrina and Hannah orders for taking care of Ian before he left, with a promise to check on his patient later that night.

"He'll need to be bathed," Sabrina said, staring at the dark red stains smeared across Ian's broad chest, sunlight glittering on the gold ring nestled against crisp black curls. He lay starkly masculine against the white sheets; black hair, dark skin, hurt and bloody. Yet even now he radiated primitive male power.

"Ah, but I never could stand the sight of blood," Hannah said, lifting the basin of bloodstained water from the mahogany chest beside the bed. "I suppose I could ask MacDoughal, but the man has the touch of an ox. I wonder if you might not help me, milady. I would be ever so grateful."

Sabrina didn't think about the impropriety of the request. She didn't notice the speculative gleam shining in Hannah's eyes. She only saw Ian lying bloody and in need. "Yes, of course, I'll help."

Hannah disappeared, returning a few minutes later with warm water, a sponge, and fresh towels. After setting the basin on the chest near the bed Hannah left Sabrina alone with Ian.

Sabrina sat on the bed beside him and lifted his hand, her fingers curving protectively around his. Slowly, she drew the damp sponge over Ian's skin, bathing the blood from his arm, from each tapered finger.

Such beautiful hands, she thought, resting his bronzed hand against the white sheet at his side, his fingers curling against the linen. Hands capable of infinite gentleness. Hands that could set her skin on fire with a single stroke. Hands that could choke the life from her. Her enemy's hands.

The water in the basin grew red as she rinsed out the sponge. She lifted the sheet, exposing the curve of his hip, the length of his leg, folding the soft linen over his belly, preserving his modesty. As if the man had any modesty, she thought. She bathed the streaks of blood from his pale hip, the skin so much lighter than his chest, and smooth, like satin stretched over solid oak.

Sunlight drew a golden line across his skin from his waist down the length of his thigh. Memories flashed in her mind, wiping the moisture from her mouth, tossing her heart against her ribs. As if controlled by strings, her hand lifted. With her fingers she traced that warm band of sunlight, tracing his skin across his smooth hip, trailing into coarse dark curls on his thigh, recalling the feel of muscle rippling rhythmically beneath her touch.

Madness to remember.

Those memories needed to be buried, she thought, tossing the sheet. It settled in a ripple of white linen over his naked hip, shielding his flesh from her eyes. If only she could shield her heart from the memories.

After rinsing the sponge she lifted his grandmother's ring from its nest of dark curls, the gold a burning ember in her palm. After a moment she lowered the braided gold to the pillow by his shoulder, draping the chain across his neck, unable to drag her gaze from that simple gold band. Who would wear it? Who would he choose? What would she be like? She knew who it wouldn't be.

Black curls swirled beneath the sponge as she scrubbed away the bloodstains. Why should she care? Why should she feel this horrible jealousy at the thought of any other woman wearing that ring? She didn't, she decided, dragging the sponge down his side. A ragged moan slipped from his lips, lashing around her heart like a whip.

"I'm sorry," she whispered, resting her hand against his cheek.

She watched the steady throb of the pulse beating in his throat. Life was so precious, so fragile. Even Ian, as strong and seemingly indestructible as he was, could be defeated by a small piece of lead.

In his sleep he turned his head toward her hand, nuzzling her palm, his breath warm and moist against her wrist. Something stirred inside her, a raw, aching hunger that drew her closer to him. She turned his head with her hand, her lips lowering until her breath fell across his lips.

One kiss. That's all. Just one kiss before he awakened. But before she could taste those sensual lips she pulled back, sinking her teeth into her lower lip. What was she doing? The man was her enemy!

She turned away, dunking the sponge in the water, her fingers trembling. Somehow she had to purge this man from her blood. She had to forget him. But how? How could she forget the sound of his voice, the touch of his hand, the taste of his lips? How did you rip your heart from your chest and live?

At six that evening the doctor returned to examine his patient. There was little change. Dr. Brimley's guarded optimism about his patient only served to strain Sabrina's taut nerves.

She sat with Ian through the long hours of the night, watching him, waving aside Hannah's attempts to coax her to bed, fearing Ian would die if she took her eyes off him. Several hours into the new day, he roused long enough to take a few sips of beef tea before succumbing once more to the darkness. Close to midnight, sleep claimed Sabrina, dragging her into restless dreams filled with Ian, always Ian.

Near dawn, she awakened, lifting heavy lids to look at the man lying motionless upon the bed. Grayish light filtered through the open windows behind her, mingling with the golden light from the lamp on the wall beside the bed, illuminating the soft rise and fall of his chest. She released the breath she had been holding. They had made it through the night.

She rose, stretching to ease the muscles stiff from long hours of sitting in the armchair. Three heads popped up as she moved. Ian's three dogs had shared her vigil, Byron and Shakespeare flanking her chair, Guinevere keeping a safe distance from her, lying on the floor at the foot of the bed.

Sabrina looked at the little female and wondered if the dog would ever trust her. Even as the thought formed she dismissed it. She wouldn't be around long enough for Guinevere to trust her. She wouldn't be around long enough to touch anyone's life. She didn't have a future here.

Regrets settled around Sabrina, thick and dark, like a cloak, smothering her. She had to stop longing for something she couldn't have, something that had never been more than a little girl's fantasy.

A lock of hair lay across Ian's brow, the wayward strands beckoning Sabrina's touch. She sat beside him on the bed and slipped her fingers through the ebony silk, brushing it back from his brow. With a sigh he opened his eyes, blinking sleepily, staring up at her, catching her with her fingers entwined in his hair.

"You're here," he whispered, his lips curving into a smile.

She pulled her hand away from his hair, curling her fingers against her palm. "And where did you think I would be, Mr. Tremayne?"

His eyelids slid shut, as though they weighed a hundred pounds. "In my dreams."

His words whispered to the need throbbing deep inside her. Who haunted his dreams? Looking at her with those sleepy eyes, who had he seen? She felt the blood drain from her limbs as she rose from his bed. She had defined her life by this man. The only future she had ever envisioned for herself had been one lived by this man's side. A future that would never become real.

Sabrina turned, staring out the windows to the rose garden, the white gazebo glowing in the light of dawn. There had to be some way to discard these feelings, this horrible need, this crippling love that refused to remain buried beneath anger and pain. There had to be some way to become whole again.

It was morning, late morning. Ian could sense it without opening his eyes; he could feel the heat of the sun on his face, see the golden glow against his closed lids. As his body crawled from sleep to waking, he became aware of the hot throb of pain centered in his side. He had been shot, he remembered that. And he remembered Sabrina, her hands on his chest, on his face, her fingers trembling, soft, gentle as she tended him.

"Sabrina," he whispered, opening his eyes, expecting to see her face as he had for the past three mornings. He blinked, bringing into focus the face of the woman who stood next to his bed. It was a kind face, a smiling face, a face he had loved since child-hood, but it was the wrong face.

"Good morning, lad," Hannah said, leaning over him, press-ing her hand to his brow. "Ah, nice and cool. The fever is past."

"Where is she?" Ian asked, trying to sit up, the torn pieces of his flesh sparking pain along his side. Hannah propped another pillow behind his head and eased him back against the smooth white linen.

"That dear child has sat with you day and night since the shooting," Hannah said, lifting a bowl and spoon from the cabi-net beside the bed. Fresh roses, every color in the garden, stood in a porcelain vase on the cabinet; red and yellow and white and pink blossoms dripping their perfume into currents of warm air streaming through the windows. "And if you ask me, you're wrong about her."

"You didn't let her go, did you?" Ian asked, feeling the first twinge of panic. Hannah ignored his question. She sat beside him on the bed and draped a napkin across his chest like a baby's bib. Dear God, she hadn't let Sabrina escape. Had she? "You didn't believe that lying little . . ."

"Eat this," Hannah said, lifting a spoonful of toast soaked in warm milk to his lips.

Ian pulled back. "I'm not sick enough to eat that stuff."

"Not sick enough! We thought we were going to lose you. Now, eat your toast like a good lad."

"Hannah, where is . . ."

She shoved the spoon past his parted lips. Ian nearly gagged. He swallowed the slimy mess and opened his mouth to complain, only to have her shove another spoonful into his mouth.

"Now I'm going to tell you something, Ian Tremayne," Hannah said, balancing a spoonful of sloppy bread at his lips. "I don't care who that girl is—Lady Julia Wyndham, Sabrina O'Neill, the queen of Egypt, I don't care. She's a fine, decent young lady. And if you are thinking you can . . ."

"Hannah, I . . ." He clamped his mouth shut as she thrust for-ward with the spoon. It bumped against his lips, spilling soppy bread and milk down his chin.

She dipped the spoon in the bowl, quickly reloading. "I don't know what happened between the two of you," she said, holding the spoon like a pistol at his tightly clenched lips. "I don't care. You're in love with that girl, and what's more she's in love with you. And I'm telling you, you're the biggest fool who ever walked on two legs if you don't marry her."

Ian had little doubt he was the biggest fool on two legs, because he was beginning to believe in that redhead. He raised his hand in surrender. Hannah slowly lowered the spoon from his lips. "Just tell me where she is. Please tell me you didn't let her go back to town," he said, using the napkin to mop the mess from his chin.

Hannah stood and gestured toward the windows. "You can see her for yourself. She's in the rose garden, with Luther to guard her, as if that darling girl were a criminal."

Ian leaned back against the pillows and stared out the windows. Below, surrounded by roses, Sabrina stood in the morning sunlight. Her wide straw hat obscured her features as she bent to clip a rose from one of the bushes, and Ian wished she would lift her head. He wanted to see her face. It occurred to him that he wished he could awaken to see her face every morning and go to bed with her face as the last image he saw.

"The house is filled with roses," Hannah said. "She told me she thought it a crime to let them die without ever having the chance to share their beauty with us."

Sabrina turned, casting her figure into sharp profile against the dark green leaves of the bushes behind her as she laid a yellow rose in the wicker basket Luther held for her. Ian traced the contour of her breasts with his gaze, garnet- and white-striped silk hugging the curves he longed to caress. He ached with the need to hold her. It throbbed inside him, more painful than his open wound. "If the woman is Lady Julia Wyndham, I doubt I'll have any choice except to marry her."

"And if she isn't?"

Ian fell back against the pillows and stared into the dark folds of the canopy over his head. What should a man do with a lying witch when he has enough proof to send her to the stake? Burn her? "Let's just hope she is Julia."

Chapter Eighteen

The sun was playing hide and seek, tossing sunlight on the skating pond in Central Park one moment, ducking behind thick, frothy gray clouds the next. Tim dipped his oar into the water, disturbing the reflection of an elm tree, watching Lucy.

She sat across from him, a porcelain doll in pink organdy and ivory lace. A smile curved her lovely lips as she trailed her fingers in the cool water, her gaze following a pair of white swans gliding near their boat.

He had seen her every day for nearly two weeks, while Lady Julia recovered from her cold. The first few times Lucy had been no more than a substitute for the beautiful countess, but no longer. Now he dreaded the day Julia would return to society.

A single ray of sun pierced the clouds, pouring golden light over Lucy, turning her hair to dark honey. She lifted her face to the sun, smiling, enchanting him. In that moment he realized he wanted to see her standing amid the falling leaves of autumn, to hold her before a crackling fire in the dead of winter, to give her the first rose of spring. Yet what of Julia?

The sunbeam vanished, snatched by the clouds. "Looks like we may get some rain," Tim said, glancing up at the sky, realizing they would soon have to head back to her house. Would Julia be waiting?

"I've always loved the rain. Especially when it falls soft and cool on a warm summer day." Lucy looked into his eyes, her smile wrapping warmly around his heart.

Tim hesitated, his oar growing still in the water as he traced each feature of her face with his eyes. How could he let her go?

"When I was a little girl I would slip out of the house to walk without an umbrella in the summer rain. It used to drive my mother to distraction."

"You drive me to distraction," he said, the words out of his mouth before he realized what he was saying. He dropped the oar on the bottom of the boat and reached for her hand, the boat swaying with his movement. "The way the sunlight glows upon your face, the way it touches your hair, that sweet way you have of blushing whenever I give you a compliment."

Color spread upward from her lacy white collar, staining her cheeks a dusky rose, several shades darker than the pink organdy of her gown. She glanced away, staring into the clear water, unable to hold his steady gaze.

He squeezed her hand before releasing her. "I shouldn't have said that."

"Didn't you mean it?" she asked, lifting her gaze to his face.

"Yes, of course I meant it." He stared down into the water, seeing his own image; the image of a man who had obligations. He had given Lady Julia every indication of his intention to marry her, and now he found himself in love with another woman. "Lucy, why did it take me so long to see how very lovely you are?"

"Why do you sound as if it's too late?"

"Julia," he whispered, lifting tortured eyes to hers.

She was quiet a moment, holding him with her huge blue eyes, eyes filled with a great sorrow. "You love her very much."

"No," he said, moving forward, wanting to take her into his arms, the boat threatening to capsize at his movement.

Lucy grabbed the sides of the boat, leaning back in her seat, her eyes wide with fear. "Perhaps I should tell you I don't know how to swim."

Her soft confession brought a smile to his lips, a smile that quickly vanished as he recalled the mess they were in. "Lucy, I all but asked Lady Julia to marry me. What kind of a cad would I be if I turned around and asked you?"

"You want to marry me?"

"More than anything in the world."

"Oh, my darling," she cried, lunging forward, throwing her arms around his shoulders. The boat tipped. Water rushed over the side. A sharp scream ripped from her lips, colliding with his low shout as the boat turned, spilling them both into the pond in a tangle of pink organdy, ivory lawn, and gray linen.

* * *

A gust of wind, heavy with moisture, rushed through the open French doors of the study at Dunkeld. Sabrina glanced up from the chess board, staring out across the terrace, watching thick gray clouds gather over the river, feeling her stomach twist.

"We're in for a blow," Luther said, rising from his perch on the sofa near a pair of tall windows, the emerald velvet carrying a dent from his heavy weight. He turned to stare out the windows, each pane a diamond beveled between strips of lead, his big body casting a shadow across the chess board.

"Kindly move, Luther," Ormsby said, glancing up at him. "You're blocking the light."

Luther shifted, standing beside Sabrina's chair, staring down at the ebony and mother-of-pearl board. "She's got you."

Ormsby cocked one white brow, looking up at Luther's grinning face. "The game is hardly over." He moved his knight, keeping his fingers on the carved and painted rosewood, his gaze darting across the board to Sabrina's soldiers. With a small nod of approval for his own choice of tactics, he released the knight to do battle.

Sabrina moved her bishop. "Checkmate."

"Extraordinary." Ormsby leaned back in his chair, rubbing his chin, studying the board, his thick white brows pulled together above his brown eyes.

Luther's deep laughter rumbled in the room. "I bet she could give the major a good run for his money," he said, slapping Sabrina across the back, the blow rocking her forward.

She smiled up at the big man who had been her guard since her arrival at Dunkeld two weeks earlier. In that time she had grown to like the affable giant, even if he did resist every attempt she had made to escape. "I might even beat him."

Luther's smile split his dark beard. "I'd like to see you try."

"So would I," Ian said from the doorway.

Sabrina glanced at the tall man leaning against the doorframe. She hadn't seen him in five days, staying clear of his room, trying to shake free of the chains binding her to this man. Tending his wound had only sharpened her own terrible need to hold him in her arms. Yet staying away from him hadn't helped.

"You look surprised to see me." His lips curved into that familiar pirate's grin. "Didn't you think I would recover?"

She might have kept her distance, but not until the doctor had told her the scoundrel would recover. Through Hannah, she had followed his daily progress, but the rogue didn't have to know that. "You are far too mean-spirited to die young."

"I've got a few things to attend to," Ormsby said, rising to his feet. Luther followed him out of the room, mumbling something about a mare needing tending in the stables.

Byron and Shakespeare both left Sabrina's side to greet their master, Byron's fluffy tail wagging high, Shakespeare strutting on his stubby legs. "It looks as though you've made a couple of conquests," Ian said, walking toward her, his usual lithe movements strained, his left arm held close to his side.

"She still won't come near me," Sabrina said, glancing at Guinevere, who limped along a few steps behind Ian, staring at Sabrina.

"It takes time."

Sabrina shifted on her chair; they both knew she didn't have much time.

The white shirt and the dark gray trousers Ian wore hung looser than they should, marking the loss of weight he had suffered. Sabrina resisted the urge to go to him, to lend her arm in support. It was best if she didn't touch him. Perhaps then she could get a rein on her emotions. Perhaps then she could resist the horrible attraction this man held for her.

He sank into the armchair recently vacated by Ormsby. After studying the board a moment he spoke. "Neatly done."

"I've been told you could do better." Lightning flashed through the panes, tossing silvery diamonds of light across Ian's face and shoulders. A moment later thunder shattered the morning air. She shivered and snatched for her courage, fighting against the stark memories stirring inside her.

"Do storms frighten you?" he asked.

As a child she had loved the storms that would rip down the Mississippi, each flash of lightning a glorious light show in the sky. Only things had changed. Now the storms evoked memories, and the deep fears she had lived with every day for months. She lifted her chin as she met his gentle gaze. Dark, purplish crescents stained the skin beneath his eyes, reminding her of how close she had come to losing him. "Should you be out of bed?"

"You have a habit of avoiding my questions."

"Perhaps you ask too many."

He lifted the black queen from the board, allowing the topic to die. "Would you like to play?"

Sabrina glanced down at his hand, the dark-haired queen rolling back and forth between his long fingers, those fingers that had touched her more intimately than she had ever touched herself. She felt too vulnerable just now, her emotions far too close to the surface to allow her to fence with him. "I don't think so," she said, rising from her chair.

He grabbed her wrist as she passed his chair. "Running away from me again?"

Her fingers curled against her palm, his hand branding the smooth skin of her wrist. "I realize this is difficult for you to understand, but I do not want to share your company."

Without releasing her he came to his feet, rising to tower above her. Sabrina tilted her head to look up into his face, feeling the heat of his body reach out to her like a beckoning flame.

"I didn't get a chance to thank you for all your help."

She glanced down at the floor, the tenderness in his eyes far more disturbing than his anger had ever been. Was he beginning to believe in Lady Julia? It struck her then how difficult it might be to see him fall in love with that Englishwoman. Her plans for revenge had been flawed from the beginning. There had never been any chance of winning this war. The only hope she had was in leaving the battlefield in one piece.

"You just might have saved my life."

"We all make mistakes."

He chuckled, the rich sound vibrating deep in his throat. "You wound me."

"No." She lifted her eyes, meeting his gaze. "But someone did. And according to Mr. MacDoughal this wasn't the first time."

He shook his head. "Mr. MacDoughal worries too much."

"Who knew you were coming here?"

"No one. At least no one who would want to kill me."

"Someone could have followed you. Someone who hated you enough to murder you."

"You say that as though you know a few of my enemies," he said, brushing his fingers over the curve of her cheek. "Besides yourself, that is."

She lowered her eyes, shielding her feelings, staring at the vee of black curls exposed by his partially open shirt. For a moment she could think of nothing but the feel of those curls against her lips, the taste of his skin upon her tongue, the scent of him in her nostrils. Biting her lower lip, she glanced away from that intriguing triangle of dark curls and golden skin, staring at a swirl of gold in the emerald wool beneath her feet.

"Do you know someone who would like to see me dead?"

Two men came to mind. One, thankfully, was on a riverboat far away from here. Thunder rumbled across the heavens. "I overheard Walter Strickland arguing with his wife. It seems he isn't happy you and Felicity are lovers."

"It seems he is under the wrong impression."

"I suppose he just took this notion for no good reason," she said, staring up at him.

"No." Ian lifted his head, staring past her to the open French doors behind her, the tendons in his neck growing rigid. "Felicity has managed to give him the idea."

"Do you expect me to believe that you and Felicity aren't lovers?" she asked, appalled at how much she sounded like a jealous wife, unable to do anything about it.

One corner of his lips curved upward, the tension draining from his expression. With his eyes he pierced her facade, seeing far too much. Yet Sabrina couldn't look away, couldn't hide anything from him at that moment.

"If I didn't know better, I would say you sound like a jealous . . ." He paused at a soft knock on the door, a look of irritation crossing his features. "Come."

Ormsby opened the door, his gaze shifting from Sabrina to Ian, a strange light of concern shining in his dark eyes, alerting Sabrina's survival instincts. "A Mr. Bainbridge is here to see you, sir. He said you were expecting him."

Ian's hand tightened on her wrist a moment before releasing her. "Show him in."

"Who is he?" Sabrina asked, stepping back from Ian, knowing the answer before he spoke it. Behind her a gust of wind swept through the open French doors, billowing emerald velvet drapes, sending shivers across her skin. As if Guinevere sensed the emotion flaring between the two humans, she crept away, taking refuge on her pillow by the hearth.

Ian held her with his eyes, his emotions carefully veiled, his voice controlled and level as he spoke. "The man with the answers."

The door opened. Through the diamond-paned windows Sabrina saw lightning streak across the darkening sky, and a moment later thunder rumbled, echoing against the stone walls of the Palisades, vibrating along her spine. A short man with copper-colored hair entered the room. He glanced in her direction as he shook Ian's hand, his eyes unreadable behind his round glasses.

"This telegram arrived this morning from the operative I sent to England to investigate your inquiry, Mr. Tremayne," Bainbridge said, handing Ian a folded piece of yellow paper.

Sabrina tried to pull air into her lungs and failed. Without looking away from Ian, she crept backward, toward the open doors, feeling like a doe caught in a lion's den. When he was done reading the telegram Ian looked at her. Smooth, expressionless, his face might have been carved from walnut, all save his eyes; those beautiful eyes burned with hatred, a fire so hot she could feel the burn of it scorch her soul.

He turned to Bainbridge, his voice low, his words lost in the roar of blood in her ears. The short man smiled and shook Ian's hand before leaving the room, closing the door behind him. Lightning flashed through the windows and thunder exploded like cannon fire behind her. Sabrina jumped, pressing her hand to her heart. Ian didn't move, standing near the chess table, the telegram crushed in his hand.

"You almost had me convinced. I actually started to believe in your little masquerade." He didn't look in her direction, keeping his eyes focused on the painting above the mantel. "What did you hope to accomplish, Sabrina? What was your plan?"

The wind lifted the drapes, brushing the skirt of her lavender poplin gown, sweeping the fragrance of moist grass and roses into the room. "Does it matter? You've won, Tremayne."

"Have I? Have I really?" Turning to face her, he let the telegram fall from his fingers. It caught the same breeze that rippled Sabrina's skirts, riding the currents a few feet before settling with a soft rustle against the carpet. "And what shall the victor do with his beautiful enemy?"

Sabrina swallowed hard, pushing past the emotions constricting her throat. The first drops of rain pelted the windows, driven by the wind. "Let me go, Tremayne."

One corner of his lips quirked upward. Yet the smile didn't touch the smoky flames of anger in his eyes. She saw a beast stir in those eyes, the same creature who had plunged cold steel into his own chest, a creature capable of killing with his bare hands.

"Should I let you go so you can try again? Something a little more deadly this time?"

He had no intention of letting her go. At least not in one piece. She turned and dashed through the open French doors. Fat drops of rain drove into her face and wind whipped her skirts as she ran down the stairs leading to the rose garden. Pain flickered in her ankle, but she knew it was nothing compared to the pain he would deliver if he caught her. Byron bounded after her, barking and darting in front of her as though he intended to shepherd her back into the house.

"Sabrina!" Ian's voice sliced like a saber through the whirling wind.

A rosebush grabbed at her skirt as she left the gravel path, tearing the soft poplin. Thick grass cushioned her feet. Through the rain pounding against her face she could see the stables, standing like a specter amid gray streaks of water at the end of the drive. Before she could reach the gravel drive Ian snagged her arm with his hand. Pivoting on her heel, she swung with her clenched fist, hitting his shoulder. Casting one arm around her, he dragged her against his chest.

"Let go of me!" she shouted, throwing back her head, tossing the last remaining combs from her hair, the heavy tresses cascading down her back to her hips.

"Why did you do it? Why did you come here?"

Blinking the rain from her eyes, she stared up at her captor. Rain spilled down his face, plastering a lock of hair to his brow, catching in plump beads on his lashes. Lightning flashed overhead, casting his face in silver, glinting on the eyes of the beast within him.

She struggled to free herself, pushing against his chest, wiggling against the steel band around her waist. She had to break free. She had to . . . a groan of pain slipped from his lips, freezing her with her clenched fist against his chest. His arms tightened around her, his eyes sliding shut, his features contorting with pain. Had he broken open the wound again?

She unfurled her fist against him, feeling the steady beat of his heart against her palm. He drew a shallow breath before he opened his eyes and looked down at her, his green eyes clouded with pain. The last thing he should be doing right now was running around in the rain. "Tremayne, let me go before we do more harm to one another. It's over. Just let me go."

"I can't do that, Sabrina."

He took her arm and began hauling her back to the house. She resisted, planting her slippered feet, sliding on the wet grass, nearly tumbling headlong into his side. In one fluid motion he bent and tossed her over his shoulder, carrying her toward the house with Byron trotting at his side.

"Put me down!" she screamed, pummeling his back with her fists.

He ignored her, carrying her through the study and into the hall. Near the stairs he staggered, grabbing for the banister to catch his balance. A dark hand of fear clamped around her heart. Immediately she ceased the blows she had been raining upon his back. "Put me down, Tremayne. Put me down before you kill yourself."

He started up the stairs, leaning heavily on the banister, his breathing sharp and ragged. He paused at the second floor, his hand tense on the carved newel post, before he continued down the hall. Once in his bedroom he lowered her to the floor.

She stumbled back from him, hugging her arms to her waist, shivering in her wet clothes, watching as he turned the key in the lock. He leaned his shoulder against the door for a moment before turning to face her.

"Are you bleeding again?"

"Is that hope or fear I see in your eyes, Sabrina?" he asked, moving toward her.

Silver light flashed in the room, followed by a deep rumble. "For pity's sake, Tremayne. If I'd wanted to see you dead, I could've killed you any time you were lying unconscious in that bed."

He paused a foot in front of her, his broad shoulders rising and falling with each ragged breath. The wet linen of his shirt molded his skin, outlining the shape of thick muscles shaded by dark hair. "What do you want?" He trembled with cold. "Why did you come here?"

"You need to get out of those wet clothes," she said, reaching for the buttons of his shirt.

He grabbed her hands. Water dripped from his hair onto the crests of his cheeks, like tears, the tears she felt rising in a hot stream inside her.

"Tell me why you came here," he said, each word forced past his throat.

"To hurt you! To humiliate you the way you humiliated me."

He drew a deep breath, staring down at her. "By marrying my nephew?"

"I never intended to marry Timothy."

He wrapped his hand around her neck, shoving his thumb into the soft skin beneath her chin, forcing her head back. His eyes smoldered with emerald fire as they penetrated her soul. "Liar."

"Bastard!"

He slammed his mouth against hers, taking her lips in a brutal kiss. He tasted of rain, of passion, of rage. She pushed against his damp shoulders, wanting to deny him, to deny her own crippling need. Yet her own desire had been too long denied.

He clasped her against his chest as though he intended to squeeze the life from her, as though he couldn't get close enough to her. Desire rose like a wild bird inside her, straining against shackles of anger and pain, swirling, lifting, struggling to break free.

A pulse flared to life deep in her flesh, echoing the dizzying rhythm of her heart. Her hands opened against his shoulders, her fingers curling into his wet shirt.

He slid his hands down her back, gripping her hips through the layers of her sodden clothes, dragging her up against his body. Yet it wasn't enough, not nearly enough. Acres of poplin and linen kept her from feeling more than a hint of his shape, more than a whisper of the heat she knew burned in his loins. She needed to feel his skin against her aching flesh, she needed to feel him inside her.

As if he could read her mind, he slipped one hand between them and grabbed the top of her bodice. With a violent tug he cleaved the garment, buttons flying, hitting his chest. He pushed the torn gown from her shoulders, pinning her arms to her sides.

"Don't," she moaned, one last shred of sanity fighting the mob of her emotions. "You are my enemy!"

"You've cast your spell, witch," he said, dragging his open palm down the center of her body, grazing her breasts. "Now live with the consequences."

His warm fingers brushed her skin through the thin layer of her chemise as he loosened the laces of her corset. The soft silk of her chemise shredded beneath his hands, baring her breasts to his lips, his tongue, his teeth.

Raking one hand through her wet hair, he cupped her nape, holding her as he kissed her. Sabrina felt the heat flow from him, his fire filling her until her blood raged with it, until she was sure he would consume her. With her arms locked to her sides, she struggled to touch him, clawing at his thighs, trying to draw him closer, when all the time her head was screaming for her to push him away.

He lifted her in his arms, carrying her to the bed, pressing her down against the velvet counterpane. Lightning flashed through the windows, spilling silver light across her naked breasts, the pink tips taut and pleading.

"Beautiful witch," he murmured, staring down at her bare flesh. He pressed his open mouth against her neck, flicking his tongue across her skin, sliding like molten lava down the curve of her shoulder.

Pressing her shoulders into the mattress, she arched toward him, offering her breasts in silent supplication. He took her offering, taking the cold skin into his mouth, swirling fire with his tongue. Sabrina shuddered, soft pleasured sounds filling the air around her, sounds she shamefully realized tumbled from her own lips.

He slipped his hands under her skirts, bunching poplin and linen high around her waist, parting her thighs with one knee. He covered her lips with his as he slid his hand along the inside of her thigh, seeking, finding the slit in her drawers. One touch of his fingers against her moist flesh and her pelvis tilted in an age-old gesture of need; a gesture she couldn't have stopped if her life had depended on it.

"Tell me you want me, Sabrina." He spoke the words softly, his breath smoldering against her shoulder, his voice a husky whisper that barely lifted above the sound of the rain pounding against the windowpanes.

Complete surrender. Unconditional. He wanted her total defeat. She had to refuse him. She had to deny him. He tightened his hand on that sensitive mound of flesh, one finger finding her sleek shaft, slipping in, sliding out, until she arched against his hand, until she moaned and writhed beneath him.

"Tell me," he whispered, brushing his lips against her ear, his hand growing still against her. "Tell me you want me deep inside you."

Sabrina arched her hips, reaching for him. Yet he eluded her, lifting his hand, hovering above her, just out of reach, allowing her to feel only the warmth of his palm against her damp heat. Her need battled her pride. Yet the contest had been lost long ago. "I want you," she whispered. "God help me, I want you."

The sigh escaping his lips was filled with anguish, as though his defeat lay in her surrender. She didn't pause to wonder at it, her faculties for thought disintegrating into mindless need. She wiggled out of her bodice and slipped her arms around his shoulders, holding him prisoner against her, pressing her aching breasts against his damp shirt. She wiggled her hips, feeling him shift, feeling his fingers brush her skin as he flipped open the buttons of his trousers. Soon she would possess him again, payment for surrendering her pride. At the moment she refused to think of the cost.

At the first touch of his hardened flesh, she arched to capture him, wrapping her long legs high around his back, crying out against his lips as he became a part of her. Memories and dreams, reality and fantasy, he was all of these things and more. And he was hers, at least for these few moments. She met each hard thrust of his body, his enemy, his equal in this battle of love.

Rain pelted the windowpanes and lightning streaked across the gray sky, a pale reflection of the storm raging between man and woman. Rage, desire, anger, love, soared between them, shattering each into glittering pieces of light, combining one into the other. His body shuddered as he plunged into her one last time, his deep moan mingling with her soft sob, lifting her against him, holding her buttocks in his hands, letting her take all his length and breadth.

Sabrina struggled to draw him deeper and deeper into her, denying the moment she would once again be forced to release him. A low growl slipped from his lips as he fell against her, his cheek pressed against her bare shoulder, his breath warm and moist against her skin. Sabrina stared at the ebony hair curling at his nape, lifting her hand, longing to touch the silky tresses.

Thunder crashed, a distant rumble of artillery, dragging her back to reality. Nothing had changed. She was still his prisoner. He was still her enemy.

She hesitated, trembling fingers curling into her palm, resting her fist against his shoulder. He lifted his head to look down into her face, his eyes the color of fresh spring leaves, clear, fathomless. A shadow flickered over his face, a specter of need so hauntingly like her own, she wanted to slip her arms around him and hold him. Yet she couldn't.

He pulled back, rising to his feet, swaying, catching the bedpost to steady himself. She came to a sitting position, her wet hair tumbling down her back, clinging to her skin like slender fingers of frost. Wrapping her arms around her damp skin, shivering now without his warmth, she watched him straighten his clothes. She waited for a word, a gesture, anything to tell her what had just happened between them was more than lust, more than an enemy's vicious revenge.

Through his wet shirt she saw the outline of the bandage that still bound his waist, a smudge of red seeping through the layers of white linen. "You're bleeding," she said, lifting her hand to his waist.

He stepped back, as though he couldn't bear to have her touch him. Sabrina drew back her hand, lowering her gaze, shielding the pain in her eyes. Why was it so easy for him to hurt her? Why did she let him?

Without a word he crossed the room, threw open the mahogany armoire, and withdrew a dark blue cashmere robe. The frown didn't leave his face as he returned to her side. "Get out of those wet clothes," he said, tossing the robe at her.

She grabbed it, crushing the soft wool to her naked breasts. The angry tone in his voice destroyed any hope she might have been harboring about what had happened. Her cheeks grew warm as humiliating images cluttered her thoughts. It was as he said it would be the next time they came together. He hadn't even given her the dignity of being able to cry rape.

She pulled the robe around her, slipping her arms into the big sleeves before coming to her feet, Ian's robe puddling on the aqua carpet around her. Under the enveloping folds she stripped away the remains of her clothes, letting skirt and petticoat and drawers fall around her feet, listening to Ian as he moved restlessly around the room.

Tying the belt around her waist, she turned to face him. He stood with his hands in his pockets, staring out a rain-swept window, his long hair curling above the damp white linen clinging to his broad shoulders. It was all she could do to keep from going to him, to keep from touching him, to keep from making a complete fool of herself, again. "What are you going to do with me?"

He didn't move, didn't acknowledge that he had even heard her. Hidden in the long sleeves of his robe, her hands formed fists at her sides. Tension vibrated in the air between them, tugging at the base of her spine. She drew a deep breath, preparing to repeat her question, when he spoke.

"Go back to your room and get dressed," he said, staring out the windows. "Be ready to leave in an hour."

"Where are you taking me?"

He didn't look at her. "Back to the city."

Sabrina felt the blood drain from her limbs. He was done with her. She could hear it in his voice, see it in the stiff set of his shoulders. It was over. All of it. He intended to walk out of her life and never look back.

Like a streak of lightning, the realization that she would never see him again ripped through her, slicing her heart. Relief, that's what she should be feeling, not this terrible sense of loss, not this horrible gnawing emptiness.

He was her enemy.

She never wanted to see him again. And yet . . . Why did she feel like slapping him? Why did she feel like screaming? Why did she want to grab him and shake him until he realized he was throwing away something very special? It could have been something very, very special. If he had only loved her.

It was over.

Never again to see his face, hear his voice, feel the touch of his hand. They were dead to one another. Tears pricked the back of her eyes. With head held high she marched from his room, before the first tear fell, before she humiliated herself once more in front of this man.

Chapter Nineteen

Rain pounded on the roof of the coach, echoing the dull throb centered in Ian's side. He shifted on the leather seat, glancing at the woman riding across from him, wondering if what he was about to do was the biggest mistake of his life.

The leather drapes were drawn at the windows, the lamps unlit, casting her in shadows. Yet he could still see her. If he were struck blind in the next instant, he would still see her; her image was etched in fire across his soul.

He felt the coach rock to a stop. His heart began pumping his blood in an exaggerated rhythm he had felt many times. Each time he had gone into battle. It was time once again.

She looked up from her hands, which lay clasped in her lap like a little girl, glancing at him before turning to the window. Gray light flowed over her face as she drew back the drape, glowing on her pale skin, illuminating the frown crinkling her brow.

"Where are we?" she asked, letting the drape fall into place.

Ian drew a deep breath and tried to shake off his doubts. What he was about to do would change their lives forever. Once done, there was no turning back. He pulled back the drape, staring through the rain at a two-story stone building. "We're in front of the magistrate's residence."

"What are we doing here?"

Letting the drape fall into place, he leaned back in his seat. He could smell her fear, as clearly as he had smelled the fear of men facing death, almost as clearly as he could smell the scent of jasmine clinging to her skin, the fragrance slipping past his defenses to play havoc with his judgment. He wanted the witch, right here in the coach, with her luscious body spread deliciously across his lap, her legs nestling his hips. With a silent oath he shoved aside the image taking hold of him.

"I've done nothing illegal," Sabrina said, moving forward on her seat, as though she were about to take flight, but Ian could see in her eyes she knew there was nowhere to run.

"What would you call masquerading as an English countess in order to snag a rich husband? Fraud, perhaps?"

Her hands formed fists on her knees. "I came here to humiliate you, to hurt you. I never intended to marry anyone."

Always ready to fight. Never cowering. Always facing him with that beautiful head held high, that lovely chin raised. She was glorious, even if she was his enemy. "You intended to marry me. Or have you forgotten?"

"I wish I could. I wish I could forget ever being that foolish."

"If you play the game, you should be prepared to lose."

"I suppose you had the right to play with my life, the way you did aboard the *Belle Angeline?* I suppose you had the right to seduce me, to humiliate me, to steal the last shred of my dignity?"

"I suppose you don't hold any blame in this little escapade?"

"The only blame I hold is having been foolish enough to believe I loved you."

"Correction, foolish enough to believe you could convince me of your devotion. The only thing you ever loved was the color of my money." Ian glanced away from her, staring at the fist he held against his thigh, knowing he couldn't keep the pain of her betrayal from his eyes. "It was your game, Sabrina."

"No. It was never my game."

The moment he raised his eyes, he regretted it. She turned her head, swiping at her cheek with the back of her hand, but not before he saw the glitter of her tears in the faint light seeping through the drape.

He felt his chest tighten as he watched her fight for control, as he fought his own urge to take her into his arms. Could anyone lie that eloquently? Was he wrong about her? Had he been wrong to leave her?

Sabrina was a consummate actress, he reminded himself. Beguiling. Deceitful. Bewitching. Vengeful. Mesmerizing. If he ever allowed himself to believe her, if he ever allowed her to see the power she held over him, she would destroy him.

"What are you waiting for, Tremayne?" She lifted her head with defiance, blinking to keep her tears from falling. "If you're expecting me to plead for mercy, you'll rot where you sit before I give you the satisfaction."

Ian clenched his jaw and threw open the door. Luther stood beside the step holding a black umbrella, one large hand extended to help the passengers from the high coach.

Sabrina pulled the hood of the black merino cape she wore over her head. Without anyone's help she climbed down from the carriage and marched toward the front door, ignoring Luther's attempts to keep her under the umbrella.

The wind whipped through the tall yew flanking the brick-lined walk, tugging at her hood, sweeping it back from her head, snatching at her neat chignon. Rain swept against her cheeks. Sabrina welcomed the rain, each cold drop cleansing warm tears from her skin, disguising her humiliation. At the oak door she stood beneath the small roof protecting the entrance, waiting for Tremayne, gathering her courage.

Feeling him approach, she kept her gaze on the door. As he grasped the shiny brass door knocker planted in the center of the weathered oak, his arm brushed hers. Sabrina stepped aside. She didn't want to touch him. She didn't want any reminder of her own folly. From the corner of her eye she saw him, standing so tall beside her; her love, her enemy, her executioner. She felt fragile, as though one touch might shatter her carefully composed facade.

The door opened and she faced a small gray-haired woman with cheeks as ruddy as ripe raspberries. Ian greeted the little woman by name. Mrs. Rawlins smiled as she looked up at Tremayne, lines flaring out from dark blue eyes, bobbing her head, welcoming them into the foyer. Sabrina allowed the plump little housekeeper to take her cape. She hung it on a wooden peg near the door, beside Tremayne's black overcoat.

"Your man MacDoughal arrived no more than a half hour ago," Mrs. Rawlins said as she led Ian and Sabrina down a narrow hall. "Put us all in a whirl, he did."

Apparently this little town wasn't accustomed to dealing with hardened criminals, Sabrina thought, following Mrs. Rawlins into the parlor. Gaslight hissed behind crystal globes overhead, casting flickering light against celery green wainscoting. The room was crowded with furniture, reminding her of a squirrel's nest filled to the brim with nuts.

A short, white-haired man rose from an Empire sofa near the black marble hearth. A smile curved his lips beneath his bushy

mustache when he saw Sabrina. James MacDoughal turned from
the windows, his gaze moving from Ian to Sabrina, a frown carving deep lines into his brow. She was surprised MacDoughal
wasn't grinning on this her judgment day.

"I must say, you surprised me, young man," the magistrate said
as he moved toward Ian, stepping around a low table and two
chairs before reaching his side. "So this is the young lady."

Ian introduced Sabrina to Judge Vernon Uttley as though she
were coming for afternoon tea. Ian Tremayne could make love
to a woman in the morning and hang her in the afternoon. The
only heart he had was black, she decided.

Would they clamp manacles to her wrists? Her throat tightened
as she imagined being tossed into a small prison cell, iron bars
caging her like an animal. It would be like the cave at Vicksburg.
Only there she hadn't been able to leave for fear of being ripped
apart by Yankee shells. She had stayed in that cave, living with
the fear of being buried alive. And now she would stay in a
small cell because of a Yankee. Resisting the urge to turn and
run like a frightened rabbit, she forced her back to straighten.
These Yankees would soon discover a few things about southern pride.

"Would you care for something to drink before we proceed?
Tea? Coffee?" Uttley smiled up at Ian. "Something a little stronger?"

Sabrina shook her head, stunned by the man's cold-blooded
attitude. The man truly enjoyed his work, Sabrina thought. He
probably attended every hanging.

Ian also refused. "I'm anxious to get this over with."

Uttley glanced to Sabrina, his smile growing wider. "I can well
understand your haste."

Uttley stepped between Sabrina and Ian, taking their arms, leading them toward the windows, chatting casually about the weather.
Sabrina felt her knees quiver with each step she took. Would she
have a trial? Or would they lock her up in a little cell and forget
about her?

The scandal.

Aunt Caroline and Lucy would be ruined. Was there any way
to keep her arrest from the newspapers? she wondered, glancing at Ian. Impossible. Keeping it quiet would spoil Tremayne's
enjoyment.

Lightning flashed and a heartbeat later thunder rumbled, shaking the windowpanes. Outside, the storm had turned morning to

midnight, summer to winter. She stared at her reflection in the windows, gaslight limning her in golden light, rivulets of rain coursing down the glass and distorting her image.

Foolish woman! Thoughtless, selfish child! Great stars above, she had made a complete mess of things.

"Mr. MacDoughal, please stand beside Mr. Tremayne," Uttley said, lifting a black book from a round table to his left. "Mrs. Rawlins, if you will take your place beside Miss O'Neill."

The little housekeeper giggled softly as she moved to stand beside Sabrina. They were all enjoying this, Sabrina thought, every one of them. Uttley took a place in front of the gathered group, opening the book he held to a place marked by a scarlet ribbon. He cleared his throat before he spoke. "Dearly beloved . . ."

He continued, his words swirling in Sabrina's mind, taking a moment to register on her shattered wits. "What's going on here? What's this you're rambling?"

Uttley paused, looking at Sabrina as though she had just sprouted an extra head. "I assure you, everything is in order, Miss O'Neill."

Sabrina looked up at Tremayne. His face was set, revealing none of his emotions, his eyes unreadable, as though he had drawn a dark green curtain, shielding his every thought. "What do you mean by this, Ian Tremayne? Is this yet another game?"

Without lifting his gaze from her face, Ian spoke. "Judge, I think the young lady and I need a few moments alone."

Uttley cleared his throat. "Ah, yes, of course. We'll just . . . we'll just wait in the hall. You give a call when you want us."

Sabrina held Ian's gaze, hearing footsteps trample the carpet, the door open then close with a soft click. "Is this some trick?"

A muscle flashed in his lean cheek. "The trick was played long ago, Sabrina."

Sabrina turned away from him, hugging her arms to her waist. "Do you expect me to believe you intend to marry me?"

"Till death us do part."

She spun on her heel, pale blue silk swirling around her. Hope flickered inside her, a glowing ember amid the ashes of hopes and dreams. "Why? Why are you doing this?"

He stood motionless, watching her, his eyes, his face telling her nothing. Rain pelted the windows. In the distance lightning streaked across the sky, a jagged lance piercing heaven's heart. He turned away from her, staring out of the small panes.

"I've decided having you for a wife would suit me," he said, his voice deep, low, devoid of emotion.

"Are you in love with me?" she asked, her voice a hopeful whisper.

Ian laughed, a coarse, angry sound in the quiet room. "Love has nothing to do with it."

He might have stabbed her, and the pain would not have been more than what she felt at that moment. "Then why? Why marry me?"

He glanced at her, his gaze lowering to the full curve of her breasts beneath the snug-fitting bodice. "You have your uses."

She moved toward him, anger and frustration trembling in every muscle. "You haven't married every woman who warmed your bed. Why me?"

"Because you know there is nothing more than lust between us," he said, glancing out the windows. "You'll be a lovely hostess for my guests, a devoted mother for my children, a tempting courtesan in my bed. And I shall retain my freedom to do as I please."

"I see. You think I will suffer your mistresses without a whimper."

He rested his shoulder against the window casement. "You wanted money, social position. I'm willing to give them to you."

"And the price is life with a man who has no heart." She bit her lower lip, fighting against the tears burning her eyes. "You really are the image of your dear father, aren't you?"

His mouth flattened into a taut line. He took a step toward her and stopped. She could see the effort it took him to control his emotions, and wondered about the consequences should he fail.

He breathed deeply, his shoulders rising beneath the black wool of his coat, his pulse throbbing against the white collar of his shirt and cravat. "I can see you will need to be broken to the bit."

"Not by you, Tremayne! I wouldn't marry you for all the gold in the world."

A dry, humorless laugh issued from deep in his throat. "You don't have a choice."

"The blazes I don't."

"Would you rather go to prison?"

Sabrina swallowed hard, an image of a cold, dark cell scrawling across her mind. "Yes."

"I see." He studied her a moment, one corner of his lips lifting. "I guess you don't care about ruining your Aunt Caroline, your cousin Lucy. I wonder what will happen when everyone finds out about your little game and the role they played."

She tried to keep her emotions from her face. Inside she was breaking, shattering into a thousand pieces.

He lifted one black brow as he played his ace. "And your father."

"What about my father?"

"I think I can manage to convince the authorities to put him behind bars. Particularly if I arrange to have him caught with a deck of marked cards in his hands."

He had the money, the power to ruin what was left of her family. "You would, wouldn't you? You would destroy everything I have left. Just to serve your perverted whim. Just to marry a woman who hates you."

"The way you hated me this morning, Sabrina?"

He would leave her nothing, not a shred of dignity, not a whisper of pride. "You'll regret this, Tremayne."

He studied her a moment, as though he were trying to see beyond the barriers she was constructing against him. "No doubt I will," he said, glancing away from her. "Shall I ask the judge to continue the ceremony?"

She nodded, her voice strangled by emotions. The judge and witnesses returned at Ian's invitation. She felt numb as she stood beside the man she had once loved and listened to the words that would bind them to each other forever. As if she stood apart from herself she watched the ceremony in the windows, her own reflection beside that of Ian Tremayne's, two lost souls hovering between heaven and hell.

She didn't look at Ian as he took her hand. His warm fingers brushed her skin as he slid cold metal along her finger. Without looking she knew that it was his grandmother's ring. It fit, as though it had been fashioned for her. Here she stood in one of Rebecca's gowns, wearing the wedding ring Ian MacClaren had once slipped onto her finger. Were they watching from above? What would they think of their grandson and his reluctant bride? What would they think of this travesty of a marriage?

After Uttley made a toast to the newlyweds with his best sherry Ian led his bride out of the house. Sabrina didn't resist as he helped her into the carriage. He took a seat opposite her, and although she refused to look in his direction, she could feel his gaze on her.

"You look as though you're on your way to the gallows. You should be smiling, Sabrina. You won."

"Did I?"

"I'm going to give you everything you wanted from the moment you tried to hook me aboard the *Belle*. You'll be one of the richest women in New York."

She lifted her eyes, staring at him, not bothering to hide the pain inside her. "Is that what I wanted?"

He was quiet a moment, caught in her steady gaze. "You really are a good actress."

"I'm going to have to be a wonderful actress to get through this." She glanced down at her hands. "If I might make one small request, as a condemned prisoner?"

He sighed. "What do you want?"

"I would like to see my Aunt Caroline. I'm sure she's worried, and I'd like to tell her what happened."

"Of course."

Sabrina rested her head against the carriage seat, staring through the partially pulled drape, blinking against the mist blowing through the window. The road stretched out before them, a ribbon of dark gray curving through gray trees under a gray sky leading her to an equally gray future.

Inside she felt as colorless as the world around her. She didn't want to feel. Not yet. Not when her emotions could tear her to shreds. Better to be numb.

In time the steady tap of rain slowed upon the roof. The clouds ceased crying. Sabrina pulled back the drape, allowing freshly scrubbed air to bathe her face, breathing in the scent of damp soil and grass and cedar.

They rounded a curve in the road and a village came into view; white and stone buildings, tall trees, all nestled in a lush, green valley. It was like a recently completed oil landscape, the paint still damp and shiny. As she watched the artist added one last stroke to his masterpiece: Sunlight slanted through white puffs of clouds, sweeping color across the sky in a bright shimmering arch. Her mother had said rainbows were a symbol of hope, of fresh new beginnings.

She sat back and closed her eyes, blocking out the rainbow. It was too beautiful, too filled with optimism, too much a contrast to her own miserable existence to endure. She drew the drape and rode the rest of the way to the city in shadows.

Sabrina refused Ian's arm as they walked up the stone stairs leading to the Van Cortlandt mansion. She was relieved to find her Aunt Caroline alone, the usual throng of morning visitors having departed. Notes flooded the hall as Dicken led the way toward the music room, sharp, sour, scraping against the ear like broken glass.

"Sounds as if someone is torturing a cat," Ian murmured under his breath.

Sabrina frowned at him. "Aunt Caroline only plays when she's upset."

Ian lifted his brows. "Let's hope she doesn't get upset very often."

Sabrina ignored his comment, staring at Dicken's back, wishing she could ignore Ian completely. It was impossible. Not while his leg brushed her skirt with every step. Not while his scent drifted to her senses, evoking memories of his warm flesh sliding against hers, of firm lips . . . She tried to banish the memories, her cheeks growing warm as she failed.

Dicken paused on the threshold of the music room, where Caroline sat playing a gilt-trimmed harp. Sunlight streaked through lace curtains behind her, striking the strings, shattering light in all directions. She rose as Dicken announced Lady Julia's arrival, the harp thumping against an Aubusson carpet in shades of apricot, brown, and ivory.

"Darling," she said, rushing toward Sabrina, green and yellow silk rustling against her petticoats.

"Aunt Caroline," Sabrina said, grasping Caroline's hands as though she were a lifeline.

"I'm so glad you're back," Caroline said, pressing her cheek to Sabrina's.

The scent of roses drifted from Caroline's skin, tossing Sabrina back into the grave of memories resting deep inside her. Time was suspended and she was back in her mother's warm embrace. The tender illusion lasted a heartbeat, only a heartbeat.

Caroline pulled back, squeezing Sabrina's hands, studying her face feature by feature, as though she were looking for bruises. "Are you all right?"

"I'm fine."

Caroline looked past Sabrina to where Ian stood near a Queen Anne chair covered in apricot silk brocade. "And just what do you have to say for yourself, young man? Tell me why I shouldn't have you arrested this very moment."

One corner of his lips lifted. "Would you arrest your niece's husband?"

"Husband!" Caroline lifted her eyes to Sabrina. "Have you married this scoundrel?"

Sabrina nodded. "We were married this morning."

"I see." Caroline stepped back, her gaze moving from Sabrina to Ian and back again. "Well, I suppose under the circumstances you had little choice."

"None at all," Sabrina whispered.

"And you, young man." Clasping her hands at her waist, Caroline fixed Ian with a steady stare. "What reason did you have for marrying my niece?"

Ian leaned his hip against the arm of the chair, the black wool of his trousers stark against the apricot silk. "I have my reasons."

Caroline studied him a moment, sharp, perceptive blue eyes stripping away pretense, piercing the soul. After a moment a smile flickered across her lips. "Yes. I'm sure you do."

Ian shifted his weight, glancing down at the tip of his black boot. He actually looked embarrassed. It seemed to Sabrina her aunt was one of the few people who could pierce Ian Tremayne's armor.

"Does your father know about this?" Caroline asked.

"I haven't had a chance to write to him."

"Darling, your father arrived in the city the day after you did. It seems he had been following you the entire time you were here."

"Why didn't you tell me?"

"I didn't know until he came to see me shortly after you disappeared. He went looking for you. Apparently, he just wasn't able to find you."

Sabrina glanced to Ian. He was watching her, his face betraying nothing. She turned away, her gaze resting on the rosewood piano near the harp. Her father had been in the city the entire time, following her. Had he also been following Tremayne? Had he found them at Dunkeld?

"There are things that need to be done." Caroline tapped the tip of her forefinger against her chin.

When had Ian been struck by that coach? James MacDoughal's voice echoed in Sabrina's memory. It had been a few weeks ago. Since her arrival in New York. Since her father's arrival in New York. No. It couldn't be her father. He would never strike at an unarmed man. He would face his enemy. He would!

"Sabrina must be introduced into society. We must think of some way to explain her masquerade as Julia."

"I suppose the truth is out of the question," Ian said.

Sabrina stared at him, righteous rage roiling in her veins. "Whose truth? Yours or mine?"

Ian held her angry glare. "And what is your version, Sabrina?"

"You know very well what it is. I wonder what everyone would think of you if they knew your penchant for lying." Sabrina moved toward him as she spoke, her hands clenching into fists at her sides. "If they knew you asked me to marry you only to seduce me."

Ian lifted away from the chair, a muscle flashing in his cheek as he clenched his jaw. "I wonder what everyone would think if they knew you and your father make a living from cheating Yankees out of their gold."

"You arrogant . . ."

"We will get nowhere this way," Caroline said, stepping between them. She took Sabrina's arm and led her a few feet away from Ian. "You must learn to be civil to one another."

"I would rather be civil to a rattlesnake," Sabrina said, glaring at Ian over Aunt Caroline's head.

"Sabrina, darling, think of me, think of Lucy, think of the scandal we could be facing."

Taking a deep breath, Sabrina closed her eyes. The man was holding all the aces. "I'll try."

Caroline patted Sabrina's arm. "I think the first thing is to hold a ball in your new house. Introduce Sabrina to your friends, show everyone how very much in love you really are."

Sabrina's groan earned a sharp look from Caroline. She glanced down at the carpet as Caroline continued.

"We can tell everyone you and Sabrina were once engaged. You argued, and Sabrina came to New York as Lady Julia Wyndham as a bit of mischief. You fell in love all over again and eloped." Caroline paused, looking at Ian. "What do you say, Mr. Tremayne?"

Ian was quiet. Sabrina could feel him watching her, waiting for her reaction to Caroline's plan. She refused to meet his gaze.

After what seemed like days Ian spoke. "I suppose we really need to peddle that piece of fiction?"

"Yes, of course we do. Now, we should plan for the ball as soon as possible." She marched toward the door, pausing when she realized no one was following. With a flare of her skirts she turned to face them, a general addressing her troops. "Come along. I must see the place if I am to plan a proper ball."

Chapter Twenty

When she felt the coach turn from the road Sabrina glanced out the window. Tall wrought-iron gates rose on either side of a brick-lined drive leading to a house from another time and place. Set amid a wide, lush expanse of lawn, chiseled limestone soared four stories, shaping a fifteenth-century chateau worthy of the rolling green hills of the French countryside. Scaffolding surrounded the east wing, lacing one tall tower like a black cobweb. Afternoon sunlight gilded the damp stone blocks, reflected on hundreds of windows, making the house shimmer like a castle from a fairy tale.

Strange, the house seemed both familiar and foreign at the same time, Sabrina thought as the carriage carried her toward that fairy-tale castle. It was as if she had once lived here. So strong was the feeling, so real were the images flickering in her mind, goose bumps rose on her arms.

When the coach pulled up under the porte cochere she turned to the man across from her. "This is your house?"

He smiled. "I know it doesn't look finished, but it's livable."

Sabrina tried to shake the odd feeling gripping her, the strong sense of familiarity, but couldn't.

"Why did you build so far away from civilization?" Caroline asked as Ian opened one of the two twelve-foot-tall oak front doors.

"I wanted some breathing space." Ian stood aside to allow the ladies to enter his house. "Unfortunately, the city will catch up with me in a few years."

White marble, veined with garnet, lined the reception hall and flowed upward, forming the base of a wide staircase. Sunlight streamed through tall leaded-glass windows at the landing, glowing on oak wainscoting, reflecting against the balustrades of lacy steel and gilt bronze that rose from the base of the stairs and swept upward, hugging the contours of the staircase.

"In ten years this part of Fifth Avenue will be as crowded as it is south of Fiftieth," Ian said.

Caroline gave him a look full of doubt. "Haven't you any servants?"

"My staff hasn't arrived from Dunkeld."

"You can't mean you shuttle all of your servants from house to house," Caroline said.

Sabrina half listened as Ian explained his staff to her Aunt Caroline. She glanced down at the simple band she wore, then at the man who had slipped that gold ring onto her finger. He was walking beside Caroline, answering another of her aunt's questions, looking a little unsure of himself. Aunt Caroline had a way of doing that to people, apparently even to extremely self-assured males.

Strange, Sabrina thought, she was married to the man she had dreamed of marrying most of her life. It should be the happiest day of her life. And yet, she had learned dreams were only illusions in the night, waiting to be shattered by the light of day.

Ian glanced at her, as though he sensed her looking at him. Caught in that green gaze, her heart did a slow tumble. Despite her intention to act indifferent, all the acting in the world couldn't save her from her own humiliating need. She glanced away from him, following a few paces behind as he gave Caroline a tour of the house.

Walking through Ian's home was like walking through a half-remembered dream for Sabrina. It was impossible to shake the eerie feeling that she had once lived here before. In a house that wasn't yet completed? Sheer lunacy.

Aside from the study, the library, and the family dining room, the first floor of the house was empty, parquet and marble floors lying naked. One room, which Sabrina supposed would become the music room, held a rosewood piano and nothing more. The house was a beautiful empty shell.

"Your father's house is full of wonderful pieces," Caroline said, gazing into the ballroom, her voice echoing in the huge empty room, which stretched more than a hundred feet along the back of the house. "When are you planning to move them here?"

"I'm not. I've taken all I intend to take from my father's house."

His tone indicated a finality that surprised Sabrina. Perhaps the memories of his father were too painful to face every day. They must have been very close.

Sabrina's footsteps rapped against polished rosewood as she crossed the ballroom floor. Six pairs of French doors lined the far wall, opening to a wide stone terrace and the gardens beyond. Two acres of land stretched out from the house in a patchwork of grass and partially planted beds. More than eighty rosebushes, their roots wrapped in canvas, sat near a stone fountain of frolicking cherubs a few yards from the terrace.

Odd, Sabrina knew there would be a rose garden beyond the ballroom, just as she could imagine each room in this house, the paintings that would hang on the walls, the furniture that would grace each room. It was as if she had come home again, to a place she had never been. At least not in this lifetime.

"We shall be able to get what we need for the ball from Stewart's," Caroline said as she led the way back to the main hall. "But you need to furnish this place in Europe. It could be magnificent with the right pieces."

Ian paused at the foot of the stairs, one hand resting on the balustrade, a smile curving his lips. "I haven't had much time to furnish the place."

Sabrina's defenses shuddered under the influence of that smile. She glanced away, staring at one of the bronze shields in the grillwork of the balustrade, the scene depicting Pegasus in flight.

"Let's take a look upstairs," Caroline said, sounding excited, like a little girl given the key to a candy store.

"I leave you in complete control, Mrs. Van Cortlandt. Please, make yourself at home." He turned and walked toward the front door.

"Where are you going?" Sabrina asked.

"Miss me already?" he asked, glancing over his shoulder.

Sabrina clenched her hands at her sides. How easy it was to betray emotions. "I was hoping you might set sail for China."

Ian chuckled. "Ah, it's nice to be loved."

Sabrina turned away, meeting her Aunt Caroline's intense gaze. "You can't expect me to be nice to him when no one is around."

Caroline's lips lifted in a smile. The door opened and closed, the sound rippling through the empty hall. "I think you are afraid of being far too nice to him."

Sabrina lifted her gown, following Caroline up the staircase, her heels tapping on marble. "What do you mean by that?"

Caroline paused on the landing, standing in the flood of sunlight streaming through the windows. The staircase branched out from the landing, soaring in two wide opposing arcs to the second floor. "Darling, you are in love with that man."

Sabrina's chin soared. "I loathe him."

Caroline shook her head. "And, what's more, he is in love with you."

Sabrina made a noise in her throat, somewhere between a laugh and a sob.

"He would never have married you if he was not in love with you."

"You really are a romantic." Sabrina glanced down at her hand, staring at the ring. "He wants a hostess, a brood mare, a whore. A wife who won't whimper about his mistresses."

"Is that what he told you?"

Sabrina flicked the ring back and forth with the tip of her thumb, braided gold glowing yellow and scarlet in the sunlight. "That's exactly what he told me."

"Masculine pride."

Sabrina followed her aunt as she continued up the stairs, taking the right branch of the staircase. "The man is a scoundrel. You don't know him."

Caroline didn't seem to hear. At the second floor she turned right down a long corridor. "Do you realize that it will take a small miracle to put this place in order?" With hands on her hips she turned in a circle as she spoke, looking at the paneled oak walls, painted white, unadorned.

"Aunt Caroline, you're wrong about him."

Caroline didn't seem to hear. "Still, I do love a challenge. I think two weeks from Friday should do it."

"Aunt Caroline, Ian Tremayne doesn't love me. You're wrong about him."

"Am I?" Caroline rested her palm against Sabrina's cheek, the scent of roses drifting from the warm skin of her wrist. "And if I'm not? What if he were to tell you how much he loved you? Then what would you do?"

The thought brought a wave of longing rushing up from deep wells within Sabrina. She shook her head, forcing back the frightening emotion, snatching at her pain. There was safety in embracing her pain. "How could I ever believe him? He's a devil. And shrewd. Believe me, if he said he loved me, he'd have another reason. It'd be a means to some twisted end. I'd be a fool to ever believe that man again."

"What you need is a fresh beginning. You and that young man need to bury the past. You need to think of the future."

"I have no future with him."

Caroline sighed. "Perhaps time will heal the wounds."

The first few doors opened to huge empty rooms. Near the end of the long corridor Caroline threw open a door and sighed. "Finally a furnished room."

Sabrina's footsteps rapped against bare oak planks, echoing against white walls. Wide plastered areas, begging for wall covering, flowed from white scrolls at the high ceiling down the walls to raised panels of oak painted white. Patterned burgundy silk draped the windows, flanked the French doors leading to the balcony, and formed a canopy above a white and gilt carved bed.

Sabrina tossed back the drapes, allowing sunlight to flood the room. "Furnished?" she asked, glancing around at the few pieces of furniture in the room.

"Compared to the rest, this room is crowded. We need to find a room suitable for the ladies' withdrawing room."

What room did he expect her to take? Sabrina wondered. She opened a door to the left of the bed and stared into an adjoining bedroom. A Brussels carpet of varying shades of blue and ivory stretched the length and breadth of the huge room. Icy blue silk flowed from the canopy of a carved mahogany bed and draped the French doors and windows. Without being told, she knew this was Ian's room. Sabrina was certain of it.

Caroline's footsteps tapped against the bare floor. "At least it has a bathroom. Of course, I would imagine each bedroom in this house has a bathroom."

Sabrina closed the door leading to Ian's bedroom and turned to face her aunt. An odd expression crossed Caroline's face as she stared into the bathroom. Her curiosity piqued, Sabrina moved to Caroline's side. A gown of pink organdy lay draped across the edge of the big white marble tub, white drawers and an ivory petticoat nearby. She moved toward the gown, drawn to it like a magnet, her blood simmering.

"One of his previous guests," Sabrina said, lifting one of the sleeves, surprised to find it damp.

Caroline frowned. "I've seen that gown before."

"I imagine I will have to grow accustomed to finding scraps of women's clothing." She dropped the gown and brushed past her aunt. "The man is a . . . a . . . pirate!"

"Darling, I'm sure . . ."

Before Caroline could finish a door opened to Sabrina's left. Lucy entered the room, wearing a white terry-cloth robe that dragged more than a foot on the floor. Her hair tumbled in wild waves around her shoulders, falling to her waist. She froze as she saw her mother. "Oh, my," she whispered, pressing her fingertips to her lips.

"What are you doing here?" Caroline asked, sounding every bit as startled as Lucy.

"I was just going to see if my gown was dry," Lucy said, her hand fluttering at her neck.

Tim materialized behind Lucy, leaving the relative safety of the adjoining sitting room to be by her side. He wore a white shirt several sizes too big for him, the shoulder seams falling at least two inches beyond his shoulders, the cuffs folded back from his wrists, his black trousers folded up at the hems. His face reflected the same shock etched into Lucy's features. "Mrs. Van Cortlandt, what are you doing here?"

Caroline clasped her hands at her waist. "I think you had better answer that question, young man."

"Mrs. Van Cortlandt." Tim glanced at Sabrina, his cheeks growing red. "Lady Julia, we . . . I mean, I can explain."

Caroline drew a deep breath. "Do so, young man."

"We were boating in the park." Tim slipped his arm around Lucy's shoulders, as though he wanted to shield her from harm. "And we capsized."

"It was my fault." Lucy glanced up at Tim. "He saved my life."

Tim's cheeks darkened under Lucy's warm gaze. "And then it started to rain. So, I thought it would be better to come here, since it's so close."

"Sounds reasonable," Sabrina said, glancing at her aunt.

Caroline shot her a dark look before pinning Lucy in her gaze. "You came to this house, unchaperoned."

"Nothing happened," Tim and Lucy said, their words overlapping.

"I'm sure it was all harmless, Aunt Caroline. Lucy would never . . ." Sabrina paused, realizing Tim was staring at her, his lips parted, his eyes wide.

"Your accent. Uncle Ian said you were from the south." He hesitated, staring at her. "It's true, isn't it? You *are* Sabrina."

"Who she is has nothing to do with this," Caroline said. "Young man, you . . ."

"You lied to me," Tim said, looking down at Lucy. He withdrew his arm from her shoulders. "Why didn't you tell me the truth, Lucy?"

"I couldn't. I promised Sabrina."

Tim shoved his fair hair back from his brow. "All of you must have had a quite a laugh. Seeing the stupid boy tumble first for Lady Julia, then for her cousin. Do you have any idea the torment I've been through the past few days?" This last he shot straight at Lucy.

"It was my fault," Sabrina said. "Lucy had nothing to do with this."

Tears glistened on Lucy's long dark lashes. "Tim, please, try to understand. I couldn't betray her trust."

"And what about me? What about my trust?" Tim backed away as Lucy reached for him, her small hand trembling. "You were a part of this." He turned, glaring at Sabrina. "What were you going to do? Marry me to get back at my uncle?"

"I never intended to marry anyone. I hoped Ian would fall in love with Julia. I intended to jilt him." She paused, swallowing back the lump of humiliation lodged in her throat. "The way he jilted me."

Tim looked down at Lucy, his face pulled into angry lines. "And you were going to help."

Lucy shook her head, tears streaming down her cheeks.

"What your uncle did was wrong," Caroline said.

Tim stared at Sabrina, hatred flickering in his dark eyes. "I'm sure Uncle Ian had a good reason for anything he did."

Sabrina took a step toward Tim. "Please don't hold this against Lucy. It was all my fault."

Tim lifted his hand to keep her away, his fingers curling into a fist. "I guess I should thank you for a valuable lesson. Nothing is as it seems." He stared down at Lucy. "Even something as lovely and innocent looking as a kitten has claws."

Lucy lowered her eyes. "I'm so sorry," she whispered, her voice cracking on a sob.

Tim turned on his heel and marched toward the door.

"You will not walk out of here, young man." Caroline turned as he passed her. "There are matters we need to discuss."

Tim didn't spare her a glance. He left the room, slamming the door behind him.

"Well, of all the . . ." Caroline's chin rose, her shoulders growing stiff. "In my day, young men were raised to have better manners."

Lucy pressed her hand to her lips, a sob slipping past her palm. Looking at her cousin, Sabrina felt awkward, knowing she was the cause of Lucy's misery. Each strangled cry escaping Lucy's lips twisted around Sabrina's heart.

Revenge.

For years Sabrina had lived with vengeance, taking it where she could. Yet nothing could bring back her mother, her brothers, Aidan, home. And in the end what had her thirst for vengeance accomplished? Lucy had been right from the beginning. Hate could only destroy. Sabrina only wished her selfishness hadn't caused Lucy pain.

Lucy looked up as Sabrina touched her arm, blue eyes swimming in tears. "I'm not sure what to say," Sabrina whispered.

Lucy's shoulders shook with great racking sobs.

"Darling, darling, don't cry," Caroline said, slipping her arm around Lucy's slender shoulders. "Right now he's angry. But if he loves you, he'll be back."

Lucy shook her head. "He . . . hates me."

"You'll see." Sabrina stroked Lucy's arm, praying there was some way to mend the mess she had made of everything.

Perhaps Ian could talk to Tim, Sabrina thought. Perhaps he could smooth the young man's ruffled feathers. But how could she hope to convince him to help? The man hated her.

Ian rested his arm along the white marble mantel of Ellen's drawing room, frowning as he watched his sister pace the length of the room. She turned at the windows, pale yellow linen swaying with the movement, her gown whipping up the hem of the lace curtains.

"I can't believe you married that woman." Ellen paused, looking up at him. "You said she was a liar, a cheat."

"So I did." Was Sabrina a liar? He thought of how she had looked this morning, her face, her eyes. He thought of how she had felt in his arms. And he remembered more.

He remembered a woman leaning over him while he lay bloody and fighting for his life. There had been a look in her dark eyes, a look of fear and desperation, fear of losing him. Was everything a lie? Somehow doubts had crept into his heart, doubts about her treachery. Perhaps because he wanted to believe she was capable of more than lies. Perhaps because he needed to believe in her. Was he a fool?

Ellen released her breath on a long sigh. "Did you do it for Tim?"

"No. I had my own reasons." He had intended to take his pound of flesh and walk away. Only he didn't want to walk away from Sabrina. Not now. Not ever.

Ellen studied him a moment, the taut lines of her face softening into understanding. "You must love her very much."

"Love?" Ian glanced down at the tip of his boot. "Mesmerized, maybe. Obsessed. Truth is, I'm bewitched by that beautiful redhead. And believe me, that's worse than love."

Ellen frowned. "And you had to marry her?"

"It was the safest thing to do." *And the only thing to do.* He couldn't let her walk out of his life. That was the only thing he was sure about.

"I'm not sure how Tim will take the news. He's been seeing . . ." She hesitated as someone slammed the front door.

Footsteps pounded on the parquet lining the hall, growing louder as they advanced toward the drawing room. A moment later Tim entered the room. He stood on the threshold, breathing hard, cheeks flushed, looking as though he had just run a mile.

"You were right, all along," Tim said, raking a hand through his hair. "That woman, Sabrina, is at your house."

"I know." Ian frowned, recognizing the shirt and trousers Tim wore as his own. "What were you doing there?"

"Long story. Got caught in the storm and . . ." Tim sank to the sofa near the hearth. "You think you know someone. You think you can trust her. You even ask her to marry you, and then she turns out to be a stranger. What a fool!"

Ian clenched his jaw. Sabrina had managed to rip Tim into shreds, the same way she had torn him to pieces months before. No matter what he wanted to believe, the truth kept coming back to bite him: Sabrina was nothing but a scheming little whore. He had to face the truth. He had to live with it and the way he felt about her.

Ellen rested her hand on Tim's shoulder. "You mustn't feel . . ."

"Not now," he said, coming to his feet. "I don't want to talk about it now."

Ian clenched his hands into fists as he watched Tim leave the room. Sabrina was an expert in teaching lessons of humiliation. Perhaps it was time someone repaid the favor.

Chapter Twenty-One

Sabrina sank to the bench planted in the center of her Aunt Caroline's maze garden and stared up at the ancient oak guarding the entrance. A few long branches stretched out above one side of the maze, casting shadows across one end of the bench. Through the thick leaves she could see the scar of a broken bough, a scar caused by a reckless little girl. Would she be in this mess today if she hadn't followed Ian Tremayne and that blond harlot a lifetime ago? Would Lucy be crying in her room?

She closed her eyes. The sun that warmed her back coaxed the fragrance from the roses surrounding her. Roses had always been her mother's favorite flower. She could hear the blooms rustle in the breeze, the scent drifting past her nostrils, tugging on her heart, pulling her back to Rosebriar, back to the glory that had once been her home, back to memories she had long tried to hide in a dark recess of her mind, memories too painful to embrace.

Three stories of red brick rose majestically from a high hill near the Mississippi River. In her mind she could see her father standing on the white captain's walk crowning the house, surveying his kingdom as he did every day. Brendan and Dennis stood tall and proud on either side of their father. Sunlight reflected on the thick Doric columns supporting white wooden galleries stretching across the back of the house on the first and second floors.

From the brick patio at the back of the house a red brick path cascaded through broad terraces to the bluff above the river, bushes of roses, camelias, and azaleas blooming in profusion, perfuming the air. As she had every day, Sabrina walked with her mother in the garden, gathering flowers.

"It's a crime to let a rose die on the vine, Sabrina," Rachel had said, smiling at her daughter as she laid a pink rose in the wicker basket Sabrina held. "We should cut them while they're still young and beautiful, allow them to share our home. You remember that when you have a house of your own. You remember to tell your daughter."

The images faded in her mind, twisting her heart with longing. If only she could see them once more—Mother, Brendan, Dennis—if only she could hear their laughter. Tears slipped from the thick fringe of lashes resting against her cheeks. Sometimes she couldn't believe they were truly gone. Forever.

This was no time to allow herself to wallow in self-pity, she thought, swiping at her tears. She needed to go back to Tremayne's house. She needed to confront the beast and ask for his help. He couldn't blame Lucy for all of this. He would see she was just an innocent caught in the cross fire of their war.

"Hiding, Sabrina?"

She stiffened at the sound of Ian's voice. How did the man manage to walk silently along a gravel walk, she wondered, glancing back at him. He stood in full sunlight, dressed in black trousers and a white shirt. Rosebushes fanned out from either side of him, blossoms of red and yellow and pink, their colorful heads bobbing in the breeze, bowing to the woodland god in their midst.

"Must you always sneak up on me?" she said, rising to her feet, leaving the shadows cast by the oak.

"Afraid of being caught?"

There was an edge to his voice, a glitter in his eyes that rallied her defenses. Must they always approach each other with swords drawn? Perhaps it was better this way. This way she wouldn't be lulled into believing he cared any more for her than he did for his last mistress; less.

She decided to ignore the call to battle. "Your nephew was at your house earlier. He . . . he was very upset. And I thought you . . ."

"I know," he said, glancing at the roses beside him. "I was at Ellen's when he came home."

"Then you know what happened."

He focused his attention on a pink rose blossom bobbing near his hip, brushing his knuckles back and forth over the petals. "He had his first lesson in a woman's treachery."

So he intended to blame Lucy for all of this. "You're quick to judge, Tremayne. Quick to hang before ever giving someone a chance to defend herself."

He caressed the rose gently, brushing his knuckles across the petals, then returning with a stroke of the pads of his fingers. "And just how do you intend to defend what you did, Sabrina?" he asked, his fingers closing around the stem.

With a twist of his hand he snapped the rose from the bush, leaving a ragged scar behind. Slowly he closed his hand around the stem of the flower, clenching his hand into a fist, sharp, beak-like thorns digging into his palm. The man didn't flinch.

"How do you justify destroying a man? He was in love with you. He would have given you anything, anything in his power."

Sabrina stared at him, struck by the intensity of his emotions. As she watched, a single trickle of blood slipped from his clenched fist, sliding across his wrist to stain the white cuff of his shirt.

"Tell me, Sabrina. How do you justify ripping a man's heart into shreds?"

"I tried to discourage Timothy."

One corner of his lips quirked upward as he moved toward her; a predator's smile as he moved in for the kill. Sabrina fought her instincts, resisted the urge to flee. She would not run from this man, not ever again. He paused inches from her, the heat of his body burning her in a way that shamed the sun shimmering all around them.

"You really are a lying little whore," Ian said, brushing the velvety petals of the rose upward across her cheek.

His words were thorns plunged deep into her heart. "Then why did you marry me, Tremayne? Why take a whore as a wife?"

"You suit me," he said, lowering the rose, brushing her neck with the petals, tracing the line of her collarbone through the blue silk of her gown, trailing the sweet fragrance.

"You like whores, is that it?"

"That's right. You always know what to expect with a whore, a nice even exchange of gold for favors."

Through her rising anger she felt a curious tingling deep in her belly as he flicked the pink petals across the tips of her breasts. He had a hunger in his eyes, the hunger of a man drawn to a woman he despises. She understood that hunger. She felt it for him.

More than vows spoken out of vengeance bound her to this man. More than a little girl's fantasy burned in her heart. They belonged to each other, as they had in countless lifetimes. Yet fate had taken a wrong turn in this, her lifetime; this man wanted only to hurt her. And he would. If she let him.

"Time to go home. Time to earn your keep, Sabrina. Time to spread those lovely pale thighs."

"Why wait?" She snatched the combs and pins from her hair, tossing them to the ground. With a shake of her head she sent the thick tresses tumbling around her shoulders.

"What are you doing?" he asked as she took his hand.

"Just what you want." She pressed her lips to his knuckles, then turned his palm upright, easing open his clenched fist. The rose lay across his palm, the green stem stained with his blood. She lifted the rose, the pink blossom bent and mutilated by his hate, dying, just as she was dying inside.

"As I recall," she said, allowing the rose to tumble to the ground between them, "I once interrupted one of your little trysts, right here, in this garden."

Ian frowned as she began unfastening his shirt. Holding his wary gaze, she slipped each button through the warm cloth with her slender fingers, scraping his skin with her fingernails.

"What game are you playing, Sabrina?"

If the man wanted a whore, she would give him one. And that was all she would give him. "You look nervous." She tugged the linen from his trousers and smoothed the warm wrinkles with her hands, sliding her palms over his hips. A muscle flashed in his cheek. "Afraid I'll bite?"

"I know you will."

"Come now, Yankee," she said, slipping her hands inside the parted linen of his shirt at his waist. "You aren't afraid of one little southern woman, are you?"

"If Lee had had more like you, we would all be whistling Dixie."

"I'll consider that a compliment." She slid her palms upward over his warm skin, traced the sleek ridges of his ribs with her fingertips, then spread her hands wide over the luxurious pelt of fur covering his chest, brushing the thick curve of muscles beneath. His muscles shifted under her hands, growing rigid, betraying the tension growing inside him.

Deep within her she felt a familiar tightening, a drawing on her muscles as heat flared. This might be his game, but she was going to change some of the rules, she thought. Slowly she skimmed the linen from his shoulders, absorbing the texture of his skin, smooth satin drawn taut over molded iron. He drew in a deep breath through his clenched teeth. She smiled and slid the shirt down his arms, allowing it to tumble to the ground.

Ian felt the gathering strength of her forces. He knew he should stop this farce now, before he lost the battle. She pressed her breasts against his chest in a slide of warm silk and firm flesh. He bit his lower lip as she pressed her open mouth against the base of his neck, swirling her tongue across his skin, brushing her fingers across the front placket of his trousers.

He felt his body respond, his blood pound in that part of him beneath her hand. She was taking control, yanking the reins from his hands. And yet he couldn't stop her. He wanted this. He wanted to claim the promise he felt in every erotic brush of her body against his. He wanted her, here, in the garden, with the sun on her naked skin.

He closed his eyes, trying to smooth the rough, uneven sound of his breathing, listening to the steady rustle of oak leaves in the breeze. Perfume swirled around him, roses and jasmine mingling into a blend more potent than wine, slipping past his defenses, intoxicating his senses with every breath he drew into his lungs.

He clenched his jaw as she lowered her lips to one dark male nipple, rolling the tiny bud between her teeth, coaxing sparks from the sensitive nub. He lifted his hands, stroking her arms, wanting to free the buttons running along the front of her gown, needing to feel her breasts in his hands. Yet she was sinking out of his grasp.

A groan crawled up his throat as she slid her cheek across the flesh throbbing for want of her. Then she touched him with her lips, exhaling against him, slow, hot, her heat scalding his skin, streaming into his blood. If she needed proof of her dominion, she had it; his hips rocked forward, pressing against her. He couldn't help it.

He was losing the battle, but it didn't matter. Not now. Not when she filled his every breath, not when she touched him this way. He had dreamed of her too long, hungered for her too long, to deny her.

He pulled her hair back from her face, watching her as she nuzzled him just above the bandage wrapped around his waist, touching him with her soft lips, flicking her tongue against his skin. She slipped the buttons in the front placket of his trousers through the warm wool, brushing him with her fingers, with the palm of her hand, releasing him to the heat of the sun, to the scalding touch of her hand.

She was woman in her essence, pure femininity, and so compelling he could scarcely breathe. With her hands against his skin, she slid the trousers and drawers from his hips, down the long length of his thighs. The breeze swirled across his flesh in eddies of fire. Slowly she pulled off his boots, his socks, then dragged the drawers and trousers from his legs, leaving him naked before her.

Kneeling before him, she lifted her eyes, her gaze roaming upward, devouring his flesh. He slipped his hands through her hair, cradling her head. She was so beautiful, this fallen angel, this witch, this woman who had stolen his soul. He felt as Adam must have felt facing Eve, aware of the coming destruction, helpless to prevent the fall.

Placing her hands on the backs of his thighs, she leaned forward, pressing her lips to the velvet tip of his arousal. Her hair lifted on the breeze, brushing the dark red silk across his thighs in a feathery caress. Clenching his teeth on a ragged moan, he tilted his head back, staring into the thick branches of the oak.

With her lips and tongue and teeth she tortured him, making him tremble and convulse under her silken touch. Dancing to her music, he rocked his hips to a primitive rhythm. Animal sounds tumbled from his throat as she drove him closer and closer to the edge of sanity.

"Sabrina," he whispered, his voice harsh from the tension throbbing inside him. He closed his hands around her shoulders, urging her to stand. He needed her now, needed to feel her sleek flesh close around him, needed to hear her soft cries of pleasure as he moved inside her.

She began to rise, flowing upward along his body, kissing him, stroking him with her hands, with her breasts, until he was choking on the fire rising within him. She lifted to meet him as he lowered his open mouth to hers. At last he had her in his arms, at last he could press himself against her, into her. Yet there had to be at least sixteen acres of silk and linen keeping him from what he wanted.

He grabbed her skirt with both hands, bunching the silk over her hips. She darted her tongue past his lips, wiggling against him, brushing his flesh with warm silk, pulling against his hips with her hands. He stepped back, the smooth stone of the bench hitting his calf.

He lifted her against him, clasping her where his pain flared. Nothing. He could feel nothing but silk and a mere suggestion of the woman beneath. "Wrap your legs around me," he muttered against her lips, seeking beneath the voluminous folds of her clothes for her thighs.

With her arms around his neck, she wrapped her legs around his waist, pressing her lush feminine heat flush against his belly. Ian sank back against the bench, her skirt billowing around him, the stone biting into his naked skin, but he felt only the pain pounding in his loins.

He pushed skirts and petticoats out of his way. He felt the soft brush of her drawers, found the moist slit and thrust inside, jolting the air from her lungs as he plunged his sword into the tight, quivering flesh of her sheath.

She sank her hands into the hair at his nape, holding him as she kissed him, nibbling his lips, plunging her tongue deep inside his mouth. Like an expert rider mounted atop an untamed stallion, she rode him, thrusting with her pelvis, meeting him as he lifted his hips, matching each slick stroke with her own furious rhythm, breaking him to her will.

The silk of her bodice slid against his bare chest. The soft linen of her drawers hugged his naked hips. The silken strands of her hair fell across his shoulders. She surrounded him.

He felt her pulsing all around him, tugging his flesh with that wondrous, luxurious feminine release, filling his senses with her tangy arousal. She tossed back her head and moaned, a long sweet shuddering sound that nearly sent him over the edge. He wanted to pour himself into her, to fill her, to plant his seed deep. Yet he wanted more. He wanted to brand her as his woman, his alone, his forever.

He ground his hips against her, pumping, pushing, pounding his straining length into her over and over, until he felt her fire flutter and flame once more, until she was clawing his back and bucking wildly on top of him. He could not contain it, not a second longer. She pulled the trigger and he exploded inside her, clasping her hips in his hands, holding her close, feeling her muscles convulse around him.

Lost deep inside her, he held her clasped to his chest, his cheek pressed to the soft cushion of her breasts, her hot puffs of breath scorching his shoulder. After a long while she took his earlobe between her teeth, squeezing until he moaned. "Did your whore perform to your satisfaction, Tremayne?"

Reality. It came cold and hard, impossible to escape. What he had thought was heaven was really hell. He released his breath in a long sigh against her shoulder. His arms trembled as he lifted her from his lap, avoiding her eyes, knowing he couldn't hide the emotions swirling inside him. She had won. And he was afraid more than the battle was lost.

He came to his feet, feeling pain sear his side, resisting the urge to touch the bandage around his waist, refusing to give her the satisfaction. And that wasn't the only place he felt pain.

"Looks like you're going to be sitting on pillows for a while," she said, pressing her finger against his backside. "You're scraped raw in places."

Ian turned, hiding his sore bottom, exposing the still stiff instrument of his own destruction to her amused gaze. Smiling, she leaned back on the bench, letting her knees fall wide to either side. With her skirts still bunched high around her waist she presented him a clear view of her feminine charms through the slit in her lacy drawers.

"Do you want to dip that a few more times until all the swelling goes down?"

Muttering an oath under his breath, he snatched his drawers from the ground. The woman really was acting like a whore. So this was her game, to show him this meant nothing to her, to prove he meant nothing to her. And the little witch had succeeded, better than she realized.

The time it took him to pull on his drawers and his trousers gave him a chance to compose his features. When he turned to face her he knew he wore an expressionless mask. She sat sprawled on the bench, watching him, smiling, her triumph glittering in her dark eyes.

From his pocket he withdrew a gold money clip. He pulled two hundred-dollar notes from the clip, then slipped them into the top of her bodice, brushing her breasts with the back of his fingers. "Nice performance. Women have been making money that way for centuries, Sabrina. I knew you would be good at it."

"You can buy anything with your precious money, can't you, Tremayne. Even a woman to warm your bed." Sabrina lifted the notes from her bodice and stared at them for a long while. "I never wanted your money. I don't want it now." She opened her fingers, allowing the notes to catch the breeze. They drifted on the current, catching in the roses, impaled on sharp thorns.

"You can't take anything else from me. My family is gone, my home."

She rose to her feet, smoothing her skirt, her hand pausing above the smear of blood his hand had left on the blue silk. "You might own my body, Tremayne, you—the man who fought to free the slaves," she said, lifting her eyes, her gaze seizing him. "But you will never own me. You will never touch me inside. Never again."

He watched her leave, her head held high and proud, sunlight stroking the fire of her hair. Words clawed at his throat, words of denial, words screaming of the emotions raging inside him. She reached the entrance.

He should say something. He had to tell her what was happening inside him. Without pausing, without glancing back at him, she left, her footsteps a steady march on the gravel.

He dropped back his head and fought the silent scream shrieking inside him. He wanted to call her back. He wanted . . . too much. More than he deserved.

Clouds were rolling in from the south, massive mountains of gray rising in thick bands toward the sun. A storm would rage by evening. He stood in the dying rays of the sun, cold, shivering, as though all the life were draining from him.

All the defenses he had built—he could feel them now, shuddering inside him. All his instincts merged with all his longing, solidifying into a single realization: He had been wrong about her. Sabrina had loved him. And he had murdered that love, killed it to preserve his pride.

He felt a fine trembling in his limbs, every muscle shaking as his defenses crumbled, caving in on him, smashing the last traces of his doubts. He should have trusted her. Lord, why hadn't he trusted her!

He closed his eyes, seeing Sabrina's image cast beside that of his brother, both staring at him with accusing eyes, eyes that had once looked upon him with love. Jon had never understood Ian's resentment, but he had tried to break through his barriers. And Jon had died because of it, because of him. And Sabrina. Ian had brought her nothing but pain.

He opened his eyes, staring down at the rose that lay broken at his feet. He knelt on one knee and lifted the rose, the blossom drooping, the neck of the stem twisted by his anger. "I wonder if you hate me as much as I do, Sabrina," he whispered, cradling the soft pink petals in his bloodstained palm.

*　　*　　*

Lightning flashed across the midnight sky in a steady march, the distant roar of thunder growing louder, like a battle drawing near. Sabrina stood beside the French doors leading to her balcony, staring into the black sky, fighting her demons. Rain ran in heavy sheets from the roof shielding the balcony, the wind whipping it against the panes of the doors.

"The war is over," she whispered. *The lightning isn't artillery. There is nothing to fear.* And yet . . . she couldn't stop the trembling inside her. She closed her eyes, the smell of damp earth invading her senses, wrenching images from the dark closet of her fear. Memories poured over her, drowning her. In her mind artillery shattered the darkness.

Stay or run? Had they dug their own graves?

Sabrina pressed her back against the wall, yet it was cold clay she felt against her spine. Night after night she had sat on her cot, with her back pressed against the cold Mississippi clay, listening to the explosions, wondering if the next one would hit their cave. Her fingers curled against the plaster behind her.

Buried alive! Dear God, please don't bury us alive.

Once she had given into the fear; she had run into the night, she had watched the shells fall from the sky like great shimmering stars. And her mother had come looking for her. Her mother had coaxed her back into that cave.

"We're safe here, darling. Please, please don't go out again. Please, Sabrina, stay with me."

Was it better to feel the hot slice of lead ripping through your body, or wait for the dirt to cave in around you?

It had never come; that shell that would bury them alive. Sabrina's fears had never come true. And yet they still tortured her.

A bright streak of light cut a jagged path through the black sky, a deep rumble shaking the air. A heartbeat later another sound pierced the darkness. Shouts. A man's shouts, low and muffled, as if he were struggling against some horrible enemy.

Ian!

Someone had broken in, someone who wanted to see Ian dead. Her bare feet were soundless against the thick carpet as she ran across her room. She threw open the connecting door leading to his room, ready to fight. Yet there was no intruder, at least none she could see.

Byron trotted toward her from his position beside the bed, nudging her hand, taking a few steps toward the bed, then coming back when she failed to follow him. The other dogs were standing beside the bed, staring at their master, as if they wanted to help the man who writhed upon the bed.

The room was cast in shadows, the gas jet beside Ian's bed burning behind a beveled crystal globe, a novel lying open, facedown beside the bed. Byron bumped her hand, nudging her until she was moving toward Ian.

The low flame cast a flickering light across Ian. He was naked except for the bandage that wrapped his waist; his restless movements had bunched the bed covers at the foot of the bed. His eyes were open, staring sightlessly into the canopy above his bed. He was shouting orders, his right arm raised as though he were brandishing an imaginary sword, fighting phantoms. Sabrina pressed her hand to her lips, watching him fight his demons.

The strange mingled roar of artillery, of screams, of moans filled Ian's ears. Such pain. Everywhere moans and screams. Lead tore past his head, ripping tender trees into pieces, slamming into the sixteen-year-old boy who fought beside him. All around men were falling armless, legless, headless; bits of flesh and blood whipped through the air, hitting his chest, his face.

Jon. Where was Jon?

Blood. So much blood; puddles of it on the rocks, soaking into the ground. The smell of it, so thick, faintly sweet, coupled forever with the stench of black powder.

He shouted to his men. The enemy had broken through their flank. The rebs were everywhere, that strange rebel yell shrieking in the air.

He felt a hand grab his arm. He turned, raising his saber. In the flash of artillery he saw her face. A woman! A woman here on the field. "Get down!" he shouted, grabbing her waist.

She shrieked as he snatched her into his arms. Cradling her against his chest he brought her down to the ground, rolling until she lay beneath him, until he could shield her with his body.

"Ian!" she shouted, pushing against his chest. "Ian, it's all right."

"They're coming. Straight over us!"

Smooth hands cupped his cheeks. "No one's coming. It's me, Sabrina. Ian, please, look at me."

Gentle words, a soft, calm voice slicing through the terror in his head. He blinked the moisture from his eyes, staring down into the face of the woman pinned beneath him.

The screams dimmed in his ears.

He heard the rain pounding against the windowpanes. He heard the ragged pants of his own breath. Gaslight flickered behind him, illuminating her features, catching fire in the cloud of hair laying in thick scarlet waves across his pillow. "Sabrina?"

"It's over, Ian," she said, her fingers sliding across his wet cheeks. "You're home. You're safe."

Fragments of the nightmare flashed in his mind. He stared down into her face, seeing pity in the depths of her dark eyes. Pity! "God," he muttered, rolling away from her.

He slid his legs over the side of the bed. He sat on the edge with no place to run. He wrapped his arms around his waist, trying to stop the trembling in his limbs. My God, she had seen him like this, seen the madness he had tried to bury. He squeezed his eyes shut, tears leaking from the corners of his eyes to scald his cheeks.

"Ian, it's all right. I understand," she whispered, resting her hand on his arm.

He curled away from her gentle touch. Inside he was shaking, and he knew she could feel it beneath that slender hand. His dogs were lying in a small cluster a few feet from the bed, looking at him with the concerned innocence of children. Dogs would love you no matter what, he thought, even if you were insane. "I suppose you think this is funny. A pirate who has nightmares."

He felt her hand hover just above his shoulder, the heat of her palm warming his skin, as if she wanted to touch him. Pity. God, he didn't want her pity.

"Sometimes the worst wounds don't show," she said, her hand touching his shoulder, just a graze of her fingers across his damp skin.

He stared at the book lying open on the carpet, the book he had hoped would distract his thoughts from Sabrina, from Jon, from all the memories he couldn't purge from his soul. She drew closer, the bed shifting beneath him as she moved, the warmth of her body radiating against his back.

"Sometimes I have nightmares too," she said softly. "There are times when I think the thunder and lightning is artillery fire. I haven't been able to sleep without a light since Vicksburg."

He dragged his hand over his face, wiping away the humiliating traces of his tears. "You were there during the siege?"

She was quiet a moment. "Were you part of it?"

He shook his head. "No. I was at Gettysburg," he said, grateful he hadn't been part of the terror she had suffered, even if it formed one part of his own nightmare.

"My brother Brendan was assigned to Vicksburg. Mother and I thought we'd be safe from the Yankees if we went there. We thought they couldn't take the city." She was quiet a moment, and when she spoke her voice cracked softly. "We were wrong."

He knew something of the siege. The city had been shelled day and night for more than a month. The citizens had burrowed into caves in the sides of hills to survive, while their supplies dwindled. Many resorted to eating horses, mules, even dogs to survive. And Sabrina had been in the middle of that hell.

"At first we stayed with friends in their house. Then, when the shelling became too fierce, we moved to a cave, three rooms dug into the side of a hill."

He looked at her over his shoulder. She was kneeling just behind him, looking as innocent as a little girl poised to say her prayers, her hands clasped against her knees, white linen and lace veiling the lush curves of her body.

She held his gaze a moment before lowering her eyes, gaslight betraying the unshed tears glittering there. He searched for words to comfort her. Yet he knew words alone couldn't touch the ragged wound inside her.

She bowed her head, her unbound hair tumbling over her shoulders in a cascade of scarlet silk that brushed his bare back. "Shooting stars—that's what the shells look like at night; they scream across the sky then explode, shaking the ground. You never know where they'll fall. You never know if you should hide in your safe little burrow or run into the open. I always feared . . . I was afraid of being buried alive." Her hands fluttered in her lap. "But nothing ever happened. So you see, it's foolish, foolish to have nightmares about something that never happened."

"No. It's not foolish." He hurt inside, ached with the need to comfort her, to love her. They had shared the horror, that baptism of blood and pain. The war had left scars upon her, just as it had left its mark on him.

Enemies. Friends. Lovers. Their past was entwined. They had been destined to meet, he was sure of it. Just as he was sure their future lay in each other. Perhaps together they could find a way to heal the wounds.

"Stay with me tonight."

She glanced up at him, her chin tilting with defiance. "Are you feeling lusty again?"

"No." He met her wary eyes with a steady gaze, lowering his defenses, allowing her to see just how much he needed her. "I'm feeling lonely again."

Lightning flashed, tossing silver light into the room. A heart-beat later thunder rattled the panes of glass in the windows. She glanced past his shoulder, staring at the darkness beyond the French doors leading to the balcony, shivering from something cold buried deep inside her.

He turned and slipped his arms around her. "Stay with me through the storm," he whispered, lowering her to the soft mattress. "Just let me hold you."

She turned, drawing up her knees, presenting him her back as he settled against her, and he held his breath. She lay tense in his embrace, like a doe trapped in a snare, but she made no move to escape him. Perhaps she needed this almost as much as he did.

He pulled the covers over them, shutting out the cold. He slipped his arm around her waist, snuggling against her, pressing his chest against her back, flowing into the curves of her body, the heat of her skin warming him through the smooth linen of her nightgown.

She was warm, soft everywhere, except the icy toes she pressed against his shins. Smiling, he rested his cheek on the pillow beside her head, breathing in the spice of her fragrance. He felt a familiar tightening low in his belly, a tingling of blood flooding his groin, and fought the rising tide of his desire.

Tonight this was all he would ask for: to hold her, to give comfort and receive his own in return. Perhaps then, in time, she would trust him once again.

For a long time he lay listening to her breathing, stroking her hair, willing her to relax in his hold. Outside the storm grew qui-et, the deep rumble fading into a steady patter of rain against the windowpanes.

In time he felt the change in her, felt her muscles soften, her breathing deepen. In time she shifted in her sleep, rolling toward him, slipping her arms around him, sliding her knee between his thighs. In time he knew the sweet torture of hold-ing the woman he loved and knowing there was a wall of hate planted between them, a wall he had erected by his own lack of trust.

"Someday, Brat," he whispered, pressing his lips against her temple. Someday he would find a way to win his lady fair.

Chapter Twenty-Two

An explosion ripped through Sabrina's consciousness. She sprang up in bed, clutching the sheet to her breasts, staring with wide eyes at the entrance to the room. Her father stood on the threshold, the door still quivering where it had hit the wall.

"Damn you, Tremayne!" Duncan shouted, storming into the room.

The dogs leapt to their feet at the sudden intrusion. Sensing Duncan's anger, Byron and Shakespeare took positions a few feet from the bed, growling, barking, the long black hair on Byron's back standing on end. Guinevere remained on her pillow by the hearth, staring at Duncan as though he were the devil come to claim her. Duncan froze a few feet into the room, glancing from the dogs back to the bed.

For the first time Sabrina noticed Ian sitting in bed beside her, his black hair tousled, falling over his brow, his chest bare, the sheet laying across his lap, exposing the curve of his naked hip. Ian ran his hands through his thick mane, forcing the waves from his brow, glancing with sleepy eyes from Sabrina to Duncan.

Memories of the night before tumbled through Sabrina's mind. There had been a storm . . . and Ian . . . he had held her through the night, with his body pressed against hers, hard, throbbing with need. And yet he had done nothing more than hold her . . . just as he had asked. And, somehow, that seemed far more intimate than if he had made love to her.

"Major, we couldn't stop him," Mac said, appearing behind Duncan. Ormsby stood beside Mac, his thin lips pulled into a taut line.

"It's all right," Ian said, frowning as his eyes focused on Duncan. With a sharp command he quieted the dogs. "You can leave us. Mr. O'Neill seems to have something he would like to discuss with me. And take the dogs with you."

After shepherding the dogs into the hall Ormsby dissolved from view, but Mac remained, staring at O'Neill like a bulldog defending his bone.

"Go on, Mac," Ian said, his gaze never leaving Duncan's face.

Mac cast one last look at Ian before marching down the hall.

"You kidnapped my daughter, Yankee," Duncan said, moving toward the bed, his movements stiff with rage. "And I demand satisfaction."

"I don't have any intention of fighting a duel with you."

"Coward!"

Ian's hand clenched on the white linen sheet. "If you weren't Sabrina's father, I swear . . ."

"Pistols or swords, Tremayne? Take your pick."

"Father, please," Sabrina said, slipping out of bed. She ran to her father, grabbing his arm, his muscles rigid beneath her hand. "Please, don't do this."

Duncan glanced down at his daughter. "I should have called him out the first time he dishonored you."

Sabrina shuddered, images of disaster flashing in her mind. One man would die. If she didn't put an end to this now, before both men were lost in this swelling storm of anger, she would one day watch one of them die by the other's hand. "Father, you can't duel with Ian."

"Like hell I can't!"

"Father, please."

Duncan shook his head. "I listened to you before, Brina. I listened to you when you said you'd handle the bastard. I listened because I knew how much you cared about that damn blue belly." He stared at Ian, the look in the dark brown depths of his eyes pure murder. "But the time has come for action."

"And what will you have me do, Father? Should I stand aside and watch as my father tries to make me a widow?"

Duncan grabbed Sabrina's shoulders, his fingers claws digging into her skin. "That man has caused you nothing but heartache since the first day he walked into your life."

"He's my husband." She rested her hands on Duncan's chest, her fingers curling against his light green waistcoat. "Please, don't do this."

Duncan cupped her face between his hands. "I can't stand to see you hurt again, Kitten."

"Then stop this now, before one of you is killed."

Duncan glanced at Ian, then looked at Sabrina. "He deserves to die."

"And what about you? What if he kills you?"

"He won't."

That old confidence. The same confidence that had led him to say the war would be over in weeks. The war that wouldn't end. Even now. "Father, please. Calm yourself; think about what you're doing."

"Brina, I . . ."

She rested her fingertips against his lips. "I couldn't stand it if either of you were hurt," she whispered. "Please, don't do this."

Duncan's eyes closed as he tilted his head back, his lips drawing into a taut line. After a long moment he looked down at her, his shoulders slumping in defeat. "I just want you to be happy."

She hugged him, pressing her cheek to his chest, fighting the tears threatening at the back of her eyes. "Why don't you go downstairs and have some breakfast? I'll join you directly."

Duncan patted the back of her head, as he had done when she was a little girl. "All right, Kitten." His arms tightened around her before he turned and left her alone with Ian.

She felt Ian's gaze on her but refused to meet his eyes, keeping her own eyes focused on the closed door. Too much; she had revealed far too much of her feelings for Tremayne already. The bed creaked softly. His footsteps were silent against the carpet, but she felt him approach, felt the warmth of his body pulse against her back, before his hand touched her shoulder.

"Sabrina, I'm . . ."

"Don't say anything, Tremayne," she said, pulling free of his warm hand.

She put a few feet of blue and ivory carpet between them before turning to face him. An image of those pagan gods gracing Henry Tremayne's hallway flashed in her mind. Yet cold marble shaped into classic male perfection paled compared to this masterpiece of golden flesh. He was magnificent, a Greek god returned to earth, all his power and beauty exposed to her worshipful eyes; a god who feasted on the hearts of mortal maids.

"If I weren't afraid of you killing my father, I would have encouraged him, I would have cheered as he faced you on the field of honor," she said, hiding behind her anger.

He frowned, a crease forming between his black brows. "Are you really that anxious to be rid of me?"

Sabrina lowered her gaze to the pelt of sable fur covering his wide chest. She hated him, hated the power he could wield over her will. "I'll dance on your grave, Tremayne."

"I don't believe you," he said, closing the distance between them.

"Your pride won't let you."

He placed his hands on her upper arms, his palms warming her skin below the lacy puffed sleeves of her nightgown. Sabrina forced her back to grow rigid.

He slipped his arms around her, drawing her to the flame of his body, scorching her skin through the white linen. She turned her head; his lips grazed her cheek. "Don't," she said, pushing on his chest to free herself, her voice humiliatingly husky.

"The war is over, Sabrina," he whispered, his arms tightening like steel bands around her waist. "Let me surrender."

Sabrina bit her lower lip. He cupped her buttock in his large hands, lifting her, pulling her closer until she could feel his desire growing long and thick against her belly, throbbing with life and promise.

"I want you, Sabrina," he whispered, his lips brushing her temple. "I need you."

The husky timbre of his voice vibrated against her need. His scent tingled her nostrils, and somewhere low, deep inside, her body tightened, like harp strings being stretched and tuned by the touch of a master. "Let go of me," she said, trying to shout, the meager supply of air in her lungs allowing no more than a shallow whisper.

He slid his fingers upward, along the column of her neck, tipping back her head, forcing her to meet his eyes. "I was a fool to ever let you go," he whispered, lowering his lips toward hers.

Moist breath, smoldering with his intriguing scent, brushed her cheek. She tried to turn away, to elude his kiss. His kisses always made her forget things, ordinary things, like who she was. He opened his hand against her cheek, his long fingers slipping into her hair, cradling her head, holding her prisoner for his assault.

Slowly, he slid the tip of his tongue along the seam of her lips, coaxing her to open to him. She resisted, pinching her lips together. With his teeth, he tugged on her lower lip, touching the smooth surfaces of her teeth with the tip of his tongue, running his hands up and down her back, molding her to the inviting planes of his body.

He moved his hips, drawing her in, pressing the thrilling pulse of his aroused flesh into her belly, pushing her away then pulling her near, over and over in an alluring rhythm, enticing her to join him in this mating dance.

Something was happening deep inside her, a slow melting of muscles, of bones. She leaned into him; she had no choice. She parted her lips beneath his, welcoming the slick invasion of his tongue. Answering the siren call of his body, she slipped her arms around his neck.

"Sabrina," he whispered against her lips.

She slipped her hand into his thick hair, her fingertips sliding sinuously through strands of cool silk. He trailed his fingers down her neck, a gentle brush of rough male skin that tingled down the length of her body. He was everything in her life, every joy, every sorrow. And she needed him, needed him more than she needed air to breathe.

Slowly he drew his hand over the lace inset below her chin. With her eyes closed, she imagined the dark masculine curve of his hand against the feminine white lace. She imagined his hands against her skin, gentle hands, strong hands, touching her as he had once, long ago, with love and tenderness. God help her, she wanted the lies.

Sabrina lifted into him, arching her back, feeling the heavy weight of his arousal press into her belly. He spread his hand wide, skimming the slope of her breast with his fingertips. He was warm, so very warm. Her blood pulsed in the peaks of her breasts, each surge screaming for his touch.

Ian kissed her face, each lovely curve and angle, the corners of her eyes, the tip of her nose, the high crescents of her cheeks, as lower he flicked open the pearl buttons lining the front of her gown. He wanted to show her how much he loved her. He wanted to surrender himself, his heart, his soul, his life to this woman.

He slipped the nightgown from her shoulders, letting it fall between them. The soft linen, still warm from her skin, brushed his chest, his belly, and drifted against his legs. He gazed at her, drawing his hands down the length of her arms, gripping her wrists. Morning light poured over the full curves of her breasts, the strawberry tips lifting with her indrawn breath, tempting him to taste her.

Pure need gripped his every muscle. The beast inside him demanded he plunge into her, devour her, quench the fires consuming him. Yet he resisted. There was much to heal between them.

He lifted her, filling his arms with her silken warmth. Her dark red hair spilled across the pillows as he lowered her to the white sheets. She reached for him. He came into her arms, sliding his arms around her, holding her, feeling the firm globes of her breasts press into his chest, the crisp curls crowning her thighs brush his swollen need.

He worshipped her, this angel he had once cast out of his life, stroking her skin, kissing her everywhere, tasting her, showing her how much he adored her. He settled between her pale white thighs, brushed his cheek across her mahogany curls, took her fragrance deep into his lungs. She cried out, arching her hips as he pressed his lips against the sensitive bud of her feminine flower.

With his tongue he dipped into her, tasting the warm nectar of her arousal. Sabrina whimpered. He drew his tongue back and forth over her soft petals. She arched and twisted as though the pleasure were pain, the same pain he felt pounding in his groin. He soothed her with his hands, sliding his palms along the taut muscles of her thighs, as he tried to calm his own desperate desire.

Beneath his lips he felt her blossom, felt her body unfurl in a delicious, trembling ecstasy. A cry escaped her lips, soft, startled, satisfying to his senses. She gripped his shoulders and arched against him in an ageless feminine demand, and Ian obeyed. He surged upward along the satin heat of her softly trembling body.

As he pressed his hardened flesh against her moist folds, he cradled her face in his hands. She had her eyes closed, shutting him out while her body welcomed him.

"I love you," he whispered, brushing his lips across her parted lips. "I've always loved . . ."

She sank her hands into his hair and pulled him to her, pressing her open mouth against his, cutting off his words. At the same time she thrust upward with her pelvis, claiming him, sheathing him with the smoldering heat of her tight, trembling flesh.

She came quickly to crisis, shuddering beneath him, moaning against his lips. Yet once would not satisfy him. He needed to give her more. And he did, over and over and over again he felt her shatter and shimmer around him, moving inside her, meeting her demands, enduring the exquisite torture of denying his own release, until she was screaming for him to follow her. Only then did he surrender completely, plunging into her pool of fire, dying in her flames.

He collapsed in her arms, resting his cheek against her shoulder, feeling the last tiny shudders ripple through her body. He didn't want to move, ever again. She was home, she was sustenance. Only with her was he whole. Only with her did he want to face the future.

She slid her open palm upward along the curve of his back. He smiled, nuzzling his cheek against the downy curve of her neck. She trailed her fingertips over his shoulder and into the hair at the nape of his neck. Never had he realized losing a war could be so rewarding, he thought, breathing in the warm musk of her skin, jasmine mingled with the pure essence of woman. Never before had he . . .

With one sharp jerk she pulled his head back, her fingers twisting his hair, until his scalp throbbed. "I hate you for this."

He stared down into her face, startled by the anger he saw burning in her dark eyes. She shifted beneath him, tugging on his hair, pushing on his chest, until he slid to her side. "You've made me a whore, Tremayne. Only a whore would enjoy having a man she despises between her legs."

He watched as she scrambled out of his bed, feeling her words slice into him. "You're not a whore."

She snatched her nightgown from the floor and turned to face him, pressing the linen to her breasts, her hair tumbling around her shoulders. "Changed your mind, Tremayne? Yesterday I was a whore, remember?"

"When you left me in the garden yesterday I . . ." He rubbed his hand over the back of his head, his scalp still stinging. "I realized I was wrong about you."

"Just like that?"

He nodded, knowing it sounded incredible, wishing he had said something last night, wondering if it would have made a difference. "This morning, when your father talked about what happened on the *Belle*, I . . ."

"You think you can manipulate me now. You think you can use my own feelings to enslave me." She stared straight into his eyes with all the emotion pulsing inside of her.

Ian felt the impact of her hate like a lead ball piercing his chest.

"I didn't find out about your father's cheating until the morning after I asked you to marry me."

"Liar!"

"Sabrina, believe me . . . ."

"I'll be the perfect hostess for your guests, the loving mother of your children, and a whore in your bed. But I will never again believe your lies."

The clock on the mantel ticked away the minutes, crashing with the rain pounding against the windows. "You're in my blood, Sabrina. And I'm in yours. We belong to one another."

She shook her head. "I hate you."

"I guess I'll have to change your mind."

"That won't happen. I'll never give you that power over me again."

"I don't want power over you, Sabrina. I just want you as my wife."

Sabrina turned and marched from the room, taking refuge in her bedroom, slamming the door between them. Did he expect her to believe he loved her? Did he really think she was that foolish? Yet a part of her still wanted to believe. A part of her still believed in fairy tales.

Foolish woman! Dangerous delusions! If she didn't find a way to guard against him, he would destroy her.

She bathed, barely taking time to enjoy the warm scented water. With Hannah's help, she dressed in a gown of green- and white-striped silk and pulled her hair into a soft chignon before leaving her room to join her father. He wasn't alone.

Duncan turned from the windows in the library as Sabrina entered. Caroline came to her feet. Lucy remained where she was, in a chair beside her mother, staring down at her clasped hands.

"I'm terribly sorry for what happened this morning," Caroline said, moving toward Sabrina in a soft swish of skirts and a delicate cloud of roses. "I made the mistake of telling your father about your marriage. He already knew where Ian lived."

"It's all right."

"That man is forcing you to stay with him," Duncan said, color rising in his cheeks. "I'll see the man dead. I swear, if . . . ."

"Father, I'm fine. Please don't . . . ."

"If you want to help Sabrina, you will change your attitude, Duncan O'Neill," Caroline said, staring up at the man as though he were a wayward schoolboy.

Duncan looked as though he intended to speak, then thought better of it. He turned toward the rain-splattered windows, pale gray light washing over him, revealing the lines of anger carved into his face.

Sabrina pressed her fingertips to her throbbing temples. She glanced at Lucy, noting the dark smudges beneath her cousin's eyes, feeling guilt wash over her once again. She had to find some way to help Lucy mend the breach with Timothy Reynolds.

"Darling, I've prepared a list of the people you need to invite to the party." Caroline handed Sabrina a folded sheet of champagne-colored parchment as she spoke.

Sabrina glanced down at the list, wondering how these Yankees would react to her masquerade. A ball was the last thing she wanted to think about, especially a ball filled with Yankees. Her gaze caught on one line, then lifted to her Aunt Caroline's. "You can't expect me to invite the Stricklands."

"It would be terrible form not to, darling."

"But that woman was my husband's mistress. That man hates Ian."

"Mistress?" Duncan asked, moving toward his daughter, raising one hand in a fist. "Has that Yankee got a mistress?"

"No," Sabrina said, surprised at how quickly she was willing to defend Ian. "She was once his mistress, but it was a long time ago."

"Sabrina, not to invite them would be admitting you know about Felicity and your husband," Caroline explained. "Believe me, not inviting them would be much worse than inviting them."

Sabrina folded the paper and met her Aunt Caroline's clear blue eyes. "You know best. I'll do whatever you think I should."

"Good girl," Caroline said, clasping her hands together. "There are a hundred things to be done, and we must start this morning."

Caroline glanced around the library, silently evaluating the mint green velvet hanging from the windows, the richly carved Empire sofa and chairs, each upholstered in the same mint velvet. "Of course, you really need to go to Europe to furnish this house."

"Good idea," Sabrina said, smiling at her aunt. "I could leave tomorrow and return in six years or so."

Caroline studied her niece a moment, her lips curving into a knowing smile. "Don't be frightened, darling. With Ian Tremayne on one side of you and me on the other, no one will dare cut you."

Sabrina had the horrible feeling Ian intended to throw her to the wolves. No matter what he said, she knew he wasn't done taking his revenge. He wouldn't be satisfied until she was broken into so many pieces, she could never fit them all together again. And if she weren't careful, she would give him the weapons he needed to do it.

"Good, I've caught you," Delia said, sweeping into the room, blue- and black-dotted silk billowing behind her, rustling like leaves in a breeze.

Ormsby followed her, announcing her arrival. With a slight arch of his thick white brows, he glanced at Delia, as much as to say he at least would observe proper decorum, before pivoting on his heel and marching from the room.

"I would have come yesterday, but I felt certain you needed time to settle in," Delia said, taking Sabrina's hand. "I had to be the first to welcome you to the family."

Sabrina had expected some reticence on the part of Ian's family. Delia's enthusiasm shocked her, as well as pleased her more than she had realized it would. "Thank you."

"When Ian told us I was shocked. We had almost given up hope of him ever marrying. Ian has all but turned into a hermit since the war."

From what she had seen of the man the only type of hermit he was turning into was a hermit intent on locking himself away with a harem, Sabrina thought.

"What a marvelous masquerade. I would have given anything to have seen Ian's face when he discovered the truth." Delia tossed back her lovely head and laughed. "Something worthy of myself."

Before Sabrina could respond Delia turned to face Duncan, demanding an introduction. Sabrina obliged, frowning when her father refused to give Delia more than a perfunctory smile, a slight twisting of the lips that looked painful.

"The resemblance is remarkable, although you hardly look old enough to be Sabrina's father." Delia smiled up at him, dimples peeking out at the corners of her mouth. "I would have guessed you to be her handsome brother."

That brought a smile to his lips. One thing about Delia, Sabrina decided, she could charm a bear, even if he had a thorn in his paw.

"We were just leaving, Delia," Caroline said, tugging on one of her blue linen gloves. "Would you care to join us? I'm afraid we will be shopping the whole of the morning and most of the afternoon."

Delia clasped her hands as if in prayer. "Now you really have found my weakness. I would love to join you."

Ian glanced up from the telegram he was holding as Elias Bainbridge entered his office. After greeting the man with a handshake Ian invited Bainbridge to take a seat.

"I was surprised to receive your note, Mr. Tremayne," Bainbridge said, sitting in one of the two brown leather armchairs in front of Ian's desk.

"I have a rather unusual request, Mr. Bainbridge," Ian said, leaning back in his chair.

Bainbridge pulled a small brown notebook from an inside pocket of his coat. He glanced across the desk at Ian, waiting for instructions.

"I want you to find a horse."

Bainbridge hesitated, his pencil poised on a blank sheet of his notebook. "A horse?"

Ian smiled. "That's right."

One copper-colored brow arched as he listened to Ian outline his request. After obtaining as many details as possible Bainbridge left, assuring Ian he would do his best.

Ian swiveled his chair toward the windows and stared out at Broadway, the pavement still wet from the morning rain, mingled sounds of people and horses and carriage wheels rising on the damp air. New Yorkers crowded the sidewalks, flowing along either side of the wide boulevard, jostling, bumping, surging from one side to the other, ladies holding their skirts above the puddles, men with heads bent, dodging carriages and trolley cars. All looking as though they were late for something important. He only prayed he wasn't too late for the most important thing in his life: Sabrina.

One mistake, one misunderstanding had led to another and another until they were Lee and Grant facing each other across a battlefield littered with wounded dreams. Yet the war was far from over.

She still cared for him. He had to believe she still cared. He had to believe there was a chance for them to find each other again. Otherwise he might as well be buried.

Chapter Twenty-Three

Sabrina left the dressing room where Lucy was being fitted for a new gown. Her cousin would look beautiful in that sapphire blue satin. Sabrina only prayed Tim would be at the party to see her. Somehow she had to find a way to bring them back together again. She would start by approaching Tremayne, even if she had to swallow her pride to get him to help. Even if she had to bed him. A curious thrill rushed through her veins at the thought. Lying with the man would hardly be a sacrifice. But it would be dangerous.

Sunlight poured through the small windowpanes at the front of Madame Duvalier's dress shop, flowing over a glass counter, shimmering against the crystal bottles littering the countertop. Threads of scent wafted from the bottles, perfume warmed by the sun, transforming the store into a summer garden filled with roses and lilies and jasmine and more. A salesclerk stood behind the counter, helping a small woman with blue hair select a scent.

How difficult would it be to get a job? Sabrina wondered. Could she change her name, apply to Duvalier, or Stewart, or someone? She wanted to show Tremayne she didn't need or want his money. But it was difficult to show your independence with fifty-two dollars to your name.

Sabrina hesitated beside one of the tables. Duvalier was the finest, the most expensive couturier in town, a fact reflected in the selection of material and accessories displayed throughout the store. Lady Julia had purchased one gown from the woman upon arriving in New York. One was all she could afford. Now she wished she had saved the money.

A bolt of emerald silk beckoned her, calling to her like a siren. She ran her hand over the lustrous material, imagining the feel of it hugging her shoulders, flowing around her legs in one of the madame's scrumptious confections.

"Yes, that would be perfect on you," Delia said, appearing at Sabrina's side. She glanced over her shoulder. "Don't you agree, Caroline?"

Caroline dropped the embroidered lace she was holding, allowing the wide band to tumble into the pool of lace on one of the other tables. "Have you found something?" she asked, moving toward the younger women.

"No, I don't . . ." Sabrina began.

"Look at this silk," Delia said, lifting one end of the emerald material, holding it up to Sabrina's chin. "Wouldn't it be divine on her?"

"Yes." Caroline tilted her head. "Yes, I think that would do nicely."

Sabrina shook her head. "I don't need another gown."

Delia gasped, as if Sabrina had just admitted to murder. "For my sake, please don't ever say that within hearing distance of Rand."

"Don't be ridiculous, Sabrina," Caroline said, keeping her voice to a harsh whisper. "You will not attend your own ball dressed in a gown people have already seen."

Sabrina felt heat rise in her cheeks. "I would rather not buy a gown right now." She didn't have the money to pay for one. And she wasn't about to use Tremayne's money. She would not be his kept woman.

Caroline gripped Sabrina's arm. "Darling, we have little time to prepare for this ball. You cannot delay."

"I . . ." Sabrina glanced down at the rich silk. "I can't afford to buy one right now."

"Do you mean to tell me Ian would begrudge you a new gown?" Delia pressed her hand to her heart. "I cannot believe it. Has he spent so much on that philanthropic nonsense of his that he cannot afford to buy you a gown?"

Sabrina's cheeks caught fire. "It isn't that. You don't understand." It was a matter of principle, a symbol of her independence. No matter how flimsy it might be.

"Have you found something?" Madame asked from behind Sabrina. "Oh, yes, with your coloring the emerald would be perfection."

"Well?" Caroline asked, her eyes speaking volumes.

Sabrina glanced back at the small dark-haired proprietress. "I'm afraid I'm just looking today, Madame."

Silence pressed in around Sabrina. The other women stared, their expressions ranging from mild surprise on the part of Duvalier to outrage by her Aunt Caroline to curiosity on the face of Delia. Sabrina wanted to turn and run, yet pride kept her rooted to the floor. Finally it was Delia who broke the silence. She ushered the madame away from Sabrina, pleading the need for assistance with choosing a few new gowns.

"You are being very foolish, young lady," Caroline said when they were alone. "You will make that young man of yours look a miser."

Sabrina drew a deep breath, forcing air past her tight throat. "I will not take his money." Ian Tremayne might do his best to make her feel like a whore, but she intended to show him she still had her pride.

That evening Ian stood in his study waiting for Sabrina. He was going to take her to the opera tonight, the theater tomorrow, the ballet the night after that. He was going to spoil her, to give her everything in his power, to erase the years of want and despair she had suffered. Maybe then he could chase away the terror still haunting her dreams. Maybe then he could win her love. Maybe then he, too, could bury his demons.

He took a thin, wide black velvet box from his coat pocket. Caroline Van Cortlandt had visited him at his office that afternoon. Apparently Sabrina refused to spend money on anything for herself. Diamonds and emeralds caught the gaslight as he opened the box, sparkling against the black velvet. He would just have to spend it for her.

He glanced up as the door opened. Duncan entered as though he owned the place, dressed in formal attire, looking entirely too pleased with himself.

He glanced at the black velvet box Ian held before lifting his gaze to Ian's face. "A gift for my daughter?" he asked, strolling to the liquor cabinet built into the wall near Ian's desk.

"That's right," Ian said, slipping the box into his pocket.

Smiling, Duncan turned from the cabinet, a decanter of brandy and a crystal snifter in his hands. "Care for a drop?"

"No, thank you," Ian said, resting his hip against the side of the sofa. "I'm glad to see you're making yourself at home."

Duncan poured a generous amount into the snifter before replacing the decanter in the cabinet. "Excellent," he said after taking a sip. "You have an excellent cellar."

The man was baiting him, tossing down a gauntlet every step of the way. "I'm glad you approve."

Duncan sat in the dark red leather chair behind Ian's desk and propped his feet on the smooth mahogany desktop. Anger prickled at the base of Ian's spine, threatening his cool reserve. Duncan wanted an altercation; he wanted to drive a permanent wedge between his daughter and her Yankee husband.

"You know it isn't going to work—all your gifts, your fancy house, the opera." Duncan sipped his brandy. "Once my daughter makes up her mind about something nothing will change it. And she's certain you're a scoundrel."

"I love your daughter."

Duncan issued a strangled laugh in the back of his throat. "You loved her enough to ruin her, to toss her away as though she were soiled linen." His eyes flashed angry fire as he stared at Ian. "She adored you. She was willing to fight me, her own flesh and blood, to make sure I didn't hurt you. And what did you do?"

"I made a mistake. A mistake I might not have made if you hadn't encouraged your daughter into your scheme for revenge. Did you think gambling on the river was a good life for her?"

Duncan slammed his glass on the desktop, spilling brandy across the sketches scattered on it. "You have no right to question me. Do you know what the Yankees left of my home, my family?"

"Did you think revenge would bring them back? Did you ever stop to think of what you were doing to Sabrina? What kind of future she would have on those riverboats?"

"Damn you!" Duncan said, rising to his feet. "I take care of my own."

"Maybe you just got too caught up in your own hatred to see what you were doing to her." Ian straightened as Duncan came around the desk. "What happens if you take her back to Mississippi?"

Duncan halted a foot from Ian, glaring at the younger man. "I won't let you destroy her."

Fighting the anger rising within him, Ian held Duncan's fierce glare. "I only want the chance to love her."

"Like hell you do! The only blue belly you can trust is one who's already in the grave."

"Dammit, O'Neill! The war is over."

"Like hell it is!"

Both men turned at a soft knock on the door.

"Come," Ian said, his voice quivering with barely contained rage.

Sabrina opened the door and paused on the threshold, her gaze shifting from Ian to her father and back again. Pale turquoise silk bared her smooth shoulders, wide ivory lace dripping from the modest round neckline, rising and falling with her every breath. Her dark burgundy hair was swept back from her face, held high at the crown of her head and allowed to tumble in thick coils down her back. She was devastating. Ian saw the confusion in her dark eyes, the flicker of pain as she stared at her father, and he swallowed his anger.

"You look beautiful, Kitten," Duncan said as he crossed the room.

Sabrina glanced at Ian as Duncan took her arm. "Father enjoys the opera, and it's been such a long time since he's been able to attend. I hope you don't mind if he comes with us."

"Of course he doesn't mind," Duncan said, patting Sabrina's hand. "There's plenty of room in that big box of his. Isn't there?"

Ian clenched his teeth as he moved toward Sabrina. He took her left arm and stared at Duncan over her head. "It will be a pleasure."

Jenny Lind had performed at the Natchez Methodist Church for one night in 1851. Sabrina had been there, sitting in the choir loft, watching, listening, falling in love with opera.

Ian had a private box, one of eighteen at the Academy of Music. They sat on satinwood chairs that were covered in scarlet velvet, nestled behind the scarlet velvet that draped the opening of the box, allowing the occupants to withdraw into privacy. Sabrina sat on the edge of her seat, watching the people stream into the big hall, magnificent gowns crowding into the aisles, jewels glittering in the gaslight.

She felt the hair on her arms tingle as the overture began, the long scarlet drapes drawing back from the proscenium arch, revealing the stage. In moments Sabrina was swept away in the music, in the drama of Faust.

The majority of the people holding boxes arrived late, just before intermission, and left early. When she remarked upon this Ian told her that most people came to the opera to be seen. For them, opera was no more than a pause between dinner and a ball.

Odd, to live with privilege and to take it for granted. Perhaps she had lived with too little for too long to understand these aristocratic Yankees. If she could, she would attend the opera or the ballet or the theater every night.

It was close to midnight by the time they arrived home. She walked the long hall toward her room, hearing her footsteps rap against the naked oak, mingling with Ian's steady tread. An intimate sound, the sound of husband and wife walking to their bed. Only this marriage was no more real than a story acted out on a stage.

Ian opened the door to her room and stood aside for her to enter. Her arm brushed his chest; the soft graze raised goose bumps along her arm. Her swift reaction to the rogue teased her anger. She wasn't even a challenge to the man. She never had been. One touch and she turned into a mindless animal, willing to surrender all self-respect for a few moments of ecstasy.

No more. She would no longer dance to his tune.

Gas jets burned on either side of the bed, creating a golden oasis in the big room, flickering across the white sheets. She paused a few feet from the bed, standing in the shadows, staring at the battlefield, marshaling her courage.

The door closed with a click. His footsteps crossed the bare floor, slow, steady, sure. The air stirred as he drew near, warmed by his skin, tinged with his scent. Anticipation rippled across her skin, tingling, prickling, damning. She drew a deep breath, trying to calm her racing pulse, and managed only to fill her senses with the tangy essence of his skin. She nearly jumped when his palms brushed her shoulders.

"You smell good," he whispered, his lips brushing the curve of her neck.

His soft breath swirled across her shoulder; a haunting tendril of heat curled around the base of her spine. He ran the tip of his tongue along the curve of her shoulder, his hands drifting upward over the turquoise silk covering her ribs, inching higher and higher, his fingers spreading, stroking her breasts, igniting fires in his wake. Pain mingled with swelling desire inside her. She reached for her anger, embracing it like a shield. Yet her shield was nothing more than smoke.

Molten gold flowed in her veins, flowing downward, collecting in the core of her femininity, melting her denials. God help her, she wanted him.

"Feel what you do to me," he said, his voice a husky whisper against her neck. He closed his hand around hers and led her to the front placket of his trousers. Beneath her palm she felt the steady throb of his desire. He moved his hips, slow and tantalizing, sliding heated wool against her hand, branding her with the rigid flesh beneath.

"Let me love you, Sabrina," he whispered, before nipping her earlobe. "Let me show you how much I love you."

Love. He made a mockery of the word. "Is it time to pay the devil his due?" she asked, moving away from him, seeking some sanctuary from his violent virility. "Let's see, where would you like me to spread my thighs, Tremayne? On the floor?"

"I think the floor is a little hard, even for me. But if you like the floor, we'll christen it just as soon as we get a carpet. You did order carpet, didn't you, love?"

She pivoted to face him. He was smiling, with his lips and his eyes. The effect was nearly fatal.

She snatched for her anger, clawing the scabs from painful memories. He had charmed her before, promised his love, pledged his devotion for the rest of his life. All an illusion. The man was a master of illusion.

"Would you like a bath? A nice, warm bath?"

"What's wrong, Tremayne? I'm not clean enough for you?"

"Clean enough, bright enough, witty enough. Enough woman to beguile me for the rest of my life."

Sabrina felt her chest tighten, her throat grow narrow with emotion. She had to swallow hard before she could find her voice. "I know the extent of your devotion, Tremayne."

"Do you?" He moved toward her.

Sabrina fought the urge to retreat. Not this time. This time she would meet him sword to sword. This time he would not defeat her.

"Do you know how much I love you?" He paused a foot in front of her, close but not touching, standing half in shadow, half in a pulsing golden light. "I've been looking for you all my life. You fill my dreams. You are my fantasy."

A breeze drifted in through the open French doors, ruffling the drapes, sweeping over her like a phantom's caress. Yet the man standing before her was real, far too real. The heat of his body surrounded her, beckoning her, coaxing her to turn traitor to her own cause. "Then why did you throw me away?"

"A mistake. A misunderstanding."

"No. I'm the one who made the mistake. I believed your lies."

"Sabrina," he whispered, brushing his fingers upward, along her jaw. "Give us another chance."

Sabrina slapped his hand aside. "Fool me once, shame on you. But I won't be fooled twice."

"Sabrina."

His single whisper held a wealth of longing. It reached inside her, stroked her own pain. So sincere. So tender. How did he manage to lie with such eloquence? She wanted to throw her arms around him, hold him, love him, believe all his lies. Great stars above, she really was a fool.

"You made it very clear what you wanted from this marriage." She began tugging off her elbow-length ivory gloves as she spoke. "You want someone to warm your bed, give you heirs. I won't stop you." She tossed her gloves to the foot of the bed. "You made it clear, I can't."

"I only said that out of self-defense."

"Is there anything special you would like this time?" she asked, pulling the combs from her hair, tossing them to the floor. "I'm still not completely tutored in the ways of a courtesan. But I'm sure I can learn."

"Don't do this, Sabrina."

She shook her head, allowing the thick waves to fall around her shoulders. "Do what? Give you what you want?"

"I want you. As my wife."

"You mean your lawfully wedded whore."

She ran her fingers over the placket in his trousers, then outward, stroking the long, throbbing length of him beneath the smooth black cloth. She felt her own arousal, a sweet flow of heat between her thighs. A sign of her own horrible weakness.

"Shall we get on with it?" she asked, managing to sound cold, as though they were about to transact business.

He was quiet a moment, holding her with his look. He seemed stripped of his defenses, his emotions laid bare, naked on his face, a soul-searching sadness stealing the haunting light from those beautiful green eyes. Her insides began to melt, her own defenses shuddering under this new attack.

"No. I don't think we shall."

He brushed his lips against hers before he turned. Without looking back, he opened the connecting door to his room and left her, closing the door behind him. Sabrina sagged against the bedpost, staring at the big empty bed.

She had won.

Or had she?

The man she had loved most of her life was within her grasp. Yet distanced. Shattered hopes and dreams were littered like jagged shards of glass between them.

With a ragged sigh, she turned and walked to the bathroom. A nice cold bath was just what she needed.

Chapter Twenty-Four

Ian studied the table a moment, trying to focus his attention on the colored balls resting against green felt, his concentration bruised by a gorgeous redhead. He should be home, he should be enjoying the sunset with his wife, not standing around a smoky room in the Union Club.

"It's been three days, Ian," Rand said, tapping the butt of his cue stick on the carpet. "And Harlem stock is still falling faster than a rock thrown from a cliff."

"It stabilized this afternoon," Ian said, glancing at his cousin. "Don't worry."

"Don't worry." Rand looked past Ian to where Tim sat on a brown leather armchair near the table. "We're about to lose a fortune and he tells me not to worry."

Tim sat with his legs stretched out in front of him, his long fingers wrapped around the full glass of bourbon that rested against his thigh. "Uncle Ian knows what he's doing."

Stocks, Ian knew. Women were the mystery. "The men who sold short aren't going to be able to gather enough shares to cover the sale. The price should start rising in the next few days."

With Duncan staying at their house, Ian hadn't had more than ten minutes alone with his wife in days. He didn't know how much longer he could go on like this, having her so close and yet not being able to touch her, really touch her. She had made it clear she would spread those ivory satin thighs for him any time he wanted. Yet he didn't want her that way. Not with a wall of hate keeping him from touching her, really touching her.

Raising his stick, Ian leaned over the table, entering the pool of light raining from the lamp suspended low over the table. He drew back the smooth satinwood cue, sent it forward into the cue ball, and watched. Soft clicks, dull thuds, one ball nudged another and another, white into red, red into yellow, yellow into green felt. Nothing dropped into a pocket.

"Thought you had the reputation for being quite a billiards player," Walter Strickland said from behind Ian. "Looks like your game is off."

Ian's hand tightened on his cue stick as he turned to face Strickland. "We all have our days."

"Wouldn't have anything to do with your wife?" Strickland smiled, his lips drawing back from even white teeth, reminding Ian of an animal who feeds on flesh. "Rumor has it all is not well in paradise."

Ian had heard some of the rumors concerning his marriage. He had felt the curious glances as he entered the Union Club, had caught shreds of conversations. It seemed people were speculating on everything from true devotion to blackmail. "I suppose you are an authority on that subject, Walter."

Walter's eyes narrowed as he held Ian's gaze. "I hear anyone holding Harlem is about to lose his shirt."

Ian resisted the urge to plant his fist in the center of Strickland's smiling face. "I imagine there will be a few men wishing they could get their hands on Harlem."

"I think most people will be able to cover their bets." Strickland turned and walked away, joining a group of men at the bar.

"Ian, what if the stock doesn't start to climb?" Rand asked.

Ian turned to meet his cousin's worried expression with a grin. "If it doesn't, then we lose a fortune."

Rand moaned and closed his eyes.

"There are worse things than losing a fortune."

Rand studied Ian a moment. "Such as being married to a lady who would like to slit your throat?"

Ian winced at the brutal truth in his cousin's words. "I think that qualifies."

"I'm never going to marry," Tim said.

Ian glanced over his shoulder, frowning as he looked at his nephew. Three days ago Sabrina had come to him, bending her pride to ask his help. It seemed he had been wrong about her, again. It was Lucy Van Cortlandt who had shattered Tim's young heart, not Sabrina. At Sabrina's request Ian had talked to Tim, trying to reconcile the two young people. Nothing he had said had helped.

"Here's to women," Tim said, raising his glass. "Put on this earth to drive a man insane."

Ian watched as Tim drained his glass of bourbon. The boy was hurting, probably as much as Lucy Van Cortlandt was hurting. "I've learned a valuable lesson, Tim. The most important thing in the world is to . . ."

Tim raised his hand. "Uncle Ian, no more lectures."

This wasn't the place or the time. Ian glanced down to the table. He wanted to go home, he wanted to see Sabrina, hold her, love her. Still, he wasn't in the mood to spend the evening watching Duncan and Sabrina play chess, as he had the past three nights.

Duncan O'Neill intended to do everything he could to destroy any chance Ian had of winning his lady. And Ian intended to fight him, and Sabrina. This was one war he couldn't afford to lose.

Gas jets hissed overhead, lighting the main hall of Ellen's house, flickering on the knights of Charlemagne marching across the wallpaper. Pain rippled from Ian's side, radiating in ever growing circles, like smooth water disturbed by a pebble. Tim hung heavily against his shoulder, his arm dangling around his neck, his hip bumping Ian's with each wobbly step he took.

"Why did we come here?"

Ian turned his head, trying to escape Tim's bourbon-soaked breath. The boy smelled like the floor of Flannery's bar. "Because you live here."

"Oh, yeah." Tim took a deep breath and began to sing loud enough to shake the globes in the gaselier above their heads.

"Quiet," Ian whispered, clapping his hand over Tim's mouth. "You want to wake your mother?"

Tim lifted his finger toward his lips, pressing it to Ian's hand, which still rested across his mouth. "Mustn't wake mother," he muttered against his uncle's palm.

The stairs stretched above them, a mountain to be conquered one step at a time. Ian started the long climb, bracing against the handrail, supporting Tim against his side, fighting the growing lethargy in his legs.

"I don't wanna go to bed," Tim shouted, pulling free of Ian. "I wanna sing! Let's have another drink." He teetered on the edge of the step, flapping his arms.

Ian grabbed Tim's shirtfront, hauling the young man against him, ramming his own back against the handrail, fighting wrenching pain from the wound in his side. He was getting too old for this, he thought, releasing his breath in a long sigh. "I think we . . ."

"Just what is going on?" Ellen demanded. She stood on the landing above them, gaslight glowing on her white satin dressing gown.

"Looks like we're in trouble," Tim mumbled, tossing his arm over Ian's shoulders.

With a sigh, Ellen descended the stairs. She took Tim's free arm and hauled it over her shoulder. Tim staggered between them as they climbed the stairs, singing, calling for another drink. After dumping him in his bed Ellen removed his shoes and threw a light blanket over him.

Ian pressed his hand to his side, trying to ease the dull throb of pain in his wound as he left Tim's room, preparing himself for the storm to come. Ellen closed the door and turned to face her brother.

"Ian Tremayne, why did you let this happen?" she demanded.

"He's a man, Ellen. Long beyond listening to his old uncle."

A lamp burned on the wall behind Ian, casting Ellen's face in flickering light, illuminating the anger carved into her features. "It's that woman; your wife."

"Sabrina isn't the reason Tim is miserable."

Ellen shook her head. "Oh, I suppose she had nothing to do with all this."

"I explained what happened."

"I know. You blame yourself for her actions."

"Ellen, I love Sabrina. I want her to be part of this family."

Ellen glanced away, refusing to hold his gaze. "And what about Tim?"

"He'll feel better as soon as he forgives Lucy for being loyal to her cousin."

Ellen drew a deep breath. "If she loved Tim, she would have told him."

Ian took her shoulders. "Ellen, Tim is a young man, a young man in love with a very dear young woman. If you want to see him happy, you'll help them get together."

She drew her teeth over her lower lip. "You don't think it's just an infatuation?"

"I think he needs to find out."

Ellen nodded, lowering her gaze to the yellow and white carpet beneath her feet. She leaned forward, resting her head against his chest. "Sometimes it's hard to think of him as being a man."

The scent of lavender rose from her skin, reminding him of all the times she had been there to help mend a scraped knee when he was a little boy. "You still haven't told me if you're coming to the party. Lucy will be there. I think it might give us a chance to bring them together."

Ellen pulled back in his arms. "You sound like a matchmaker."

"I suppose I do."

"Of course we'll be there. We wouldn't want people to think I don't approve of your bride."

"I had hoped you might visit her before the party, to give her some support. Delia has welcomed Sabrina like a sister."

"Of course. They're both cut from the same cloth."

Ian's hands tightened on her shoulders. "Sabrina is my wife. I would hope you could at least try to accept her."

Ellen looked up at him. "You trust her?"

"Right now I trust her to do everything she can to end this marriage." Ian dropped his hands and leaned back against the wall. "If I'm very lucky, I just might convince her to love me again." He glanced at his sister, a smile hovering on his lips. "I could use some help."

Ellen studied him a moment, a frown digging deep lines into her brow. "I can't promise to treat her like a sister, but I suppose I can at least be civil."

Ian laughed. "At least it's a start."

The drawing room down the hall from Sabrina's bedroom was the same as most of the rooms in the house—empty. Moonlight slanted through the three floor-length mullioned windows that faced the front drive, carving silvery squares on the oak-plank floor, casting phantom picture frames upon the bare walls. Sabrina leaned her back against the center window casement, her silhouette framed in shadows on the wall across the room.

Where was Tremayne? It was past midnight. If he were really having dinner with his nephew and cousin before spending the evening at the club, he would have been home by now. Delia had left hours ago to be home when Rand returned.

Tremayne had probably left Tim and Rand at the club. The liar was probably with one of his mistresses. At this very moment he was holding her, kissing her, sliding his hands along the curves of her body while he moved inside her.

Sabrina crossed her arms at her waist, trying to shut out the painful images flickering in her mind, staring out across the front drive. The macadamized surface reflected the moonlight like a smooth, curving river. Beyond the tall front gates, across Fifth Avenue, stretched the dark acres of Central Park. With a crowded city inching toward him, Ian had built his home where he would always have the park as a calm slice of the country. Yet he would never have peace at home. Not as long as he was married to her.

A warm breeze drifted through the partially open window, brushing her nightgown and robe against her legs. How long would he play this game? He could divorce her any time he pleased, toss her aside like a soiled piece of linen. And if they should have children, she wouldn't stand a chance of keeping them. She was no better than a slave. Still, Tremayne would find even a slave had dignity.

She stiffened, watching a horse and rider pass through the open front gates, emerging from the shadows into the moonlight. The golden horse was a pale apparition in the silvery light, the rider a dark specter from her past. An odd sensation gripped her as she stared down at him, time seeming to fold in on itself, and once again she felt touched by memories from a life she had never known.

Her blood surged, spreading a tingling excitement through her veins. Would he always be able to do this to her? she wondered, resting her hand over her heart. Would he always make her ache for all the things he had once promised her, all the lovely lies?

He was her enemy. Yet alone in her bed at night she found her thoughts drifting to the man who had once held her through a storm-ravaged night, to the man who could turn her blood to fire with one glance of his pale green eyes. After midnight it was often difficult to remember that he was a black-hearted pirate.

She followed him, hurrying from one window to the next, her shadow passing through the silver squares of light, as he took the bridle path leading to the stables. He looked tired, she thought, noting the way he rode with his shoulders hunched forward, one hand pressed to his side, as though his wound was troubling him. Had his mistress tired him? Had she . . .

Her thoughts died on a gasp as Ian's horse stumbled. A sharp whinny sliced through the night, penetrating the windowpanes. Caught unaware, Ian sailed over Cisco's lowered head. He soared through the shafts of moonlight streaming through the leaves of the elm tree, standing tall beside the path. His body jerked and his arms flew wide in a vain attempt to stop his forward plunge.

A moan filled Sabrina's ears as Ian hit the ground, the sound issuing from deep in her own throat. She pressed her fingers to her lips. "Get up," she whispered. Yet Ian remained motionless, a dark, twisted shape amid the shadows.

One thought raged with the pounding of her blood in her brain: He might be dead. A fall like that—with nothing to cushion the impact—he could have snapped his neck. "Dear God," she murmured, turning from the window. She ran from the room, her slippers slapping against the oak planks, the pale blue silk of her robe billowing behind her.

A warm breeze rushed against her face as she threw open the front doors. She darted across the drive, her feet sinking into damp grass as she ran toward the bridle path. A deep moan carried on the breeze, and Sabrina nearly wept with relief. At least he was alive. As she approached, he shifted in the shadows, struggling until he was sitting on the cedar chips lining the path.

"Ian," she whispered, sinking to her knees by his side. "Are you all right?"

With his hands cupped to his face, he leaned forward into a shaft of moonlight, resting his elbows on his thighs, a shuddering groan slipping from his lips. She braced her hand against his back, riding the steady rise and fall as he drew long, deep breaths.

"What happened?" he asked, looking at her with dazed eyes, like a little boy who has been thrown for the first time. Blood trickled from a gash above his right brow, streaming past his eye, down the curve of his cheek.

Sabrina felt his pain, a slow sting of agony that wrapped tightly around her heart. "Cisco stumbled," she whispered, touching his cheek, feeling the warm smear of his blood beneath her fingertips. "You were thrown."

Cisco stood a few feet away in the moonlight, holding one foot at an angle above the ground, his breathing rough and ragged through his mouth.

"Cisco," Ian murmured, rising to his feet. He swayed, reaching out for something to steady his sudden dizziness.

Sabrina came to her feet and grabbed his arm. She supported him as he closed the few feet that separated him from his horse, his body brushing her side with each wobbly step, a trace of lavender drifting from his coat, invading her nostrils. Lavender!

Sabrina's hand tightened on his arm. So, he really had been with another woman tonight, she thought. She sank her teeth into her lower lip. She wouldn't say anything. She wouldn't show this man how much he could hurt her. Never again.

Once they reached Cisco's side he sank to one knee in front of the horse. The horse sidled, bobbing his head, snorting loudly. "Easy," Ian whispered, stroking the stallion's chest.

Sabrina stood behind Ian with her arms crossed at her waist, watching him. She hated this, hated this need to keep a guard over her emotions. Who was she? Who was the woman who had held him in her arms, who had cushioned his muscular thighs? It didn't matter. It shouldn't matter. She wouldn't let it touch her. Except she couldn't stop the hurting. Dear God, if only she could stop the hurting.

Seemingly oblivious to the storm of her emotions, Ian continued speaking softly, calming the horse with assurances that everything was fine, as he examined the gash in Cisco's foreleg. "Thank God, his leg isn't broken."

Sabrina stared at that narrow slash just below Cisco's knee. "How would he cut his leg like that?"

Ian didn't answer. He stood and started walking the bridle path back toward the elm tree, moving carefully. Sabrina followed him. A few yards down the path Ian hesitated, then dropped to one knee on the cedar.

"This is how it happened," he said, plucking at a wire that stretched across the path.

The deep hum vibrating from the wire scraped along Sabrina's spine. She stared down at the slender piece of metal, the deadly strip barely visible in the pinpoints of moonlight streaming through the leaves overhead. Someone had anchored it a foot above the ground at the base of a tree beside the path, then stretched it across the path and tied it securely to a dark-colored stake. "That wasn't there when you rode out this evening."

Ian glanced up at her, his face catching a shaft of moonlight. "No. It was done some time after I left."

"Who?" Sabrina whispered, the possibilities churning in her brain.

"Someone who doesn't like me very much," he said, rising to his feet. "Someone who knew I would be returning home late. Someone who knew I would be on horseback."

Sabrina took a step back, slipping into the heavy shadows near the trunk of the tree. "My father didn't do this."

Ian stared into the shadows, as though he was trying to see her expression. The mellow tang of cedar swirled around them with the breeze. "You know him better than I do. If you think he didn't do this, then it's good enough for me."

"He didn't. He would never strike like this, like a coward in the night."

"No. Pistols at dawn are more your father's style," he said, pulling a handkerchief from his coat pocket. He began dabbing at the blood on his cheek as he continued. "Honor is something he lives and breathes. He built his life on codes of chivalry."

Sabrina felt a small measure of tension drain from her limbs. "You understand him well," she said, falling in beside him as Ian started walking down the path toward Cisco.

He glanced down at her. "Surprised I can understand the meaning of honor?"

"You might understand it, but you don't live by it."

With his hand on Cisco's bridle he began leading the horse toward the stable, which stood next to the carriage house at the end of the path. "You suppose that's why someone is trying to kill me? Because I have no honor?"

She was surprised the word didn't lodge in his throat. An honorable man did not force a woman to marry him. An honorable man did not swear his devotion to his wife and then jump into another woman's bed. So much for his words of love.

She didn't want to stay with him another minute. If she did, she would lose her temper. And if she lost her temper, she would end up revealing too much of her emotions. The man didn't need to know he could still hurt her. "I'll send someone for the police," she said, turning toward the house.

He grabbed her arm. "I don't want the police involved in this."

"But someone just tried to kill you. And it wasn't the first time. The next time you might not walk away."

"You're worried," he said, his lips curving into a smile. "That's a start, Brat."

Sabrina released her breath in a frustrated rush between her clenched teeth. She stared at the torn shoulder of his coat and fought to control her anger. "Don't change the subject. This man doesn't fight fair. He'll come at you again. You have to do something to stop him."

"I'll have Bainbridge look into the matter." He folded his bloody handkerchief and stuffed it into his coat pocket as he spoke.

"That's all?"

"Aside from digging a hole and hiding, I don't know what else I can do."

Sabrina cringed at the image his words conjured in her mind. "You need to tell the police."

Ian shook his head. "I don't want the police trampling around in my business."

She lifted her chin and stared straight into his eyes. "Afraid they'll discover you have a mistress?"

He stared down at her, moonlight revealing every nuance of his expression. She saw bewilderment in that handsome face and a flicker of wariness. Or was it guilt?

"What are you talking about?"

"Who was she, Tremayne?" she asked, glancing past him to where the stables rose in the moonlight, two stories of limestone fashioned into a small chateau. The elegant stables of a noble lord, a conquering knight, a man who took what he wanted and trampled anyone in his path. "Who were you with this evening? Felicity Strickland? Maybe her husband is tired of being made a fool. Is that what you're afraid the police will discover? I suppose I should be pleased. At least you haven't demanded I service you. I suppose she keeps you more than satisfied."

"I haven't been with another woman since the day I met you on the *Belle*."

"Liar," she said, lifting her eyes, her gaze striking his. "You smell like a spring garden. Apparently Felicity has a taste for lavender."

He smiled, as if he were enjoying her display of emotion. "If I smell like lavender, you have my sister to blame. I saw her this evening."

"Am I supposed to believe that?"

"It's the truth." He cupped her cheek in his warm palm and brushed his thumb over the full curve of her lower lip. "Sabrina, you are the only woman I want."

She slapped aside his hand. "You wouldn't know the truth if it jumped up and bit your nose."

"I know one thing in this life, one truth—we belong together."

He stood in the moonlight, looking down at her, blood smeared along one side of his face, hair tousled, looking so sincere, so utterly unhappy, that she felt her defenses shudder.

"But I'm not interested in playing any more games," he said. "The next time we make love will be after you are willing to admit you love me. Because I won't settle for anything less. I can't."

The smooth satin of her robe rippled in the breeze, sliding against her skin, lifting to brush his legs. "You are my enemy, Tremayne," she said, stepping back from him.

"No. I'm not your enemy, Sabrina. And one day, one day, I'll make you realize the truth."

More lies! When would they end? When he was in his grave? "If you don't do something to stop this man, you're not going to be around to prove anything to anyone."

He tilted his head, glancing down at the cedar chips beneath his feet, before meeting her eyes. "And here I thought you intended to dance on my grave," he said, his lips curving into a smile.

"I was angry." Sabrina glanced away from his perceptive eyes, staring at the open doors of the stable. "I don't want you dead, Tremayne. But that doesn't mean I want to live with you."

"Don't worry, Brat, I'm not going to let anyone make you my widow until I've had fifty or sixty years to show you just how good it feels to be my wife." Cisco bumped his arm and whickered softly. Ian turned away, leading the horse toward the stables.

Sabrina stared after him, a slight limp marring Ian's usual long, graceful stride, a panther with a bruised hip. Someone was trying to kill him. A world without Ian Tremayne—it was unthinkable. For years he had filled her life with hope, with love. For months he had filled her with vengeance. And now . . . could she believe in him?

She felt the ground crumble beneath her, like sand shifting in the advancing tide, drawing her toward the sea, toward surrender. She snatched for her anger, her pride, seeking a hold, knowing she was close to plunging headlong, fearing she would drown in her own emotions.

Chapter Twenty-Five

"I wish this wasn't necessary," Walter Strickland said as he settled into one of the two leather wing-backed chairs in front of the desk in Ian's study.

Ian had been expecting a visit from Walter for the past three days. Still, it was a visit he didn't expect to enjoy. "Would you like a drink?" he asked, opening the liquor cabinet.

"Yes."

"Brandy?"

Walter nodded. His hand shook as he took the snifter from Ian's hand. Ian noticed and wished he hadn't. He sat on the other side of the desk, watching Walter, waiting for the man to make the first move, wondering if he already had. Had Walter tried to kill him? First at Dunkeld, later here, on a darkened bridle path?

Walter drained his glass before looking across the desk at his host. "You know why I'm here."

Ian leaned back in his chair. "I have a pretty good idea."

"I underestimated you." Walter glanced down into his empty glass. He twisted the crystal in his hand, catching the sunlight streaming through the open doors behind the desk, hitting Ian's face with a bright shard of light. "I should have known better."

"You forced my hand."

Walter nodded, keeping his eyes focused on his glass. "Jealousy can make a man do some pretty stupid things."

"Women have a way of bringing out the best in men." Ian swirled the brandy in his glass, staring down at Guinevere, who lay on the carpet beside his chair. She glanced up at him as he spoke, soft brown eyes filled with affection. "They can also bring out the worst in us."

"Ian, I'm going to lay all my cards on the table," Walter said,

leaning forward in his chair, resting his forearms on his thighs.
"I . . ."

"I want a few words with you, Mr. Tremayne," Sabrina said,
storming into the study. She slammed the door behind her, rattling
a country landscape hanging in a gold frame on the wall, bringing
Guinevere to her feet.

Ian stared at the red-haired whirlwind sweeping toward him.
She was breathtaking in her fury, her cheeks stained scarlet, her
dark eyes flashing fire, her breasts rising and falling beneath
pale blue poplin with each angry breath. For a moment he forgot Walter sitting across from him, lost in her wild beauty.

"How dare you!" she shouted, planting her hands flat on his
desk. "If you . . ." Her words halted as she noticed Walter
Strickland sitting beside her. She straightened, lifting one slender hand to the base of her neck. "Oh, I didn't realize you had
company."

"Mrs. Tremayne," Walter said, coming to his feet.

"Nice to see you again, Mr. Strickland," Sabrina said, offering
her hand. "I hope you don't mind if I steal my husband for a few
moments."

Walter glanced at Ian as he took Sabrina's hand. "No, not
at all."

"Ian, dear," she said, walking toward the door leading to the
adjoining library.

Ian followed, searching his brain for the cause of her anger,
watching the sway of her skirt, feeling desire clutch at his loins.
It had been an eternity since he had held her.

Sabrina closed the library door and turned to face him. "How
dare you!" she said, keeping her voice a harsh whisper.

He stood in front of the jade marble hearth, looking at her in
a way that sent her heart careening against the wall of her chest.
"I'm not sure what you mean."

"Duvalier delivered that gown this afternoon." She marched
forward until she was less than a foot from him, tossing back
her head to stare into his eyes. "Did you think I'd embarrass you,
showing up at your party in one of my own gowns?"

Ian frowned. "Can't a man buy a gown for his wife?"

"I'll not be a kept woman."

"A kept . . . of all the cockeyed . . . You're my wife."

Sabrina shoved aside his words with her hands. "I don't need
your gowns." Great stars above, she couldn't believe she was

making such a fuss over a gown. But it was more than a gown. This man had scraped her emotions raw.

Her skin prickled all the time, as though she had stood naked in the sun, the way she had when she and Becky Sheridan had gone skinny-dipping in the pond behind Becky's house. Ten years old and sunburnt from head to toe. It had been difficult to explain. So was this. "I don't want your money, Tremayne."

"I know."

"I have gowns, fine gowns, gowns good enough for any of your Yankee friends."

She paced to the French windows and stared out at the garden. Hundreds of roses swayed in the warm summer breeze, blossoms of pink and yellow and white and red dancing to the whim of the wind. She felt nervous and restless. She hadn't slept through the night in weeks. The man invaded her dreams, coming to her bed, pressing the long length of his warm, muscular body against her, holding her, kissing her, loving her. And when she awoke and found herself alone, hugging a pillow and aching deep inside, it was all she could do to keep from running to him.

"I've been working days for this party. Though lord knows it won't matter." She hugged her arms to her waist. "Your friends want to eat me alive; that's the only reason they're coming."

"What's this? Is my beautiful rebel afraid of a few Yankees?"

"I'm not afraid," she shouted, glancing over her shoulder at the infuriating scoundrel.

"I think you are," he said, advancing toward her in slow, purposeful strides.

Sabrina turned to face him, forcing her back to grow rigid, fighting to hold her ground. She wasn't a coward. She wouldn't turn tail and run. She wouldn't!

He paused a few inches in front of her. "I think you're afraid of me."

Sabrina squeaked as he grabbed her waist. Just like a little mouse, she thought, pushing against his chest. "I am not afraid of you."

The sunlight streaming through the open French doors slid along the curve of his lazy pirate's smile. "I think you're afraid of this," he said, lowering his lips toward hers.

Sabrina pushed against his shoulders with clenched fists, fighting him, fighting her own need, as his lips whispered across hers. He held her with one arm around her waist. He cupped her head in one large hand when she tried to turn away from him, as he kissed her, as he slipped the tip of his tongue along the tight seam of her lips.

She wouldn't open to him. She wouldn't surrender to the demands of his mouth. She wouldn't welcome the slick invasion of his tongue. She wouldn't drown in the promise lingering in that kiss. Great stars above, he felt so good!

He was a spark to kindling. Heat flared inside her, hundreds of shimmering, pulsating flames springing to life. Each beat of her heart sent spurts of fire sprinting through her veins. Her fists opened on his shoulders. She slid her hands along the smooth white linen of his shirt, wanting to feel the warm velvet of his skin. She sank her hands into the thick hair at the nape of his neck, her fingers closing on the silky waves, locking them in her fists.

Ian growled deep in his throat, a primitive sound that whispered to that part of her that she couldn't tame. He slid his arms around her waist. She slid her arms around his shoulders. He held her close against him, yet not close enough. Not nearly close enough to satisfy the need pulsing inside her.

She wiggled against him, pressing her aching breasts against his hard chest. She needed more. She needed to feel the delicious friction of his flesh against hers, the rasp of crisp curls, the heat of smooth skin. She needed to feel his power throbbing deep inside her.

"Do you know what you do to me, Sabrina?" he whispered against her lips, the husky timbre of his voice sending shivers skimming across her breasts. He drew his hands down over her hips, bunching blue poplin in his hands, pulling her against the heat throbbing in his loins.

"I love you. I love you so much I ache." He pulled back, just far enough to look into her eyes. "I go to bed wanting you. I wake up wanting you."

His tender lies snapped the spell he had spun. All at once she remembered every reason for not believing this man, every reason for not surrendering her heart and soul once more. She turned her head as he tried to kiss her, pushing against his chest, his heart hammering against her palm, echoing the same dizzying rhythm as her own. His breath came quick and ragged against her cheek, hot and moist, conjuring images of him lying naked and warm in her arms. Her back stiffened.

"Any woman can ease that ache throbbing in your drawers," she said, her hand balling into a fist against his chest.

His chest rose and fell against her hand as he drew a ragged breath. She could feel his arms tremble before he released her. When she lifted her gaze to his face the raw pain she saw in his green eyes lashed her heart like a leather strap. She wondered at the effort it took him to force his lips into a smile.

"Would you like me better if I didn't get aroused by being near you? Would that show you how much I love you?" He lifted his arms at his sides. "What do you want, Sabrina? A eunuch?"

"I want to be free of you." She spun on her heel, brushing his chest with her shoulder as she marched toward the open door leading to the hall.

"I think you're afraid, Sabrina. Afraid of discovering your enemy is really your love."

Sabrina hesitated on the threshold, drawing a deep breath before she turned to face him. "I discovered the truth a long time ago. I discovered the man I loved, the man I trusted, was a lying scoundrel." She left, slamming the door behind her.

Liar! Scoundrel! Rogue! Closing her eyes, Sabrina sagged against the library door. He expected her to believe him again. He expected her to tumble into his arms.

And she wanted to.

Worse. Far worse. She was already starting to believe the lies, the lovely warm lies of love. Already she craved his touch, his strong arms, his kisses, his lovemaking. Already she was well along the road to destruction. Or was it salvation?

Someone cleared his throat, loud enough, deliberate enough, to break her reverie. Ormsby stood not more than ten feet away, with a guest. Sabrina pulled away from the door, her heart crawling into her throat, her gaze riveted on Ellen Reynolds.

The library door had been open during that entire battle. From the look in her green eyes, Sabrina had the sinking feeling the woman had heard everything.

"Mrs. Reynolds has come to see you, madame," Ormsby said, his voice calm and cool, a lifeline tossed out to Sabrina. "Should I have tea prepared?"

Dear Ormsby, always an island of calm within any storm. "Yes," Sabrina whispered.

"No," Ellen said, her voice colliding with Sabrina's.

Sabrina cringed. "Thank you, Ormsby."

Ormsby turned, his dark gaze grazing Ellen before he walked away from the two women.

Ellen attempted a smile. "I know you must be terribly busy this morning. I came only to . . ." she glanced to the ceiling, "to welcome you to the family."

Her words were even less convincing than her smile. "Thank you."

They stood for a moment, facing yet not looking at each other, unspoken words crackling between them. Sunlight seeped into the hall from open doors along the length of the hall, forming a checkered pattern of light and shadow against the red-veined white marble. Her Aunt Caroline's voice rolled down the mahogany-lined hall from the distant ballroom, soft, yet firm, giving orders like a general, preparing for the ball that would take place tomorrow night. The ball to prove to all of New York how happy the newlyweds were.

"Are you sure you wouldn't like something to drink? Tea? Lemonade?" Sabrina asked, breaking the uncomfortable silence.

Ellen shook her head. "I have to be honest with you. The only reason I'm here is because Ian asked me to come."

Sabrina's back stiffened. "And if it were up to you, you'd send this gold-digging rebel back to Dixie where she belongs."

Ellen's lips parted, then closed, before pulling into a tight line. "My brother is very dear to me. You came here to hurt him."

"I came here to deal him the same hand he dealt me."

Ellen's chin rose. "I don't know exactly what happened when you first met. I do know Ian blames himself for your actions."

"Yet you know better. You know your darling Ian could never have done anything dishonest."

"Ian doesn't have a dishonest bone in his body." Ellen moved toward Sabrina as she spoke, a tall, slender knight defending her brother's honor. "He's a fine gentleman. A wonderful man."

"Your brother proposed marriage only to seduce me into his bed. Is that your idea of an honorable man?"

"My brother would never do such a thing."

"Your brother is a scoundrel."

Ellen sucked air between her teeth. She was quiet a moment, holding Sabrina with an intense gaze, breathing like a boxer after going six rounds with his opponent. "As I said before, I don't know what happened between you and my brother. I do know Ian loves you very much. For that reason I am willing to accept you into this family."

Ian had told his sister he loved her. Hope surged in Sabrina's heart, ramming headlong into her doubts, threatening the last shreds of her defenses. To believe in him would mean surrendering her sword, laying her soul bare to Ian Tremayne. She couldn't do that. "I realize you may find this a shock, but this peasant has no desire to be a part of your royal family, Mrs. Reynolds."

"Yes, so I heard." Ellen pivoted, ivory linen swirling around her. Like a soldier on parade, she marched toward the main hall, pausing after going only a few feet. After hesitating a moment she turned to face Sabrina. "When I first met you I thought you would be ideal for my brother."

Ellen paused and Sabrina stiffened, waiting for the condemnation to follow.

"I know you won't believe this, but I still do think you are the woman for Ian." Ellen smiled. "I really do hope you can resolve your differences. He is a very special man. He deserves so much . . . I want to see him happy. And you are the woman who can do that. I feel it."

And Ian was the man who could destroy her. Sabrina hugged her arms to her waist, watching Ellen leave, doubts swirling in her head.

Guinevere was waiting near the door when Ian entered the study. Walter turned from the liquor cabinet, raising the brandy decanter. "I hope you don't mind."

"Not at all," Ian said, bending to rub Guinevere's head.

"Would you like some?" Walter asked, sloshing brandy into his glass.

Ian shook his head. Brandy wasn't going to make him feel any better. He sank to his chair behind the desk and waited for Walter to find his courage. Behind him the drapes fluttered in the breeze, a spicy-sweet scent of roses drifting into the room.

"I'm in a great deal of trouble," Walter said, closing the cabinet doors. He lifted his glass from the cabinet and returned to the chair in front of Ian's desk. "If I'm forced to stand by the shares I've contracted to deliver, I'll be ruined." He paused, staring into the brandy. "They'll send me to jail."

Ian studied him a moment, knowing what Walter would do if the situation were reversed. "That happens when you sell what you don't own."

Walter rubbed the crystal glass between his hands, staring into the swirling brandy. "I need your help."

Ian ran his hand over Guinevere's smooth head. The dog closed her eyes and lifted her nose to brush Ian's wrist. "You were hoping to ruin me."

Walter nodded, keeping his eyes focused on his brandy. "I thought Felicity might finally get you out of her blood if you were a broken man."

Another man destroyed by his love for a woman. What would his love for Sabrina do to him? Ian wondered. "How many shares have you promised?"

The glass grew still in Walter's hand. "Five hundred."

Ian released his breath through his teeth. "It opened this morning for two hundred and forty a share. Can you cover the cost?"

Walter nodded. "It'll hurt, but I can manage, if I can get my hands on the shares."

"I have the shares and the promise of what you intended to sell." Ian withdrew a book of checks from a top drawer of his desk. He leaned forward, handing the book to Walter. "Make out a check and I'll cancel your contract."

Walter stared at Ian, his eyes wide, confused. It took a moment before he set his glass on the desk and lifted a pen from the gold holder on the desk. As Walter filled out the check, Ian drafted a note canceling Walter's contract.

"Is that it?" Walter asked, handing the check to Ian.

Ian glanced at the amount, then shoved the check into the center drawer of his desk. "That's it."

"It seems I've underestimated you, again. I expected to be roasted for this."

"I'm not your enemy, Walter," Ian said, meeting Walter's eyes. "I never was."

Walter stared across the desk, his features molded by hate. In extending a helping hand he had trampled the man's pride. Ian felt the fine hairs rise at the nape of his neck. The man would try again. He wouldn't be satisfied until Ian had fallen flat on his face.

"How much do you stand to gain from this, Tremayne? A million? Two million?"

"If it's any consolation," Ian said, leaning back in his chair, scratching Guinevere behind one ear, "I would rather have had the merger pass than the money."

"It's not much of a consolation." Slowly, Walter rose from his chair. He left without a backward glance, his shoulders stiff, his head cocked at an aggressive angle, looking like a rooster ready for a fight.

Ian swiveled his chair toward the open doors behind his desk. Outside gardeners were cutting the grass, grooming the gardens for the party tomorrow night.

Walter had paid a high price for loving Felicity, a much higher price than the check sitting in Ian's drawer. He only wondered what price he was going to pay for loving Sabrina. His heart? His pride? His life? No matter the cost, he would pay it if it would only win her love.

Howard Nealey stared at the woman as she left his store. He hadn't been able to see much of her face past that black veil, and all that black lace and satin left him with little more than the suggestion of the feminine form beneath, but he had a good imagination. The dying rays of the sun pierced the windows near the door, shimmering on her hair. Yes, sir, he always had been partial to redheads.

"You think she really wants all that arsenic to kill rats?"

Howard glanced at his young clerk, smiling. "Now, lad, she's already a widow. What else would she be needing arsenic for?"

Chapter Twenty-Six

Sabrina glanced from the open book on her lap to the gold and crystal clock on the mantle. It was half past midnight. If she didn't get some rest, she would look like a hag tomorrow. Facing a pack of hostile Yankees was bad enough, but facing them with purple smudges under her eyes was worse. She closed the red leather-bound book and laid it along with five other identically bound journals on the table beside her chair: eighteen years in the life of Everett Jonathon Tremayne.

She had taken the journals from the library three days ago. Sabrina knew so very little about the man who had haunted her most of her life. She hoped the journals might give her a glimpse into the man she had married. And they had. Perhaps too well.

Entry after entry in the journals spoke of Jon, spoke of Everett's pride and hopes for his son's future. Yet few references were made of Ian. It was as if the man had only one son. It was not what she had expected to discover.

She glanced at the door connecting her room with Ian's. Was he asleep? As her mind formed the question, soft notes drifted into the room through the open French doors. The stars were crying, raining crystal tears upon the earth. Someone was playing the piano, the haunting melody lifting on the warm breeze, twisting around her.

As if in a trance, she followed the whisper of music, the notes echoing along the corridor outside her room, beckoning. Marble chilled her bare feet as she descended the stairs and followed the hall to the music room. At the entrance to the room she paused.

Ian sat in a shaft of moonlight, his fingers drifting over the keys of the piano, his melody streaming down her spine. His white shirt glowed in the moonlight. A breeze flowed in through the open

French doors, billowing the dark drapes, ruffling his thick mane, lapping the hem of her nightgown against her legs.

Safe in the shadows, Sabrina stood, his music spinning a sultry web around her. She had never before heard the melody. Yet it spoke to her like an ageless friend, stroking her pain, echoing the longing lingering deep inside her, linking her to the man who played in the moonlight.

Sensing her, Ian glanced up from the keys, his eyes piercing the shadows, finding her. He seemed of another place and time, another world, shadow and moonlight, power and grace. Sabrina's breath hovered in her throat. She resisted the urge to retreat. Only a coward retreated.

"I heard the music," she said, her voice husky in her own ears.

"I didn't mean to disturb you."

She wondered if he knew just how much he did disturb her. Byron left Ian's side, trotting toward her, his nails tapping on the oak parquet. "I didn't know you played," she said, bending to stroke Byron's fluffy head.

Ian slid the bench back from the piano. He rose, moonlight shimmering around him. "I suppose there are one or two things we don't know about one another."

There were times when he looked at her, when she felt he knew her better than anyone had ever known her, when she felt he knew her every secret, every hope, every dream. He had a way of making her feel vulnerable and safe all at the same time.

"Did Bainbridge have any news for you this afternoon?" She had wanted to ask him earlier, yet they had never been alone; her father had always been there, protecting her against the enemy.

Ian shook his head. "Nothing more than I already knew." He glanced at her, smiling. "There are a few people who don't like me."

She wondered how he remained so calm about all of this. It had been nearly a week since someone had stretched that wire across the bridle path. Each day he left the house she wondered if this would be the day the blackguard would strike again. She wanted to lock Ian in his room and post a guard at the door. Wouldn't he laugh if he knew *she* was thinking about keeping him captive.

"We spent a small fortune the past few days," she said, straightening. Byron trotted away from her, flopping on the floor beneath the windows, near the sprawled form of Shakespeare. "So don't be surprised when the bills arrive."

"You've done wonders with the place. It's actually starting to look like a home." He grinned, a wide boyish grin that tugged at her heart. "I kept meaning to furnish the house, but I just never got around to it."

"Aunt Caroline is the one who worked the miracle." She was learning things about this man. He was splendid at business, yet he often neglected simple things, like keeping his hair at a fashionable length. "This house—it's a copy of another, isn't it? One built in France."

He seemed startled by her question. "How did you know?"

She shrugged. "I'm not sure."

"I saw it when I was touring Europe the summer I got out of college."

An odd sensation crept along the column of her spine, like mist rising in the light of dawn. Memories drifted in her mind, memories she had never made. She saw Ian with his black hair tied back in a queue, his clothes the leather breeches and white linen shirt of another century.

"I knew before seeing it how the stone would rise to shape the walls and towers. I knew there would be a rose garden." He was quiet a moment, focusing on a distant point beyond her shoulder, as though he, too, were being drawn into misty memories. "And I felt . . . For some reason I felt as though I had lived in that house all my life."

They had lived in this house, she was certain of it, in some distant lifetime. She was also certain they had been happy then.

He shook his head, as though he were trying to clear it of memories. "I guess you think that's pretty strange."

"No." She understood, too well. She stood for a moment, a captive of his gaze, fighting the odd current of feeling wrapping around her, threatening to pull her into his arms. She should leave. Yet she didn't want to leave. She didn't want to return to that lonely bed. Not yet.

"Aunt Caroline is insistent that you go to Europe to furnish the house properly," she said, walking to the piano.

"When would you like to go?"

"Just like that?"

"We could visit the original. Would you like that?"

Something twisted deep inside her as she looked at him. Something good. Something disturbing. She let her fingers drift over the black and white keys, a Beethoven sonata filling the air. It had been a long time since she had played. Yet her fingers remembered the movements. "I suppose you would have to come along."

She heard his footsteps above the soft notes of the piano, slow, steady, moving toward her.

"Is my company so distasteful?"

"Yes," she said, wishing it were true. She felt him pause behind her, his warmth wrapping around her.

"I enjoy being with you, Sabrina," he said, running his hands lightly across her shoulders. "You belong here, in this house. You belong in my arms."

She continued playing. "You mean your bed, don't you, Tremayne?"

"I won't lie, Sabrina. I do want you in my bed," he said, slipping one arm around her waist. With his free hand he pulled back her unbound hair, exposing the curve of her neck. "I enjoy holding you."

Sabrina closed her eyes, feeling his warm breath stream across her shoulder. Memories flared inside her, memories of his breath against her breasts, her belly, her thighs.

"My hands long to caress you, to feel the warm satin of your skin," he said, sliding his hand upward, across her ribs. "My lips long to taste you, all of you. God, Sabrina, you have no idea how good you taste." He pressed his parted lips against the base of her neck, his damp mouth scalding her skin.

Sabrina's fingers paused against the keys. Her breath hovered in her throat as his hands inched upward, stroking her ribs. She should pull away, she should show him he meant nothing to her. Yet something kept her planted where she was, that undefinable power he could wield over her will. The breath she had been holding escaped in a soft rush between her lips as his thumbs brushed the underside of her breasts.

"Tell me you don't feel it too. Tell me you don't lie awake in your bed at night thinking of how good it would be to lie with me, to have my hands on your flesh, to feel my body sliding against yours, moving inside you."

"Lust," she whispered. "Nothing more than lust."

He spread his hand wide, his fingers curling around the curve of her breast. "Is it lust? A fire that burns swift and hot and dies as quickly as it rages out of control? Is that what burns between us?" He brushed his lips against her temple. "Or is it more? Is it a slow-burning flame that sears the soul? Were we destined to find each other, Sabrina? Were we destined to love each other?"

She drew a sharp breath as he stroked his fingers across the tip of her breast. "I didn't know you believed in fairy tales."

"I believe in this," he said, sliding his cheek against hers. He pressed his open palm against the curls at the joining of her thighs. "I believe in you and me, together. I need you, Sabrina."

The longing in his voice was too much like her own. Sabrina snatched for her anger, her pride, seeking a hold, knowing she was close to sinking into the sea of emotions swirling inside her, sinking right into his arms. If she surrendered now, she would surrender everything to this man. She couldn't! Yet her anger broke like a dried twig beneath her grasp, leaving her with nothing to keep her from plunging into disaster.

He insinuated his hand between her thighs, cupping her flesh through the soft cotton of her nightgown, his warm palm flush against her aching mound. "You want me, Sabrina," he whispered, flicking open the top button of her nightgown. "I can feel your need against my hand."

As if to prove his words, he pressed his fingers more fully against her. A warm wave of desire washed over her. Sabrina dropped her head back against his shoulder, allowing the current to take her.

He tilted his pelvis, pressing the hard ridge of his own need into her buttock as he flicked open tiny pearl buttons, as he made tight circles against the flesh that would gladly open all her secrets to him. "Let me hold you. Let me give myself to you."

Night after night he had haunted her. Night after night she had awakened with this horrible ache inside her, an ache only he could soothe.

"Let me love you."

She needed him. She wanted him. She would have him, at least in this small way. At least for tonight. "Yes."

"Sabrina," he whispered as softly as a prayer as he slipped one hand between his. She felt him free the buttons of his trousers, felt the luscious weight of him fall against the small of her back. She opened her eyes to the sight of his hands drawing back the folds of her nightgown. White cotton parted beneath his touch, exposing her breasts, the curve of her ribs, the dark shadow of her navel, and lower she saw the darker shadow of feminine curls.

"You're so very beautiful," he whispered, cupping her breasts in both hands, lifting them to the soft glow of moonlight, stroking his thumbs over the dark pink tips.

A low shuddering moan escaped her lips. She rotated her hips, brushing her buttock against his groin. He sucked air between his teeth and released it in a hot sigh against her shoulder.

Slowly he slid one hand down her chest, his fingers spread wide. Leaning against him, she watched as his dark fingers brushed back and forth across her pale skin, his hand sliding lower and lower, past the small cup of her navel until he was slipping into the dark curls below.

He rolled her nipple between his thumb and forefinger, squeezing while he slipped one finger into her. She gasped with the sudden surge of sensation shimmering inside her, spiraling upward and downward and sprinting in all directions. He moved his fingers against her, playing her, until his music filled her, until she was moaning and thrusting against his hand, until she thought she would die if she couldn't feel him inside her.

"Now," she whispered, turning in his embrace, like a puppet on strings, her movements strained with the tension rising inside her.

He clasped his hands around her waist and lifted her. The piano sang loudly as he sat her back against the keyboard. "My beautiful witch," he whispered, sliding his hands along her thighs wrapping her legs around his waist.

She slipped her arms around his shoulders, her skin sliding against warm white silk, holding him, needing to embrace every inch of him.

"My own sweet angel," he murmured against her lips.

He slid the tip of his tongue over her lips and she parted for him. Lower, she felt the delicious stretch of her body, a slow tingle, as he slid into her welcoming warmth. Sabrina arched against him, pressing her hands down on his shoulders, lifting her hips, possessing him fully. Ian leaned into her, his hands cradling the smooth curves of her bottom, holding her clasped against him for a long moment, as though he were absorbing her, pressing every detail of this moment into his memory. And then he began to move.

The music she had heard playing inside her sparkled around them as they moved together. It was a symphony to Sabrina's ears, the most beautiful music she had ever heard. The melody built slow and steady, ripples of notes gathering, expanding, the tempo growing faster and faster until it ended in one crashing crescendo.

Sabrina arched against him, crying out his name, holding him captive with her arms, with her legs, with every sinew of her body.

She felt him shudder, heard his deep moan as the last notes of music faded in the moonlight. She knew that it could never be like this with another man. Not in this lifetime. Not in a hundred more.

Ian stood with his face pressed to the curve of her neck, his soft hair cushioning her cheek. As her blood cooled, reality trickled into her brain. She became aware of the uncomfortable press of his fingers and the hard thrust of the piano keys against her buttock, the ridge of wood against her back. And, with an awful clarity, she realized the price she had paid for this rhapsody: her dignity, her pride, her soul. It was a high price to pay for lies.

She lifted her head, her gaze resting on Guinevere. The little dog was sitting in a shaft of moonlight near the open French doors, watching her. For days she had tried to win the little creature's trust. For days she had failed. Perhaps the dog was wiser than she was, Sabrina thought. She could learn from the dog's caution. It was wise not to give your trust to anyone.

Ian turned his face, brushing his lips against her skin just below her ear. "I don't think I've ever heard a more beautiful melody."

She could hear the smile in his voice, feel the curve of his lips against her skin. A victor's smile. She pushed against his shoulders, wanting to break free of his hold.

He glanced up, his green eyes silently questioning as he looked into her face.

"It hurts," she whispered. In more ways than she wanted to acknowledge.

"Sorry." He lifted her against him and turned, slipping away from her before setting her lightly on the floor.

"Please, don't," she whispered, turning her head when he touched her cheek.

"I love you, Sabrina. Please, don't turn away from me."

She couldn't stand this. She wasn't strong enough to survive his lies, not if she believed them. She walked to the French doors as she closed the buttons of her nightgown, her fingers trembling. She stared out into the rose garden, the warm evening breeze bathing her flushed cheeks. Behind her she heard the soft sounds of a man straightening his clothes.

"I wonder what brought about this change in you, Tremayne. Why did you decide to play this new game?"

He moved behind her, his warmth radiating against her back. "This isn't a game, Sabrina," he said, resting his hands on her shoulders.

She curled her shoulders away from him. Moonlight flirted with the garden, sprinkling silver light across the rosebushes. The cherubs in the fountain stood frozen in the light. No water bubbled. No sign of life. Just cold white marble. "What do you expect to gain from your lies? You can have me in your bed. You've proven that."

"I want more than just your beauty, Sabrina. More than your lovely legs wrapped around my waist."

"What do you want from me?"

"I want a real marriage, a home, a family."

He wanted to destroy her, destroy her with her own foolish longing. He wouldn't be satisfied until she was broken of will, a slave of body and spirit. Cool granite chilled her feet as she crossed the terrace. She grabbed the stone balustrade, trying to catch her sense of balance. "Keep your tender declarations, Tremayne. You waste them on me."

"You still love me, Sabrina."

"I did love you." Emotions crowded her chest, pressing against her lungs until she could scarcely draw a breath. "I loved you so much it hurt. For nine years I dreamed about you. You were my prince from a fairy tale." A single tear escaped her tight control. She slashed at the glistening droplet, loath to show him any weakness. "Foolish, isn't it?"

Ian moved toward her, his arms reaching for her. She pressed her hand against his chest, pushing, trying to deny him, to deny her own horrible longing. He hesitated, his arms dropping to his sides, his eyes searching hers.

"When we met on the *Belle* I thought it was destiny. After all those years of dreaming about you, there you were." She glanced away, unable to hold his gaze, ashamed of the pain she could no longer hide. "And you loved me, or so I imagined."

"I did love you, Sabrina. I do love you."

Sabrina shook her head. "You used me."

"Sabrina, you don't understand . . ."

"I was going to tell you what we'd been doing. I prayed you'd understand what drove us to seek revenge. I thought you'd understand how it felt to lose everything. But it didn't matter. It never mattered." The breeze slipped into his thick mane, brushing the ebony strands against the white silk of his open collar. "Because you were just playing a game."

Frowning, he shook his head. "I'm a man, Sabrina, not a prince from a fairy tale. I made a mistake. I can't promise I won't ever make another one. But it won't be like this." He reached for her. She stepped back. "We have to put the past behind us. We love each other. Our future is together."

"You destroyed any love I once had for you."

Ian stood a few feet away, his features carved white marble, his eyes glittering emeralds in the moonlight. "It's still there, deep inside, wounded but alive."

She turned away from those penetrating eyes. "What's wrong, Tremayne? Can't accept the fact that I've grown up? Does your pride ache to know at least one woman has managed to see you for the deceiving scoundrel you are?"

"Dammit, Sabrina!" He grabbed her shoulders and spun her around to face him. "I married you because I didn't want to let you go. I couldn't let you go again."

"You told me just how you felt the day you walked out of my life. You told me why you were marrying me on our wedding day. Why should I believe you now?"

He was quiet a moment, his hands burning into her skin, his eyes penetrating her soul. "Because you once told me you would give your heart to one man. I'm that man, Sabrina."

"No," she whispered, trying to break away from him.

"I know I've hurt you," he said, holding her with a gentle strength she couldn't resist. "I haven't escaped without a few wounds of my own, but it's time to mend. If you refuse to forgive, if you refuse to try to forge a life with me, you're throwing away our one chance to be whole."

Sabrina closed her eyes, shutting out the beauty of his eyes. She saw too much in those eyes, her own hopes, her own dreams, her own desperate longing. Was she seeing only what she wanted to see? "I don't trust you."

His hands tightened on her arms, then vanished, leaving a warm imprint against her flesh. "I guess I don't blame you."

Sabrina shivered in the warm night air.

"Let me prove it to you. Let me show you how much I love you."

She shook her head. She couldn't believe in him again. She couldn't. "I just want you to let me go."

"Is that what it will take, my love?" he asked, slipping his hands around her clenched fists. "Must I set you free to win your heart?"

The sincerity she saw in those glittering green depths shook her faith in his treachery. He was a worldly man, she reminded herself, capable of lies. She knew all too well how he could lie. "Yes."

He lifted her hands, his eyes closing as he pressed his lips to the knuckles of her clenched fists. He held her hands an eternity, his breath warming her skin.

"All right," he said, his voice barely lifting above the rustle of the leaves in the breeze. "Since I can't convince you of my love I'll let you go."

He might have slammed his fist into her chest. Never had she expected him to agree. "When?"

"I'll arrange passage for you and your father and Aggie back to Mississippi on Monday."

Her heart squeezed painfully as reality swept over her like a tidal wave. He was willing to let her go. Still, where would she find the strength to leave him?

"Is that what you want, Sabrina?"

She nodded, her voice deserting her. The breeze lifted a lock of her hair, the slender strands brushing his arm in a silent caress.

"All right, we'll play by your rules," he said, his hands drifting down her arms. Her skin tingled beneath the soft caress. "When you decide you want me come back to me. Because I'll be waiting, Sabrina." He lifted her hand and pressed his lips to the pulse throbbing wildly in her wrist.

She pulled her hand away from the flame of his kiss. "That won't happen, Tremayne."

"Won't it?"

Not trusting her voice, she shook her head.

"I hope you're wrong, my love. Because if you leave me forever, you leave me an empty shell. Living, without feeling. Existing on memories. Lost in shadows."

Sabrina swallowed hard, forcing back the tender words crawling up her throat. "I'm cold. I'm going to bed," she said, brushing past him.

"It won't be any warmer there," Ian whispered.

Chapter Twenty-Seven

Sabrina stared at her reflection in the mirror above the vanity in her bedroom. It wasn't the first time she had faced a pack of Yankees, she assured that frightened young woman in the mirror. Yet she couldn't quell the flock of savage butterflies swarming in her stomach.

Aggie moved behind her, her reflection marching across the mirror as she crossed the room, emerald silk fluttering across her arm. Frowning, Sabrina turned to face her. "I told you I wasn't wearing that gown."

Aggie didn't look at her. "It's a shame what the two of ye've been doin' te that poor young man," she said, laying the emerald silk across the burgundy counterpane.

Sabrina turned back to the mirror as Aggie moved toward her. Aggie had been staying at the same boardinghouse as Duncan. She had moved into Ian's house the day Sabrina's father had, and she hadn't stopped scolding Sabrina since. "Why, whatever are you talking about?"

Aggie grabbed the brush from the vanity. "Ye know darn well what I'm talkin' about," she said, dragging the brush through Sabrina's thick waves. "With himself tryin' te make amends, and yer pa followin' ye around as though ye were in need of a chaperone." She shook her head, clucking her tongue in disgust. "Ye should be ashamed of yeself, Brina."

Sabrina hadn't told Aggie Ian had agreed to let her leave. She hadn't told anyone, perhaps because she wasn't sure she wanted her freedom. "Has he got you in the palm of his hand now, Aggie?"

Aggie tugged on Sabrina's hair, gathering the silky strands in her thin hands. "I trust him, if that's what ye're askin'. Why, yer just as stubborn as that old mule MacDoughal. I'll tell ye, he and I have gone a few rounds since I came here."

"I think you like him."

"The devil ye say."

"If you pull any tighter, you'll stretch my eyes shut," Sabrina said, glaring at Aggie in the mirror.

"Yer eyes have been shut fer a long time, Brina."

Sabrina's lower lip jutted out until she looked like a spoiled child to her own eyes. "I can't believe you're siding with that Yankee over me."

Aggie shook her head. "I'm on yer side, child. I just want ye te give the man a chance. Ye're not goin' te be happy without him."

Sabrina glanced down at her hands, pressing her palms flat against the white vanity. She spread her fingers, staring at the simple gold band. Truth. It was sometimes difficult to face. But the truth was, she didn't want to leave Ian Tremayne. She wanted to give this marriage a chance.

"I've never known you te be a coward, Brina."

Did she have the courage to risk her heart once more? "How do I know he's really changed? He left me once after telling me the sweetest lies you could ever hope to hear."

"Was it all his fault? If he knew about the gamblin', then he had reason not te believe ye."

"How do I know he doesn't just want to see me humiliated? Maybe he just wants to feed his pride." Sabrina pressed her fingertips against the smooth wood, arching her fingers. "When he married me he told me he only wanted a . . . he wanted me in his bed. And now . . . now he says he loves me."

"I think he does, child. I think he's finally opened his eyes. I think he finally realizes the gem he has in his hand."

Perhaps he did regret abandoning her on board the *Belle*. Perhaps he did love her now. She drew a deep breath, shivering with her doubts. Could a pirate turn into a prince? Did she have a choice but to find out the truth? Sabrina glanced up, meeting Aggie's eyes in the mirror. "I think I will wear that gown, Aggie."

Aggie pressed her cheek against Sabrina's, her thin hands squeezing the younger woman's shoulders. "Ye're goin' te be all right, Brina."

Sabrina closed her eyes and drew a deep breath. "I hope so, Aggie." She hoped she could trust Ian Tremayne as much as she loved him.

After Aggie fashioned Sabrina's hair into soft coils at the nape of her neck she helped her into the gown Ian had chosen for her. A thin band of delicate, embroidered cream-colored lace edged the round neckline. One wide band of black silk emphasized her tightly cinched waist. Sheer emerald gauze, dusted with diamonds, formed the overskirt of the gown, sparkling in the gaslight, frosting the emerald silk below.

Hannah came to see how everything was going just as Aggie was fastening the last few buttons running down Sabrina's spine. "No man will be able to take his eyes from you tonight. Ah, Aggie, you did a fine job with her pretty hair," Hannah said, clasping her hands below her chin. "Lovely. How very lovely."

There was only one man she wanted to impress, one man she wanted to live with her whole life through. A man she prayed she could trust.

"The master will be proud," Hannah said, fussing with silk roses clustered at one shoulder of the gown. "Lord, but I'm happy for you two young people. I knew things would work out for the best. You're just what that young man has been needing."

But was Ian Tremayne what she needed? Sabrina left her room, needing to move, to walk off some of her anxiety. With critical eyes she surveyed the ballroom. Gaslight glittered against the cut crystal of six chandeliers, reflecting in twelve gilt-trimmed mirrors, shining on rosewood parquet polished to a glassy finish. White roses and mums stood in tall gold vases along each of the three refreshment tables; tall palms in porcelain pots sat in the corners of the room. The room, with its white paneled walls and gold and white chairs and sofas, might have graced Versailles.

Servants scurried everywhere, carrying trays of pastries and other refreshments. A unicorn sculpted in ice graced the center of the main refreshment table. Gold plates filled with chilled lobster, plump pink shrimp, caviar, fruits, chocolates, gold buckets filled with champagne, twin fountains each fashioned from gold, one flowing with pink lemonade, the other with white wine stretched the length of the table. They had spent Ian's money well.

Everything would soon be ready. Everything except the hostess. She turned away from the room, rubbing her damp palms together.

At the library Sabrina paused in the hall, watching Ian search through the leather-bound volumes on the far wall. Except for his coat he was dressed for the ball. Gaslight flickered overhead, shimmering on his hair, the once shaggy tresses neatly trimmed to graze the top of the collar of his crisp white shirt, inviting her fingers to trail through the silky strands. Before she knew what she was doing, she was entering the library.

"Have you seen my father's journals, Mac?" Ian asked without turning from the bookcase.

"I have them," Sabrina said.

Ian spun on his heel, facing her. His gaze touched her face before lowering to sweep the length of her figure. Although his look was not overtly suggestive, he triggered a pulse deep in her flesh. One glance and she came alive.

A smile lifted one corner of his lips as he met her eyes. "Thank you."

With one look he could make her feel as though she were the most desirable woman on the face of the earth. Sabrina glanced down to the tip of her emerald silk slipper, peeking out from beneath her gown. "I should be the one thanking you. It's a beautiful gown."

"Made all the more beautiful by you."

Like a tide of fire, her blush rose from her waist to the crown of her hair. "I hope you don't mind me reading the journals."

"I don't mind at all. I'm just a little surprised."

"I wanted to learn more about you," she said, moving toward him, aware of the candor of her admission.

Ian watched her approach, his emotions carefully veiled. "I doubt you'll learn much from my father's journals."

She paused a few feet from him. "You can learn by what isn't there, by what isn't said."

She glanced up at the portrait hanging over the hearth. Beside a tall gray stallion, a young man stood, one hand poised on the horse's shoulders, sunlight streaming over him, shining on thick golden hair. Dark blue eyes looked down at her from a face carved with strong, even features, his lips quirked into a gentle smile. "That's Jon, isn't it?"

"It was started the year we joined the army. The artist finished it after his death." Ian was quiet a moment, staring up at his brother's portrait, his eyes betraying the grief he still carried in his heart.

"You volunteered for dangerous assignments after he died, didn't you? It was then you became a spy."

Ian didn't look at her as he replied, "It was work that needed to be done."

Ian hadn't wanted to come home from that war. Sabrina knew it without having to hear him say the words. "He was a grown man, Ian. He made his own choices. It wasn't your fault he went to war. It wasn't your fault he didn't come home."

He glanced at her, seemingly startled by her words. He held her gaze a long while before glancing down at the carpet beneath his feet. "I'm not always sure that's true."

She wanted to go to him, to throw her arms around him, to tell him how very glad she was he had survived that war. Yet she couldn't move, torn between two terrible needs: the desire to give, to surrender heart and soul, to become one with lover and mate; and the instinct to protect, to shield heart and soul, to spurn the traitor of her love. Dear God, she wanted to trust him.

"Mrs. Van Cortlandt has arrived," Ormsby announced from the entrance of the room.

Sabrina glanced to the door, grateful for the interruption, the reprieve from decisions too soon to be made. "Aunt Caroline wanted to be here before anyone arrived."

"Wait," Ian said as she turned to leave. He moved to his coat, which lay across the back of one of the green velvet chairs. After pulling a black box from an inside pocket he moved toward her.

Sabrina watched him approach, trying to quiet the sudden surge of blood pounding through her veins, the excitement she felt at just being near him.

"I've had this for almost two weeks, but there never seemed to be a good moment to give it to you," he said, handing her the velvet box.

She stared down at the box for a moment before finding the courage to open it. Her fingers trembled as she lifted the lid. Glancing inside, her breath froze in her throat. "Great stars above," she whispered. And it seemed as though the box contained all the stars in heaven.

A necklace lay nestled against black velvet, a necklace more beautiful than any she had ever seen. A large marquis-cut diamond winked up at her from the center. Square-cut emeralds nestled against the center stone, then alternated with round diamonds to each end of the first tier. Diamonds formed a second tier of shimmering loops, a tear-shaped emerald dripping from a round diamond at each lacy swag. Three glittering half moons of diamonds cascaded from the center stone, ending in a large teardrop emerald.

Ian lifted the necklace, the gems catching the light, sending sparks of color in all directions. "Will you wear it?"

She nodded, closing her eyes as he draped the necklace around her, diamonds hugging the base of her neck, the last emerald teardrop dipping to just above the neckline of her bodice. His warm fingers brushed her skin as he closed the clasp.

"There you are," Caroline said as she entered the room, breaking the delicate spell.

Ian stood away from Sabrina as Caroline drew near. She looked from Sabrina to Ian, her eyes sparkling with understanding. "Turn around, Sabrina, let me have a look at you."

Sabrina obeyed, emerald silk flowing gracefully around her as she pirouetted.

"Charming, simply charming," Caroline said, clasping her hands to her chest. Her gaze lowered, catching the brilliance of diamonds. "And what is this?" She moved closer, critically examining the necklace.

Sabrina glanced over her aunt's shoulder to Ian. He stood watching her, a smile curving his lips. "A present from . . . my husband."

"Exquisite," Caroline declared, turning to face Ian. "You have an eye for beauty."

Ian grinned at Sabrina. "Yes, I do."

Caroline surveyed Ian critically, her gaze resting on the black waves curling above his collar. "I see you trimmed your hair."

Ian shoved one hand through his thick mane. "You wouldn't have anything to do with the barber who appeared on my doorstep this afternoon."

"I might have given him your address." Caroline smiled, glancing from Sabrina to Ian. "Now, come along. You don't want to be late for your own party."

The combined power of the Van Cortlandt and Tremayne families was too much for the elite of New York to resist. Six hundred people flowed into Ian's house to welcome his bride. Ian kept his arm firmly around Sabrina's waist, a very real symbol of his support, as they greeted their guests.

A few of the men who had once courted Julia greeted Sabrina coolly, but they couldn't withstand her charm. Soon she had even her most ardent critics smiling, laughing over the playful trick she had played on Ian. No one walked away from the beauty thinking of the trick she had also played on them.

A few of the women remained aloof, particularly those who had hoped to wed the very eligible Ian Tremayne. But New

York society had many southern ladies in its midst, ladies who had preached secession while their husbands had been trying to keep the union together. They immediately accepted her into the fold, admiring her courage in attempting so daring a masquerade.

Ian watched his wife whirl around the dance floor in the arms of Peter Warren, pride swelling in his heart warring with the jealousy coiling there. His southern lady had conquered the Yankees with her wit, her beauty, her enchanting smile. He was proud of his bride. Yet he resented every second she spent in another man's arms, every lovelorn look cast in her direction, every smile she gave away; there might be so few hours left in which to enjoy her smile.

"She's a great success," Delia said.

"Yes, she is." He glanced toward Sabrina, who was dancing a few feet away. As if she sensed his gaze, she turned her head, looking in his direction. Their eyes met, and his world narrowed and expanded, centering on Sabrina, everything else around him dissolving into a blur of color and noise. In her eyes he saw mirrored all of his dreams, all of his endless longing. All too soon her partner swept her away, breaking the tension throbbing between them, leaving him with more hope than he had known in years. Maybe, just maybe, his beautiful red-haired angel intended to stay.

"Does the poor woman know you married her only as a substitute for me?"

Ian dragged his gaze from his wife to glance down at Delia. She was staring at him, her lovely head at an angle, her full lips curved into the mere hint of a smile. He suspected Delia believed, or at least partly believed, that to be true. "Let's keep it our secret."

Delia followed, her movements lithe and effortless, as he led her through a series of dips and turns. "Your bride tells me she used to go hunting back in the woods of Mississippi. Maybe now Rand and I can get you to join us. You might even invite us to Dunkeld for a few days of hunting pheasant."

"You're welcome any time. But I've lost my interest in hunting." He had seen enough killing to last twelve lifetimes.

"You'll feel differently when you see the trophies we bring in from the fields."

"Maybe."

Ian glanced at Sabrina, remembering the warmth in her eyes. Tonight he would see if the war could be ended once and for all.

He couldn't let her walk out of his life. Not without showing her everything she was leaving behind.

"I was so worried about tonight," Lucy said, lifting a glass of lemonade from one of the refreshment tables. "I should have known you would be a great success."

Sabrina smiled. "I'm surprised no one asked what that terrible knocking was as I greeted them."

Lucy looked up at Sabrina with wide eyes. "What knocking?"

"My knees."

Lucy laughed, the bright sound mingling with the music flowing from the minstrels' gallery. "They weren't really."

Sabrina nodded. "I'm sure to have bruises tomorrow."

"You can handle . . ." Lucy hesitated, her smile slipping as her eyes focused on something behind Sabrina.

Sabrina glanced over her shoulder. Timothy Reynolds stood near the end of the refreshment table, talking with Alisa Rensellaer. As Sabrina watched, the little blonde laughed and tapped her lace-edged fan against his chest. Tim glanced in their direction, the look in his eyes telling Sabrina all she needed to know.

Sabrina had tried to approach Tim earlier, but he had walked away from her. Now she was beyond feeling empathy for the young man, she thought, turning to face Lucy. "I'm sure he's just trying to make you jealous."

Lucy glanced down at her lemonade. "I only wish he were."

"It's time to stop wearing your heart on your sleeve," Sabrina said, taking Lucy's glass. She set it on the table and took Lucy's arm. "The young man won't listen to reason, so maybe we need to stir his blood a little."

"What do you mean," Lucy asked, allowing Sabrina to lead her away from the table.

"I mean, I see a very nice young man standing alone by the edge of the dance floor, a Mr. Peter Warren. I'm sure he'll only be too delighted to dance with you."

"I don't feel much like dancing."

"And Timothy Reynolds knows that." Sabrina glanced down at her cousin. "You're going to be the belle of this ball. You're going to smile and laugh and have a marvelous time."

Lucy looked doubtful. "But I don't know how."

"Of course you do. Smile. We're going to see if Mr. Reynolds can swallow his own medicine."

Sabrina introduced Lucy to the tall, dark-haired young man, and as she had suspected, Peter immediately invited Lucy to dance. Sabrina turned, glancing at Tim, smiling as she saw the sudden intensity on his face. The young man would soon discover that this was war.

"Sabrina, darling, there's someone you really must meet," Caroline said, taking Sabrina's arm.

"Aunt Caroline, I can't right now. I need to . . ."

"You need to come with me," Caroline said, ushering Sabrina toward the main entrance of the ballroom.

Sabrina's breath thickened, strangling her throat as she looked down at her aunt. Her voice was barely a whisper when she spoke. "What is it? What's wrong?"

Caroline didn't reply until they were in the hall, walking away from the ballroom, their heels rapping in quick staccato against marble. "Your father is playing cards with your guests," she said, in a voice for Sabrina's ears alone.

"Great stars above!" Sabrina said, pressing her hand to the base of her neck.

"Stay calm, darling," Caroline said, steering Sabrina down the hall. "But get him out of there. He could ruin you."

Sabrina only prayed he hadn't already ruined everything.

Chapter Twenty-Eight

Sabrina paused on the threshold of the billiard room, her hands clenching into fists at her sides. Flames flickered behind crystal globes, the brass fixtures hanging on mahogany panels, the walls glowing a rich reddish gold in the gaslight. The billiard tables had yet to be purchased. Twelve round tables sat on the gray-green marble floor, each occupied by gentlemen wishing to escape the dancing for more adventurous sport. Each potential prey for her father.

Duncan sat at a table near the French doors leading to the terrace, a cigar clamped between his teeth, a stack of chips in front of him. Three other men sat with him at the table. As Sabrina approached, Duncan hauled in a pile of chips from the center of the table, his three companions groaning, remarking on his remarkable string of luck.

Duncan glanced at her, a silent question in his dark eyes. The other men at the table greeted her as she drew near, their warm smiles reminding her of how completely they had accepted her. She noticed their meager stacks of chips and fumed inside.

"Father, I must speak with you for a moment," Sabrina said, smiling down at him.

Duncan's eyes narrowed against the smoke curling from his cigar as he looked up at her. "I'm in the middle of a game, Brina."

"Gentlemen, would you mind terribly if I stole my father for just a few minutes?" she asked, bestowing upon the men her most beguiling smile.

"As long as you bring him back," Louis Remsen said, smiling up at Sabrina. "We can't let him walk away without a good run at trying to break his luck."

"Oh, I'll bring him back," Sabrina said, placing her hand on

Duncan's shoulder. "And I have a feeling your luck is about to change."

Sabrina welcomed the cool air against her warm cheeks as she stepped onto the terrace. Music flowed from the ballroom, filling the gardens with the soothing strains of a waltz, the melody failing to calm the anger roiling inside her. Her gown swished softly, silk against satin petticoats, as she led the way into the shadows at the far end of the terrace.

"I was cleaning their closets, Kitten," Duncan said, once they were out of hearing range of the card room.

Sabrina raised her finger to her lips. "Keep your voice down," she said, glancing around the terrace. The drapes of the music room fluttered with the breeze, gaslight streaming through the open French doors to splash across the terrace. She wondered if anyone was in that room.

"Just what was so important you needed to drag me away from the table?" Duncan demanded, keeping his voice just above a whisper.

"Father, those men are our guests."

Moonlight filtered through the leaves of the sycamore near the terrace, drawing silvery ribbons across his face. "Humph! Those men are your Yankee husband's guests."

"My guests! These people have accepted me, and . . ."

"Why the devil do you care if a pack of jackals accepts you?" He studied her face, his own pulling into sharp lines of anger. "It's that Yankee. You're still under the man's spell."

Sabrina turned away from his hate, moving to the balustrade, resting her hands on the cool granite. "I still love him, Father."

"Dammit, Sabrina! The man wants to hurt you."

Sabrina drew a deep breath, the sweet scent of freshly cut grass rushing past her nostrils. "I don't think so. Not now."

Duncan's footsteps fell heavily upon the granite terrace and his arm brushed her shoulder as he stood beside her. "The man is a devil. Once he knows how much you care for him, he'll destroy you."

"You don't understand." She turned, looking up at him. "Without him, I'm dead inside. I exist, I breathe, I eat, I wander through the day. But I'm not alive. Not without him."

He grabbed her upper arms, his fingers biting into her flesh. "You haven't given yourself a chance to get over him."

She shook her head. "You haven't given yourself a chance to accept him."

"Never," he said, dropping his hands to his sides. "I would rather see him dead."

"Father, please," she said, reaching for his arm.

Duncan stepped back, away from her pleading hand. "What will you do when he throws you out? How long do you think you'll interest him when he knows he has you in the palm of his hand?"

Doubts fluttered in her heart, doubts she was trying hard to bury. "He says he loves me."

"He's a liar."

Ian Tremayne had lied to her so many times, she wasn't sure what to believe. Yet she wanted to believe him. She wanted to believe he had changed. "Father, please understand that I have to try. I have to find out if we can make a real marriage."

"If you live with that Yankee, you do it without my blessing."

She grabbed his coat sleeve as he turned to leave. "Father, please. Don't make me choose between my father and my husband."

He stared at her, his eyes chunks of ebony set in a face molded from hate. "You already have, Brina."

Sabrina stumbled back against the balustrade as Duncan marched away from her. She lifted her hand to her lips, fighting the urge to call to him. It would do no good. He would accept nothing but her complete withdrawal from her husband. And that she couldn't give him, not while there was a chance to make a life with Ian.

She turned, staring out across the lawn, tears blurring her vision, conjuring images of her home as it once had been: Rosebriar, full of laughter, of hopes, of love. Her hands tightened against the granite.

They couldn't go back. The past needed to be laid to rest, but could she trust the man she loved?

Caroline stood near the open French doors of the music room, listening to Duncan's footsteps, his heels slamming against the granite terrace. She had heard part of his argument with Sabrina, the loud, angry words he had not tried to contain. She only prayed the argument hadn't carried to the adjoining drawing room, where people from the ball might have overheard.

She stepped onto the terrace as he drew near, blocking his way. He halted a few feet from her, staring at her as though he had half a mind to run her over. "We have a few things to discuss," she said, taking his arm.

"Do we?" he asked, refusing to budge as she tried to usher him into the room.

"Duncan O'Neill, you can give me a few minutes."

He was quiet for a moment, the muscles in his face taut as he held her gaze. "All right."

Once inside she closed the French doors, hesitating just a moment before turning to face him.

"What is it, Carrie?"

He had shaved his face, leaving a neat fringe of hair above his lip. It made him look young, and very rakish. Just as she had remembered him. "How dare you try to separate those two young people?" she said, moving toward him, trying to smother the excitement smoldering in her veins. "And don't try to tell me you haven't. I saw you just now. I heard everything."

"I won't stand by and watch that Yankee hurt my little girl. I did it once. I'm not about to do it again."

Caroline paused a few inches in front of him, tilting her head back to look into his eyes, standing so close she could feel his warm breath against her face. "Do you know she loves him?"

"She'll get over him."

"Do you know he loves her?"

Duncan sniffed loudly. "So he's got you convinced, has he? I seem to recall another Yankee that had you convinced."

Was he still holding that grudge? Did he still care? "My husband has nothing to do with this."

"Tell me, did you ever have any regrets? Ever wonder what it would have been like if you had accepted me instead of Templeton Van Cortlandt?"

Caroline lowered her gaze to his shoulder. Too many times she had thought of the wild young man she had left behind. Too many times she had wondered what it would have been like to lie once more in his arms. "You consoled yourself quickly enough."

"Only after you agreed to marry that rich Yankee."

"I was young. I wanted more than Natchez could give me."

"More than I could give you."

She moved away, feeling her armor crumple under his steady attack. "You were happy with Rachel."

"Rachel was a wonderful woman. Beautiful, gentle. Not at all the spirited hellcat her younger sister was."

Caroline rested her hand on the back of a Queen Anne chair near the hearth, one of the many things she and Sabrina had purchased in the past few days. With the tip of her finger, she traced the red wool stitches in the crewelwork that formed a red rose on the top of the chair. Nice things, beautiful clothes, power, wealth. These had all meant a great deal to her at one time. Too much. "How do you think I felt every time I saw you with her?"

"I don't know. How did you feel?"

As though she were dying. As though she were shattering into a thousand pieces. "Can't we let the past rest?"

He was quiet. She could feel him watching her, and she tried desperately to repair the facade of cool elegance that had served her for so many years. She was too old to feel these dreadful emotions, this churning of heart and soul.

"You're still one of the most confounded women I have ever met. Beautiful, spirited, high-handed, and damn stubborn. In many ways Sabrina is more your daughter than she ever was Rachel's."

"I love her like my own." And it was more because Sabrina was Duncan's daughter, not her sister's child. A terrible thing to admit. Wicked. Shameful. True. "You are going to cause her harm, Duncan O'Neill." She turned to face him. "If you love her, let her find her own way."

His lips tightened into a grim line. "Like you did, Carrie?"

She looked into his eyes, this man who had held her, had loved her, had taught her what it meant to be a woman. This man she had left behind, along with her heart. "Aren't we old enough to forgive each other?" *Are we too old to start again?*

He moved toward her, love and anger colliding with an ancient longing in his eyes. With both hands, he cupped her face, lifting her for his kiss.

Caroline opened to him, curling her hands against his arms, tasting him again after an eternity. Long-smoldering embers flickered into flames deep inside her. She was sixteen again, standing in her mother's rose garden with the most handsome man in Adams County. Lord, how she had missed him.

"I never stopped," he whispered, his voice strained with emotion. "Never."

Neither had she. Caroline sagged against the chair as Duncan walked toward the door. "Sabrina?"

"I'll do anything I can to convince her to leave that Yankee bastard."

Caroline knew there was little she could do to stop him, but she was going to try, for both Sabrina's happiness and her own.

*   *   *

Ian moved through the ballroom like a panther after prey. Half the evening was gone and he had danced only once with his bride. Where the devil was she? The last time he had seen her she was dancing with Colin Reed. As he glanced around the room, he noticed Colin on the dance floor, leading Lucy Van Cortlandt through the steps of a mazurka.

"Look at her," Tim said from behind Ian.

Ian turned to face his nephew. Tim's fair hair was parted in ridges, as if he had run both hands through it. "Who?"

"Lucy. She's been flirting with different men all night."

The young man was staring at the girl as though he wanted to toss her over his shoulder and carry her to the nearest cave, Ian thought. "Did you think she was going to join a convent?"

Tim made a harsh sound deep in his throat. "She never cared about me."

"I think you're wrong. But since you don't care about her I guess it doesn't matter."

"If she thinks she can tell me she loves me one minute, then the next flirt with half the men in New York . . ." Tim's jaw clenched, cutting off his words. "I'll show her."

Ian shoved his hands into his pockets, frowning as he watched his nephew head straight for Alisa Renssellaer. He hoped the boy wouldn't do anything foolish, such as proposing to one woman to spite another.

"There you are," Felicity said, resting her hand on Ian's arm. "I've been looking for you."

"What do you want?" Ian asked, glancing down at her.

Seeing the look in his eyes, she dropped her hand and took a step back. "I need to talk to you."

"About what?"

"In private."

Ian knew Felicity would hound him the rest of the night until she got what she wanted. It was better to get it over with quickly. He had other things that needed tending tonight. She fell into step beside him as he left the ballroom. As they approached the hall leading to his study, the door to the music room swung open and Duncan O'Neill stepped through.

Duncan came to a halt when he noticed Ian and Felicity, his dark eyes snapping from the small blonde standing beside his daughter's husband to Ian's face. "I swear to God, Tremayne," he said, advancing toward them. He paused a foot in front of

Ian, his sides heaving with barely controlled rage. "If you hurt my daughter again, I'll kill you."

Ian held his angry stare. "I don't intend to give you any reason."

"I'll be watching, Tremayne."

Ian turned and watched Duncan march toward the ballroom. Just what had set off that explosion? he wondered. A few people peeked out of the drawing room a few feet away, casting curious glances in his direction. An audience. That's just what he needed.

"He doesn't like you very much," Felicity said, rushing to keep up with Ian's long strides as he walked down the hall toward his study.

Ian didn't reply. After ushering her into his study he closed the door. "All right. What do you want?"

She smiled, yet he noticed the smile didn't touch her eyes. "I'll pour you a drink."

What mischief was the woman up to now? he wondered, moving to the hearth. Ian leaned his forearms against the mantel and rested his brow on the cool garnet marble. If Felicity did something to upset Sabrina, he might seriously consider strangling the woman.

Behind him he heard her moving, the soft rustle of ruby satin, the gentle swish of liquor being poured into crystal. Nice sounds. Homey sounds. Too bad it was the wrong woman making them. The cabinet closed and a moment later he felt her touch his arm.

"Brandy," she said, offering him the snifter. "You see, I remember what you like."

Ian's fingers slid against the deep beveled edges of the cut crystal. "What is it, Felicity?" he asked, frowning as she stroked her fingertips across his hand.

She moved closer, running her hand along his arm, a cloying scent of spices and gardenias invading his nostrils. He noticed her neckline was particularly low, even for Felicity. The snug red satin revealed a deep valley between her white breasts, and he wondered how she kept from popping right out. Whatever she wanted, she was dressed to bag a bear.

He placed his free hand on her waist, feeling the ribs of her tightly cinched corset beneath his palm. She smiled, a smug little grin that said things were going according to her plan. "Get to the point," he said, pushing her away.

She stumbled back a step, her lips parting, her eyes wide. "How dare . . ." She caught herself, biting her lower lip.

Whatever she wanted, she wanted it desperately, Ian thought, taking a sip of brandy, the amber liquid slicing a fiery path across his tongue and down his throat.

"Ian darling," she said, molding her lips into a smile. "I need help."

"With what?"

"I overheard Walter talking to Mr. Elsbury the other day," she said, toying with the golden curl that rested against one pale shoulder. "It seems my husband has managed to sell more stock than he owns. I'm afraid we'll be ruined."

"And you thought you might come here to bargain."

"He said you held the contracts." She sauntered toward him and pressed her open palms against his chest. "Ian, I'll do anything. Anything you want. You can't let this happen to me."

"Felicity . . ."

"Please, Ian," she whispered. "I meant something to you once."

"Relax, Felicity. Walter was here yesterday. We made an arrangement." He smiled, glancing down at her ample display of bosom. "So you see, there's no reason to play the prostitute."

"I see." She took a step back, twitching her skirts with her hands. "You must find this all very amusing."

"On the contrary." Ian set his glass on the mantel and stared into the crystal. "I don't find any of this amusing." He glanced at her, wondering just how much of the devil dwelt inside her. "You know, Felicity, I almost think you wanted Walter to ruin me. Maybe you wanted to go even farther. A duel? Did I wound your pride enough to want to see me dead?"

"If I thought Walter would stand a chance, I would encourage him. I adored you, Ian."

"It's not too far a step to go from love to hate, is it, Felicity?"

She turned, her wide skirt swaying with each angry step she took, gaslight rippling along the red satin. Pausing at the door, she turned. "One day you'll pay for the way you've treated me," she said, before leaving him alone.

Ian walked to the open French doors. Leaning his shoulder against the casement, he breathed in the cool night air, trying to cleanse his senses of Felicity's perfume.

Women. One of these days he was going to figure them out. Now that really would be worth a fortune.

*   *   *

Awash in moonlight, the lawn rolled away from the house, shimmering like waves on a rippling river. Sabrina stood in the shadows of the terrace. Somehow she had to pull on a mask of calm; she had to return to that ballroom, she had to smile, to pretend her life wasn't a tangled mess.

Was she making a mistake? Maybe her father was right. Did Ian want to hurt her? Did she have any choice but to stay with him, to try to make a life with him? There was only one thing she was certain of: Love was a gamble.

She hugged her arms to her waist, her gaze resting on the fountain gracing the center of the rose garden. Frolicking cherubs tossed water into the air, where moonlight transformed it into glittering silver. It was exactly as she had imagined it would be, as it had been in that distant corner of her memory.

Without warning, reality faded; the reel tumbling from the ballroom dissolving into the tinkling notes of a minuet. Amid roses in full bloom, two specters moved through the steps of the dance. A woman dressed in white brocade, her powdered hair piled high above her head, smiled at her partner. The tall, broad-shouldered man bowed, his white satin coat brushing his white satin breeches. His hair was unpowdered, the shiny black tresses tied at his nape with a black ribbon.

Sabrina felt as though she were floating, suspended in a void of time and space, caught by memories made in a distant past. Drawn to a half-remembered dream, she descended the steps at the end of the terrace. Thick grass cushioned her slippered feet as she moved toward the garden. As she drew near, the lovers faded and the blossoms of the past disappeared, fading into the roses of the present.

Sabrina closed her eyes, willing the vision to return. For a long time she stood, quiet, aware of every breath of wind against her face, every whisper of the fountain. With her heightened senses she felt him approach. Without opening her eyes, she knew who moved toward her; his scent drifted on the breeze, his warmth reached for her.

"Tell me, what's the belle of the ball doing hiding from her admirers?"

Sabrina opened her eyes to find Ian standing a foot away, much too far. "Do you think they've accepted me?"

One corner of his lips curved upward. "They couldn't resist your charm."

She glanced away, staring at the rosebush near her side, feeling awkward and horribly vulnerable. What words did you use to end a war? How did you begin to heal the wounds? How did you find the courage to trust again?

In his presence she never seemed to think, just feel; terrible, conflicting emotions. Love. Hate. Trust. Doubt. Desire. Obsession. A waltz drifted from the house, violins spinning the notes into a delicate, floating fabric of sound.

"Dance with me, Sabrina," he whispered, his deep voice mingling with the soothing notes of the violins, the sparkling sound of the fountain.

She lifted her gaze to the hand he offered, his palm up, his fingers long and reaching. Her hand moved, as if pulled by a string. His fingers closed around her hand, warm and sure, drawing her into his arms, where she belonged, where she had always belonged.

Moonlight kissed his midnight hair, caressed the crests of his cheeks, brushed the thin line of his nose, painting him in silver and shadow. He was a phantom of her past; love lost, love waiting to be claimed.

Her skirt brushed his legs as he swept her around the fountain. His hand warmed the small of her back through the layers of silk and linen, layers she would gladly discard to feel the warmth of his touch against her skin.

"Do you remember the last time we danced in the moonlight?" he asked, slowing their movements.

She had been trying very hard to forget those few days aboard the *Belle Angeline*. She stared up into his eyes; they reflected light and shadow, mystery and desire. Why had he dredged up the past? Why, when she was willing to face the future? Like a hurricane rushing in from the sea, memories swept over her, stirring the sleeping anger deep inside her, calling back her doubts.

"Of course I remember," she said, breaking free of his embrace. She turned toward the fountain, watching the sparkling streams of silver rise and tumble. "It was the night you seduced me with tender words, with promises of love, of marriage." She had to forget those few days. She had to forgive.

He rested his hands on her upper arms, his palms branding her bare skin. "Sabrina, I meant every word I said that night," he said, his lips near her ear, his warm breath whispering across her shoulder.

Standing in his warmth, Sabrina shivered. Why was he doing

this? Why was he lying? Dear God, was he lying about everything? She felt as though she were drowning, caught in a whirlpool, pulled beneath her hopes, smothered by doubt.

"I think it's better if we don't talk about what happened," she said, hugging her arms to her waist.

"I think we need to talk about what happened," he said, smoothing his fingertips across her temple. "Sabrina, when I asked you to marry me I meant every word."

"So you were lying then, but you're telling the truth now," she said, pulling away from him. It was true; you couldn't change what you were inside. And he was a lying scoundrel. "I was a fool to ever think this could work." She lifted her skirts and ran toward the house, needing to escape this disturbing man, needing to be alone.

"Sabrina, wait," he said, catching up with her at the base of the stone stairs leading to the terrace below the ballroom. "Let me explain. I want you to understand why I . . ."

"There's nothing to explain," she said, turning to face him.

"I think there is," he said, running his hands down her bare arms. "If we are ever going to have a future, we need to heal the wounds of the past."

"I don't think we have a future, Tremayne. You see, I just realized I could never live with a man I can't trust." *No matter how much I love him.*

Above them, music flowed from the open doors of the ballroom. Several couples, who had been enjoying the moonlight on the terrace, moved to the stone balustrade, gazing down at their hosts.

Ian's hands tightened on her arms. "I fell in love with you the first moment I saw you. I didn't find out about your father until the morning after we made love."

"Why are you doing this?" she asked, slapping away his hands. "Why must you lie?"

"Sabrina . . ."

"It's over, Tremayne."

She lifted her skirts and rushed up the stairs, with Ian right behind her. He grabbed her arm, halting her in the middle of the terrace, in a wedge of golden light tumbling from the ballroom.

"Dammit, Sabrina! I'm getting pretty tired of being called a liar."

"When were you telling the truth?" she asked, staring up into his face, the face she had loved all her life, the face that hid a pirate's soul. "The day on board the *Belle* when you told me it was all a game? The day you told me you wanted a whore for a wife?"

Her voice rang above the music, attracting the attention of several people in the ballroom. They moved close to the door, drawing the curiosity of more guests.

"When? Just when were you telling the truth?"

"The day I told you I loved you," he said, his low voice a velvet counterpoint to her shout.

"I'm not that big a fool." Sabrina spun on her heel. She would never believe this man again. Never!

"You aren't walking away from this," Ian said, grabbing her arm.

"Oh, yes, I am," she shouted, swinging around to face him. "I'll be on the first train headed south."

"Like hell you will!"

Anger filled her until she was shaking. "You said you'd let me go."

Ian grinned. "I lied. What do you expect from a liar?"

Without a thought to their growing audience, Sabrina drew back her hand and slapped him, so hard she knocked his head to one side, so hard her palm screamed in agony. A collected gasp rippled through the people surrounding them. In the light from the ballroom she could see the brand of her hand blazing across his dark cheek.

"Enough," Ian whispered.

Sabrina screamed as Ian tossed her over his shoulder. Guests parted, like the Red Sea before Moses, as he carried her into the ballroom.

"Let go of me!"

Pins and combs tumbled from her hair, bouncing on the polished rosewood floor, releasing her hair; it cascaded in thick waves, brushing his calves with every step he took. She pounded his back with her fists, wiggled, kicked, all to no avail.

"Is there some trouble?" Caroline asked, meeting them at the main entrance of the ballroom.

"Nothing I can't handle," Ian said.

Sabrina raised up on Ian's shoulder, pushing the hair from her face. "Aunt Caroline, help me."

Caroline smiled. "Duck, dear, or you'll bump your head on the archway."

A frustrated scream escaped her lips, the sound strangled with anger. "This man . . ." Her words ended in a shriek as Ian shifted her, tipping her back until she had to grab his waist to keep from falling headlong to the floor. He carried her across the threshold, followed by a tide of guests.

"You're insane!" Sabrina screamed as he started up the stairs.

"No doubt about it."

Sabrina's hair swung in an arc as Ian turned on the landing. More than a hundred people crowded the hall, staring up at them as though they were the entertainment for the evening.

"Please, stay," Ian said, his deep voice filling the hall. "Enjoy your evening. I assure you, I intend to enjoy mine." With the last word he turned and took the stairs two at a time.

Laughter followed in Ian's wake, pricking Sabrina's wounded pride. "How dare you!" she said, her words strangled with rage.

"You'll soon find I will dare a great many things, sweet, gentle wife."

Sabrina let loose with a string of curses, peppering the air, pounding on his back with her fists as Ian carried her down the long second-floor hallway.

"Just where did you learn such language?" Ian asked, his deep voice colored with humor. "Is that any way for a lady to talk? Especially to her husband."

"Put me down," she shouted, ramming both her fists against his back.

"Sabrina, remember, I'm an injured man," he said, entering his bedroom.

"You wait until I get my hands on you."

"Sounds enticing."

Sabrina parted the curtain of her hair to look around the room. The wall lamps had been lit; they cast a golden glow on the mahogany-paneled walls. The bed sat like a throne upon a figured carpet in shades of blue and ivory and an icy blue counterpane lay folded across the foot of the bed, the top sheet drawn back, revealing an inviting lair of white linen. Excitement tingled across her skin; she groaned with frustration. "Put me down!"

He complied, dropping her on her feet so quickly she nearly fell. With a growl she attacked, leaping at him with her clenched fists. She managed to land a blow on his shoulder before he snatched her wrists in his big hands. In one movement, he brought both her arms down, pinning her hands to the small of her back, thrusting her upward into the oak wall of his chest.

"Blackguard!" she shouted, tossing back her head, spearing him with her eyes.

"Magnificent witch," he whispered, before his lips claimed hers.

He tasted of brandy and something else, something far more potent—his own intoxicating essence. Flames flared deep inside her, fueled by love too long denied, fanned by desire too strong for chains. She twisted her head, breaking their union, scraping her lips against his smooth chin, denying her own throbbing need. "God, I hate you."

"I can feel how much you hate me," he whispered against her temple.

She wasn't even a challenge to him. The muscles in his chest shifted against her breasts, brushing, teasing, as he changed his grasp. Gripping both her wrists in his left hand, he slid his hand upward, along the column of her spine, flipping open silk-clad buttons. Sabrina felt her gown surrender under his marauding fingers, the fragile barrier giving him no resistance. "Let me go," she shouted, trying to twist free of his grasp.

"Never." He cupped her skull with his right hand, tilting back her head, forcing her to look at him. A wealth of emotions smoldered deep within his eyes, filling them with a haunting light, so beautiful she ached.

"You're mine, Sabrina. You own my heart. I could never let you go, not while I have breath in my body."

In contrast to his words, he released her. She stumbled back, lifting her hand to her lips, her gown sliding from one pale shoulder.

Grinning, he turned the key in the lock and removed it from the door. "We don't want any interruptions," he said, moving toward her.

"Just stay where you are, Tremayne," Sabrina said, backing away from him.

He paused, tossing the key to the top of his armoire before continuing his march toward her in slow, steady strides. "I've played by your rules long enough, Sabrina," he said, stripping off his coat. "It's time to play by mine." He tossed the coat to a nearby chair.

He filled the room with his vitality, with his strength, with his maddening masculinity. She backpedaled. If he thought she was going to submit to his pawing, if he thought she would become his docile little concubine, he would soon learn she was made of stronger stuff. "I'm through with your games."

His grin turned devilish, his eyes sparkling with mischief. With one tug he loosened his white cravat. "Sabrina, the game hasn't even begun."

"You lied to me!"

His cravat hit the floor. "Only because I thought you had lied to me."

He pulled the studs from the front of his shirt, letting them fall to the carpet, where they bounced in all directions, littering the floor in a steady trail of mother of pearl, revealing a growing wedge of dark curls and warm-looking skin. That widening vee was stark and masculine and so riveting Sabrina lost track of her next step. She tripped over a footstool, tumbling to the floor, landing in a puddle of emerald silk, hurting nothing but her pride.

He paused, standing above her. "Tell me the truth, Brat. Why are you fighting me?"

"Because I hate you," she said, scrambling to her feet. Her gown sagged away from her breasts, giving him an unrestricted view of her white camisole, her breasts clearly outlined beneath the sheer silk, the taut, pleading peaks betraying her. She snatched the garment to her shoulders.

He raised his black mutilated brow. "Now who is the liar?"

She glanced around the room, her gaze catching on the connecting door to her room.

"I'm going to make love to you, Sabrina."

His deep voice reached inside her, stroking her low, like warm fingers sliding against her flesh. Her body responded, a shameful rush of liquid heat flowing thick and sweet from that part of her growing flush and swollen with need.

"All night. Until you realize just how much I love you. Until you admit you love me. Until you swear leaving me is the last thing you ever want to do."

She had little doubt he could wrench that confession from her. Lifting her skirts, she ran for the door leading to her room.

He pounced, grabbing her around the waist, lifting her off the floor. She clawed at the arm wrapped around her waist, kicking, connecting with his shin, his low groan giving her a moment's satisfaction before he tossed her to the bed. She landed in a twisted heap of silk and hair, sinking into the lush depths of down and feathers.

"Arrogant Yankee," she mumbled, pushing the hair from her

face, realizing her gown was twisted around her hips, revealing white silk stockings and garters adorned with pink rosebuds.

He stood beside the bed, smiling down at her, pulling the shirttails from his trousers, deep creases marring the starched white linen. He lowered his eyes, his gaze sliding over her, so warm, so intense, so full of promise, she felt it like a lover's caress. His gaze lingered a moment where the gown drooped from her pale shoulders, brushing the swell of her breasts exposed so temptingly above the lacy edge of her camisole.

Soon he would touch her. Soon he would clasp her against his naked body, stroke her skin with his hands, his lips, fill her with his power. Her skin tingled, her breath sputtered, her heart refused to come under rein. And he knew exactly what he was doing to her. She could see it in the crooked curve of his lips, in the lush emerald depths of his eyes.

"My beautiful, fiery witch." He pulled the shirt from his shoulders and tossed it to the floor. "Sear my soul with your fire."

Gaslight flickered across his broad shoulders, the width of his chest, burnishing his golden skin, glistening on tempting black curls. With her eyes she traced the thin white scar down his chest, her gaze lingering on the savage wound in his side, still red and puckered, a stark reminder of their mortality. Something twisted low inside her, a blade of desire honed as keenly as a razor.

"Do you have any idea how many nights you've haunted me? How many nights you came to me, here in my bed?" He flipped open the top button of the placket in his trousers. "This is where you'll stay, Sabrina. Where I can hold you at night. Make love to you in the light of dawn."

She would be no man's whore. "Go to blazes!" she shouted, scrambling off the other side of the bed.

She ran for the door. He got there first, blocking her way with six feet three inches of infuriating male strength. "So it's to be rape, Tremayne," she said, backing away from him, using the only weapons she had.

He grinned. "Do you believe for one minute it will be rape?"

The truth was far too humiliating to face. He could steal her will, turn her into a creature ruled by emotion, enslaved by passion. In the end he would steal every shred of her dignity. "I hate you!"

"No, you don't. I almost came to believe you. But I know you. I know the only reason you're fighting me is because you won't take the risk of loving me."

"You're a bad bet, Tremayne."

"No, I'm not. I love you, Sabrina." He smiled, that smile radiating a warmth, a tenderness that couldn't be counterfeited. "I'll love you until I die. And if it's possible, I'll love you beyond the grave."

Sabrina stood frozen as he moved toward her. His words spun around her in a sultry web.

"Let me love you." He ran his hands across her shoulders, sliding the gown from her skin. It fell in a whisper, billowing around her feet. "Let me . . ." He hesitated, sucking in his breath.

"What is it?"

He shook his head, bending at the waist, clutching his abdomen with both hands. He tried to straighten but couldn't. "I . . . don't know." His face contorted with pain, his hands twisted into his clothes. "Feel . . . hot coals . . . in my belly."

"If this is some trick to . . ."

He clasped his hand over his mouth and staggered toward the bathroom. Fear knifed through her heart. She ran after him, throwing her right arm around his waist, grabbing his elbow with her left hand, trying to steady him, feeling his entire body tremble. As they reached the bathroom his body convulsed. With a deep groan, he collapsed to his knees and vomited against the cold marble floor.

She stroked his shoulders as spasm after spasm racked his body, his skin growing damp beneath her hands with a thin sheen of sweat. After an eternity he leaned back against the wall, his breath coming in ragged gasps, sweat beading on his brow, above his upper lip.

"Ian," Sabrina whispered, smoothing his damp waves back from his brow. "My God, what's wrong?"

His Adam's apple bobbed as he swallowed hard. He dragged the back of his hand across his mouth before he spoke. "Better send for a doctor. I think I've been . . ." He hesitated, looking up at her through watery eyes. "Quickly, love."

Chapter Twenty-Nine

Ian dragged himself toward the side of the bed, trying to contain the moan of pain crawling up his throat, the warm milk and toast Sabrina had just coaxed him to eat chasing that wayward sound of pain. He felt her arm slip around his shoulders. She supported him as he leaned over the edge of the bed, the smooth silk of her gown absorbing his sweat. His muscles convulsed, emptying the contents of his stomach into a porcelain chamber pot, squeezing until dry heaves shook his body.

When at last the seizure subsided he collapsed against the bed, his head hanging over the edge, blood pounding in his temples. He couldn't remember ever feeling this ill. And he had the uneasy feeling things were going to get worse before they got better.

Sabrina helped ease him back against the pillows, dabbing at his lips with a lace-edged handkerchief. Jasmine drifted from the soft cotton, the enticing fragrance soothing the sour smell in his nostrils.

Ian blinked away the water clouding his vision. Lamplight caressed Sabrina's face, gold flickering against white satin. She looked angry and frightened and determined, the way she had that night she had pressed a knife to his throat. Only this time she was on his side. Together they could move mountains, he thought, his lips curving into a smile. "Thanks, Brat."

"Do something," Sabrina said, glancing to where Dr. Wentworth stood beside her.

Wentworth's brown eyes looked troubled behind the oval lenses of his glasses. He shifted his ample weight to the opposite foot, like a draft horse at rest, his ruddy face pulling into long lines. Beneath his black coat he wore a red-and-white-striped nightshirt, one shirttail tucked into dark gray trousers, the other dangling free. "Mrs. Tremayne, there's very little I can do."

That wasn't what he wanted to hear, Ian thought. He felt Sabrina's fingers stroke his hair, her fingertips grazing his scalp, warm, fiercely tender. She looked so vulnerable, this angel, his very own. She had seen so much, suffered so much, watched her mother die, her brother. He wanted to reassure her, to hold her, to shield her.

"Don't worry," he whispered, lifting his hand, wanting to touch her face. It took more strength than he had; his hand fell to the sheet beside his hip.

Sabrina lifted his hand between both of hers, holding him in a firm grasp, as though she wanted to fill him with her own strength. "Dr. Wentworth, there must be something more you can do besides feed him burnt toast and warm milk."

Dr. Wentworth pushed his glasses against the bridge of his thin nose. "Mrs. Tremayne, the milk and toast will help bind the poison."

"Poison!" Sabrina sat back, as though the doctor had slapped her.

Poison. Ian had known it; his body had told him the frightening truth. He had to fight it, this enemy he couldn't see, this enemy that threatened to rip him away from Sabrina. God, he couldn't die now. He couldn't leave her. Pain rose in waves of fire, washing over him, stripping away his strength like sand succumbing to the sea. Fight it! Fight it!

"Poison." The word echoed from the small group huddled at the foot of Ian's bed. Caroline stood in the center, surrounded by Aggie, Hannah, and Mac.

"My guess would be arsenic," Wentworth said.

"But how would he get arsenic?" Sabrina asked.

"Someone gave it to him," Mac said, his eyes growing narrow as he stared at Sabrina. "The same someone who stretched a wire across the bridle path."

"James MacDoughal," Aggie said, turning to face him with her hands planted on her bony hips. "Ye can stop lookin' at her like she was some kind a street baggage right now, ye can."

"Listen to me, Agatha Fitzpatrick . . ." Mac hesitated as Ian's moan cut through the room.

Ian pulled his knees against his chest and shuddered, his breath coming in short, ragged pants. Sabrina sank her teeth into her lower lip, fighting the tears pricking her eyes, stroking his hair, his back, his shoulder, his body convulsing beneath her touch. Twice she had felt this helpless. Both times she had lost someone she loved. Her hand tensed against Ian's bare shoulder. She couldn't lose him. He couldn't die. He just couldn't. "What can I do?"

"Feed him more burnt toast soaked in warm milk, I'm afraid. And a half ounce of this every hour." Wentworth handed Sabrina a bottle labeled hydrated peroxide of iron. "There's little else we can do," he said, closing the black bag he had resting on the cabinet near the bed.

Sabrina had the gnawing suspicion Wentworth had already given up on his patient. She smoothed the waves back from Ian's brow, the black strands of silk curling around her fingers. "He's a strong man, doctor. He'll fight. He'll be all right." He had to be all right.

In a voice low enough for her ears alone, Wentworth spoke. "Mrs. Tremayne, your husband was recently wounded. You need to realize his body may not be strong enough to fight the effects of the poison."

Sabrina lifted her gaze to the doctor. "He'll be all right."

Wentworth sighed. "I hope you're right."

"And just where do you think you are going?" Caroline asked, blocking the doctor's way as he started to leave the room.

"There's nothing more for me to do. I'll be back in the morning," Wentworth said.

"You will stay right here." Caroline took the bag from his hand and directed him to a Queen Anne chair near the white marble fireplace.

The doctor looked at the chair, then glanced at Caroline, as if weighing his options. Caroline stood with her hands planted on her hips, glaring at the man. With a sigh he sank into the icy blue brocade, his hips squeezing snugly between the arms, the chair groaning under his weight.

"I've sent someone for the police," Mac said, staring at Sabrina. "They should be arriving any time."

Sabrina glanced at her Aunt Caroline. She stood looking at her niece, her eyes revealing the same fear gnawing at Sabrina's belly. The police would suspect her father. The realization did nothing for her already stretched nerves.

Sabrina rested her cheek against Ian's hair. "We're going to get through this. You're going to be all right," she whispered, determined to make those words reality.

*   *   *

Two hours later Caroline sat on the edge of a dark red leather chair in Ian's study, watching Inspector Ewing walk toward the liquor cabinet near the desk. His grayish brown hair reflected an indentation from where his hat had rested; his blue-and-gray-striped coat looked as though he had slept in it, his brown trousers faring no better. Yet beneath shaggy brown brows his dark eyes were bright and piercing, like a ferret smelling blood. This man might look like an unmade bed, but she had the feeling he was as sharp as a razor's edge.

Beside her, Duncan shifted in his chair, tapping his fingers impatiently on the leather arm. She glanced at him, her gaze tracing his profile, sharp, classic in line, like a noble prince. Suddenly she realized how much she wished she could protect him. He couldn't have done this. He just couldn't have.

"Would you care for some brandy, Mrs. Van Cortlandt? Mr. O'Neill?" Ewing asked, lifting a decanter from the liquor cabinet, the crystal catching the light, sending shards of color in all directions.

Duncan frowned as he met Ewing's gaze. "Inspector, if the man was poisoned, is it a good idea to be drinking his liquor?"

Ewing nodded, a satisfied smile curving his lips. "I suspect it wouldn't be a good idea at all, Mr. O'Neill. Very perceptive of you."

Caroline glanced at Duncan, wishing he had accepted that glass of brandy.

"Inspector, I've told you all I know. If you don't mind, I'd like to be with my daughter."

"I understand you and Mr. Tremayne didn't get along well," Ewing said, sitting on the edge of the desk.

Apparently Ewing had already questioned the servants, Caroline thought. Smart man. If you wanted to know anything about a family, the servants were the ones to ask.

"It's not a secret. I don't approve of my daughter and that Yankee."

Ewing smiled. "You've even threatened to kill him."

Duncan's hand clenched into a fist on the arm of the chair. "I didn't poison the man. It's not my way to strike like a viper in the night."

"But it would solve your problems if Mr. Tremayne were to die."

"I'm telling you," Duncan said, leaning forward in his chair, "I didn't have anything to do with this."

Caroline rested her hand on Duncan's arm. "Inspector, I'm sure a man like Ian Tremayne must have enemies, men who envy his wealth. Men jealous over the affection their wives still hold for the man."

Ewing rested his hands on the desk, leaning back, smiling at Caroline. "Suppose you can give me any names?"

Caroline thought of one of the men sitting in the library, one of the many lined up for questioning. Walter Strickland believed he had reason to want Ian Tremayne dead. Still, she didn't want to participate in a witch-hunt. "It is your job to discover these things. Not persecute innocent people."

Ewing was quiet, watching her, waiting. Caroline's fingers tightened on Duncan's arm. She felt his hand cover hers, warm and strong. She noticed Ewing's smile grow a little more smug as his gaze dipped to their clasped hands.

"Did you know we found a bag of arsenic in the kitchen, Mrs. Van Cortlandt?" Ewing asked. "Did you know the housekeeper, the staff, no one seems to know how it got there? Do you know how it got there, Mrs. Van Cortlandt?"

Caroline's lips parted, her breath vanishing in a gasp.

"How dare you imply she had anything to do with this?" Duncan demanded, coming to his feet. "She's a fine lady. Anyone who would . . ."

"Duncan," Caroline said, tugging on his hand. He glanced down at her, his dark eyes flaming with anger. This is what the inspector wanted: a show of anger, a display of violence. "Please, the inspector is just doing his job." With pressure on his hand, she coaxed him back to his chair.

Duncan took her hand between both of his. "Do your job, Inspector. Find the scoundrel who hasn't enough honor to meet his enemy face to face."

Ewing nodded, a smile curving his lips. "We'll do our job, Mr. O'Neill. You can be sure of it." He held Duncan's angry stare a moment, smiling as if he saw exactly what he wanted to see. Shoving away from the desk, he turned to the detective standing beside the connecting door to the library. "Show in our next guests, Bailey."

The first rays of dawn were creeping like a specter into Ian's room through the open French doors, the morning song of the birds drifting in with the breeze. It all seemed so normal. Except this morning Ian was fighting for his life.

Sabrina lifted a spoon toward Ian's parted lips. "Take this, darling."

No response.

She tipped the spoon, allowing the medicine to drizzle into his mouth. It slid in a narrow rivulet from the corner of his lips, flowing across his cheek to stain the pillowcase.

"Ian," she whispered, pressing her fingers against the pulse point in his neck. His skin felt cold, damp against her skin, his pulse sluggish, as if every beat might be his last.

She stood, the three dogs lying beside the bed scrambling to their feet at her sudden movement. "Doctor," she shouted, rushing to where Wentworth sat sleeping in the chair, Byron and Shakespeare trailing her skirts. "Doctor," she said, shaking his shoulder.

Wentworth awakened with a start, surging upward in the chair. "What is it? What's happened?"

"He's worse. Much worse."

Wentworth followed her back to the bed. After examining his patient he turned to Sabrina. "I'm sorry, Mrs. Tremayne. The poison is taking its course. If he's strong enough, he'll survive. If not . . ."

The unspoken words plucked at Sabrina's heart. She clenched her hands at her waist. "Do something."

Wentworth shrugged. "There's nothing I can do."

She felt a cold nose brush her arm and glanced down to find Guinevere looking up at her, as if the little dog were pleading with her to help her master. Sabrina sat on the bed beside Ian, cupping his face in her hands. "Listen to me, Ian Tremayne, don't you dare die on me. Show me just how stubborn you can be. Show me you can fight this thing as fiercely as you fought me. Do you hear me?"

Nothing. Not a whisper. Not a flutter of lashes.

He was cold, so cold, she thought, running her hand across his shoulder. Her mind churned, leafing through all the home remedies her mother had always dispensed at Rosebriar, all the treatments they had used at the hospital. No one had ever been poisoned. Yet for a fever she had seen people plunged into cold water. Cold water to reduce their temperature. Warm water might . . .

"Hannah!" she shouted, coming to her feet.

The little housekeeper was holding vigil in the sitting room, along with Mac, Aggie, and Luther. They all came running at Sabrina's call.

"Prepare a bath," Sabrina said, grabbing Hannah's shoulders. "A hot bath. Right away."

Hannah blinked. "Will you be wanting jasmine scent?"

Sabrina shook her head. "The bath is for Ian. Please hurry."

"For Ian?"

"That's right, he needs . . . Hannah, please just hurry. I don't have time to explain."

Hannah ran from the room, and a few moments later the sound of running water drifted from Ian's adjoining bathroom. While Hannah prepared the bath, Sabrina rubbed Ian's arms, coaxing the blood to flow in his veins. She tossed back the sheet and blankets and began rubbing his legs, sliding her hands against the white linen of his drawers, working her way down to his feet and back up again.

When the bath was ready Luther took Ian's shoulders and Mac his ankles, and the two men lifted him from the bed, his dead weight sagging between them. Sabrina slid her arms under Ian's waist, bracing the unconscious man. Wentworth watched, scratching his chin, staying well out of Sabrina's path. With Aggie and Hannah and Ian's three dogs following, the little group carried Ian into the bathroom and lowered him into the big marble tub.

Sabrina knelt beside the tub and began rubbing Ian's skin, lifting one arm and then the next, hoping the combination of friction and hot water could coax his blood to circulate. Water lapped against his chest, dark curls swaying, swirling with the ebb and flow created by her hands. The white linen shielding Ian's modesty dissolved into a transparent veil in the water, exposing the dark-shaded length of his legs, the relaxed curve of muscle and flesh crowning his thighs.

Heat flared in her cheeks, and it had little to do with the steam rising from the water. "I can manage from here, thank you," Sabrina said, glancing back at the people gathered in a small group behind her.

Their footsteps rapped against marble as they left her alone with her husband. She pulled the drawers from his hips and dropped the sodden linen in the sink. She began massaging Ian's legs, his skin firm, resilient, beneath her hands, crisp curls teasing her skin.

Time. She had wasted so much time. Time she could have spent in his arms. And for what? Pride.

Pride couldn't keep you warm at night.

She lifted her hands, dripping water across his chest, stroking his cheeks. Steam drifted from the water, beading on his chin, his cheeks, curling the wisps of hair around his face. Words swirled inside her, words spoken in anger, words armed with steely claws that sliced into her heart. He could die believing she hated him. "I'm sorry," she whispered. "So very sorry."

"For what?"

Sabrina glanced over her shoulder to find Delia standing in the doorway. Ian's family had stayed the evening, as had Caroline and Lucy. They had taken turns the night before, sitting with her, lending quiet support.

Raspberry red satin flowed around Delia as she moved, the elegant dressing robe trimmed in gold braid across the shoulders and down the front. Raspberry red slippers trimmed in white fur peeked out with each step she took. "Be careful what you say, darling. The police are desperately seeking a suspect."

"I hope they find the stinking coward."

"That little Inspector What's-his-name took each one of us into Ian's study last night and tried to feed us poisoned brandy." Delia swept the long length of Ian Tremayne with her eyes as she spoke, steam and water little protection from her thorough perusal. "I never realized he had been scarred so badly in the war. Still, the scars don't take anything away from him, do they? He's really quite splendid."

Sabrina grabbed a towel from the gold rack on the wall beside her and draped the white linen across the tub, shielding Ian from his waist to his knees.

Delia laughed, the bright notes bouncing against the white marble walls. "Sabrina, I never realized you were so stingy."

Sabrina rested Ian's damp hand against her shoulder, his fingers curling against her neck. "Was there something you wanted?" she asked, rubbing Ian's upper arm between her hands.

"You're going to ruin that gown."

"Delia, I'm sorry to sound impatient, but . . ." She didn't finish, too little sleep and too much worry robbing her of words. "Please."

"Yes, of course I understand." She swatted Byron's nose as the dog nudged her arm, sending the curious mutt back to his position behind Sabrina. He sat on the marble between Guinevere and Shakespeare and stared at her. "I couldn't sleep. So I thought I would take over for a few hours."

Sabrina shook her head. She couldn't leave Ian. Not until she was sure he was out of danger.

"You look as though you could use some rest. And I don't mind giving Ian a bath."

She had the feeling Delia would love to get her hands on Ian. "I'm trying to warm him. He's so cold."

"Sabrina dear, you'll want to be awake when he regains consciousness. The way you're going, you'll be half dead."

"I wouldn't be able to sleep."

"Does this mean you two have finally resolved your differences?" she asked, slipping the sash of her robe through her fingers. "That was quite a scene last night. You and Ian set a few tongues wagging."

Sabrina's hands grew still against Ian's shoulder, her cheeks scorching from the memories. "I said some things . . . things I didn't mean."

Delia patted Sabrina's shoulder. "Well, I'm sure Ian will be more than forgiving."

If he survived. Sabrina traced the line of his collarbone with her fingers. "I hope we have . . ." She hesitated as someone called her from the bedroom.

"Mrs. Tremayne," a tall, sandy haired young man said, sticking his head into the bathroom. He glanced at the bathtub, then at Sabrina. "You're giving him a bath?"

"I'm trying to raise his . . . just who are you? And what are you doing in my husband's room?"

He smiled, small lines flaring out from his light brown eyes. "I'm Detective Yardley, George Yardley. I've been assigned to watch over Mr. Tremayne."

"In other words, you're here to make sure no one tries to finish the job," Delia said, smiling up at Yardley.

"Ah, well, I guess you could put it that way, ma'am."

"Well, Sabrina, you should feel safe now." Delia assessed the detective from the crown of his thick brown hair to the tips of his black shoes. "I certainly feel much better."

Sabrina frowned, rubbing her thumb over Ian's knuckles. "Do you think he'll try again? So soon?"

Yardley pulled his gaze from Delia, his lips curving into a slight smile as he looked down at Sabrina. "Mr. Tremayne is vulnerable right now."

So was she. All her defenses were gone, shattered, ground to dust by her need for Ian. And right now she didn't care. She didn't care if she ended up a bloody casualty of this war. All she wanted was Ian healthy and strong and in her arms.

Lucy sat on a Chippendale armchair in Ian Tremayne's drawing room, clenching her hands in her lap, watching Henry Tremayne pace back and forth in front of the cold hearth. The man reminded her of the scarecrow she had seen in the cornfield at Rosebriar, so thin the bones made little peaks beneath the shoulders of his expensive black coat.

Behind her a warm evening breeze drifted in from the garden, carrying the perfume of roses. The drawing room had become a waiting room for the family. For two days Lucy had lived with these people, feeling their tension as keenly as her own.

Henry paced when he was worried. Delia and Rand played piquet at a round table across the room. Ellen read, or at least stared at the open book in her hands . . . she hadn't turned a page in the last half hour. Uncle Duncan stroked his right brow while staring at the tip of his shoe. And Tim . . .

From beneath her lashes Lucy glanced at Tim. He sat on a Queen Anne chair across from her, his forearms on his thighs, his shoulders curled forward, clasping and unclasping his hands. She wished she could go to him. She wished she could slip her arm around his shoulder and offer comfort. But she knew he didn't want her comfort. He didn't want anything from her. He hated her, she thought, glancing down at her tightly clenched hands.

She felt her throat grow tight, her eyes sting with gathering tears. How could she be sitting here feeling sorry for herself when Ian might be dying? The thought brought a fresh wave of feeling rolling through her. She drew a deep breath and fought against her emotions. She would be strong, for Sabrina.

All heads turned toward the door as it opened. Caroline entered the room, glancing around at the people gathered there, shaking her head. "There's been little change, I'm afraid," she said, before taking her place on the sofa beside Duncan, the pale blue silk of her gown billowing around her.

"How is she?" Duncan asked, his voice husky from hours without sleep.

"Exhausted. I doubt she slept more than a few hours since it happened." Caroline lifted her embroidery from the rosewood table beside the sofa. "Yet she refuses to leave him, even to change. I just hope she doesn't make herself ill."

Duncan frowned and stared down at the tip of his shoe.

"I'll stay with her a little while," Ellen said, coming to her feet. The rustle of her skirts screamed in the quiet room, the soft click of the door a gunshot on ears long strained for any encouraging news.

"Who do you suppose Ewing suspects?" Rand asked, sitting back in his chair, glancing at his father.

Henry paused in front of the black marble hearth, his gaze darting to Duncan before lowering to the floor. "I don't know. I don't know who would want to see Ian dead."

"I think he suspects nearly all of us," Caroline said, without glancing up from her sampler.

"He's an absurd little man," Delia said as she shuffled the cards. "What possible reason could any of us have for killing Ian?"

The room grew quiet, except for the soft click of the rosewood clock on the mantel and the crisp sound of cards sliding together.

"Money."

The single word pulled everyone's attention to Tim. He glanced up from his hands, looking straight at Duncan. "Uncle Ian is worth a great deal of money."

Duncan held the young man's stare with a steady gaze, tension crackling between them until Tim glanced down at his hands.

Tim couldn't believe Uncle Duncan had done this, Lucy thought. Yet he did. She could see it in his eyes. Doubts twisted her stomach. Was it possible? Hate could lead a person to do horrible, wicked things.

"I personally believe it was Walter Strickland." Delia began dealing the cards. "He despises Ian. And he certainly looked nervous when he went in to be questioned yesterday. Almost as nervous as Felicity."

"I suppose that's only natural," Caroline said, glancing to Delia before once again focusing on her sampler. She jabbed her needle though the smooth cotton as she continued. "He must realize he's high on Ewing's list."

"It's a terrible way to die," Rand said, sliding one card into place in his hand. "Like being eaten alive from inside. And Ian was always so strong."

"You shouldn't talk as though he's dead," Henry said, his voice cracking with emotion. The sudden outburst seemed to drain all his strength. "He'll be all right." He lowered his head, as though he was too weary to hold it upright any longer. "He has to be all right."

Rand nodded and lowered his gaze to the polished rosewood tabletop. Yet Lucy could see the doubt in his face, the doubt that was in everyone's heart.

"I once heard of this man in France who would marry these rich women then poison them with arsenic." Delia paused, glancing down at her cards. She rearranged one card before she continued. "He went though six wives before he was caught and hanged."

Duncan surged forward in his chair. "My daughter had nothing to do with this."

Delia glanced at Duncan, her lips forming a little *o.* "Why, of course she didn't."

Yet the suspicion was there, hanging as thick as smoke in the room. Lucy looked from one face to another, realizing this was not the first time the possibility had occurred to Ian's relatives. Fear congealed inside her, filling her chest until she could barely breathe. If Ian should die . . . if they suspected Sabrina . . . Dear God, she could be hanged.

"If you think Sabrina had anything to do with this horrible thing, you're wrong," Lucy said, coming to her feet. "You don't know her. She's kind. She's . . . honorable. She would never, never hurt anyone."

Lucy turned, rushing from the room before anyone could say a word. Warm evening air bathed her damp cheeks as she ran across the terrace. Violet organdy and ivory silk billowed behind her, scraping the stone stairs leading to the rose garden. Once within the fragrant arms of the garden she collapsed, sinking to one of the three stone benches circling the fountain.

They were wrong! Sabrina was innocent. Uncle Duncan was innocent. They were! A warm hand touched her bare arm, breaking her tortured reverie. She knew who it was without seeing his face. "Go away," she whispered, turning her head to hide her tear-streaked face.

"Lucy," Tim whispered, sitting beside her.

"Go away," she shouted, shoving aside the arm he slipped around her shoulders. She came to her feet, staring down at him through her tears. "You think she did it. You think Uncle Duncan did it."

Tim came to his feet and reached for her. She stepped back, eluding him. "Lucy, I didn't mean . . ."

"You don't understand her. You never tried to listen to me. You just condemned her. You condemned me."

Moonlight washed his face of color. He stood staring down at her, his eyes dark and turbulent, deep lines etched into his brow, into the skin beside his lips. "I want to understand."

Lucy shook her head. She turned away from him, staring at the fountain, dismissing him the way he had dismissed her days ago. "Go away."

"I can't. I can't leave you like this."

Lucy swiped at the tears streaming down her cheeks. "Why not? You left me crying once before."

He fell quiet but didn't move. She could feel him standing a few feet away from her, feel the warmth of his body, feel the tension of his muscles. Water bubbled from chubby cherubs, rising high in the air in spurts of exuberant silver, tumbling in soft rhythmic splashes. She tried to concentrate on the fountain, tried to ignore the man who refused to leave.

"I love you. I realize how fragile love can be. Uncle Ian taught me that."

She tried to concentrate on the pain he had caused her. Yet she kept thinking of the way his arms had felt that one day he had held her, so warm, so strong.

Tim took her arm, holding her when she tried to break free, forcing her to face him. She lifted her gaze to his face, determined to be stubborn. "I thought I told you to leave me alone."

Tim sank to the thick grass beneath their feet, dropping to one knee before her, grabbing her hand in both of his. "Don't turn me away, Lucy. Marry me."

Lucy was so startled, she forgot about breathing. She stood like a statue, staring down at his upturned face, a face she had loved for as long as she could remember. "I couldn't marry any man who thought my family capable of murder."

"I don't. Not really." He rested his cheek against the back of her hand. "I'm just so worried about Uncle Ian. I . . . I wasn't thinking."

Moonlight painted silvery streaks in his golden hair. She slipped her fingers through the silky strands, sweeping back a wayward lock from his brow. She never was very good at being stubborn.

He looked up at her, his love naked in his eyes. "Marry me," he whispered.

"Do you mean it this time?" she asked, a smile curving her lips.

He pressed his lips to the palm of her hand. "I love you, Lucy," he whispered, his voice melding with the bubbling fountain.

Inside Lucy hope and love chased away her fear, her anger. "Off your knees, Timothy Reynolds."

He hesitated a moment before rising to his feet, staring at her with uncertain eyes, waiting as though she were a judge who could send him to the gallows or free him. Sliding her hand across his cheek, she smiled. "Do you think we should wait to tell the others?"

A great sigh escaped his lips as he pulled her into his arms. "No. I think Uncle Ian would want us to tell the world."

Lucy shuddered, sliding her arms around his lean waist, holding him close, absorbing his warmth. Silently she prayed once more for the man fighting for his life. She knew if Ian died, a part of Sabrina would be buried with him.

Chapter Thirty

A breeze drifted in through the open French doors in Ian's room, brushing Sabrina's face, lifting a slender strand of her unbound hair. She glanced at the rosewood clock on the mantel. It was close to midnight, close to another day, the third since the poisoning. She had begun to live each day minute by minute, giving thanks for every second Ian lived.

She sat on the edge of Ian's bed, holding his hand, stroking his hair. Light spilled over him from the lamp on the wall beside the bed, gilding his skin, finding blue highlights in his midnight hair. With her eyes she traced each feature of his face, etching his image on her heart. He could be snatched away from her, leaving her with nothing but her memories.

She had shaved his cheeks after dinner, scraping away black stubble, leaving smooth, bronzed skin. With her fingertips she stroked his brow, his cheek, the full curve of his lower lip, his breath warm and moist against her skin. Resting her fingers against his neck, she held her breath. He seemed better, she assured herself; his breathing was less erratic, his skin warm, dry, his pulse steady beneath her fingers.

"He's getting better," she whispered, glancing at the little dog sitting on the floor beside her. "We'll look after him, won't we, girl?"

Guinevere laid her head in Sabrina's lap. Sabrina bit her lower lip as she stroked the dog's smooth head, fighting against the sudden tears searing her eyes. They were friends at last. She glanced at Ian, wishing he could share this one small triumph. In time he would, she thought.

The doctor was making his nightly raid on the kitchen, leaving her alone with Ian; alone except for Yardley. She didn't mind Yardley. In fact, she felt secure with him. Unlike the other detective, the one who had come to relieve Yardley for several hours this afternoon, the one who looked at her as though she were about to smother Ian at any moment. Did they really suspect her of trying to kill her husband? But she had given them reason to believe in her hatred. That haunted her more than their accusing eyes.

A movement behind her made her glance over her shoulder. Yardley sat on one of the chairs in front of the fireplace, an open book in his lap, Shakespeare and Byron sprawled at his feet. He was staring toward the sitting room, his gaze fixed on James MacDoughal, who stood on the threshold.

Mac nodded to the detective as he moved toward the bed. "How is he?"

"I think he's better." Sabrina's fingers tightened on Ian's hand. "Or maybe I just see what I want to see."

Mac was quiet, standing at the foot of the bed, watching her. "I see how things are with you." He glanced over his shoulder to Yardley, then moved closer to Sabrina. When he spoke he kept his voice just above a whisper, his words meant only for Sabrina. "You love him very much."

Not trusting her voice, Sabrina nodded.

"I've been with him since he was a boy. Miss Brenna, she was always afraid someone would kidnap Miss Ellen and the boys, so I was the watchdog. Always looking out for trouble, trying to keep them safe." Mac glanced down at the floor. He was quiet a long moment before he spoke. "I'm thinking I might have gone too far with you."

Sabrina smiled up at Mac. He looked tired and worried, his face drawn into deep lines, shadows darkening the skin beneath his eyes. He was hurting, maybe as much as she was. "I understand why you didn't trust me."

Mac shook his head. "I'm wishing I'd never given that deck of cards to the major. If I hadn't, then the two of you would have been married a long time ago, and happy."

Sabrina felt the blood drain from her limbs. "What cards?"

Mac lifted his gaze to her face. "I got a deck of your father's cards from the barkeep. I only showed it to the major after he told me you was going to be married."

"After. You mean the morning we arrived at St. Louis?"

Mac nodded. "I was thinking you were only after his money," he said, his voice a harsh whisper, the sound of a man who wasn't accustomed to keeping his voice low. "He's had a few gold diggers aiming for him."

"My God." Through gathering tears, Sabrina glanced down at Ian. "He was telling the truth," she whispered.

"I'm real sorry. I know it can't ease the trouble I've caused you, but I was only trying to protect him."

Sabrina lifted Ian's hand to her lips. All the angry words, all the misguided hate, all so destructive.

"I hope you can forgive me."

Sabrina nodded. *Forgive me*. She wanted forgiveness. She needed forgiveness. She could forgive this man who only wanted to protect Ian. "It doesn't matter." The only thing that mattered was getting Ian well.

"Thank you," Mac whispered, resting his hand on her shoulder. "You're a fine lady." He stayed a few moments, looking down at Ian like a lost puppy, then returned to the sitting room.

Sabrina leaned over Ian, sliding her hand through his thick mane, the soft strands curling around her fingers. Tears fell from her eyes, dropping on his face like summer rain. He had been telling the truth. He loved her. He had meant to marry her all along. And she . . .

She bit her lip, clenched her eyes shut, trying to stem the storm of tears, to no avail. Her shoulders shook with silent sobs, tears coursing down her cheeks in slender rivulets, falling on his bare chest, his cheeks, his eyes, puddling in glistening pools on his skin.

Don't cry.

The words were softer than a whisper, so soft that at first she thought they were only in her mind. Then they came again, and she felt his fingers come to life in her hand, squeezing weakly in an attempt at giving comfort. Through blurry eyes she saw him smile, his lips curving into that devilish pirate's grin that could steal her breath.

"Ian?"

"Why are you crying, Brat? Don't you know I hate to see you cry?"

With a sob she fell upon his chest, pressing her cheek against his shoulder, weeping, too tired to control her relief, her joy. He slipped his arms around her, holding her, his embrace lacking his usual strength, yet filled with a tenderness that made her weep all the more.

"Mrs. Tremayne," Yardley said, touching her arm. "He hasn't . . ."

"No," Sabrina said, her voice muffled by Ian's shoulder and her own tears. She pulled back in Ian's arms, swiping at her tears with her fingers. "He's alive."

"What's happening?" Hannah asked, rushing into the room. "Dear lord, he isn't . . ."

Mac, Aggie, Luther, and Ormsby followed Hannah, swarming around the foot of the bed. Sabrina backed away from the bed as Hannah swooped down on Ian, cupping his cheeks in her hands, her joy pouring out in tears and squeals. Ormsby, Luther, and Mac crowded around Hannah, each expressing their relief. Amid the confusion, Yardley slipped out of the room.

"Looks like ye're gonna get a chance," Aggie whispered, slipping her arm around Sabrina's waist.

A chance to live with Ian. A chance to show him how very much she loved him. There was nothing more she could ever hope for, Sabrina thought, looking past Mac's shoulder to her husband. Ian glanced up to meet her eyes, smiling, telling her without words everything she needed to know. Her future was in his eyes, a future beside him, a future filled with warmth and hope and love.

"What have we here?" Wentworth asked as he entered the room.

"He's conscious," Sabrina said, feeling fresh tears of joy well up inside her.

"Well, I never expected . . ." Wentworth shooed everyone to the foot of the bed. He set a tall glass of milk and a plate piled with slices of cold roast beef and bread on the cabinet beside the bed before bending over Ian. "How are you feeling, young man?"

Ian's stomach felt as though an angry mule had been kicking him for the past two days, his throat felt as though he had been eating cinders, and he was sure if he tried to stand he would end up flat on his face. He glanced past the doctor to where Sabrina stood, her eyes glistening with unshed tears and unspoken words. He smiled. "All things considered, I'm feeling more than a little lucky."

"Well, it didn't look as though you were going to make it. If not for . . ." Wentworth paused as Ewing and Yardley entered the room. Hitching his thumbs in his bright red suspenders, he stared at the advancing policemen. "Inspector, I don't believe this is the time to ask your questions. My patient has only . . ."

"It's important I talk to him, Doctor." Ewing stood at Ian's bedside, across from Wentworth. "Mr. Tremayne, I'm Inspector Nehemiah Ewing and this is my associate, Detective George Yardley. We would like very much to talk to you about the events that have taken place in the past two months."

The inspector looked like the type of man who didn't intend to take no for an answer. The quicker Ian got done with the good policeman, the quicker he could get back to holding his beautiful bride.

"Inspector, can't this wait until morning?" Sabrina asked, moving to Wentworth's side. In spite of her wrinkled gown, her tired face, she looked like a princess. "My husband has been through a terrible ordeal."

"I will only take a few moments of his time, Mrs. Tremayne," Ewing said.

Ian didn't like the look in Ewing's eyes as he stared at Sabrina. It was a little like watching a cat who thinks he is about to pounce on a rather plump mouse. Sabrina was a suspect. Ian was sure of it.

"Inspector Ewing, I insist . . ." Sabrina began.

"It's all right," Ian said, smiling at her. "I don't mind. Please, I want to get this over with."

Sabrina hesitated a moment before bowing to Ian's wishes. Upon her insistence, Wentworth was allowed to stay while the rest of them were banished from the room. She cast Ian one last look before she closed the door. Ian leaned back against his pillow, anxious to collect on all the promises he saw in his wife's beautiful eyes.

"Your wife is a very lovely woman," Ewing said, smiling down at Ian. "She seems to care a great deal for you."

"I'm sure you've spoken to enough people to know we've had some problems, Inspector. Misunderstandings, really."

Ewing nodded. "I understand this isn't the first time someone has tried to kill you, Mr. Tremayne. There's a matter of a coach that tried to run you down, and a poacher in the woods."

Ian glanced from the inspector to the younger detective, who stood at the foot of the bed, making notes in a brown leather notebook. "Accidents."

"Perhaps." Ewing scratched his head just above his right ear. "But a wire stretched across the bridle path and arsenic in your brandy can hardly be called accidents."

Ian clenched his jaw. He had doubts the shooting was an

accident either. Still, he didn't like the possibilities that came to mind.

"We found a bag of arsenic in your kitchen, Mr. Tremayne. The bag was from a store on Broadway." Ewing stood beside Ian, watching him for any reaction. Ian didn't give him any. After a moment he continued. "We interviewed the clerk at the store. He remembered a lady coming in a few days ago to buy a bag of arsenic for ridding herself of rats. A well-dressed lady who wore a black-lace veil over her face."

Ian felt his stomach tighten. "Please, get to the point."

"The lady had red hair, Mr. Tremayne. Dark red hair."

"My wife had nothing to do with this," Ian said, rising up in the bed. His head reeled at the sudden movement, blood swimming before his eyes.

"Mr. Tremayne, please," Wentworth said, laying his plump hand on Ian's bare shoulder. "You mustn't get upset. We don't know how much damage may have been done to your heart."

Ian fell back against the pillows, breathing hard, trying to clear his head of the dark mist gathering behind his eyes.

Wentworth bent over Ian, shaking his head, before glancing at Ewing. "Inspector, I think you should leave now."

"No." Ian dragged air into his lungs. "I want to hear what you have to say."

Ewing pursed his lips as he studied Ian for a moment. "We have every reason to believe your wife and her father are behind the accident with the coach and the shooting, as well as the poisoning. I'm afraid I will have to arrest them."

Ian surged upward, the blood pounding in his temples. "You will do no such thing."

"Mr. Tremayne," Wentworth said, grabbing Ian's arm. "That's enough, Inspector. I will not allow you to kill my patient."

Ewing nodded and turned to leave.

Fighting the dizziness that gripped him, Ian shook off the doctor's restraining hand. "Not yet, Ewing. I have a few things to say."

Sabrina leaned back against the wall in the hall, resting her head against smooth oak, staring at Ian's door. Words clawed at her throat, words she needed to give to Ian. Why couldn't Ewing have the decency to wait? How much longer would they be?

"Do you think I should be waking the others, milady?" Hannah asked.

"Let's wait a little." She wanted Ian to herself. She wanted to hold him, to tell him just how much she loved him. What was taking Ewing so long?

"There's no sense in standin' here," Aggie said, touching Sabrina's arm. "Why not take a nice bath and change yer clothes?"

Sabrina glanced down at her gown; the emerald silk was stained and wrinkled. Had she really spent two entire days in this gown? Unconsciously, she ran her hand over her tangled hair. "I must look horrible."

"Tired," Aggie said, smiling up at her. "Very tired."

Sabrina glanced at Ian's door. "I need to . . ." She intended to sleep beside her husband tonight. Perhaps she should bathe and change. "All right."

As Sabrina turned to walk toward her room, Ian's door opened. Inspector Ewing entered the hall, followed by Yardley. She glanced from Ewing to Yardley. Their grim expressions sent dread coiling around the base of her spine like a serpent. "What is it?"

"Mrs. Tremayne." Ewing moistened his lips with the tip of his tongue. "I'm sorry I have to tell you this."

Sabrina curled her hands into fists at her sides. "What's happened?"

Ewing glanced down at the floor, then lifted his gaze to her eyes. "I'm afraid your husband has died."

The words slammed into her chest. "No."

She rushed to the open door, peering past Yardley into the room. Wentworth stood beside Ian's bed, his head bowed, staring down at a man's figure shrouded by a white linen sheet. "Ian," she whispered. They had come too far, fought too long and hard. It couldn't end like this.

She moved toward the lifeless body of her love, feeling her strength drain from her limbs like water through a sieve. Darkness reached for her, cool and comforting. She felt a strong hand close around her arm before the world vanished into a black void.

Sunshine.

It streamed through the leaves of the trees overhead, warming the white roses arranged in a cluster atop the coffin, wafting perfume in the air. It shouldn't be, Sabrina thought. The sun shouldn't be shining. Not today. Not ever again.

How long had it been since the world ended? Had yesterday been filled with hope? The day before? This morning they had awakened her from blessed oblivion. They had dressed her in black and brought her to this place.

Sabrina looked through the black lace of her veil, staring at the name etched above the door of the mausoleum, listening to the deep, steady voice of the minister, not understanding the words. From nearby she heard the sound of weeping; sharp, erratic sobs.

She lowered her eyes. Sunlight shimmered on the long mahogany box, brass handles glowing a deep gold, reflecting a woman dressed in black.

Numb.

It was as if every emotion had deserted her. Leaving her empty. So empty.

She felt a hand on her arm and looked up at her father, his image distorted by the heavy veil over her eyes.

"It's time, Sabrina," Duncan whispered.

She hesitated when he tried to steer her away from the shiny casket. He wanted her to leave Ian. Leave him here in this lonely place. Six men lifted the casket and began to walk toward that house of white marble. She pulled against her father's hand, trying to follow Ian.

"Sabrina, you have to let him go," Duncan said, slipping his arm around her shoulders.

"No." She couldn't leave him, not here, not alone.

A single rose tumbled from the lid of the casket as they carried Ian up the three marble stairs. Sabrina lifted the white rose from the bottom step of the mausoleum, pressing the dewy bloom to her breast, watching as they carried Ian into the shadows.

She had to stay. She had to tell Ian. She had never told him. Strong arms closed around her. She had no strength to fight. Not now. As if in a dream she allowed those strong arms to lead her away from her only love.

Caroline crossed Ian's bedroom, glancing at the untouched dinner tray on the cart near the hearth, her footsteps muffled by the thick carpet of blue and ivory. She paused at the door, looking back at her niece.

Sabrina sat on a chair in front of the French doors, Ian's three dogs sitting nearby. In her hand Sabrina held a white rose. She stared out at the setting sun, soft shades of gold and rose painting her lovely face. She had come here directly after the funeral this morning and hadn't moved since.

Since Ian's death two days before, Sabrina hadn't shown any emotion. She hadn't shed a single tear. It was as if she had retreated inside herself, barely recognizing or acknowledging the people around her. With a sigh, Caroline opened the door and left Sabrina alone with her memories.

In the hall, Duncan stopped his pacing when he saw Caroline. "Will she come down for the reading?"

Caroline shook her head. "I'm worried about her. She should cry. She should let some of that emotion out. It's going to destroy her if she keeps it inside."

Duncan drew a deep breath before he spoke. "She's a strong woman. She'll be all right."

She could see the doubts in his dark eyes, the same doubts she had in her heart.

Duncan took her arm as they started to walk down the hall. "Do you think she'll be allowed to stay here? I don't think it would be good to take her away right now."

Caroline shook her head. "It all depends on what's in the will." She studied his profile, her fingers curling against the smooth black wool of his coat. "Perhaps you should think about staying in New York."

He paused on the landing, looking down at her with those intense dark eyes. "And what would I do here, Carrie?"

Caroline glanced down at the tip of her shoe, peeking out from beneath the black satin of her gown. "I could use help in running the shipping company. It's hard on a woman alone."

"You've been doing fine for the past three years."

She wouldn't beg him, she wouldn't get down on her knees and ask him to marry her. "If you can't think of any reason to stay, then I suppose there isn't one."

He held her as she tried to continue down the stairs, his hand growing tight on her arm. With his fingers under her chin he forced her to meet his eyes. "You're the one who left the first time, Carrie. You're the one who threw my love back into my face. You tell me why I should stay now."

Caroline opened her mouth to speak, but the words just wouldn't come. The last rays of the setting sun streamed gold and scarlet through the etched windows behind him, sparking fire in his dark hair. She wanted to touch him. Yet she couldn't move.

He brushed the pad of his thumb over her lips, a smile lifting the corners of his mouth. "What do you want from me, woman?"

She had to swallow the pride in her throat before she could

speak. "You know. You've always known. I was foolish once. Don't be foolish now."

"Were you foolish?"

She nodded, pressing her hand to his chest, feeling his warm skin through white linen. "I didn't realize. I never knew one love could take hold of you, could haunt you all the days of your life."

Duncan closed his eyes, feeling her words slice into his heart. When he opened his eyes she was still there, still looking up at him with those huge blue eyes, eyes that had haunted him for nearly thirty years. He turned away, grabbing the carved newel post at the corner of the balustrade.

He had tried with Rachel. He had cared for her. Yet when he had held his wife in his arms it had been Carrie's lips he had kissed, Carrie's smooth skin beneath his touch. She touched his back, her small hand spread against his coat, her fingers tense, pleading. Why now? God, it wasn't fair.

"Duncan, I want to be with you. If not here, then anywhere you go."

"Dammit," he whispered, spinning to face her. "Why now? I have nothing. Nothing! Do you understand?"

"I don't care."

"You didn't want me when I had Rosebriar to give you, when I had land and money. Why now?"

"I sold my youth for money." She lowered her eyes, a single tear sliding beneath the fringe of black lashes laying against her pale skin, glistening gold in the sunlight that kissed her cheek. "Please, don't let pride get in our way."

As if he had no will, he lifted his hand to her face, cupping her cheek in his palm. She was no longer a child of sixteen, but a woman. A very lovely, very wise woman. Slowly he slid the pad of his thumb over her cheek, sweeping away her tear, trying to smooth away all trace of her pain. "I love you, Carrie."

Her lashes flickered against her cheeks, then lifted. Tears glittered in her dark blue eyes, tears and a fierce determination. "If you love me, stay with me."

"As a pet?"

"Now you listen to me, Duncan O'Neill." She grabbed his arms. "I prefer to run matters of importance, like the entire social circle of New York, rather than that boring old shipping business."

Unless he missed his guess, the lady could run a fleet of shipping companies and the entire social circle of New York and still have enough energy to run the rest of the country.

"If you think I'm going to let your stubborn pride keep us apart, think again. I'll follow you. I'll haunt you day and night. Whenever you look over your shoulder I'll be there. And when you go to bed at night I'll be there, too, in your dreams. And when you wake up in the middle of the night, cold and lonely with only your stubborn pride to keep you warm, you'll think about how it could be lying next to me." She dropped her hands, a smile curving her lips. "So, what do you say, Duncan O'Neill? Are you going to try to get away from me this time?"

She was right. He had lived too many years without her to throw away what happiness they had left because of pride. "Why, Miss Carrie Buchannon, are you asking me to marry you?"

Her lips parted as she sucked in her breath. "Why, of all the . . ." Her words dissolved on a sigh. A smile slid across her lips, then lifted to her eyes. "I suppose I am. Seems only fair. You asked me the first time."

He pressed his lips to her brow, breathing in the heady scent of roses clinging to her dark hair. "Are you sure you want me?"

Caroline threw her arms around his waist and pressed her cheek to his chest. "I've been wanting you since I was six years old."

He held her, at last filling his arms with her soft, trembling form. After a long time he pulled back, cupping her face in his hands as gently as he would cradle a rose in his grasp. "I would be honored to be your husband, my love."

"Duncan," she whispered as softly as a prayer.

He brushed his lips across hers, taking only a sip of the wine he would have years to savor. "I think we'd better go."

The family was gathered in the library, each swathed in black, each turning to look at the doorway when Caroline and Duncan entered the room. Caroline noticed Lucy sitting beside Timothy Reynolds on one of the two velvet sofas, and gave her daughter a slight smile. How difficult it must be for those two young people, she thought, to have their love shadowed by tragedy. She also noticed Inspector Ewing and Detective Yardley standing in the back of the room, watching every move Duncan made.

Duncan informed Ian's solicitor, Jay Woodhouse, that his daughter would not be attending the reading. The man nodded, his balding head catching the lamplight. He sat behind a table near the windows and opened a black leather portfolio.

Caroline sat on an armchair near the hearth, and Duncan stood behind her, his warm hand resting on her shoulder. This time they could make it right, she thought. At last she would live with the man who had haunted her over the lonely years.

Woodhouse cleared his throat before he began reading the will. The terms were simple. It took less than three minutes for him to tell the people gathered that all of Ian Tremayne's estate was left to his wife, Sabrina Kathryn O'Neill Tremayne.

Caroline felt Duncan's hand tighten on her shoulder, an echo of her own surprise.

"All of it?" Delia asked, moving to the edge of her chair.

Woodhouse nodded. "According to the latest will."

Henry turned from the windows. "Does that include his shares in the bank?"

"Everything." Woodhouse closed the portfolio.

"But the shares in the bank are supposed to stay in the Tremayne family," Rand said.

"According to the papers regarding the origination of the bank, the controlling votes must be held by a direct descendant of the founder, James Everett Tremayne. And they shall remain with you and your father." Woodhouse folded his arms on the table. "But the dividends derived from those shares shall be distributed to Mrs. Sabrina Tremayne. Should Sabrina Tremayne die without issue the estate will be divided among Ian Tremayne's remaining relatives. In this case, Mrs. Tremayne will also relinquish the estate should she remarry."

Heads turned, stares directed at Duncan. Caroline lifted her gaze to Ewing, who stood watching Duncan, his lips pulled into a hint of a smile. He thought Duncan had poisoned Ian. He was just waiting for proof before arresting him. Caroline was sure of it. And Ian's will was motive enough.

"Excuse me. I would like to tell my daughter," Duncan said, offering Caroline his arm.

Caroline slipped her arm though his, her fingers growing taut on his arm as they left the library. If they arrested him . . .

"I never expected that Yankee to do something like this," Duncan whispered as they reached the staircase.

Caroline looked up at Duncan's profile. The war had changed him, had hardened the young man she had known. Yet she loved him now as she had the first time she had set eyes on him. "He loved her very much."

His lips tightened. "I guess maybe he did."

Duncan knocked on Ian's door and waited. When he received

no answer he opened the door. The room was empty. Sabrina's chair still sat in front of the French doors, a single white rose on the seat.

They searched the house. She was gone.

"Where could she have gone?" Caroline asked, looking up into Duncan's worried face.

He shook his head.

"The way she was feeling . . ." Caroline clasped her hands together. "You don't think she would hurt herself, do you?"

Duncan closed his eyes. "Tell Ewing what happened. The maniac who killed Ian might have the same idea about Sabrina."

"Where are you going?" she asked, grabbing his arm as he started toward the main hall.

He covered her hand with his. "I'm going to look for her."

Caroline pressed her hand to her lips, watching Duncan march down the hall, praying he would find Sabrina before it was too late.

Chapter Thirty-One

Sabrina paused on the bottom step of the mausoleum, moonlight spreading like cream over the white marble arch, the oak door a dark shadow. A cool breeze swept in from the river, rustling the leaves of the trees overhead, billowing her skirts as she climbed the few stairs and gripped the brass handle. With a groan the door swung open, releasing into the night the scent of roses and dust.

Moonlight drifted into the tomb in a silvery wedge, illuminating the smooth walls lined with wide drawers, sleeping places of the dead. She hesitated on the threshold of the narrow crypt, so like the cave that had been her home; cold, dark, like death itself. And Ian was here, locked in this lonely place.

I love you, Sabrina.

Ian's words seemed to sigh on the breeze. She closed her eyes, listening to the sweet memory.

I'll love you until I die. And if it's possible, I'll love you beyond the grave.

Fighting her fear, she followed that silvery trail of moonlight to Ian's side. The black silk of her skirt brushed the brass vases lining the base of the walls, each filled with roses, their perfume failing to mask the dark scent of decay.

Ian rested beside his mother, encased in marble, his beautiful eyes forever closed to the sun, their haunting light no more than a memory, a memory that would live forever in her soul. She ran her fingers over the letters etched into marble, tracing his name. If only she could touch his face, just once more. If only she could . . .

"I didn't mean it," she whispered, her words echoing softly against the marble. "I should have trusted you. I wanted to . . . but I was afraid."

Let me love you, Sabrina.

Regrets. They collected inside her, like brittle pieces of broken glass. She had fought him. And now . . . she pressed her palm flush against the cold stone. Nothing but memories remained.

"All those terrible things I said . . . I wish I could . . . I . . . you didn't know how I felt. You didn't know . . . how much I loved you. How much I love you." She pressed her cheek against marble, seeking his warmth, feeling only the cold stone.

He was gone.

Gone. Not just for a day or a month or ten years, but . . . forever. That reality seeped like ice into her bones. She would never touch his face again, never hear his voice, never know the wonder of feeling his child grow inside her.

Tears spilled through her lashes, the marble beneath her cheek growing slick. Her life stretched out before her, cold, bleak, empty. She would never marry again. She would never look into another man's eyes and imagine they were the pale green of fresh spring leaves. She would never feel another man's touch and imagine it was his. To live that lie would be unbearable.

"I love you, Ian. God, how I love you," she whispered. She knew he couldn't hear her. He would never hear the words she wanted desperately to tell him. It was too late.

He was gone.

She curled her fingers against the smooth stone, tearing the black lace of her gloves. Coming to this place couldn't help ease the pain twisting inside her, tearing her into pieces she would never be able to mend. There was nothing here, nothing but cold marble and the shell of the man she loved.

He was gone. Forever.

"Ian . . . oh, God . . . no."

"How very touching."

Sabrina jumped at the sound of that husky whisper. Pressing her hand to her throat, she stared at the doorway, where a figure cut a black outline in the moonlight. He wore a black hat pulled low over his face, a black coat and trousers. Obscured by shadows, Sabrina could see nothing of the stranger's face.

"Who are you? What are you doing here?" Sabrina whispered, trying to see the man's face. Did he even have one, this dark phantom of the night?

"Someone who is going to grant your wish."

Chills crawled over Sabrina's skin. Fears buried in that part of the mind seldom recognized, in that part believing in ghosts and demons and the grim reaper—those fears nibbled at her spine. "You have no right to be here."

The stranger moved his hand, moonlight shimmering for a moment on the barrel of a gun. "I'm going to send you to Ian. That's what you want, isn't it?"

Fear wiped the inside of her mouth dry. Sabrina took a step back as the stranger approached. No dark spirit this, but a man; the man who had stolen Ian from her side. "You did it. You killed him."

A laugh, strangely muffled, rattled against the walls. "I had that pleasure. Though the police will think you did it. You and your father. I made sure of that."

He was about her height and slight of build. "Who are you?"

"It doesn't matter." He moved forward. "You'll be dead in a few moments. Suicide, I'm afraid. Later, your father will be hanged."

Anger flashed like lightning inside her. "Bastard!" Sabrina shouted, moving toward the stranger.

"Don't move," he said, shifting the gun, pointing it at Sabrina's heart.

She froze, her gaze lowering to that deadly pistol. She couldn't let him get away with this. He had murdered Ian; she couldn't let him murder her father.

"On your knees."

Steady, Sabrina warned herself, sinking to her knees. There had to be some way to stop . . . Her hand brushed a brass vase. The stranger lowered the gun toward her temple. Sabrina slipped her hand around the slender neck of the vase, solid brass cold against her palm. A click, stark, metallic, a bullet lodging into place. Her heart stopped. Now!

She tossed the vase at his face. Water and roses spilled over the stranger, followed by the dull thud of brass against flesh and a muffled moan.

Gunfire ripped through the air, ricocheting off the marble walls. Sabrina felt the ball pass by her head, heard it slam into the marble in the heartbeat before she scrambled to her feet. Ramming her shoulder into the stranger, she dashed past him, knocking him off his feet. A curse followed her as she ran from the tomb.

Threads of silver streamed through the trees, shimmering spotlights on granite and marble. Lifting her skirts, Sabrina dashed through the light and shadow, her footsteps cushioned by thick grass, her heart pounding at the base of her throat. Her carriage stood on the path, the pair of bays standing with their heads bowed, nibbling at the grass beside the gravel drive. Just a few more yards.

Gunfire ripped open the quiet night, sending crows fleeing their nests, squawking in protest. Sabrina felt the blaze of the ball scrape her upper arm. She stumbled from the impact, falling headlong against the damp grass, pain screaming along her nerves, stealing her breath.

The stranger was desperate, Sabrina realized. He no longer cared if it looked like suicide. He had to make sure she didn't get away. She came to her feet, grabbing her arm, blood flowing warm and sticky against her palm.

Ducking behind a granite vault, she paused long enough to drag air into her lungs. Her stomach soured from the pain. Her body shouted to hide. Yet she couldn't. He would find her and kill her. She had to get away. She was her father's only chance.

Crouching, she ran, keeping to the shadows, using monuments and tombstones as cover, her black clothes transforming her into a creature of the night. If she could make it to the main road, she might be seen by someone. Just which way was the main road? There were so many paths, each winding in a different direction.

A stone wall, no higher than her knee, came into her view. She emerged from the cover of trees into the stark white light of the moon. Beyond the low wall the ground dipped sharply, moonlight skipping over stones and clumps of weeds and grass. A few brave saplings clung to the steep slope.

More than a hundred feet below her, railroad tracks gleamed in the moonlight, stretching out on a bed of gravel beside the steadily flowing river. Great stars above, she had gone the wrong way.

She turned to retrace her steps, her heart slamming into her ribs as the stranger materialized from the shadows. Sabrina stepped back, her leg brushing the stone wall as he moved toward her.

"Going to jump?" he asked in that strange hoarse whisper.

"It's not going to look much like suicide," Sabrina said, turning, keeping her face to the stranger as he stepped near the wall. "Not with a gunshot wound in my arm."

The stranger cocked his head. In the moonlight Sabrina saw the reason for the muffled sound of his voice. He wore a black scarf stretched across the lower part of his face. Who was he?

"Not more than a scratch. Something a rock might do." He raised the pistol, aiming at Sabrina's head. "By the time they find you, it will hardly be noticed."

Sabrina closed her eyes, expecting the next sound to be the sound of the gunshot that would end her life. Instead she heard a deep voice, a voice that could only be in her imagination.

"Drop the gun."

She opened her eyes to see a ghost standing at the edge of the shadows. Moonlight flowed over him, painting the planes and angles of his face, glowing against his white shirt. Had the stranger shot her already? Had death reunited her with her love? Yet the stranger seemed just as startled to see the specter as Sabrina.

"You're dead," the stranger whispered.

Ian shifted the gun, pointing it a little higher, aiming at the stranger's head. "Not as dead as you'll be if you don't drop that gun."

Staring at him, Sabrina felt dizzy. Was he real? Or had grief plunged her over the edge into madness?

"Sabrina, come over here," Ian said, keeping his gaze on the stranger.

As Sabrina started to move, the stranger thrust the gun muzzle against her cheek, snapping her head to one side. "One move, Tremayne, and I kill her."

Ian's gaze moved over Sabrina's face before turning back to the stranger, his eyes growing narrow. "You can't get away with this. The police are searching the cemetery."

"I think I can. Drop your gun."

"He'll kill both of us," Sabrina shouted, her voice strangled by emotion. "Shoot him. Save yourself."

Ian hesitated a moment, glancing at Sabrina, before dropping the gun to the ground. The stranger laughed, the sounds strained through the cloth, sounding eerie in the evening air.

"You're a difficult man to kill, Ian Tremayne," he said, swinging the gun, pointing it at Ian's chest. "Let's see how you survive a bullet in the heart."

"Run, Sabrina!" Ian shouted, surging forward, but Sabrina knew he would never reach the stranger in time, not before a bullet had ended his life.

With a shriek Sabrina leapt toward the stranger, hitting his arm, throwing her weight against him. The gun fired, the bullet impotent in the air. The stranger plunged backward, hitting the stone wall, toppling over it, taking Sabrina with him.

"Sabrina!" Ian felt his heart turn over in his chest. He ran, yet he seemed to move by increments, each second stretching a lifetime, each movement an eternity as he watched Sabrina disappear in a sweep of black silk.

A woman's scream pierced the evening air, plummeting into the distance, slicing into his chest. Groans clawed the air, colliding with the sound of rocks tumbling against rocks. Ian staggered, his body still weak from the lingering effects of arsenic poisoning.

"Sabrina," he whispered, reaching the stone wall, staring down the slope, expecting to see her body twisted at the bottom of the cliff. He saw one body, cloaked in black, lying beside the railroad tracks. "Sabrina!"

A rock tumbled down the slope, skipping in the air, before hitting with a dull thud on the gravel below. He saw a movement, a reflection of pale skin in the moonlight, as Sabrina lifted her face. She was caught a few yards down the slope, clinging to the root of a young oak tree. Alive! He felt the sting of tears in his eyes that came with a sudden surge of joy.

"Ian," she shouted.

"Hold on, sweetheart. Just hold on," Ian said, stepping over the low wall.

Pebbles gave way under his feet. He slipped, falling against the slope, sliding on his back toward the gravel below.

"No!" Sabrina shouted, reaching for him.

Stones bit into his skin; dirt and pebbles passed through his hands as he sought an anchor. With one hand he snagged a half-buried boulder, grinding his slide to a halt. He lay on his back, snatching for breath, waiting for the dizziness to clear his head. Any sudden movement sent his equilibrium straight to hell these days.

"Go back," Sabrina shouted.

He looked over his shoulder to where Sabrina clung for her life. She couldn't last much longer. The realization pumped fresh blood into his veins. Digging footholds into the slope, clinging to clumps of weeds and rocks, he edged toward her.

"Take my hand," he said, reaching for her.

Sabrina pulled herself closer, wrapping one arm around the slender trunk of the tree, reaching for him with the other. A sharp crack ripped through the air, followed by Sabrina's scream as the sapling snapped.

Ian's breath froze as she began to tumble backward. Releasing his hold, he snatched for her, grabbing her wrist. They slid several feet before he anchored them with his hand against one of the roots of the fallen oak. He closed his eyes, feeling her struggle to find solid footing, dangling from his hand like a trout on a fishing line. Taking a deep breath, he began to drag her upward, until she could grab the tree with her free hand.

"It's all right," he said, slipping his arm around her waist.

"Ian," she whispered, turning her face to his. "You're really here."

"I can think of other places I would like us to be," he said, glancing up the slope, holding her tighter.

Together, they inched their way upward until they could climb over the stone wall to safety. Once on solid ground, Ian pulled her against his chest and kissed her, savoring the taste of her, absorbing the heat of her body into his blood. She sank her hands into his hair and responded as though she intended to draw him into her skin, pressing against him with enough enthusiasm to nearly knock him off his unsteady feet.

"Ian," Sabrina whispered, pulling back in his arms.

She cupped his face, staring up at him, moonlight streaming over her beautiful face, revealing her emotions. The love he saw in her eyes filled him, crowding the spaces in his soul that had too long been empty.

"You're alive," she whispered. "How? I don't understand how."

He grinned. "It's a long story."

"Long story?" In a blink, her expression shifted, relief and elation and love dissolving into raw anger. "Why didn't you tell me?" she shouted, pushing against his chest. "Why did you let me go through hell thinking you were dead?"

He grabbed her shoulders, holding her when she tried to pull away. "They were going to arrest you and your father."

"Did you think I did it? Did you think my father did it?"

Ian shook his head, regretting that movement immediately. He grasped her shoulders tighter, steadying himself. "I made a deal with Ewing. I told him I'd play dead and help him catch the real murderer."

Her lips plumped into a pout. "You could've told me. You should've told me. Do you have any idea the torment you put me through? I thought you had died without me ever getting the chance to tell you . . ." She bit her lower lip.

He cupped her cheek, sliding his thumb over the corner of her mouth. "Tell me what?"

She slapped away his hand. "You're a cruel, worthless, no-good . . ." She stuttered, looking for words. "Yankee!"

"Sabrina," he said, following her as she started back toward the cemetery. His pistol lay glittering in the moonlight, reminding him of the man lying at the bottom of the hill. He retrieved the pistol, slipping it into his trouser pocket as he jogged to catch up with his wife. "What did you expect me to do? Let them take you to jail?"

Sabrina rubbed her left arm just below the shoulder, her hand sliding against blood-soaked silk. "You should be tossed in jail."

"You're hurt," he said, resting a hand on her arm, below the torn silk. He pulled a handkerchief from his pocket, intending to bind the wound.

She pulled her arm free of his grasp. "This is a scratch compared to what you did, Ian Tremayne."

"Listen to me," he said, grabbing her uninjured arm, halting her progress on the edge of the shadows. "If you think I'm going to . . ."

"Mr. Tremayne!" Ewing shouted from the shelter of trees in front of them. "Mr. Tremayne!"

"Damn," Ian muttered under his breath. He was tempted to disappear into the night, with his bride, but there was the matter of the dead man at the bottom of the hill. "Over here!"

A few moments later Ewing stepped into the moonlight, followed by Yardley. Both men were holding pistols.

"Mr. Tremayne, I thought we agreed you would let me handle this." Ewing glanced at Sabrina, then back at Ian. "I believe you are supposed to be in the east wing of your house, in bed."

Ian felt Sabrina stiffen beside him. "I never was good at following orders I didn't believe in."

Ewing cocked his head, his glasses reflecting the moonlight. "Mr. Tremayne, there is a murderer loose. We heard gunshots."

"The man you're looking for is at the bottom of the hill, Inspector. I suggest you take the stairs," Ian said, pointing toward the stone stairs fifty yards to his left.

"See to it," Ewing said, glancing over his shoulder at Yardley. The young detective started toward the stairs on a run.

Ewing drew a deep breath, glancing from Sabrina to Ian. "It was foolish to come out in your condition, Mr. Tremayne."

"Your condition," Sabrina whispered, glancing up at Ian. She searched his face with worried eyes. "Are you all right?"

It occurred to Ian that a wise man might not try to hide the fact that he was having trouble staying on his feet. Still, he wasn't anxious to play the role of an invalid. "That depends."

Sabrina frowned. "On?"

Before Ian could answer someone emerged from the trees. Duncan O'Neill paused for a moment when he saw the group of people gathered in the moonlight. His gaze fastened on Ian's face, his lips parted in shock. "What the devil is going on?"

Ian felt his strength ebb, like a tide drawing back to sea. "Mr. O'Neill, word of my death was premature."

"Inspector!" Yardley shouted from the base of the hill.

As a group, they moved toward the stone wall. Yardley knelt beside the black-clad figure, a hat and a scarf in his hand, the silk swishing in the breeze, like the tail of a black cat. On the ground, the stranger lay in the creamy light of the moon, face up, eyes staring blindly at the people peering from high above.

"Delia," Ian whispered, feeling his knees begin to buckle. It was odd, this sensation that came with knowing someone you cared for, someone you thought cared for you, wanted to see you dead, like a blade twisting in your heart.

Ewing and Duncan rushed toward the stairs. Ian sank to the stone wall, putting his back to the woman lying dead below him. He felt tired. Weary in body and soul. After a moment warm lace touched his face, gentle fingers curving against his neck. He looked up into Sabrina's face, her lovely features mirroring his pain.

"I'm sorry," she said, her voice taut with emotion.

"Sabrina," he said, his voice a haunting whisper. He turned his face, pressing his lips against the black lace covering her palm. "Love me."

"I do love you." She sank to her knees before him. Sliding her arms around his waist, she pressed her cheek against his chest. "I love you more than my life."

He held her, filling his arms with her soft warmth, pressing his face against her hair, breathing in her fragrance, feeling her tears soak his shirt, the emotions shaking her slender figure. This is what he had been searching for all his life. He had found love in this spirited young woman. And he would never let her go. "Looks like the war is over."

Ewing and his team investigated further, needing to be sure Delia had acted alone. For a few tense days Rand was under suspicion. During that time Ian supported his cousin and his uncle, lending a strong arm to the man devastated by his wife's death. The day after her death, the police found a dark red wig in a locked drawer in Delia's bureau. They also found a diary. In it, she chronicled her plan for Ian's demise.

Ian took the diary after the police completed their investigation. The idea of obtaining all of the Tremayne wealth had occurred to Delia after Jon's death. She had pushed Everett Tremayne, had watched him fall, had watched him gasp his last breath. It chilled Ian to read about her enjoyment of the murder. After Everett, Ian was the only one standing in her way.

It was close to midnight. Ian sat in a chair in his sitting room, staring at the last page in Delia's diary.

We buried Ian today. He was so young, so very handsome, so difficult to kill. Oh, I've done it! I've finally done it. All of the plans, the waiting, over at last. The bank will be mine and all that delicious money. Every bit of it! And all because of me.

Those fools; Ewing with his clever little eyes, he and all the others suspect the lovely widow and her angry father. Because of me. Only me! Oh, I only wish I could tell someone. I did it. I did it! I planned it all, every detail. And now I shall take my reward. It's time to hear the reading of the will, time to look suitably upset at dear Ian's departure.

"Ian, are you all right?" Sabrina asked from the doorway of his bedroom.

Ian turned to look at his wife. She stood framed by the white-painted oak, dark shadows filling the space behind her. Her hair tumbled to her hips, gaslight from the lamp beside the door flickering on the rich burgundy waves. She looked sleepy, like a little girl roused from slumber. Yet her figure was anything but childlike.

Sheer ivory silk clung to her breasts, rippled down her legs. A lace panel plunged in a deep vee from the hollow beneath her chin to the dark shadow of her navel, giving him a tempting view of pink nipples and smooth skin. He rose, dropping the diary on the table near his chair. He had made love to her less than an hour before, loved her until she fell asleep in his arms. Yet seeing her stirred the slumbering desire in his loins.

A smile curved her lips as he drew near. "Just what's on your mind, Yankee?"

He paused a few inches in front of her, close enough to feel the warmth of her skin reaching out to him. "Surrender, my beautiful rebel." With the back of his fingers he stroked her breasts, wringing a soft sigh from her lovely lips. "Complete and unconditional."

She leaned forward and nipped his chin while her hand trailed across his bare chest, tracing the thin white scar to the waistband on his trousers. "Just who is the one surrendering, Yankee?"

Ian smiled against her hair. "Does it matter?"

Sabrina slipped her arms around his shoulders and stepped into his warm embrace. "Not one bit."

Epilogue

A warm August breeze swept in from the river, setting the rose blossoms of Dunkeld swaying. Sabrina rested her hands on the smooth white balustrade of the gazebo that was planted in the center of the garden and looked past the roses, out across the sun-dappled lawn. A few yards away a man lay on the emerald grass beneath a chestnut tree, his three-month-old son nestled upon his chest. The sight was enough to make Sabrina believe in miracles again.

She loved it here. Most mornings in the summer, she and Ian would sit in the gazebo to share a few quiet hours, watching the river roll by their own private paradise, talking of the future. But Ian was gone this morning. She was alone in the gazebo, except for her Aunt Caroline and the three dogs. Guinevere lay stretched beside her; Byron and Shakespeare had both claimed shady corners.

Sabrina took a deep breath of the fragrant air, embracing the memories awakening within her, memories of her mother, of her brothers, of Rosebriar. She still missed them; she always would. Yet she could remember them now without the blinding pain. She could remember their joy, their laughter. With Ian, she had healed the wounds; he had given her back her memories, and together they had found peace.

Together they had made a home, filled with the love and security Sabrina thought never again to know. Together they were whole once again. No longer haunted by demons. No longer trapped by the past. No longer lost in shadows.

"I have enjoyed this week with you here in the country more than you can imagine. It's given us a rest from all those curious people who keep dropping by to pay their respects," Caroline said, pushing back with her heels, the white wicker rocker swaying gently beneath her. "You know, darling, I believe your father and I have scandalized New York."

Sabrina leaned her shoulder against one of the posts supporting the roof. "Do you mean by your little miracle?" she asked, smiling at her aunt.

"I suppose Connor is a miracle. But then, I have always believed in miracles," Caroline said, rising from her chair. She squeezed Sabrina's arm as she continued, "As much as I believe in fresh beginnings."

Sabrina watched her Aunt Caroline descend the steps of the gazebo, the roses bowing to her as she passed through their ranks to cross the lawn. Duncan lifted his hand to his wife as she approached, beckoning her to join him in the shade of the chestnut tree. The violet silk of her gown billowed around her as Caroline settled on the dark green grass beside her husband and her infant son.

Sabrina hugged her arms to her waist, embracing the baby she wouldn't see until the new year. Fresh new beginnings; she believed in them with all her heart.

"Where's Uncle Ian?" Tim asked, resting his forearms on the balustrade across from Sabrina. "I thought he was going to lead us all on a picnic this afternoon."

"A telegram came for him last night," Sabrina said, smiling as her cousin peeked over the balustrade. "He said he needed to take care of business in town this morning, but he would be back in time for lunch."

"We were thinking we might take a ride," Lucy said, resting her hand over Tim's arm, her gold wedding band catching the sunlight. "Do you think Ian would mind if we didn't wait for him?"

Sabrina smiled, understanding the need for newlyweds fresh home from their honeymoon to be alone. She had been married more than a year, and she still felt that need every day. "No, I'm sure he wouldn't mind."

Tim and Lucy walked across the lawn, hands clasped, moving in and out of the sunbeams slanting through the leaves overhead. As they approached the drive, Ian stepped out of the shadows near the side of the house. Sabrina felt her heart bump against the wall of her chest as he looked in her direction. One glance and the man could still add a beat to her pulse.

Tim and Lucy stopped to exchange a few words with him. Ian smiled and nodded before leaving them to continue his path to his wife. The dogs sensed his approach. Guinevere was the first to scramble to her feet and set off to greet her master. Byron followed, then passed her, barking, dashing toward Ian with his fluffy tail wagging; then came Shakespeare in the rear, strutting on his bowed legs.

Sabrina followed her husband's every move. Soft buff-colored breeches rippled over the thick muscles in Ian's thighs with every long, loose-limbed stride that brought him closer to her. He paused on the grass long enough to give his dogs a soft word of welcome and a quick pat before heading once more toward his wife.

He took the two steps leading up to the gazebo in one stride, his three little waifs trotting behind him. "Hello, Brat," he said, grinning down at Sabrina, offering her his hands.

He wore no coat, and his shirt plunged open to midway down his chest, exposing an intriguing expanse of black curls and golden skin. The man had no regard to propriety. It was just one of the reasons she loved him so fiercely. "Seems to me I asked you not to call me Brat," Sabrina said, slipping her hands into his warm grasp.

"So you did." He tugged her toward him and kissed the tip of her nose. "But you'll always be my beautiful Brat."

"You are maddening," she said, tugging on the thick hair that waved just above his broad shoulders. He needed a trim, but Sabrina didn't feel any impulse to remind him. She liked his shaggy mane.

He smiled, seemingly pleased with himself. "I have a surprise for you," he said, tugging a light blue silk scarf from his pocket. "But first you have to put on this."

She brushed her fingers over the scarf, the silk fluttering in the breeze beneath her touch. "A blindfold?"

He nodded. "Trust me?"

She frowned at the piece of silk. "Of course I trust you, but . . ."

"Good," he said, stepping around her. "Because there isn't anything in the world more precious to me than my wife, and my baby growing inside her."

Sabrina bit her lower lip as he tied the cool silk over her eyes, stealing her sight. She trusted him. She did! But as he led her down the stairs, it was all she could do to keep from snatching off the blindfold.

Sunlight splashed across her face; she could feel the warmth, see bright crimson against her closed lids. Gravel crunched beneath her slippers, then her feet sank into a thick carpet of grass.

"You're cutting off my circulation," he said, gently loosening her grip on his arm. "I thought you trusted me."

"I do," she said defensively. Cool shadows cast by the trees stole the sunlight from her face. She felt one of the dogs brush her skirt and prayed she wouldn't trip.

It was silly to be nervous, she thought, fighting to relax. She knew Ian wouldn't let her trip. She knew he wouldn't let her run into anything. And yet . . . oh, it was difficult to put your trust completely in the hands of another person. Sunlight streamed across her face, and she judged they must be somewhere near the drive leading to the stables.

"Wait here," he said, prying her hand from his arm. "And don't peek."

Sabrina drew a deep breath, trying to steady her nerves. Yet a few moments later, when Ian touched her arm, she jumped.

"Easy, love." Ian took her hand, his long fingers wrapping warmly around her wrist. As he lifted her hand, she curled her fingers defensively, afraid to touch what he offered. "I'm not sure you do trust me, Brat," he said, brushing his warm lips across her taut knuckles.

"I do," she whispered, and she would prove it. She unfurled her fingers, touching Ian's smooth cheek, giving him her trust, just as she had given him her love. She felt his long fingers move against her palm, then something soft and firm and warm brushed her fingers.

A soft nicker whispered near her ear, and something nudged her arm. It was all so familiar. Yet it couldn't be. She pulled off the blindfold. Sunlight blinded her. She blinked, clearing her eyes, focusing on the chestnut stallion standing beside Ian.

"Great stars above," she whispered, pressing her knuckles to her mouth.

Aidan tossed his head, his long red mane rippling in the breeze. He bumped her arm, nuzzling at the skirt of her blue- and white-striped gown, searching for the lump of sugar she had always had for him.

"Aidan," she screamed, throwing her arms around the stallion's neck, pressing her face into his thick mane. She breathed in the earthy scent of horse, of home, tears welling in her eyes. The horse stood quiet in her embrace as her tears dampened his coarse hair; tears shed for love lost, for love found.

"Hey, I thought this would earn me a smile," Ian said, touching her shoulder.

She spun away from Aidan and threw her arms around the man who had rescued a part of her past. She clung to Ian's neck, sobbing against his shoulder. He held her, stroking her back, absorbing her tears, murmuring soft words of comfort and love. When the storm had passed she pulled back, giving him a watery smile. "How did you do it?"

The breeze tossed a lock of his long, midnight hair over his brow, like a pirate on the deck of his ship. He grinned, completing the roguish image, smoothing away her tears with his fingers. "I hired Bainbridge."

"Thank you," she whispered, cupping his face in her hands, capturing his pirate's smile.

Laughing, she spread damp kisses across his cheeks, on the tip of his nose, and finally on his lips. There she lingered, drinking in the taste of him, welcoming the thrust of his tongue. She pressed against him, hoping he could feel the love glowing as brightly as the sun inside her.

"Lucy and Tim went riding," Ian murmured against her lips.

She caught his lower lip between her teeth and tugged gently. "I know."

"I don't think your father and Caroline would mind if we went on a picnic without them."

Sabrina leaned back in the circle of his arms. "Why, Mr. Tremayne, are you thinking about taking me to that secluded little glade a few miles from here?" she asked, toying with the black curls just below his collarbone. "The one with the swimming pond your grandfather made?"

He rested his hands at her waist and pressed his lips to her brow, his smile curving against her skin. "I am."

"You do remember the last time we went you came home with a bright red backside?"

"It was worth it."

She brushed the silk scarf back and forth across his neck. "Will you let me blindfold you?"

He pulled back, giving her his devilish grin as he slid his hands upward, along the curve of her back. "I'll let you do anything you want, Brat."

She laced her fingers at the nape of his neck, beneath the silky fringe of his hair. "Then what are we waiting for, Yankee?"

Dear Readers,

I hope you enjoyed the time you spent with Sabrina and Ian at least half as much as I enjoyed bringing their story to life. In my next book for Leisure, which will be released in 1994, I have the pleasure of sharing with you a search for a mythical city hidden in the depths of Brazil. *A Quest of Dreams* brings together a woman who fears commitment and a man who has been searching for a home and family all of his life. Through the mists of the jungle Kate and Devlin find a love neither can deny, and a secret as old as civilization. If you enjoy a love story filled with adventure and sprinkled with fantasy, I think you will enjoy *A Quest of Dreams*.

I love to hear from readers. If you would like a reply, please enclose a self addressed stamped envelope.

Debra Dier
P.O. Box 584
Glen Carbon, IL 62034

NATIONALLY BESTSELLING AUTHOR OF *REJAR*!

DARA JOY

Tonight Or Never

They call him "Lord of Sex." He is a rake, a rogue, a libertine, and a scoundrel. With his wicked sense of humor, keen intelligence, and charming ways, the Viscount Sexton is an expert in the art of seduction. But little does he know his days of debauchery are about to come to an end. For Chloe intends to have him for her own, forever. Now she'll just have to get the stubborn devil to realize that they belong together. And the feisty redhead has the perfect plan, for what could be better than beating Don Juan at his own seductive game...

___52216-0 $5.99 US/$6.99 CAN

DEBRA DIER
LORD SAVAGE
Author of *Scoundrel*

Lady Elizabeth Barrington is sent to Colorado to find the Marquess of Angelstone, the grandson of an English duke who disappeared during an attack by renegade Indians. But the only thing she discovers is Ash MacGregor, a bounty-hunting rogue who takes great pleasure residing in the back of a bawdy house. Convinced that his rugged good looks resemble those of the noble family, Elizabeth vows she will prove to him that aristocratic blood does pulse through his veins. And in six month's time, she will make him into a proper man. But the more she tries to show him which fork to use or how to help a lady into her carriage, the more she yearns to be caressed by this virile stranger, touched by this beautiful barbarian, embraced by Lord Savage.

_4119-7   \$4.99 US/\$5.99 CAN

Dorchester Publishing Co., Inc.
P.O. Box 6640
Wayne, PA 19087-8640

Please add \$1.75 for shipping and handling for the first book and \$.50 for each book thereafter. NY, NYC, and PA residents, please add appropriate sales tax. No cash, stamps, or C.O.D.s. All orders shipped within 6 weeks via postal service book rate. Canadian orders require \$2.00 extra postage and must be paid in U.S. dollars through a U.S. banking facility.

Name_____
Address_____
City_____ State_____ Zip_____
I have enclosed \$_____ in payment for the checked book(s).
Payment <u>must</u> accompany all orders. ☐ Please send a free catalog.

Scoundrel

Debra Dier

"A sparkling jewel in the romantic adventure world of books!"
—*Affaire de Coeur*

Emily Maitland doesn't wish to rush into a match with one of the insipid fops she has met in London. But since her parents insist she choose a suitor immediately, she gives her hand to Major Sheridan Blake. The gallant officer is everything Emily desires in a man: He is charming, dashing—and completely imaginary. Happy to be married to a fictitious husband, Emily certainly never expects a counterfeit Major Blake to appear in the flesh and claim her as his bride. Determined to expose the handsome rogue without revealing her own masquerade, Emily doesn't count on being swept up in the most fascinating intrigue of all: passionate love.

_3894-3 $5.50 US/$7.50 CAN

Rejar

DARA JOY

Lord Byron thinks he's a scream, the fashionable matrons titter behind their fans at a glimpse of his hard form, and nobody knows where he came from. His startling eyes—one gold, one blue—promise a wicked passion, and his voice almost seems to purr. There is only one thing a woman thinks of when looking at a man like that. *Sex.* And there is only one woman he seems to want. *Lilac.* In her wildest dreams she never guesses that bringing a stray cat into her home will soon have her stroking the most wanted man in 1811 London....

___52178-4 $5.99 US/$6.99 CAN